# Everything Changes But You

Maggie Alderson was born in London, brought up in Staffordshire and educated at the University of St Andrews. She has edited four magazines, including British *ELLE*, and worked on two newspapers, contributing to many more.

She has published four collections of her columns from *Good Weekend* magazine and her children's book, *Evangeline the Wish Keeper's Helper*, was short-listed for the 2012 Prime Minister's Award.

She co-edited two anthologies of short stories in aid of the charity War Child and also *In Bed With*, a collection of erotic stories by well-known women writers. This is her seventh novel.

She is married, with one daughter, and lives by the sea – and virtually on Twitter @MaggieA

## Also by Maggie Alderson

# Everything Changes But You

## MAGGIE ALDERSON

MICHAEL JOSEPH

*an imprint of*

PENGUIN BOOKS

MICHAEL JOSEPH

Published by the Penguin Group
Penguin Group (Australia)
707 Collins Street, Melbourne, Victoria 3008, Australia
(a division of Pearson Australia Group Pty Ltd)
Penguin Group (USA) Inc.
375 Hudson Street, New York, New York 10014, USA
Penguin Group (Canada)
90 Eglinton Avenue East, Suite 700, Toronto, Canada ON M4P 2Y3
(a division of Pearson Penguin Canada Inc.)
Penguin Books Ltd
80 Strand, London WC2R 0RL England
Penguin Ireland
25 St Stephen's Green, Dublin 2, Ireland
(a division of Penguin Books Ltd)
Penguin Books India Pvt Ltd
11 Community Centre, Panchsheel Park, New Delhi – 110 017, India
Penguin Group (NZ)
67 Apollo Drive, Rosedale, North Shore 0632, New Zealand
(a division of Pearson New Zealand Ltd)
Penguin Books (South Africa) (Pty) Ltd
24 Sturdee Avenue, Rosebank, Johannesburg 2196, South Africa

Penguin Books Ltd, Registered Offices: 80 Strand, London, WC2R 0RL, England

First published by Penguin Group (Australia), 2012

1 3 5 7 9 10 8 6 4 2

Text copyright © Maggie Alderson 2012

The moral right of the author has been asserted

Cover design by Emily O'Neill © Penguin Group (Australia)
Text design by Emily O'Neill © Penguin Group (Australia)
Cover photograph by Rob Palmer
Author photograph by Adrian Peacock
Typeset in 11.5/16 ot Fairfield Light by Post Pre-press Group, Brisbane, Queensland
Printed and bound in Australia by McPherson's Printing Group, Maryborough, Victoria

National Library of Australia
Cataloguing-in-Publication data:

Alderson, Maggie.
Everything changes but you / Maggie Alderson.
9781921518140 (pbk.)
A823.4

penguin.com.au

For Katy and Lottie Watts

# Before

'Are you sure you can leave all this behind?' she asked him one last time, as they stood taking in the view across to the city from the balcony of their Potts Point apartment.

It was early evening and the bats were starting to fly east from the Botanic Gardens, but the sky over Sydney Harbour was still a vast intense blue. For a moment, Hannah thought to mention that the sky was never that colour in Hackney. And never that big. Most of the year the London sky sat on your head like a tight lid.

But they'd been over it all so many times she decided not to go into the details again. Their bags were packed, sitting ready in the hallway. Some large boxes had already gone on ahead as freight. They had an hour spare until they would need to leave for the airport and had come out for one last look at the city where they'd fallen in love. Then there would just be time for a final coffee at Fratelli Paradiso and that would be it. Goodbye Paradiso. Goodbye paradise.

As they stood looking at that view, so familiar yet suddenly as vivid again as the first time she'd seen it, three years before, when she'd come out to be beauty editor on the Australian edition of *Glow* magazine, Hannah knew they were both thinking the same thing.

There were the Bridge and the Opera House, so iconic, but as familiar to her now as her own front door. There was the CBD skyline, its unique shapes framed by a psychedelic Sydney sunset. Then her eyes panned down to the more personal landmarks. Harry's Café de Wheels, where they would sneak off for a pie on a Sunday afternoon. The old wharf, now a swanky hotel where they'd once spent a crazy night after partying in the bar downstairs. Boy Charlton Pool where Matt swam every day and the Art Gallery which had been her brain-cooling haven on unbearably humid February weekends.

Such a beautiful city, with a character and energy all its own. Smart, cheeky, warm, irreverent, sexy. Just like the man standing next to her. Her gorgeous Australian husband, whom she'd persuaded to leave all this for some one-bedroom dump in London, which they hadn't even found yet.

'Of course I can leave it,' said Matt, putting his arm round her. 'I already gave up Bondi and moved to Potts Point for you, didn't I? Moving to London is just a more extreme version of that. It's an amazing place and much better for me professionally. I know too many people here; I need a challenge.'

He pulled her closer and kissed the top of her head.

'And anyway,' he continued, 'what does it matter where we are on this big blue planet, as long as we're together?'

She smiled at him.

'You always have the right words, don't you, Matt?' she said, running her hand gently down his cheek.

'I have my moments,' he said. 'I'm just waiting for some other people in the music business to appreciate them a bit more.'

'It'll happen,' she said and meant it.

# Chapter One

The moment she heard the third crash, Marguerite knew that Anthony was visiting. The first two crashes Charlie was more than capable of making on his own. He might have tripped over a dog, or missed his step with the ice tray somewhere between the fridge and the sofa. But as soon as she heard the third one, which sounded as though it had involved broken glass, she knew Anthony was there. It was only a matter of time until they started singing.

Sighing deeply, she wove the needle through the worked part of her needlepoint and gazed out through the open French windows at her garden, now coming gloriously into its May bloom.

She knew she should turn on a lamp to save her eyes, but couldn't bear to; every second of the exquisitely fading light was to be savoured. And now bloody Anthony had to come along and ruin it.

How had he slipped past her? She hadn't heard a car on the gravel, so it was a mystery how he'd got round the house and into Charlie's 'granny flat', as he called it, at the back, before she could intervene. The last time he'd tried to make one of his surprise visits she'd sent him packing before Charlie had even known he was there.

Now she thought it was probably already too late to step in. They were in full flow and going over to try and stop them at this stage would only lead to a big scene. Charlie was just so impossible when he was drunk. Such a charming gentleman when sober, Sir Charles

Berry-Downing QC, a silly childish idiot under the influence. It was almost as though he had to try and get it all out while he could, with the booze to blame afterwards.

She sighed again, remembering the first time she'd met Charlie's new friend, Anthony, who she'd been hearing so much about: another bright apprentice barrister in neighbouring chambers.

One night, way back in the mid-1960s, before Hannah was born, she'd come home late from work at the museum to find the two of them in the drawing room of the flat in Cadogan Gardens, already well away, jackets and ties off, empty champagne bottles lying around. They'd been properly drunk all right, but such good company.

Anthony immediately filling a glass with champagne for her – and never letting it get empty. Stan Getz on the record player, Charlie dancing with a cigar clamped between his teeth, his arms around his own back, feeling himself up, slapping his own hand when it crept down to his bottom. So funny. Then more champagne and laughter and both of them taking turns to dance with her.

It had been binge-drinking, really, she understood that now, but it had seemed a joyful, carefree thing then, just laughing and dancing, being young and relishing life, until the champagne was all gone. Then Marguerite had made Welsh rarebit – amazing she hadn't set the place on fire, more than a bit pie-eyed herself by then – and they'd sat around the kitchen table eating it and talking with great intensity about who knows what, but it had seemed very important at the time, until exhaustion set in.

Then Anthony had disappeared into the night, Charlie passed out on the sofa and Marguerite went to bed alone, for the first of so many times in her married life.

But those had been glorious days, when Charlie was still working his way up in the legal profession, with Anthony as his partner in crime, as he called him. The men who put the bar into barrister. They did drink far more than was good for them from the outset, but it had seemed innocent high jinks then, without any knock-over effects into their real lives, apart from the hangovers.

But gradually it had turned into this darker thing that made Charlie so impossible until he was sober again. It had happened gradually over the years, getting much worse when he retired to the country, far younger than he should have. Until finally, five years before, she'd had ask to him to go and live over in the granny flat – or clear off altogether.

Should she have insisted on the latter? Had she been weak about that? For a moment she let her head, with its cloud of pale grey hair swept up in a French pleat, slump down – but only for a moment. Then she lifted it up sharply and after taking a deep breath in, pulled back her shoulders and set her expression. She hadn't lived this long to be daunted by a pair of old drunks now.

It was a bore, though, she allowed herself to admit, as she closed and locked the French windows, then headed across the hall and along the kitchen passage to the back door.

She'd really thought that once she'd thrown Charlie out of the house – although only across the yard at the back to what had once been a coach house, admittedly – she wouldn't have to endure this any more. He could binge-drink as much as he liked, as long as she didn't have to witness it.

But Anthony's presence always kicked things up several gears. After fifty years it was as though Charlie was still trying to prove he was as much of a player as his friend. She would happily have left them to it, but really didn't feel like spending four hours in the waiting room at A & E, until Charlie could get something stitched up, or X-rayed. Not again.

'Damned stupid child in an old man's body,' she muttered, taking her quilted gilet from a hook and shrugging it on.

Two black shapes came out of the darkness of the kitchen and rubbed their heads against her legs, as she slipped her feet out of house shoes and into gardening clogs.

'Hello, you two,' she said, fondling the Labradors' silky black ears, 'did I wake you up and it's not even breakfast time? Well now you're up, come and give me moral support while I sort out Daddy.'

But after setting out across the brick-laid yard, a sleepily wagging tail on either side of her, she came to an abrupt stop as a bottle sailed out of the brightly lit first-floor window of the granny flat and smashed

5

on to the bricks just in front of her feet, the contents splashing her legs. The dogs immediately sprang to attention, barking at whatever had threatened them and their beloved pack leader.

'Ssshhh, you two,' said Marguerite, touching their heads reassuringly, 'and sit. We don't want those silly men to know we're out here and I don't want any cut paws either.'

With the dogs reluctantly sitting and growling quietly, she turned on the torch she kept in her pocket and saw that the courtyard was strewn with broken glass and running with red wine.

She was quite relieved to realise the crashing sounds she'd heard earlier hadn't involved soft human tissue impacting with hard objects, and looked down again at the pieces of shattered glass lying all around, her eyes automatically starting to organise them into groups. Which shards would fit neatly together, how you would start to make the broken bottles whole again.

Marguerite had been putting broken things perfectly back together – porcelain, china, terracotta – for even longer than she'd been picking up the pieces after Charlie's drinking binges. Her mind flitted to her studio and the piece she was looking forward to getting started on in daylight. A very pretty Coalport teapot, spout and handle broken off, lid lost, just the kind of challenge she loved. Not one of the priceless artefacts she still sometimes worked on for museums, but a domestic object with special meaning to its owner.

But then a burst of loud laughter from the granny flat window snapped her back to the moment and realising she was standing in a place of some danger, she grabbed the dogs by their collars, and hastened back towards the house.

She made the threshold just in time to avoid the flight and catastrophic landing of another bottle, followed by raucous cheers from the flat. After locking and bolting the door, she leaned back against it for a moment with her eyes closed, willing her heart rate to slow.

Then, after carefully checking eight paws for splinters of glass, she went up to bed and put her ear plugs in. A very happy black Labrador lying on either side of the bed next to her.

# Chapter Two

Hannah was driving the bus. That's what her four-year-old son Hector called it every time he got to sit in his favourite spot: upstairs, front seat, right-hand side.

Hannah loved that seat too. Bowling along Old Street on the number 55, looking down on all the people scurrying out of the Tube, she felt as though she owned London. It was a small compensation for having to be on the bloody bus at all, when she would so much rather have stayed at home with her family.

She lifted up her phone to take a snap from that vantage point and texted it to Matt's number:

> Look Hector! Mummy's driving the bus today! Put a red
> sticker on your bus chart xxxxxxxxxxx

As the phone confirmed the message had been sent she could picture him so clearly, still tucked up in the big bed with his dad and baby sister, where she'd left them. She felt every extra inch the bus moved her away from the three of them like a physical pain.

'Go out and help save the women of Britain from bad eyeliner and last season's nail polish,' Matt had joked, as she'd stood in front of the wardrobe glumly deciding what to wear.

It had to be something pretty special that would segue from a day at her desk to that night's important dinner with the big shots from French brand Nèriade, one of the most prestigious of all the beauty companies.

Hannah sighed, even as she picked out a gorgeous new Erdem dress she hadn't worn yet, knowing she should be more geared up about it all. Nèriade was a key brand for ChicClick.com, the luxury online boutique where she was now beauty director, and she'd always had a great relationship with them in her *Glow* days.

But on top of not being home in time to put the kids to bed yet again, there was another thing that was making her feel less than excited about the evening ahead: none of her beauty writer pals would be there. It would just be her and her boss, Veronica – the website's dynamic founder – with the Nèriade people at the dinner.

Beauty events used to be social outings for Hannah, but these days it was all business, with the trappings of conviviality pasted over the top. Gone were the days of giggling hysterically over several glasses of champagne too many, with the clan of beauty editors she'd known since they were all junior assistants together.

She'd quickly understood that in her new job she couldn't afford to let wine loosen her lip when deals were being done, even if it was during a fabulous dinner by a celebrity chef.

So, following Veronica's steely discipline, she'd learned to drink no more than one glass of wine through the meal, while appearing to partake enthusiastically of her corporate host's generosity. The secret was to drink only tiny little sips of whatever wine was offered. It wasn't a very relaxing way to spend an evening.

'Hey, Matt,' she called out, looking back at him and the kids snuggled up in bed together, reflected in her dressing table mirror, as she sat down to do her make-up, 'what do you think is a good collective noun for beauty editors? A compact of beauty editors? A spritz of beauty editors?'

Matt paused from blowing raspberries on his daughter's tummy and smiled at Hannah. He loved a word game. And Hannah thought a bit of light banter would help get her out of the morning funk she was sliding into.

'A top note of beauty editors?' he suggested. 'A cliché of beauty editors? A freebie of beauty editors? A make-up bag of beauty editors?'

'A bag of beauty editors,' echoed Hector, always eager to join in, 'a blag of beauty editors, a blag of blooty bleditors!'

He had no idea why both his parents immediately burst out laughing, but was thrilled just the same and beamed at them.

'That's great, Heccie,' said Matt, 'do you know what it means?'

'Bag, blag, blaggety, blag, waggety, wag, maggoty, mag . . .' Hector was now chanting, jumping up and down on the bed in a state of high excitement Hannah feared could only lead to tears, but he looked so happy doing it she didn't say anything.

'Actually, I think you had it right off the bat, Hanns,' said Matt, putting out a hand to restrain Hector, whose jumping was now getting perilously close to his baby sister's head. 'Calm down, mate. A spritz of beauty editors nails it. Fragrant, delightful . . .'

'But fundamentally lacking in substance?' said Hannah, pressing her lips together after applying her lipstick. 'Bit of a grump of a beauty editor for this one today, I'm afraid. I've got that dinner tonight, remember? A thrilling new development in the field of mascara – and, more importantly, how we can sell more of them . . .'

When he didn't respond to her sarcasm, she glanced back in the mirror and saw that the three of them were now fully under the duvet and from the noises Matt was making, she gathered they were playing a game of sharks. He was humming the theme from *Jaws* and Hector was starting to squeal with delighted terror.

Tears of tenderness pricked Hannah's eyes. She longed to jump back into bed and join in, but a glance at the clock reminded her she had no time for such self-indulgence. She had a job to do – a pretty amazing one at that – and a family to support. She needed to get on with it.


Hannah was passing the time on the bus, thinking about gold eyeshadow. She liked the new Guerlain compact she'd tried out that morning, with its four different shades of gold, and was sure there was a good idea in there. François Nars had done some great new lip glosses with flecks of gold in them, she remembered, and then inspiration struck – Nèriade had a really great gold liquid eyeliner in their range. Perfect.

Put together it would make a great visual spread for the beauty 'pages' Hannah did for the magazine section of the website – and the credit to Nèriade would be the perfect thing to drop casually in to the conversation at the dinner tonight. Tick, tick, tick.

Feeling enthused, Hannah pulled her laptop out of her bag, to make notes. Just the day before she'd seen a new Dutch model with extraordinary matt black skin. The gold would jump out against it brilliantly. They could do multiple shots of the stages of gold being layered on her eyes and then run it together as a video, so it looked as though it was growing on her. It would be amazing, exactly the kind of project which had made her excited about taking the job at ChicClick – her first one not on a print magazine – just under a year before.

But then she reminded herself, with a slightly sinking feeling, that she'd need to find at least two more gold-themed beauty products that ChicClick already stocked to sell the 'Gold Standard' idea – her first thoughts for the headline – to her boss.

On *Glow*, three had been a trend, but on ChicClick there had to be at least five products they could sell off the page, or Veronica would say it didn't justify the cost of the photo shoot. And, as she routinely analysed the sales of units against every spread Hannah produced, there was no fudging it.

Nothing was pleasantly random on ChicClick, thought Hannah. Everything came back to pounds out versus pounds in and that was the end of it. Magazines were businesses too, she did understand that, but there was a looser attitude on them that allowed creative ideas to be the guiding force, rather than the bottom line, with the idea that excellence in the first would lead naturally to results in the other. That concept was simply not accepted on ChicClick and Hannah still wasn't used to it.

If she'd understood that at the outset, she wondered, not for the first time, as the bus sat at the long lights outside Holborn Tube station, would she have been so quick to accept the job when Veronica had offered it to her? She'd been rather swept off her feet when the glamorous website founder had taken her – and Nancy, who'd been just two months old at the time – out to lunch and asked her if she would like to be the first beauty director of the site.

They were about to start selling high-end cosmetics and scent alongside the already very successful designer fashion business and Veronica said she needed a beauty director with 'a flawless international editorial reputation, to win the confidence of the big brands'.

As well as being very flattered at that description of her professional status, Hannah knew that websites, where you could use video as well as static images to express your vision and get new ideas out really quickly, were the creative future for beauty, just as they were for fashion. ChicClick was already the most glamorous and successful of them all, Veronica something of a celebrity in her own right, and it was all very exciting.

So when, on top of all that, Veronica offered her a salary that was nearly double what she was getting at *Glow*, with the prospect of bonuses on top – woohoo! – it was a done deal.

It was only as they were getting towards the end of the lunch that she'd dropped a bombshell which might have tipped Hannah off about just how business-focused her new employer was.

'I'm so delighted you're going to join us,' Veronica had said, 'and of course, the sooner you come on board the better. I'll need you from the beginning of June at the latest.'

Hannah's eyes had immediately dropped down to look at Nancy, so tiny and vulnerable, asleep in her pram next to the table, as her brain did an instant calculation that her baby daughter would only be four months old in June. Veronica saw her and laughed kindly, patting Hannah on the back of her hand.

'And don't worry about bubba,' she said, 'with that salary you'll be able to afford plenty of help. I've got three kids, as you know, and it works perfectly for us. I was back at work after a few weeks with all of them. So much better for everybody than if I was at home all the time. I'd be so grouchy, they'd beg me to go back to work. I'm always there for the important stuff – sports day, school plays and all that – but they also respect how important my business is to me.'

Still taking it in, Hannah said nothing, but seeing the small frown that appeared momentarily between Veronica's immaculately groomed brows before she chased it off again with a smile, what she was thinking must have been obvious.

'Really, Hannah,' she said, leaning across the table towards her, 'ChicClick is a very woman-friendly set-up, just like magazines are, so you don't need to worry about any of that. Kids' doctors' appointments, the dentist, school stuff, you just take the time for them, no problem. And you know you'll be a better mum if you're reaching your own full potential.'

She was still smiling as she spoke and Hannah could see she was sincere. It wasn't a hard-headed posture covering up her real feelings; the set-up clearly did suit Veronica and her family. Hannah made herself smile back at her new boss, hoping it would work equally well for her, Matt, Hector and Nancy.


Eleven months on, as the bus crossed over into Oxford Street and she started to put her laptop away ready for her stop, she thought it was probably working well enough.

Just.

# Chapter Three

Matt was the only man in the baby signing class, but there was only one girl in it for him. He had his eyes firmly fixed on Nancy, who was picking up her sipping cup and waving it in the air while making the sign for drink with the other hand. Clever possum!

'Good stuff, Nance,' he said, rewarding her with a kiss on the head and then making the drinking sign himself, his thumb to his mouth. 'Daddy's thirsty too, darling, can I have a drink?'

She laughed heartily, clearly said the word 'dink' and handed him her cup. He pretended to drink from it, putting his head back and making loud glugging noises, which made her laugh even more and as he handed the cup back to her, he took the opportunity to give her a good tickling under the arms, setting off another cadenza of throaty giggles.

He just loved to hear Nancy laugh. It was his favourite sound in the world. He had it as his ring tone and he'd given a recording of it to his best mate and song-writing partner, Pete, to sample into a tune, completely unfazed by his eye-rolling response and suggestion he recorded her farts as well.

But the tickling turned out to be one thrill too far for little Nancy and he had to lift her up and put her over his shoulder for some gentle back patting, as the laughter turned to choking coughs. That was when he realised everyone in the room was looking at him.

He glanced over at the teacher.

'Sorry, Janie,' he said, 'we were making rather a lot of noise, weren't we? I'll calm down.'

'That's all right, Matt,' she said, looking up at him from under her eyelashes, 'you two are simply adorable together, aren't they, girls?'

Matt looked round at the nine women sitting in a circle with their babies on their knees, and was horrified to see them all smiling dopily back at him. Oh shit, why had he drawn attention to himself? It was bad enough being the only bloke in the class and now this.

Why had he ever agreed to bring Nancy to this course? She was starting to talk now anyway, but Hannah had seen something in a magazine saying that even if you started later, baby signing helped speed the development of language or some such crapola, so here he was.

And not for the first time, he was wondering if the teacher could show him the sign for: 'I'm very happily married, thanks, and my wife is much hotter than any of you and she's really smart and has truly magnificent tits so forget it.'

And I wouldn't even have done any of them when I was single, thought Matt, doing an instant chick reccie – a checcie, as Pete called it. Well, maybe the redhead. He'd always been partial to a ginga. Hannah's hair was very dark auburn, the most perfect colour.

As his gaze lingered accidentally a little longer on the woman opposite him, with the strawberry-blonde hair, cute freckles and nice long legs, he saw her nipples harden under her T-shirt and then the unmistakeable sign of milk leakage. Oops.

He looked away quickly, trying not to smile, as she hurriedly pulled her cardigan over her chest, her cheeks pink with embarrassment. And he adjusted his sitting position as he felt a dangerous twinge in his jeans. Bastard cock, treacherous dog dick.

Of course it was Hannah's tits he was thinking about; the breast-feeding thing had always got him going in a pervy way. Well, he hoped it was Hannah's. He was thinking about them now anyway and that wasn't a good idea either.

He forced himself to concentrate on what Janie the teacher was saying and put Nancy back down on the floor in front of him. Looking at her innocent little face always calmed his filthy mind. The idea of some bastard ever having thoughts like that about her was an instant turn-off. He imagined smashing her first boyfriend's face into a wall. Boom!

But just as he was getting himself together, he realised that the woman next to him was tapping him on the shoulder. He turned round to see her smiling eagerly at him. Oh no.

'We've got to partner up,' she was saying, inching closer to Matt. Much closer.

'Right,' said Janie, 'are you all in pairs? Oh good, Rose is taking care of Matt.'

They all giggled. Matt smiled weakly. He was never coming here again. End of story. What was wrong with these women? Didn't they have men at home to service them? And wasn't having kids supposed to put most women off sex?

He'd always been intensely grateful that Hannah seemed to be a glorious exception to that accepted piece of parenthood lore, but these chicks definitely seemed more than up for it. Maybe he'd get Pete to bring Nancy next time. He could work his way through them. And tell Matt all about it ha ha ha.

He turned round to face the woman he was supposed to be 'partnering' so they could test each other on all the signs they'd learned so far and tried not to think about what a dickhead he must look.

When the class was over several of the women tried to involve him in their plans to head as a group to the nearest baby-friendly café, but Matt bolted for the door instead, taking the stairs down to street level at a run, with Nancy on one hip, her buggy in his other hand.

He decided to get the supermarket shop over with, but even in there, he felt harassed. With Nancy riding shotgun in the trolley, happily waving around a celery stick he'd broken off for her, every woman he passed gave him a version of the soppy smile which seemed to be specially reserved for a man with a baby.

He wouldn't have minded if he thought they were getting clucky at the sight of Nancy. That would be understandable. But it was definitely him they were smiling at. Was having a baby with you proof you had been able to maintain an erection at least once in your life? Was that it?

He'd certainly never been so blatantly cruised like this when he was young, single and pretty bloody fit. Not even strutting around Bondi with his shirt off. He'd always done all right with the girls but he'd still had to work to pull, like the next bloke. That was how it was supposed to be. This was just wrong.

Maybe it was London. Maybe all the women here were sex starved, their men's bits shrivelled up by a lifetime of damp and cold. He didn't get it – when it was that bloody cold going to bed was the best thing to do. You'd think these Brits would be at it non-stop.

He started writing a text to Pete with one hand, grabbing things off the shelves with the other, pushing the trolley with his knee. Pasta twirls, pasta bows, pesto. Sweetcorn, spaghetti hoops, tomato soup. Apple juice, jelly snakes, rice cakes. All Hector's favourites. He knew the family shopping list off by heart. Or hoped he did, because he'd left it at home.

He stopped for a moment to load up with cherry tomatoes, which seemed to constitute a food group in their own right for Hector, then finished the text and sent it:

**I'm going to lend you Nancy for a day mate. She's a total chick magnet. I'm in the supermarket fighting them off.**

He knew his friend wouldn't read it straight away, as it was only 11.30 and he'd still be flat out sleeping, but they'd have a laugh when he did see it.

The shopping done – and was he imagining it, or had the middle-aged woman on the till been flirting with him too? – he decided to brave a coffee in the supermarket's café. Not that he thought of it as coffee. He and Pete called it 'ceeffo', a warm milky drink, with some similarities to coffee, rather as rooibos was to real tea. A tolerable drink in itself – just – but not the same thing.

Nancy was getting grizzly, so he gave her some bread sticks to chew on in her buggy, rocking it backwards and forwards with his foot to lull her to sleep while he sipped his ceeffo latte and flicked through the *Guardian*.

He was pleased to see a four-star review of a gig by a band he and Pete knew quite well, with a particular mention of a song they'd actually helped them out with a bit. They hadn't got any credit for it, but Matt didn't mind. It was always good to work with different people and he was happy for them, but he knew Pete would puke when he saw it.

Matt closed the paper, stretching out his legs and leaning back in the chair, wondering what to do next. He had some time while Nancy slept but didn't want to risk waking her up, bumping her back up the stairs to the flat. Maybe he'd go for a run round the park with her, or maybe he'd just stay where he was and wait for Pete to call, so they could plan what they were going to do later. Matt never felt his day had quite started until he'd had contact with his best mate.

He checked his phone to see if Pete had replied to the text yet and had familiar mixed feelings when he saw one from his model agent, confirming a big catalogue job in a couple of weeks.

Matt had been earning good money modelling since his early twenties, but still didn't feel comfortable with it. He knew he was lucky to have the income – and it was still really his only income, whether he liked it or not – he just didn't want it to define him. The words 'male model' made him shudder. When Pete really wanted to piss him off he called him Zoolander.

Hannah always told him not to be so silly, she knew lots of lovely, interesting models with full lives and Matt's attitude was insulting to them, but he couldn't help it. He didn't want to be Matt Constantinos the Model. He wanted to be Matt Constantinos the Songwriter – who did the odd bit of modelling.

He just couldn't accept it as a proper job for a man. Standing around like a ponce in some stupid outfit. He made a point of never looking at what he'd done afterwards. Just took the money and ran. He'd give the whole thing up in an instant if only his songwriting career would take off properly. It would happen, he knew it would, but sometimes the waiting got a bit tough.

He clicked the link on the text and chuckled to himself when he saw exactly what was involved with this job. Pyjamas. Or 'premium gentlemen's sleepwear' as the company described it. The only consolation was that no-one he knew was likely to see it. And the pay rate was pretty good. Enough for them to be able to afford a nice holiday in the summer, even once he'd paid a babysitter to look after the kids for the duration of the three-day shoot. So he'd be Matt the Himbo one more time and dry his tears with the cash.

He went up to the counter to order another ceeffo, picking up a copy of the *Daily Mail* another customer had left behind on the way back, and trying not to think about the flat whites at Paradiso.

# Chapter Four

Ali was lying on the sofa in her underwear watching TV, with the blinds down, all the lights off and the air conditioner on full.

'What are you doing?' asked her flattie Mel when she got home from work, turning off the air con and pulling up the blinds. It was still light outside. She came over to the couch and peered closely into her friend's face. 'It's May, Ali, not February. Look at you – you're all goosie bumps.'

'I'm acclimatising to dark and cold,' said Ali, pulling a throw rug off the nearest chair and wrapping it round herself. 'Make me some tea, would you, Mels? I'm freezing.'

Melanie raised her hands in the air palms out, shaking her head in disbelief, as she headed for the kitchen at the end of the room. Although, having been friends with Ali since kindy, she should have been used to such dramatic behaviour.

'Explain what you're doing and I will,' she said.

'I'm trying to get my body used to colder temperatures, or I'll spend my whole time in the UK getting sick. You only get two years legal working holiday visa and I don't want to waste any of it. Imagine being sick in bed with the whole of London out there waiting for you.'

'You're already sick,' said Mel, holding the kettle under the tap, 'sick in the head and you'll be going into summer up there anyway.'

Ali grinned and jumped up off the couch, coming over to the breakfast bar and perching on a stool, still huddled inside the blanket.

'Miss Mellie speak not with forked tongue,' she said, 'but you are really going to miss me, aren't you?'

'You know I will, but when do you think you're actually going to go? How are your savings coming along?'

'They're right on target,' said Ali, rubbing her hands with glee – and to warm them up. 'That's why I've cranked up my acclimatisation program. I'm really close to my goal and I'm going to get some big tippers in tonight, I can feel it in my bones.'

'Well, good luck with that on a Tuesday night and you better warm those bones up before you go to work, or you'll be too stiff to "dance", as you call it.'

'It *is* dancing, Miss Melanie,' said Ali, hopping off the stool, swinging the blanket around her head and coming to a stop looking fetchingly over one shoulder, with a foot extended behind. 'I'm an exotic dancer. And a very good one.'

She turned back towards Ali, stood up straight and lifted her right leg up very slowly until her knee was nearly level with her head.

'All right,' said Mel, shielding her eyes, 'you don't need to show me the merchandise. An exotic dancer with a first-class degree . . . Like I said, a lovable head case.'


But Ali had been right about the tippers. It was unusual on a Tuesday but a crowd of money boys had come in and competed to trash the most cash.

As she went into a deep forward bend and looked back at them from between her splayed legs, to a chorus of hormonal howls, they reminded her of displaying gorillas banging their chests. Although gorillas were more attractive.

But as long as they didn't touch her any more than was necessary to slide banknotes into the side of her g-string – and there was a burly security guard to make sure they didn't – she didn't care. Every $10 note was another ride in a London black cab. A fairly short one, from what she'd heard, but she might not have to wait too long to find out for herself now. Her savings were coming along nicely.

As she handed her tips to the club's owner at the end of the night and waited to see how much she'd get back – 50 per cent if she was lucky, but it depended on his mood – she did a mental check. If she carried on building up her savings at her current rate, she was only thirty days off her goal. Then it was buy the cheapest ticket and fly away. She wasn't going to tie herself to a date by booking the ticket first; it all depended on saving up the cash. As soon as she had it she'd be on her way to London.

London, England. She loved rolling the words around in her head, like the beginning of an old movie. She could see the shot panning over Big Ben and along the Thames to Tower Bridge, the classic London location set-up. Oh lordy, she couldn't wait to be part of that big picture.

Her massive extended family made her feel so suffocated in Sydney. It was a big city, but she couldn't seem to disappear into it. Wherever she went there was a bloody cousin, which wasn't surprising, really, because one of her mother's sisters had married one of her father's brothers. Her family tree was as complex as the DNA helix and made even more intense with her father's side being Greek Cypriot and her mother's Aussie Irish, all of them big into clan loyalty. Sometimes Ali felt it was eating her alive.

Whatever she did in Sydney some member of the family had an opinion about it and usually not a good one. And since one of them had helpfully told her mum she was working at a pole-dancing joint in the CBD – while managing to obscure the small detail of how he'd found that out, the sleaze – she'd felt simultaneously suffocated and vilified, which was a uniquely uncomfortable place to be.

That night's pay stashed in her bag, she caught a cab to Newtown, wondering which Tube line she'd be using for her London commute. She knew all the colours of the different ones off by heart and felt they must somehow reflect their characters. The Circle line was sunny yellow. The Central line was sassy red. The Northern line was sombre black. The Jubilee line was elegant grey. The Piccadilly line was sensible dark blue and much cheaper into the city than the Heathrow Express, which was a rip-off.

The number 55 bus took her straight from Holborn Tube station to her cousin Matt's place on Hackney Road. You had to pay your fare at the machine at the bus stop, or have an Oyster card at the ready. She was going to buy one when she got off the plane at Heathrow, her badge of honour as a local.

She was London-ready, shit yeah. But was London ready for her?

# Chapter Five

Hannah's mobile rang as she was about to go into a meeting with Veronica to 'strategise' – as she put it – their approach for the dinner that night.

She was also going to present her Gold Standard idea, in the formal way Veronica expected, so she knew she should ignore the call, but there was always that little tug of anxiety in case it was Matt ringing about a problem with the children.

Looking at the phone's screen she saw it was her mother and hesitated for a moment. Should she let it go? But, no, another kind of hard-wired anxiety made her answer it.

'I hope I'm not disturbing you, Hannah,' said Marguerite, 'are you at work?'

'No, no, it's fine, Mummy,' said Hannah, hoping it sounded convincing, as she glanced at the clock on the wall across the office. She had exactly eleven minutes. Being late for Veronica just wasn't an option. Neither was taking this call in the open-plan ChicClick offices. 'Just give me a moment,' she said and scooted across to the stairwell where she could have a little privacy.

'Is everything all right?' she asked, once the fire door was safely shut behind her, wondering, as she said it, if that would have been every daughter's first question to their mother, on receiving such a phone call. But with her dad the way he was it had become a natural reflex, all part of what had prompted her to move home from Australia seven years before.

It had been at their wedding reception, in a marquee in her parents' garden, that Hannah had first started to feel she needed to come back permanently. After making a father-of-the-bride speech of such beauty, humour and elegance it reduced the entire marquee to tears, her beloved Daddy had proceeded to get so legless he'd sat down in the middle of the dance floor and refused to move, until Matt and a couple of other strong young men had to carry him up to bed.

Seeing the pained look on her mother's face as they'd hauled him out – and not feeling exactly thrilled about it herself – Hannah had realised that, much as she adored her life in Sydney, she couldn't leave Marguerite alone to cope with Charlie's excesses any longer. So she'd made some discreet enquiries and a few months later, when the beauty director of the London edition of *Glow* handed in her resignation, Hannah was offered the job. It was a big promotion and her ticket home – bingo!

To her great relief Matt had been immediately enthusiastic about the idea, because his best buddy, Pete, had made the move to London a year earlier and he couldn't wait to hook back up with him. It had still been a big wrench for them to leave their blissful Sydney life, but as she sat on the cold concrete fire stairs in the ChicClick offices her mother's next words were the latest of many confirmations that they'd done the right thing.

'Anthony was here last night,' said Marguerite grimly.

'Oh, no,' groaned Hannah, 'Mr Party Animal himself. Was it very bad?'

'No A & E this time, at least,' said her mother crisply, 'that was a relief, but the courtyard is absolutely covered in broken glass. I have no idea how many bottles they threw out of the window, but it was a lot.'

'Full or empty?' asked Hannah, slumping down with her elbows on her knees at the thought of it.

'Some of each, I think,' replied Marguerite, 'I'll have to sweep it all up before I can take the car out. It is a bore.'

'Oh, Mummy,' said Hannah, realising she'd raised her voice and hoping it wasn't audible through the fire door, 'you know it's more than a bore – it's appalling, they're like a couple of vile superannuated teenage delinquents. You should get ASBOs on both of them – and make them bloody sweep it up.'

'Fat chance of that,' said Marguerite. 'Anthony's already gone. I saw him sneaking down the drive first thing, but I certainly didn't stop him. As long as he's going in the right direction – away – I'm happy. And your father won't be good for anything for days. I presume he's still alive. I haven't been over to check yet.'

Hannah let that one sail over her head.

'Well, I still don't think you should sweep it up,' she said, 'you could hurt yourself. Ask the gardener to do it.'

'Why should he? It's hardly what he's employed for,' said Marguerite, 'and he's new. He's only been here once before, what would I tell him? "So sorry, Gary, my husband has thrown a large part of his cellar out of the window, would you mind sweeping up half a ton of broken glass before you start on the weeding?" It would be so embarrassing.'

Hannah paused to think. Her mother had a point. What could she tell the gardener? That her husband had a mental age of fourteen as soon as alcohol passed his lips? Supply yet another humiliating story about him to entertain the regulars in the local pub: Heard the latest about Sir Charlie Soak-It-Up, the septuagenarian lager lout?

'I see what you mean,' she said eventually. 'I'm so sorry you've got all that to deal with. It's pathetic the way Daddy allows himself to be led astray by Anthony, but keep your pecker up, we'll be down to see you in a couple of weeks. Hector's so excited he put his wellies in the dishwasher last night so they'd be nice and clean for you.'

'Oh, bless him,' said Marguerite, 'but that's why I was ringing you actually. Just to check you really want to come. I thought you might not want to expose him to it.'

'Of course we want to come,' said Hannah, cutting her off, slightly sharply, because there was a hint of truth in what her mother had said and she felt guilty about it. Hector adored his grandfather and it some-times worried Hannah that they were rather too alike in their belief that a good joke was worth taking any risk for.

'I'll ring Daddy later,' she said, 'and tell him that if he pulls another stunt like this we won't come down, but have you up to London instead – without him. I don't mean it, of course, but it might work as a threat.'

'That would be wonderful,' said Marguerite. 'The prospect of missing out on Hector and Nancy might make him see sense.'

'I hope so,' said Hannah, 'and remember, if he does act up while we're there, you'll have me and Matt to back you up, OK?'

'Thank you, Hannah,' said Marguerite, 'and do give them all my love.'

And she hung up, in that brisk way she always did, without giving Hannah the chance to say goodbye.

Hannah rubbed her temples and closed her eyes, immediately opening them again and realising she'd better get her head back in gear – and her body back in the office – sharpish, when all she wanted to do was ring Matt and tell him about it. He always knew the right thing to say to calm her down when things got too weird with Charlie and her mum, but there wasn't time for that now. Or for wondering what Hector and Nancy were each doing at that very moment, which was the next thought that had come into her head. That part of her life would just have to wait.

And so, lifting her chin, she keyed in the code to open the door back into the ChicClick offices and headed over to her desk to collect her things for the meeting, bestowing her best poised Beauty Director smile on her colleagues as she went.

If she'd learned one thing from her mother, it was how to put up a good front.

# Chapter Six

Marguerite decided to allow herself a couple of hours with the Coalport teapot before she went to check on Charlie.

What she would find in the granny flat, when she eventually went over, was unlikely to be conducive to quiet concentration, so she wanted to start while she had a clear head and was still feeling buoyed up by the short phone conversation she'd just had with Hannah.

Although she didn't like to think she was burdening her daughter with her woes, especially when she was at work, telling her what Charlie and Anthony had got up to the night before – and not having to explain why it was so upsetting – had really helped to bring it into the real world and stopped it going round and round in her head, like a record with the needle stuck.

Living for so long with someone as impossible as alcohol made Charlie could make it hard to keep a grip on what was normal. Especially as one of his favourite themes in the midst of a binge was telling Marguerite that she was the crazy one.

'Unnaturally calm and poised,' he'd say, 'classic elements of the sociopathic profile.'

Putting all that old rubbish out of her head and feeling very cheered up at the prospect of seeing the children as planned, Marguerite rang the new gardener to cancel him – she'd find a way to deal with that glass herself – and got to work.

With infinite care she took the pieces of broken china out of the cardboard box they'd arrived in, unwrapped each one from copious bubble wrap and lined them up on her baize-covered worktop.

This was going to be very enjoyable, she thought, looking at the pieces. It was the kind of job that required all her different skills, including making a whole new lid. Lovely.

She reached for her hardback notebook, opening it at a fresh page and writing in the date and details of the commission. On shelves behind her were rows of identical notebooks, which she'd been keeping since she first started training at the British Museum in the late 1950s. They'd been very useful over the years when she'd been putting together her various books on the art, craft and science of mending ceramics.

Picking up a digital camera – given to her by Hannah – she photographed the broken pieces of china, with a pencil next to them for scale, ready to stick in to the notebook later. With that all done she could really get to work, starting with the ugly brown glue lines on the shattered pieces from an earlier repair, which would have to be cleaned off before the new mend could start. She pulled on her rubber gloves and started to assemble the necessary materials.

The next time she glanced at the clock an hour had passed. She smiled to herself, thinking how lucky she was to have the joy of concentrated work to take her mind off the messier aspects of her life, which couldn't be so satisfyingly mended with glue and filler. Then, with the teapot pieces coated with solvent, sealed inside separate plastic bags, and resting between small sandbags in case of accidental knocks, it was time to research the lid.

She stood up to look at the row of china teapots on the top of her bookshelves. She had eight different examples, but none were right for this particular job, so she'd have to look in her books and auction catalogues to be sure. Maybe take a trip up to the V&A. Just the thought of that gave her spirits a lift. Perhaps she could meet up with Hannah for lunch in the café there . . .

But even as she imagined that pleasant prospect, she found herself glancing guiltily over at the laptop sitting firmly closed on the small desk next to her worktop. Her son-in-law Matt had set it up for her, taking several afternoons of their Christmas visit to show her how to work the thing. It was truly extraordinary how you could access the archives of the greatest museums in the world with just a few taps of the keyboard, as he'd shown her. She'd been properly amazed and knew she could probably find one of these early nineteenth-century Coalport teapots on there in about ten seconds.

She just didn't want to.

She hadn't been able to bring herself to tell Matt, who'd been so kind and patient with her – or Hannah, whose idea it had been to make her a 'silver surfer' – but doing this kind of research her own old-fashioned way was one of her greatest pleasures.

Neither did she want to use wretched email. The treat of hearing the grandchildren's voices – or giggles with the odd word in Nancy's case – down the phone was not something she was willing to relinquish.

And supporting her secret determination to stick to the old methods, so tried and tested, she found exactly the right teapot in the first book she opened.

Feeling quite renewed by such a satisfying morning's work she hung her apron on a brass hook on the back of the studio door, then went to the kitchen to make Charlie a mug of very strong tea with two sugars. She put two chocolate digestives into her pocket and Escoffier was at her side in a moment.

'No, Scoffie,' said Marguerite, 'these biscuits aren't for you. Or you Beetie, although you do have much better manners than your greedy son, don't you darling? Come on, let's go and see if Daddy's still alive – although we'll have to go the long way round, to avoid all that nasty glass.'

The dogs followed her, trotting about and sniffing, as she turned right out of the back door and walked down the drive for a few yards, before heading up a path to the left, with the vegetable patch on one side, the tennis court on the other. She'd ask the gardener to weed it and help her put the net up, when he eventually came. Matt was a marvellous player and it always cheered everyone up to watch him.

The four of them might even have a little knockabout together, with Hector as ball boy. Wouldn't that be fun? And if Charlie could be occupied with some distractions like that, his thoughts were less likely to drift towards the idea of opening a bottle.

With that kind of forethought, Marguerite had found that she could manipulate events so they could still enjoy some form of happy family life together. It was so important for the little ones. All of them, really – especially Charlie. If he could have a few days of drink-free fun with them, it would knock on for a quite a while after they left, until boredom drove him back to it.

That was what made Charlie drink now. Boredom. Marguerite had never thought he was the classic alcoholic; it was just once he'd got the taste he couldn't stop. He was more of a serial binge drinker.

When he was younger it had been all tied up with the high-adrenaline nature of his profession. Like the actors they were so often compared to, barristers came off their 'stage' buzzing on a biochemical high and what would have been a couple of relaxing post-court drinks for Charlie's peers tended to turn into a binge for him. He just didn't have a middle way.

She paused to pull up some dandelions growing in the cracks in the path, putting off her arrival at the granny flat just a little longer. She hated him living in there, like student digs, but it was the only way they could maintain a relationship. Near, but not on top of each other. If only he'd listened when she'd told him it was a mistake to retire at sixty. She'd done everything to try and get him to have medical treatment instead, to go to AA or whatever, but he wouldn't have it.

He'd been convinced that geographical distance from his professional pals and preferred drinking dens was the answer. So he'd insisted on retiring and moving full-time to the house in the East Sussex countryside where he'd grown up and which they'd used for weekends after his parents had died.

It was a lovely house and Marguerite had always understood Charlie's deep connection with it and with that particular bit of country; the problem was it had condemned them both to an overly quiet life and the looming presence of a third member of the marriage, in the shape of a bottle.

Steering the dogs round the near side of the tennis court, Marguerite was able to get over to the steps up to the granny flat without going near the broken glass. With them waiting keenly at her heels she gingerly pushed open the door, wondering what cocktail of noxious smells would assail her nostrils.

Sometimes a really serious binge made Charlie incontinent, which was particularly unpleasant, especially if vomit was also involved, but this time she was relieved to smell nothing worse than old cigar smoke and stale wine. She went into his bedroom without knocking and was surprised to find him sitting up in bed reading. Catullus. One of his favourites. In the Latin.

'Morning, my ministering angel,' he said, smiling fondly at Marguerite as she handed him the mug of tea and the biscuits.

The dogs rushed to greet him and Charlie immediately rewarded them with a biscuit each.

'Oh, Charlie,' said Marguerite, 'you know chocolate makes them sick.'

'Ah, but look at their happiness now,' he said, raising his mug in a toast, before draining it, 'and what's a little suffering later, for bliss in the living moment?'

'Well, you should know,' said Marguerite, her hands finding their way to her hips, in a posture she knew was a motif of their fifty-plus years together.

'Marvellous,' said Charlie, wiping his lips and holding out the mug to her, 'the healing power of tea. I don't suppose you'd make me another, would you, Marguerite, my darling?'

'You can't go easy with any kind of liquid can you, Charlie?'

He grinned and shook his head, raking his still-thick grey and white hair back from his face. Even after all the years of raddling drink, he was still a strikingly handsome man.

Bones. It's all bones, thought Marguerite, picturing how the separate bones of Charlie's skull combined to make up the particularly lovely planes of his face and head, just as the broken pieces of the teapot would come back to the round shape of the whole as she pieced them back together.

She was making more tea, after picking her way through the sitting room strewn with full ashtrays and dirty glasses, when Charlie came through, scratching his tummy inside his striped pyjamas.

He went over to the window and stood looking down at the courtyard. Marguerite brought the mug over to him.

'You haven't got any milk,' she said, 'so you'll have to have it black. I've put extra sugar in it.'

He turned to take the mug, a miserable expression on his face.

'I was hoping I'd dreamed this,' he said, gesturing out of the window with his head.

'Ah, yes, the bottle-throwing,' said Marguerite, 'I was going to ask you about that. What on earth were you doing, Charlie?'

He looked sheepish.

'You know Anthony was here . . .' he said, tentatively.

'I assumed it was him last night,' said Marguerite, 'when I heard the brutish laughter, then I saw him sneaking off down the drive this morning. Presumably after picking his way round the devastation. Charming.'

'Hmm,' said Charlie, 'well, he did want to sweep it up actually, but I told him just to make himself scarce. Didn't think you'd be too thrilled to find him here. Anyway, he said my wine was rubbish, so I threw the bottle out of the window and it was such fun hearing the crash it was then hard to stop.'

He turned to look at her, with the piercing blue eyes which had once made criminals tremble in the dock. They'd had the same effect on her in their early days.

'That's why I like going to the bottle bank,' he said, a faint smile at the corner of his finely moulded mouth, the grey moustache on the upper lip immaculately trimmed.

At least he wasn't a scruffy drunk, thought Marguerite. He even smelled nice, a hint of his Czech & Speake cologne detectable beneath the cigar smoke and alcohol vapours.

'It's such marvellous catharsis smashing the bottles into the big metal bins,' he said and the smile became an irresistible grin.

And although she was shaking her head at him, she found that she couldn't help smiling back.

# Chapter Seven

Ali reckoned it was possible this could be her last night at the club. It was a stretch, but if she could take $200 home, she'd be up to her target and off to buy a plane ticket the next morning. London, England . . .

But although Thursdays were normally good nights, this one was turning out to be a major flop. There were hardly any punters in and none of them were sitting at her table. She was dancing for no-one.

There was a big football match on, which usually kept them away, although depending who won, things could pick up later. If the Sydney team triumphed, there would be an influx of jubilant drunken blokes about an hour after the final whistle. If they lost, there wouldn't be.

'What's the score?' she asked Bill, the massive Samoan guy who was the dancers' security guard on the nights she worked.

'Not good,' he said, looking at his phone, 'reckon the idiots are going to lose again.'

'Oh shit,' said Ali. 'I really needed a good night tonight.'

'Well, don't worry, Sweetie,' said Bill, 'when some punters do come in, I'll make sure they sit at your table. You're a good girl. I'll look after you.'

Ali knew what this meant, about her being a good girl. It was because she gave him a cut of her earnings every week. One of the more experienced dancers had told her to do that when she'd started there. She'd felt instinctively it was good advice and had noticed since that some dancers didn't get such attentive protection as she did. The one time

33

a couple of punters had tried it on with Ali, Bill had come down on them immediately. He was like a block of flats looming up and the blokes in question had immediately backed off – giving Ali a huge tip, by way of an apology, which she'd later split with Bill.

He was true to his word and when a couple of guys came in a few minutes later, Bill ushered them straight over to Ali and she immediately got moving, jumping up to the top of her pole, arcing her legs over in a full scissor split and then down, one leg round the pole, the other straight out, turning all the way, giving them tantalising glimpses of what they'd come to look at. Snap! She had them. They sat at her table, grinning like the losers they were.

Energised by the thought that this could be her last night, Ali danced like a diva, pulling all her best moves with extra verve, but the blokes weren't coming forward with the goods. She'd been dancing for about ten minutes and they still hadn't slipped her any cash.

Eventually she caught Bill's eye and gestured with her head for him to come over.

'What's up, Sweets?' he said, leaning in close and whispering. 'These guys giving you trouble? They look pretty quiet . . .'

'They're not tipping,' said Ali.

'Hey,' said Bill, leaning over the nearest one, 'aren't you gonna show this lady some respect?'

'What lady's that?' said the man, with a snide grin, which suggested he was even more stupid than he looked.

'You have to tip the dancers, smartarse,' said Bill, moving his enormous head in closer.

'Where does it say that?' said the punter. 'We paid to come in. We paid for our drinks. Where does it say we have to pay this slag as well?'

'That's it,' said Bill, 'you're out. Nobody talks to my girls like that.'

He twisted the man's arm up behind his back at what looked like a very painful angle and frogmarched him towards the exit. His friend stood up, his mouth open like a fish, and watched them go. He glanced back at Ali, then towards his friend, who was now yelping with pain and then he picked up both their schooners of beer and threw them at her.

One glass hit her on the shoulder, the beer drenching her, the other bounced off her arm and smashed on the table.

The other security guard came rushing over from the back of the room, but the glass-thrower was already out of the door at a run.

For a moment, Ali just stood there, in a state of shock. It hadn't really hurt, but she wanted to get off the table fast, get dry, pull herself together. But more shaken than she'd realised, she stepped awkwardly in her towering platforms, skidding on the beer and fell, hard, on to the wooden table and the shattered glass. Then she blacked out.

It was Bill who took her to St Vincent's. And in his own car, because no taxi would have picked her up. A practically naked woman, covered only by an old towel which was already turning red with blood from the gashes on her stomach, chest and thighs, where she had landed heavily on the broken glass. She was lucky she hadn't split her head open on the raised edge of the table, but she'd knocked it so hard she was still dizzy. A huge lump had formed on her forehead, but the skin wasn't broken.

She sat in the passenger seat, groaning and weeping quietly, while he made soothing noises in what she realised, even in her distress, was probably Samoan.

'Thanks, Bill,' she said. 'You're being very good to me.'

'Don't worry. I look after my girls.'

But when they got to the hospital, he stopped the car and pointed towards the entrance.

'That's where you go in,' he said, turning to look at her, but not unbuckling his seat belt.

Ali blinked back at him, trying to understand.

'I can't take you in,' Bill was saying. 'Too many questions. I'm not legal.'

He shrugged, looking pained, then he got out his phone.

'Give me the number of a friend,' he said.

Ali managed to stammer out Mel's mobile number and Bill tapped it in, then passed the phone to her. To her intense relief, Mel answered.

'Hello?' she said, clearly not recognising the caller's number.

'Mel, it's Ali,' she croaked out.

'Oh my God, what's happened? You sound terrible.'

'Can you come to St Vinnie's A & E?' whispered Ali, as another wave of dizziness swept over her.

'On my way,' said her friend.

She handed Bill his phone, slumping back on to the seat's headrest after the effort of making the phone call. Seeing the state of her, he relented, heaving himself out of the car and coming round to open the car door for her. He half-carried her over to the entrance and propped her against the wall outside.

'Like I said, I can't take you in,' he told her. 'I'm real sorry. You're a good girl, Sweetie. Get my number off your friend's phone and let me know you OK. OK?'

Ali had a moment of clarity.

'But I'll see you back at the club tomorrow,' she said. 'It's Friday, always my best day.'

'Don't worry about the club, darling,' said Bill, 'just let me know you OK later. Now, in you go.'

Then gently lifting her away from the wall, he turned her round, opened the swing door into the hospital with his foot and pushed her through it.

Ali took two steps into the waiting room and felt her legs give way.


After stitching up the wounds – with Mel there to hold her hand – they kept Ali in overnight. Mel was back at her bedside as soon as she could get there the next day – ranting about how she'd been telling Ali to give up the pole dancing.

Ali had her fingers in her ears. She really wasn't in the mood for a lecture. When Mel's lips stopped moving she took them out and reached over to take her hand.

'Thanks for being such a good mate, Mellie,' she said. 'I really do appreciate it. Can't tell you what it meant to have you here last night.'

'But tell me something,' said Mel. 'How did you get here from the club? I couldn't get a straight word out of you last night.'

'Oh!' said Ali. 'Good point. The security bloke brought me and I need to thank him – is the number I rang you on last night in your phone?'

Mel nodded.

'Give it here,' said Ali, glancing around to make sure there were no nurses in the ward. They weren't supposed to use mobiles in there.

She rang the number and Bill's deep voice answered.

'Yeah?'

'Bill, it's Sweetie, from the club – you helped me out last night.'

'Ah, Sweetie,' he said, sounding pleased. 'You OK, babe?'

'I'm still alive, Bill, thanks to you. I'm pretty cut up, but I'll be OK, and my friend is here with me. I just wanted to say thank you.'

'Good you tell me, Sweetie,' said Bill. 'You get better. Take care.'

'I'll be fine and I'll see you soon. I'll probably be well enough to come back in a couple of weeks. I can put concealer on the cuts.'

'No,' said Bill, abruptly, 'don't come back. No table for you here now. I had to tell the boss what happened and he said he doesn't want no girls that cause trouble. Sorry, Sweetie.'

'But I didn't do anything . . .' started Ali.

'Just the way it is, babe,' said Bill, 'and take this number off that phone, would ya?'

And then he hung up. Ali sat looking down at the phone, quite stunned.

'That was weird,' she said.

'You're not kidding,' said Mel. 'Sweetie?'

'Well, you don't think I'd give them my real name do you? But get this – he told me the boss doesn't want me to go back. I've been fired from my pole dancing job for getting glassed by a customer. That doesn't seem very fair.'

Mel looked at her, shaking her head.

'I can't believe you. After what happened, you'd go back to that shithole? You're lucky it wasn't worse.'

'But I'm only $200 off my savings goal, Mel. It would only take another night, two at the most.'

'$200?' asked Mel. 'Is that all you're holding out for? $200 between

37

you and your dream of London? Are you nuts? We'll have a whip-round party. I'll set it up as a Facebook event. Invite a load of friends over for cheap food and drink and ask them to give you $10 each – you'll get more than that.'

Ali grinned at the idea. Why had she never thought of that? It was the perfect solution, a goodbye party – and the last bit of cash for her London fund. And although she'd never admit it to Mel, the prospect of no more pole dancing was a much bigger relief than she'd realised it would be.

# Chapter Eight

Veronica loved the gold idea. Hannah showed it to her as a PowerPoint presentation, featuring not only six gold-themed beauty products already available from the site – including the Nèriade eyeliner, which made Veronica give her a delighted thumbs-up – but also fabulous gold accessories from the fashion side of the business.

Hannah felt as though she'd just been declared top of the class, as Veronica bestowed her warmest smile on her. That broad, genuine grin always made Hannah want to try harder to please her, just as she remembered doing for her favourite teacher – making it the perfect moment to tell her about a little marketing coup she'd managed to pull off. She was rather pleased with herself about it.

'And there's another exciting development with Nèriade I want to tell you about,' said Hannah.

Veronica immediately looked more serious.

'Which is?'

'I've been talking to their PR, you know, Daisy . . .'

Veronica nodded, her shiny dark brown eyes locked on Hannah.

'. . . about this amazing new mascara they're launching in September. They've used this new technology which makes it catch the light as you move, so your eyes appear to twinkle. It's called *Cils Etoilé* – starry lashes – and it's really good stuff, look.'

She fluttered her eyelashes at Veronica, who nodded again, with a 'fancy that' expression on her face.

'It's a real innovation in mascara, which is much rarer than they'd have us all believe, ha ha, and I think it has the making of a cult product,' said Hannah, knowing she was babbling now, but too excited to stop. 'And the really amazing thing is they're going to let us have an exclusive on it for the first month. So any magazine or blog which features it for the launch will have to credit us as the exclusive stockists.'

She grinned at Veronica waiting for the returning smile of approval, like a dog waiting for a treat, but it didn't come. Instead, Veronica pursed her lips and looked very thoughtful. She didn't look cross exactly, but Hannah began to wonder if she'd said something wrong.

'I mean, only if you think it's a good idea,' she said, trying to cover her tracks. 'I was just thinking it would start to plant the idea into people's heads that we are their first base for the latest luxury beauty innovations. Not just another option, but the first and best destination.'

More wittering. Time to shut up. But then it all seemed OK as Veronica finally did smile again. Not the full beam, but better than nothing. Worth a small tail wag.

'That's great, Hannah,' she said, 'that is exactly what we're trying to do, to get the beauty offer to the point we're already at with the ready-to-wear, you're spot on. But I was just thinking about the dinner with Nèriade tonight – is this mascara sales exclusive a done deal? Will they all know about it, or is it just something you've been chatting to the PR about?'

She paused for a moment, looking at Hannah very intently. Although the urge to start wittering again was very strong, she managed to keep her mouth shut, knowing she needed to let Veronica get to the point now. Having a barrister for a father did have its advantages sometimes, if she could just remember to use them. Charlie always said knowing when to keep quiet was as big a part of winning cases as what you said.

'Because,' Veronica continued, 'it would be very uncool if we brought it up tonight and the CEO didn't know anything about it. I would hate to make her feel on the back foot – although on the other hand, if it is all confirmed, I will want to make a very big deal of it with them.'

She paused again, putting her hands behind her neck and turning her head slowly from side to side. Hannah felt she could almost see Veronica's brain working, looking at the situation from every angle, calculating all the possible outcomes for her business, good and bad, like a super computer analysing millions of numbers in a split second.

'But if it is happening,' she continued, bringing her arms down again, 'I'm wondering why they haven't been talking to me about it, because obviously I would need to agree a contract. And surely it's a sales decision from their end, not a publicity one and I just can't help thinking this kind of sales exclusive is not something they would give away lightly – because in effect they would be giving the finger to Selfridges, Harrods etc in favour of us.'

She paused yet again, giving Hannah one of her piercing looks before speaking.

'Are you sure she didn't mean just an online exclusive, Hannah? Or perhaps an exclusive freebie offer for a few of our customers?'

Now Hannah had no trouble keeping quiet. She was stumped. Eek. She'd definitely had the impression Daisy was talking about a fully exclusive sales deal, but maybe she had only meant online, or a 'reader' offer, and she'd misunderstood. She didn't have anything in writing. It had all been discussed over a lovely chatty breakfast at the Riding House Café. Oh dear. In her excitement about impressing Veronica with her business smarts, she'd got ahead of herself – and done the opposite. What a moron.

'Well, I did think she meant a total exclusive . . .' she fudged, knowing that kind of wishy-washy thinking never played with Veronica, who had just displayed her ability to see every implication of a situation at warp factor speed, but at a loss what else to say.

Veronica looked at her watch – a rare vintage Rolex – then back at Hannah. Not unkindly, but there was a definite coolness.

'Well, I'll need to know exactly where we are with all this before the dinner this evening,' she said. 'So give the PR a ring and let me know the score, OK?'

'I'll get right on it,' said Hannah standing up and starting to walk towards the door.

'And one other thing,' said Veronica, 'ask her if she's going to be there tonight.'

'Oh, I'm pretty sure she is,' said Hannah, realising as she spoke that she'd done it again. Pretty sure just wasn't sure enough. 'OK, I'll ask her,' she added quickly and hurried off to her desk.

Hannah called Daisy's number at the Nèriade office, then her mobile. Both went to messages. She called her assistant and it was the same. She texted her, emailed her, Tweeted her, Facebooked and even Linked In her. She left messages everywhere, but by five-thirty, she still didn't have any of the information for Veronica. They were meeting the Nèriade people at the restaurant at seven, so she thought she'd better go and tell her.

Taking a deep breath, she walked towards Veronica's office, only to see as she got closer that it was empty. Her PA, Lexie, wasn't there either. She was wondering what to do when Lexie came back to her desk.

'She's already gone,' she said.

'Oh,' said Hannah, 'I'll send her a text then and see her at the dinner.'

'Hang on,' said Lexie, handing her a blue envelope, 'she left a note for me to give you. I was just about to bring it over.'

Hannah opened it to find one of Veronica's signature correspondence cards, with her initials printed at the top in shiny raised ink.

Dear Hanns,
Don't worry about coming to the dinner tonight. It's just
going to be me and the CEO and a couple of suits after all.
Daisy isn't coming either. Go home early and see your babies.
Hugs, Ronnie

Hannah stared down at it with mixed feelings. The 'Ronnie' sign-off was a great honour, as no-one was allowed to call her that in the office. It was strictly for friends. 'Hugs' was nice too, so things couldn't be too bad, but the bit that really freaked her out was Veronica knowing Daisy wasn't going to be at the dinner – the piece of information Hannah had so woefully failed to glean despite all her efforts.

Had she been disinvited from the dinner for failing on that front, on top of being so flaky earlier about what she'd thought was her great mascara exclusivity coup? Or was it just a different kind of dinner from what had originally been planned?

Although it had all been a bit odd, Hannah couldn't help feeling euphoric an hour later, as she walked up the steps to the front door of the Victorian terrace house where their flat was on the first floor. It was always a treat to be home from work in time to see her children before they went to bed; she just wished Matt didn't have to go out the minute she got back.

In the time it took for her to open the internal door to the flat, he'd already slipped on his leather jacket and put his iPod earbuds in. They literally passed in the doorway, with Matt giving her a kiss on the lips and a squeeze of her bottom as he went.

'Hello extremely beautiful and goodbye!' he'd said, running down the stairs. 'They've had their dinner and I just changed Nancy. See you later, babes.'

Hannah didn't have time to answer before she heard the front door of the house slam shut and felt Hector grab her round the legs.

'Mummy!' he said, joyously. 'Come and see my bus I've made you. It's only got one seat.'

He grabbed the hem of her dress and was trying to physically drag her to the kitchen. Hannah was so pleased to see him she dropped everything and scooped him up in her arms.

'A bus, is it?' she said, nuzzling her nose against his. 'This I have to see. Is it red by any chance? And is the only seat our favourite one?'

He nodded, putting his forehead against hers while gazing into her eyes. Hannah felt like a hand was squeezing her heart as she smiled back at him.

'Let's get Nancy and you can show us both, OK?'

The welcome from the baby was equally rapturous, so shifting Hector on to one side, she lifted her up and with a child on each hip, waltzed them out of the hall and into the kitchen.

'Tonight's going to be a good good night!' sang Hector as she jogged them round and round to the music Matt had left blaring out and Nancy joined in with her throatiest laugh.

Hector's bus was a splendid construction of cereal packets and egg boxes, rendered the appropriate red with poster paint, which also freely covered the small kitchen table and chairs and parts of the floor. The remains of their meal were still strewn around too, pots and pans stacked in the sink.

Hannah sighed, feeling slightly irritated that she had to see to all that after a rather peculiar day at work, then decided she'd damn well enjoy some time with her kids before she started on it. She put Nancy into her high chair, gave both children a drink and some rice cakes and sat down at the table with a mug of tea. It was so lovely to be with them, yet at the same time she couldn't help feeling a little flat.

This was exactly the scenario she dreamed of all through the evenings she had to make small talk – and look like she was enjoying it – at strained dinners and cocktail parties with beauty brand executives, so why did she feel oddly short-changed?

But she knew what the problem was really. Matt wasn't there. Although being with the kids in the light of the May early evening was lovely, it wasn't the proper family time that she craved. That meant all four of them together. This was more like a relay race, with Matt passing the childcare baton to her the minute she got home.

She knew she couldn't complain; she was very lucky that Matt had agreed to look after Nancy until she would start nursery at two and a half, as Hector had done. Hannah knew lots of hard-working couples and single mums who didn't have any choice about putting their babies into full-time day care as soon as they finished maternity leave, but as she was the major breadwinner and Matt was 'self-unemployed', as he put it, apart from the occasional days of modelling, they'd had another option. The downside of the arrangement was that he got his adult time out of the house when Hannah came home.

While Nancy napped after lunch, he did the same, so that when Hannah came home from the office, he could go out and do his day's work. Or rather, his night's work. For some reason, songwriting was something that could only be done at night for him and Pete. It wasn't only because their marathon sessions frequently involved copious drink and/or reefers, it just seemed like those two could only get into the creative zone when the real world was asleep.

So living in separate shifts the way they did – and childless, single, man-about-Shoreditch Pete didn't understand the bourgeois concept of 'weekends' either – Hannah did sometimes wonder quite how she and Matt kept their bond intact.

But apart from the fact they really loved each other, there was one very good reason their connection was still watertight, as she was reminded much later that night when Matt came in and she was still up.

She'd had every intention of going to bed early, but whilst doing a hasty sort-out in the sitting room, which was practically knee-deep in Hector's toys, she'd come across an a box of old photographs underneath the sofa, when she was fishing out some stray bits of Lego.

She vaguely remembered pushing it under there with a lot of other 'treasures' when they'd moved in nearly five years before and hadn't given it a thought since. But from the moment she started flicking through the contents, all her tidying and early-night intentions were blown. It was like turning on the telly randomly and finding your favourite movie playing. With you as the star.

She was so immersed in it she had no idea how much time had passed when Matt eventually came back.

'Still up, babe?' he said, leaning against the door frame, pulling his earbuds out and stuffing them into the pocket of his jeans.

'Look at this,' she said, holding up the picture she'd been looking at when he walked in.

It was the two of them standing at the top of King's Canyon, squinting into the sun, a brisk breeze blowing hair all over their faces, grinning with dopey happiness. He had one arm tightly around her shoulder; the other was holding the camera out in front to take the picture.

'Wow,' he said, flopping down on the floor next to her and taking the snapshot from her hand. He put one arm round her and extended the other out in front of him, just like in the picture.

'Shows how long we've been together, babe,' he said. 'We've got photos together that are prints. And now I've got to hold it out in front of me like this to see it.'

He laughed, but Hannah was still feeling a bit misty, after coming across this one and all the other pictures she hadn't looked at for years. It had brought back the memories of their first days together so vividly. That trip to Alice Springs and beyond had marked the start of their relationship getting serious.

'Don't we look happy?' she said quietly.

'We were,' said Matt, kissing her neck.

'Were?' she replied with mock outrage, pretending to push him away.

'We were happy then and we're delirious now,' he said, returning to the neck-nuzzling, which very quickly involved areas lower than the neck, and simultaneously shrugging off his leather jacket.

Hannah was feeling weary after the odd day at work, followed by a fairly frantic evening with the kids, but even in that state Matt could still rev her engines in no more time than it took his lips to make the journey from head to breasts, which he was now enthusiastically investigating. And he knew exactly what that did to her.

'Mmmm,' he was saying. 'I think we should have two more children. I love what it does to your nipples.'

Hannah loved what he was doing to them and sinking back on to the cushions Hector had thrown on the floor when making a camp earlier, she pulled him down with her.

'Filthy London carpet,' he said, pulling up her dress. 'Kinky. I like it.'

# Chapter Nine

Mel came back from work for the fifth night in a row to find Ali still lying where she'd left her in the morning – on the sofa watching rubbish television – and decided it was time to get firm with her.

She'd been home from the hospital for two weeks now, but had spent all of it so far in that position, hardly eating, quite often with a blanket pulled right up over her head. It didn't matter how many times Mel told her friend that the scars would fade with time and that she should go to London as she'd planned to help her get over it, she just couldn't shake her out of the funk she'd fallen into.

'I'm shop-soiled,' Ali would reply, 'damaged goods. What's the point of doing anything? And I haven't saved up enough to go to London anyway.'

Mel had abandoned the idea of the fundraising party, as Ali had declared she wouldn't come to it. Her suggestion that she lend Ali the last $200 of her self-imposed savings goal, or that she put in a claim for criminal injuries compensation, had also been rejected. As had her hints that maybe Ali should move home with her mum until she was better. Apart from anything else, her share of the rent was due, and with the state Ali was in, Mel didn't feel she could nag her about it.

'You are, without a doubt, the dumbest genius I've ever met,' said Mel, tugging the blanket away from her friend's face, to get her attention. She pulled harder than she meant to and it fell on to the floor, revealing Ali's body clad only in undies, because she said getting dressed was still too painful. Mel winced silently. The scars on her thighs and stomach were so horribly livid, she still got a shock every time she saw them, but they would fade in time – especially if Ali would only use the skin-healing oil a beautician friend had given her. She hadn't even opened it.

'You make no sense, Ali,' said Mel, softening her tone. 'You're giving up your dream to go to London – which you've been talking about since we were twelve – because of injuries some random arsehole imposed on you? You've given that idiot control of your life. Can't you see that?'

'No,' said Ali, snatching the blanket back up and pulling it over her head.

Mel felt beaten. She had enough on coping with her job as a junior lawyer at a big Sydney practice. Mothering her friend as well was stretching her too thin and although she knew she'd miss Ali heaps when she was in London, she did need a flatmate who paid her share of the rent.

That's when inspiration struck. Seeing Ali's mobile on the coffee table she quietly picked it up and snuck off to her bedroom. Scrolling through the names, she found it easily: Matt, with a UK number, so it had to be her cousin, the one she was going to stay with. A quick look at the world clock told her it was 9 a.m. in London. Perfect. She called the number and the deep Aussie voice that answered confirmed it was the right one.

'Yeah?' it said.

'Oh, hi,' said Mel, feeling strangely nervous. 'Is that you, Matt? It's Melanie here, from Sydney. Ali's friend?'

'Oh, yeah, hi, Mel, how're you doing?'

'I'm OK, Matt, but Ali's not so good.'

'What's the matter?' he said. 'She's supposed to be coming over here. I've been waiting to hear from her. Is something wrong?'

'Well, a couple of weeks ago she had a bit of an accident. She's all right, but she got a lot of nasty cuts on her stomach and, er, legs. The thing is, Matt, it's made her pretty depressed and she's got it into her head that she can't come to London because of it. In fact, she won't get off the sofa.'

'That sounds like our Ali,' said Matt. 'Never one to miss the chance of creating a drama. But is it really bad?'

'Well, it's not great actually, but the scars will heal over time and I think an adventure like coming to London would take her mind off it.'

'Do you want me to speak to her?'

'Oh, yes, please,' said Melanie, her voice full of the gratitude she felt.

'But you don't want her to know about this call, right?'

'So right,' said Mel.

'OK. Give me her number and I'll call back in a minute – and thanks, Mel. You're a good friend.'

Mel went back into the sitting room, where Ali still had the blanket over her head, slipped the phone back on to the coffee table and then made herself busy in the kitchen area.

Five minutes later Ali's phone started up, with its unmistakeable whip bird ringtone. She didn't answer it.

'Phone, Ali,' Mel called brightly from the kitchen.

'Fuck it,' said Ali from beneath the blanket.

'Fuck you!' said Mel, darting over to answer it and suddenly furious. 'I won't let you carry on like this. I've had enough!'

She grabbed the phone and after saying a quick 'hold on' to the caller – whom she assumed was Matt – she thrust it under the blanket in the general direction of Ali's ear. She didn't even take it from her, so Mel held it there, cursing Ali in her head. She was properly pissed off now.

She could hear the low hum of Matt's voice, but not what he was saying. Whatever it was, it did the trick.

Ali suddenly took hold of the phone and sat up.

'Can I really?' she said, with the first trace of enthusiasm Mel had heard in her voice since the glassing. She crossed her fingers behind her back. And then her legs. Finally Ali started talking.

'But the thing is, Matt, I've got these shithouse cuts all over my stomach and legs and tits and I feel so fugly . . . I don't want to come to London looking like a car smash. That's why I'm so depressed. I was always going to come in May so I could have a bit of summer before my first winter, but I feel like if I put it off another year, I'll have to get any boring old job just to live and then I'll lose my mojo and never come . . .'

There was a pause while Matt spoke and then Mel saw an expression of delight dawning over Ali's face.

'Shit! I never thought of that. That's great. OK. I'm coming over. I'll email you as soon as I've booked my flight. Thanks, Matt. And give my love to Hannah and the kids. I can't wait to see the little buggers. Big kisses.'

Then she leaped up from the sofa and started dancing around.

'I'm on my way to London, I'm on my way to London . . .' she sang, doing conga moves around the room and over to Mel, putting her hands on her hips to make her join in. Mel was so relieved at the instant change in her she did for a few moments.

'All right, enough,' she said eventually, turning round to face her friend, 'I'm so happy you've changed your mind – you can't imagine how happy – but what happened? What's cheered you up so suddenly?'

'My cousin Matt. That was him on the phone wanting to know when I was coming to London. He says I can stay with them as long as I like, until I find a job and my own place and best of all – I told him about this . . .'

She lifted up her singlet and pointed at the still-gory cuts on her stomach.

'And he told me not to worry because even in summer it never gets warm enough over there to take your clothes off anyway, so no-one will ever see it, and I'll never have to explain how I got like this. Result! Right, I'm going to start packing. Come and help me, Mels.'

She skipped along the corridor to her bedroom and after sending up a silent prayer of thanks to Matt and whatever god had wrought this miracle, Mel did.

# Chapter Ten

Hannah arrived at work the next morning to find a beautiful bouquet of fragrant white flowers on her desk. It wasn't unusual for beauty directors to get flowers, but her eyes widened when she read the card on this bunch:

**We've got the mascara sales exclusive. Well done, Ronnie xxx**

Making her feel even better, she and Veronica had a lunch booked in that day with the PR from the beauty division of Giorgio Armani and they went to it together, travelling in great luxury, in the back of the gleaming Mercedes supplied by her boss's car service.

It wasn't far from the ChicClick offices in Great Titchfield Street to the Soho Hotel and Hannah would normally have walked, changing into her heels a few yards from the hotel entrance, but Veronica never wore anything but towering heels and never arrived anywhere on foot. She was strictly car to kerb.

She exercised with a private trainer in her home gym before work every morning, so didn't need the aerobic hit of a lunchtime walk that Hannah always seized upon, and would never waste ten minutes she could better use Blackberrying in the back while someone else drove. And having the car door opened on arrival and emerging, long toned legs first, was all part of her image.

It wasn't that she was up herself, Hannah thought, as they arrived at the venue and Veronica sat looking straight ahead waiting for someone – whoever – to open the car door. She just instinctively understood the theatrics of success. Stumbling out of the car behind her, forgetting to let the doorman come round to her side to open her door, Hannah was reminded yet again just how much she had to learn from her boss.

Her journey home that night was a lot less glamorous. She didn't get her favourite seat on the bus, in fact, she didn't get a seat at all. There was a problem at the depot which meant there were hardly any buses running on her route and she'd had to push and shove to get on at all when one had finally come along. If she hadn't had a text from Matt saying he and Pete had a meeting with someone and he needed to head out as soon as he could, she would have gone for a look round Liberty until the crowds thinned out.

Instead she spent the entire journey standing, squashed in with other people, trying to stay upright as the bus laboured along in the traffic, while holding all her bags. After being thrown backwards and forwards on to other grumpy commuters a few times by the driver's particularly lurchy style of driving, she gave up and squashed the bags between her feet, leaving her hands free to hold on.

It was when they were getting near to her stop and she started gathering up her stuff that she realised her laptop bag was missing. She looked all round, letting the bus pull away again, while she checked under seats and had a crafty look to see what bags other passengers had on their laps and between their feet. The crush had thinned out a bit now, but there was no sign of it. After missing another stop she had to accept it was gone.

Feeling stunned, she got off at the next opportunity and trudged back towards home, constantly looking back over her shoulder for a bus going that way, the bags that were left feeling heavier with every step. Her head was reeling as she tried to remember what had been on the laptop that hadn't been on her work computer as well. Most of it, she was horrified to accept.

She'd always known she should back it up after every single session to the memory stick Matt had given her to hang off her key ring, but she hadn't. She'd just been careless. What an idiot.

As she came up to the newsagents near the flat, she decided to treat Hector to some of the really nasty cheap sweeties he craved, so at least somebody in the house would be happy. She picked out two each of his favourites – flying saucers, false teeth, bananas, fizzy coke bottles and strawberry laces – and handed the bag to the man behind the counter.

But when she went to pay the 50p it came to, she couldn't find her wallet. It wasn't in the zip pocket of her handbag where she normally kept it. It wasn't in the other interior pocket or the front one. Eventually she crouched down and looked in every compartment of her stupidly complicated handbag, taking practically everything out. Where the hell was her wallet?

It must be in her tote bag, she decided. She must have forgotten to put it back in her main bag, but a quick trawl through there was fruitless too. In desperation, she even looked through the bag of food she'd bought in John Lewis food hall, but it wasn't there either. Finally, she stood up and explained to the man behind the counter – the man she had bought her newspaper from every morning, along with numerous pints of milk, emergency loo roll, comics, sweeties and so on for the past five years.

'I can't find my purse,' she said, 'but I only live a few doors down, so can I take these now and give you the 50p when I get my paper tomorrow?'

The man didn't answer. He just pointed at a notice on the wall by his head:

**Please don't ask for credit, as refusal may offend.**

She read it and looked back at him.

'I'm not asking for credit,' she said. 'I just can't find my purse and I'll give you the 50p in the morning, when I buy my paper here – like I do every day. OK?'

'No credit,' said the man.

53

'I'll bring it from the house in two minutes, then,' said Hannah, unable to stop her voice rising. 'I just want to take these sweets home for my little boy. You know him! I bring him in here all the time.'

The man shook his head and looked past her at the next customer.

'Are you serious?' said Hannah. '50p?'

'You are bothering my customers,' said the man, and he reached over and took the small plastic bag from Hannah's hand, putting it out of sight behind the counter. 'Next please.'

'Fine!' said Hannah, realising there were quite a few people behind her now and that she was going into London Loony mode – but she didn't care.

'You can keep your 50p worth of crap sweets,' she said, raising her voice, 'and I'll buy my paper somewhere else every morning. Goodbye.'

And then, after grovelling around to pick up her stuff, and dropping everything several times, she stomped out of the door, her cheeks flaming.

Even before she'd got home she regretted it. Buy the paper some-where else – where? On the bus? She'd just condemned herself to a life of great inconvenience. And where would she buy loo roll when they ran out on a Sunday evening now? Or an emergency pint of milk?

Then, as she kicked the front door of the flat open, after putting down and picking up all her bags again, the first sight that greeted her was Matt slipping on his jacket and picking up his keys.

'Bye bye baby, baby goodbye,' he sang, pecking her on the cheek as he passed her in the doorway.

'Stop!' shouted Hannah.

Matt came to an abrupt halt halfway down the stairs and turned to look at up her, one ear bud in, the other hanging down.

'What?' he asked, looking bewildered.

'Please don't go straight out tonight, Matt,' she said, furiously.

'But Pete's waiting for me,' he said, looking slightly pained. 'I told you I had to meet him and you're really late back, babes. I should have been there thirty-five minutes ago.'

'Well, I'm sorry I'm late,' snarled Hannah, 'but the buses weren't running properly and someone stole my laptop and I can't find my purse and that horrible man in the newsagent wouldn't let me take 50p worth of sweets for Hector even though I buy my newspaper there every single day and I told him I'd bring him the money right away and he still said "no credit" and now you're just going out, as usual, and leaving me on my own again.'

She threw her bags on the ground and plonked herself down beside them, bursting into tears. Hector was at her side in a moment, with Nancy following him at her fastest totter. Matt came back up the stairs, closed the door behind him and joined them all on the floor. He put his arm round Hannah's shoulder and looked into her face.

'Hey, babe,' he said. 'What's going on? Did I hear you say your laptop's been stolen?'

'Don't cry, Mummy,' said Hector, trying to lick the tears off her cheeks.

'Oh Hec, darling, don't do that. I don't want your spit on my face,' said Hannah, wiping it off and hefting Nancy on to her lap, as she started crying too, 'and don't you start crying, Nancy, no-one stole your laptop. This isn't about you, for once.'

Matt gently took Nancy from Hannah's arms and placed her on Hector's lap.

'Go on, Hec,' he said, 'be a big boy and look after your little sister while I look after Mummy.'

'But Mummy cleans my face with spit sometimes,' protested Hector.

'Not now, Heccie,' said Matt, firmly, 'cheer Nancy up for me, OK?'

Hector started pulling faces at his little sister and when that seemed to be working, he went into his full routine, culminating in dropping his shorts. She loved it. Matt pulled Hannah into his arms and stroked her hair.

'Tell me all about it, babe,' he said.

Hannah sobbed on to his jacket's leather shoulder.

'Some git has stolen my computer on the bus and possibly my wallet too. I can't find it.'

'Oh, what?' said Matt. 'That is crap. Come on, let's go and sit somewhere more comfy and I'll make you a cup of tea, OK? Or would you like something stronger?'

'Strong tea, please,' said Hannah. 'Builders.'

Hannah sat at the kitchen table, wiping her eyes and blowing her nose, while Matt put on the kettle, simultaneously texting Pete, distributing drinks to the kids and settling them in front of a DVD.

Once Hannah was fixed up with her tea and a packet of ginger biscuits, he brought all her bags through to the kitchen and methodically tipped them out on to the floor. There was no sign of the wallet.

After checking every inch of every bag three times he looked up at her and wrinkled his nose.

'Not looking good,' he said.

'I thought so,' said Hannah, 'what a monumental drag. And it was my new Anya Hindmarch one too. It was made of eel skin.'

Somehow the eel skin was the last straw and she dropped her head into her hands in despair. Matt gave the bags one last pat-down and then came and sat opposite her, taking her hands in his. She lifted her head to look at his face, gazing so tenderly at her.

Suspended in the strange vacuum that follows shock, Hannah felt as though she was seeing it afresh. The high cheekbones, the straight bony nose and square jaw coming into a perfectly symmetrical squared-off point, with a dimple in the middle. The deep-set dark brown eyes. The full mouth with the finely chiselled curves on the top lip. Heavy dark brows and a day's growth of stubble. Matt was such a beauty, she thought. He didn't really know how much, which was probably a good thing.

'They're only material objects,' he was saying. 'At least you weren't hurt. You could have been robbed at knifepoint.'

Hannah nodded, smiling weakly at him.

'It's just so horrible knowing that someone who was on that bus with me, someone I shared air with and probably looked at, took my laptop bag from between my feet and then went looking for my wallet. They knew who it all belonged to. It wasn't random.'

'That's big cities for you,' said Matt. 'Lots of people so desperate they lose their sense of humanity.'

Hannah looked back at him.

'So just remind me again why we live in one?' she asked.

# Chapter Eleven

Charlie was sitting in the bath singing. The smell of Badedas mingled with the fragrant smoke curling up from the fat cigar he was holding in his right hand.

'Fly me to the moon,' he warbled, clamping the cigar between his teeth as he picked up a large loofah and scrubbed the back of his neck. Then he remembered why he was so happy and paused for a moment before resuming. 'Because all the bears that ever there was . . .'

Carefully placing the cigar in an ashtray lifted many years ago from the Hemingway Bar in the Paris Ritz, he stood up and vigorously lathered himself all over.

'Hello, old boy,' he said, looking down at his penis, before giving it and his testicles a good going-over. 'Still a bit of life in you, I see,' he said with satisfaction as it responded to his touch. 'Well, save it 'til later, champion. No time now.'

Standing up straight, after rinsing off the bubbles, he looked at himself in the steamy mirror on the wall at the end of a bath. He liked what he saw. Yes, it was all heading south and a bit soft round the middle, but the broad shoulders he'd developed rowing at school were still with him and provided a fine frame for a man's body to age around.

He ran a hand through his thick hair and blew himself a kiss, before stepping out of the bath and pulling on a thick towelling bathrobe, also stolen from the Paris Ritz. That had been a very funny weekend.

After another quick puff on the cigar, he settled himself in front of the mirror for his shave. Shaving was a serious ritual for Charlie, to be taken slowly and with great care for a perfect result, offering the chance for some clear-headed thinking, the busy part of his mind occupied with not cutting himself, or accidentally shortening one end of his moustache, so the deeper part could really think. He'd come up with some of his most brilliant defences while shaving.

It also offered an opportunity to admire the bone structure he had inherited from his Irish mother. He always sent up a little prayer of thanks for it.

'Thanks Mummy,' he said aloud, 'very grateful for the boat race.'

Taking the scissors he'd had for over fifty years he gave his moustache a careful trim, then inspected his nostrils and ears for unwanted sprouts of wiry white hair. Finding his tweezers in the bone cup he kept on the shelf over the sink, he plucked out a few eyebrow hairs which were getting a bit Brezhnev.

He'd always believed his immaculate appearance had played a large part in his success at the Bar. He'd been famous for it. The male members of the jury wanted to be him, the female ones wanted to . . . well. And he'd always flirted with all of them in the way that came completely naturally to him, because they had to like you as well as be convinced by what you said to them. But it all had to be done with finesse. If you came over as a Flash Harry that wouldn't have helped at all and judges didn't like it. The secret was to be the madly dashing chap who was their new best friend.

After checking the top of his nose for hair growth – he'd known men who'd grown virtual beards on there and was always on alert for signs of it – he slapped on some aftershave, shuddering pleasurably at the sting. Then he scrubbed his nails and round his gold signet ring, which his grandfather had given him on his twenty-first birthday.

He saved the teeth-cleaning for after breakfast, so this stage of ablutions ended with the hair, to which he applied a little oil of limes and then attacked vigorously with an ivory-backed brush in each hand. They'd belonged to his father and he was planning to leave them to young Hector.

Very important for a man to give his hair a good brushing twice a day, stimulate the scalp, boost the blood supply. He was sure that was why he still had a full head of it. And never a trace of dandruff on his shoulders.

With the cigar back in his mouth he headed into his drawing room, looking pristine after a visit from the marvellous Fiona earlier that morning, just as Escoffier appeared at the door with a newspaper in his mouth.

'Oh, you good boy,' said Charlie, taking the paper, which was only slightly damp and chewed at the edges, and giving the Labrador a vigorous rub around the head and ears. 'Now wait a moment, Scoffie.'

Opening out the *Telegraph* to read the front page as he went, he headed to the kitchen and found a cold sausage in the fridge, which he threw to the happy dog. Then he rootled through the pile of post Fiona had left on the kitchen counter, opened a dull-looking letter – a newsletter from the London club he never went to any more – and wrote on the empty envelope: 'Thank you, my precious xxx'.

Going over to the dog, who had swallowed the banger in two gulps and was hovering by the kitchen door keenly hoping for another, he held the envelope in front of his shiny black nose. Escoffier opened his mouth and Charlie placed the note gently between his jaws.

'Now take that over to Mummy and I'm sure you'll get another treat, OK? Biscuits, Scoffie! Biscuits!'

With his tail wagging wildly Escoffier jumped up and ran back down the stairs, as Charlie chuckled to himself and turned to fill the kettle. Time for several cups of tea and an assault on the crossword.

Marguerite was helping Fiona make the beds in the nursery.

'I'm so looking forward to seeing little Nancy again,' said Fiona, tucking the sheet round the mattress of a cot Hannah had slept in as a baby. It had bunnies and teddies painted on a panel on the side.

Marguerite could remember buying it in Peter Jones when she was heavily pregnant. Charlie had joined her there after a long lunch and had pinched the salesgirl's bottom. Luckily people hadn't sued for things like that in the 1970s.

'Does she still sleep in that little padded bag, buttoned on her like a dress?' Fiona was saying. 'I thought that was very comical, but a clever idea. Babies so often wake up because they've kicked the covers off, don't they? They get cold, little lambs.'

'I believe she does still sleep in her bag,' said Marguerite. 'I wish those had been around when Hannah was little, she was a terrible sleeper.'

'Oh, my girls were great sleepers,' said Fiona. 'The hard bit was waking them up for school, even when they were tiny. Their kids are exactly the same, but it's when they get on to other things you have to start worrying, isn't it?'

She laughed heartily and Marguerite smiled at her, amused as ever by the non-stop chat and the merry sight of her pillar-box red hair around the house. It was short and spiky on the top and she had glasses to match, with red sparkly frames in a cat's-eye shape. She was wearing a tunic top in a bright swirling print over red leggings and thick-soled rubber flip-flops, also red. Her toenails were bright blue.

Marguerite always wondered how Fiona managed to clean so quickly and thoroughly with large rings on every finger. Charlie had given her various lovely rings over the years – usually by way of apology for some outrage – but she found they got in the way of her work, so she only ever wore her slender gold wedding ring. And there were times when she'd taken that off. It was one of the more dramatic techniques she'd used to make him calm down for a while.

Once Hector's bed was made with a new set of linen featuring a bright circus print, Marguerite went down to the kitchen, arriving there just as Charlie came to the open back door.

'Permission to enter Ma'am,' he said, saluting and snapping the heels of his deck shoes together. He was wearing brick-red sailing trousers and a Jermyn Street shirt in a bright multi-stripe, a yellow cashmere jumper draped around his shoulders. She could smell freshly applied cologne. He could have come straight off a knitting pattern, she thought, not for the first time.

'Don't be so daft,' said Marguerite. 'Do you want some coffee, or will you wait until they get here? I'm going to the station to meet them in ten minutes.'

'Can I come with you?' he said, his face brightening at the idea. He looked about ten years old. 'Make it more of a welcoming committee.'

Marguerite thought for a moment. She wanted this week to be perfect and if she left Charlie at home on his own in an overexcited state, there was a chance he could have his first little celebratory drink before they got back. Which would be the first of many. Holding off the first one was the trick of it.

'Good idea,' she said. 'It would be lovely to give them a proper welcome.'

'Marvellous! Can we go now? Have a cuppa at the station buffet while we wait? I can be Trevor Howard to your Celia Johnson.'

Marguerite had to smile. Charlie's enthusiasm for life was unquashable and still, she found after all the years and all the excesses, fairly irresistible.


Hector saw them first.

'Charlie!' he shouted, frantically pressing the open button on the train door, well before the train stopped. 'Charlie's there! Look! Hello Charlie!'

Charlie hadn't seen him yet, but the minute the train door opened and despite his parents' protests to wait, Hector leapt off the train and ran up the platform to jump into his grandfather's arms.

'Hello Hector, my boy,' said Charlie, swinging him round and then putting him down again rapidly, a bit red in the face. 'Right, let me inspect you. Stand up straight. Have you grown?'

Hector looked up at him, face bright with excitement, as he squared his shoulders and held his breath, standing up as tall as he could.

'I think you have! Catch!' cried Charlie, pulling a toffee out of his pocket and throwing it in the air. When Hector didn't catch it, he pulled out another and put it straight into his hand, ruffling his hair at the same time.

Marguerite rushed to help Matt and Hannah, who were battling to get their luggage, a pushchair and Nancy off the train, before it pulled off again. Matt put the baby straight into her arms.

Marguerite's eyes filled with tears as she looked at her granddaughter's face, so like Hannah's at the same age, with the same creamy skin, from her side of the family, but with Matt's deep-set dark eyes.

'Hello, my little darling' she said. Nancy gazed back at her and then gave her a beaming smile, which made her suddenly look exactly like Charlie.

Marguerite blinked with surprise. The games genetics played.

# Chapter Twelve

Ali was in London. She was kneeling on the sofa in Matt's unit looking out of the window down on to Hackney Road. Every time a red double decker bus trundled by, which was often, she felt like punching the air. It was proof she was really there. Looking to the left she could see a red post box on the corner. More proof. If a Beefeater could just stroll past . . .

The low grey sky was another reminder she was no longer in Sydney, but Ali was thrilled with it. It had been raining when she arrived at Heathrow that morning and she was delighted. The more clothes she could wear, the better.

She got up and turned on the TV, relishing the accent of the woman smiling out at her. It sounded like Scottish, rather than the plummy BBC English she'd been expecting, but she wasn't complaining. It wasn't Aussie, that was the thing.

The screen changed to ads and Ali went over and sat cross-legged on the floor in front of the TV to eat her toast and Marmite, every commercial seeming like a lesson in understanding her new country. Her new home. Yay!

The toilet roll advertised with puppies here was called Andrex. Interesting. But what on earth was Cillit Bang? That was weird.

She looked down at her toast after the first bite. Bloody oath, it really was different from Vegemite. Not quite so sweet? A bit more tangy? She liked it, but she could see how it would always be a surprise to put the so familiar-looking bit of toast in her mouth and be greeted with that just very slightly different flavour.

Her tea tasted different too; probably the milk. And the water. People had warned her that London water tasted horrible. And the coffee was the worst, she'd heard. She could hardly wait to try some. Surely it couldn't be that bad? She didn't care anyway. It was *London* coffee, that was the thing.

It was a shame Matt wasn't at home when she arrived – he'd told her they would be away staying with Hannah's parents – but she'd got in using the keys he'd mailed to her in Australia.

Now what? She'd unpack a bit, but not too much, because the flat wasn't exactly spacious and once they all got back on Sunday, she'd be sleeping in the sitting room and didn't want to be a nuisance, cluttering the place up. She couldn't imagine how four of them fitted in there really, even though two of the residents were only tiny.

She couldn't wait to see the kids – Hector had been over to Sydney when he was little but she'd never seen Nancy before – and had been looking at all the adorable paintings stuck up around the kitchen. Hector seemed to have a thing about the red buses too.

After pulling out an outfit she thought suitable for her first day in London and finding her wash bag, Ali headed for the bathroom to scrub the flight out of her hair.

It was very cramped in there and there wasn't a separate shower stall, just one of those crappy things attached to a bendy metal tube, hanging from a hook on the wall over the bath.

She turned it on and was surprised to see just a thin spray of water coming out of it. It was more of a mist than a shower, tiny droplets like you get off a waterfall, but without the cascading water bit underneath.

She turned round to grab her shampoo, thinking it might get going if she gave it a moment, but when she looked back, it was exactly the same. How was she supposed to wash her hair in mist? She stepped underneath what flow there was and it took ages even to get her hair properly wet.

She finally lathered it up and then, as she tried to get the shampoo out again, she felt the water starting to get cooler. She turned the temperature knob higher, which made a difference for a few moments, but then it cooled again until she was standing under a cold shower, with a head still full of shampoo.

'What the fuck?' she said, hopping out on to the bathroom floor and grabbing the shower head off the wall so she could rinse just her hair over the bath without cold water also pouring over her body, which had made her barely healed cuts start to burn and throb.

She gave up on the idea of conditioner and after wrapping her freezing head in a towel, very gently patted her body dry then applied the healing oil which Mel had insisted she bring with her. Hurt like hell rubbing it in.

Dressed in a 1960s shift dress which came just to her knees, hiding the marks on her thighs, and a very washed-out denim jacket, her hair hastily zapped with Hannah's drier, which she'd spotted on top of the wardrobe, she drew a thick line of black eyeliner on her top lids and pulled on her boots. A pair of vintage Vivienne Westwoods which were her best ever eBay find.

She looked at herself in the long mirror in the bedroom. Maybe she should dye her bleached blonde hair back to brunette to mark the start of her new life. She ruffled it with her hand to make it messier, pushing her fringe over to one side. No, she still loved her Blondie hair. She'd dyed it on her first day of uni and it felt like part of her now.

As she turned to leave the room she noticed the huge array of make-up on Hannah's dressing table. It was all perfectly arranged with a Perspex box full of lippies, another of eyeshadows and so on, and all really amazing brands, like Chanel, Guerlain and Dior.

Of course, Hannah was a beauty editor, so it wasn't surprising her dressing table looked like David Jones' beauty hall. It couldn't hurt to have a little look. She carefully opened lipsticks until she came to one she couldn't resist trying – a fabulous matt fluoro pink. She put it on and stepped back to check out the effect. Yeah. That was the finishing touch. She was ready.

Now what?

Ali went back into the lounge room and slumped on to the sofa. All those years of dreaming about London and now she was here. But what to do first? Trafalgar Square? The Tower of London? TopShop?

She picked up the folder of pages she'd printed off from her months of internet research, so crammed and bristling with post-it notes it was threatening to burst out and fall over the floor, and put it straight down again. The last thing she needed was more information; she was overloaded with it already. What she needed was a phone. A UK phone. So that's what she'd do, she'd go out and get herself a phone.

She gathered up her things, taking out what she didn't need, like her passport and Australian money, then as she picked up the flat keys, she remembered the welcome note Matt had left for her on the kitchen table.

She went back and read it again:

> **G'day Ali! Welcome to London. You're going to love it. We're at Hannah's folks, back Sunday. Number on fridge, my mobile doesn't work down there. Sleep in our bed – then it's the sofa, sorry! If you get lonely ring my friend Pete. He's a good Aussie. Number also on fridge, under Toxic Pete. See ya Sunday. Matt xxx**

Ali wondered if she should ring to tell him she'd arrived safely, but didn't want to intrude on their family time. Maybe later. Meanwhile, she sent him a text using her Aussie phone – he'd get it eventually – before turning it off with a sense of finality.

Pausing to write down the phone numbers from the list on the fridge, she stuffed the piece of paper in her bag and headed out, still wondering exactly where to go. There didn't seem to be much in the way of shops in the road where Matt's place was, except a newsagent. She went in and asked the man behind the counter if he could tell her where she could buy a phone. He didn't seem to understand what she was asking him.

'No phone here, no phone here,' was all he would say to her polite request, reaching past her with his hand out to take money from the customer behind her.

Feeling rather disoriented by his unhelpfulness, she turned to leave the shop. She was standing in the doorway, wondering whether to go left or right, when someone touched her arm. It was the woman who'd been behind her in the shop.

'If you want to buy a phone, go that way up to Mare Street,' she said, 'or head back the other way, towards the City. Get a bus.'

She had a distinctive Australian accent. Sounded like Melbourne. The way she'd said 'goy' for 'go'.

'Hey,' said Ali. 'Are you Aussie?'

'Yeah,' said the woman, 'and I can tell you are. Just arrived?'

Ali nodded, half embarrassed, half still completely overexcited.

'Well, good luck,' said the woman and walked off before Ali could even thank her.

Ali watched her go, grateful for the advice, but it was odd she hadn't even asked Ali where she came from in Oz or anything. They might know people in common. Oh well. She carried on standing on the street as buses went by in either direction, still wondering which way she should go. She could remember that to the left was the way she'd come to Matt's earlier in the morning and decided that seemed a better bet, not entirely new territory.

So she got on the next bus that came along, slapping her Oyster card against the reader with a great sense of satisfaction. It was heading back the way she'd come that morning, and once she got into her seat, she wrote the number – 48 – in her notebook, next to Matt's address. Not having a pocketful of crumbs to leave a trail with, that seemed her best bet for finding her way back.

Ali loved her seat, front right on the top deck, which she'd chosen because she reckoned it would have the best view. Plus she so loved the idea of a bus having an upstairs, it would have been rude not to sit there.

As it trundled along she scoped the landscape like a big game hunter, looking for signs that might indicate a phone shop, and generally checking it all out, trying to drink it up and make it part of her while every individual brick still seemed interesting. It was grimey and grungy and urban, pretty much like Newtown, where she'd lived in Sydney, but with a much older feeling. The grunge here looked historic.

After a while, they passed an old church with a mad-looking steeple which she was pretty sure meant she was in Shoreditch. She'd read up keenly on that area, which was meant to be where everything cool was happening in London now, and she was thrilled Matt lived near it. Forget Camden and Portobello Road, Ali knew they were just for tourists these days and she planned on becoming a Shoreditch local as quickly as possible.

She could see there were a lot of interesting-looking bars and restaurants in that bit, but it didn't look like good phone shop territory, so she stayed on the bus until it got more CBD-ish, with big office buildings and people in suits and ties, rather than rolled-up jeans and trilbies. When she saw the sign for Liverpool Street Station she hopped off the bus and there, right opposite, was a phone shop.

Forty-five minutes – and more money than she'd hoped to part with on her first day – later, Ali had a new mobile phone. She immediately texted Mel back in Sydney. A crazy use of credit, but she had to.

> Here's my new number . . . my LONDON number ha ha ha.
> Don't forget the 001144. Miss ya heaps Als xxxxx

She jumped up and down with excitement a couple of times after sending it and then wondered who to call next.

She did have a few contacts in London, mainly friends of friends, but she'd left all those numbers back in the folder at Matt's place. Then she remembered the note in her handbag and decided to give his mate Pete a call. Just because she could really.

He answered on the second ring, sounding pretty groggy.

'Yeah?'

'Oh, did I wake you?' said Ali.

'Only dozing,' said the voice. A very Australian voice, which Ali found more reassuring than she'd expected to. 'Who wants to know?'

'Name's Ali,' she said. 'I'm Matt's cousin.'

'Oh, yeah,' said the person she assumed was Pete, 'he said you might call. Welcome to the snake pit, Ali.'

'The snake pit?'

He laughed.

'Welcome to East London. Where are ya?'

'I'm opposite Liverpool Street Station.'

'You wanna have a coffee? I only live round the corner. I could do with a ceeffo.'

'That would be great,' said Ali, kneeling on the pavement to write down the details of where to meet him and wondering what the heck a ceeffo was.

She soon found out.

'So what do you think of your coffee?' asked Pete, a mischievous look in his heavy-lidded eyes.

Ali paused before answering, but something about the look in those eyes, gleaming beneath his tatty old corduroy cap, told her she could be herself.

'It's shithouse,' she said.

Pete burst out laughing.

'Oh, you're not wrong,' he said. 'Me and Matt call it ceeffo – like coffee in some ways, but not quite the same thing.'

'Is it like this everywhere?' said Ali, having another tentative sip and pulling a face. It was bitter and sickly and tasteless at the same time.

'No, this is a good one,' said Pete. 'Just kidding, I brought you here because it was handy; there are a few places – all run by Aussies and Kiwis – where you can get a decent cup, but this is OK by most standards here. And don't even think about going to Starbucks. That's like a bowl of water someone washed some coffee cups in. The day before.'

Pete leaned back balancing precariously on two legs of his chair, booted feet on the low table, arms behind his head, the glint of his half-closed eyes just visible as he checked her out. He wasn't good-looking in a conventional sense, but there was something about his face that made you want to keep examining it. He looked a bit like a lizard with a couple of days of beard growth. Maybe a cane toad.

'So, what are you doing here, Matt's young cousin?' he said after a moment.

'Being somewhere else,' said Ali.

'Fair enough,' said Pete. 'Got any plans beyond that? Big ambitions? Paying the rent?'

'No big ambitions,' said Ali. 'I just want to live in different air, have new experiences. I don't want to take over the world. Not like you and Matt.'

Pete laughed.

'Is that what we're trying to do? I do wonder sometimes.'

'How's it all going?' said Ali. 'The songwriting thing.'

Pete crashed the chair back on to all four of its legs and leaned forward, scratching his head underneath his cap.

'The thing?' he chuckled to himself. 'Oh, it's fun doing the thing, love all that, just doesn't make us any fuckin' money. Matt likes to give ideas away for free – says you have to give it out to get it back, karma coma stylee – but I'm more of your old-fashioned type. If you want some of my shit, pay me for it, kind of thing.'

Ali nodded. She was with Pete on that one.

Talking about work seemed to have made him restless. He drained his coffee – his ceeffo – in one, then clapped his hands and rubbed them together.

'Ready to go, Sydney chick? I'll give you Aussie Pete's tour of Shoreditch, if you like. Introduce you to the 'hood. Sound good?'

'Sounds great,' said Ali, forcing herself to finish her coffee, to make sure she stayed awake. Sitting inside the dimly lit café, her head had started to feel a bit woozy.

'I'm going for a leak,' said Pete, standing up. He turned away and then looked back at her, one eyebrow raised, his hand in his jacket pocket.

'Can you roll a joint?' he asked her.

'Sure,' said Ali. 'How many papers?'

Pete's face broke into a ragged grin.

'Your call,' he said, throwing her a packet of tobacco and heading off.

# Chapter Thirteen

Hannah was ecstatic about the flowers. There was a whole table of sweet peas – she had no idea there was so many different colours, from white to dark wine-red – and another of lilies, so the scent in the room was intoxicating. Hannah closed her eyes and drank it in, trying to remember a perfume launch that had made her so excited by a smell, and all the flowers looked so beautiful to her. How could the judges possibly choose between these entries?

Matt was with Hector checking out the cakes, deciding which order they would eat them in if they could have all of them. Marguerite had promised her grandson he could help her make whichever cake he most liked the look of and he was agonising between three tiers of chocolate and a Victoria sponge with a thick filling of jam and cream.

Charlie was outside keeping an eye on Nancy, who was in an informal crèche of little ones crawling and tottering around on blankets laid out on the grass outside the village hall. His role was to turn her and the others back every time they were about to leave the confines of the lawn and head towards the gate and the road.

It was quite tiring work – the little blighters were very determined – and he was delighted when one of the grandmothers brought him a cup of tea and a slice of coffee and walnut cake.

After consuming that he chatted to the lady who'd brought it out to him long enough to repay her kindness, and for her to go sufficiently pink in the way he was used to, and had been used to since he was nineteen. Job done.

He did sometimes wonder when it would wear out, this ability to inspire pinkness in ladies; surely it had to one day, but as long as he still had it he was going to use it. Spreading a little happiness, the fairy dust of flirtation, and making his own life that little bit easier at the same time. Win win win.

With this one sufficiently charmed to take over on the crawler/toddler monitoring, he scooped Nancy up and headed into the hall to find the rest of his family. They were gathered in front of the cakes.

'Here's Charlie,' said Hector, rushing over to grab his hand and pull him over to the tiers of sponges and fruit loaves. 'He'll know. He knows everything.'

'I don't know about that, Hector,' said Charlie, passing the baby to her mother, 'but what's the story here? What do you have on the case so far?'

'I'm choosing a cake to make with Granny,' said Hector, 'which is your favourite?'

'Well,' said Charlie, putting his hand up to his chin and considering the options, 'I've just had rather a good slice of coffee and walnut, but I'm not sure you'd enjoy the coffee aspect. My all-time favourite cake is Granny's Dundee cake. Especially the almonds on the top, all toasted from the oven. Yum . . .'

'Are those nuts?' said Hector, looking suspicious.

Charlie nodded.

'No way,' said Hector, 'I hate nuts. They're nuts. People who like nuts are nuts.'

He laughed loudly at his own joke and everyone joined in.

'Well, in that case,' said Charlie, 'your granny also makes a very fine Victoria sponge – but then, on the other hand, chocolate is never a cake to be dismissed without due consideration.'

As they continued to debate the merits of the various options, Matt came over to Hannah, relieving her of Nancy.

'So, how much longer do you reckon we're going to stay here?' he asked. 'I feel I've covered all the entries in the Cranhurst Spring Flower and Cake Show and Church Spire Fund-Raising Fête in some depth.'

'What else do you want to do?' asked Hannah, disappointed at the idea of leaving before she'd had the chance to sit outside with some tea and cake, enjoying the bunting-tastic village scene. It was a beautiful sunny afternoon, a gift. She remembered many previous spring fêtes which rain had forced to be held inside.

Matt shrugged.

'I dunno. Read the paper? Play some tennis? Ping pong? Tiddly-winks? Go for a run? Gnaw my own arm off?'

'Oh, Matt,' said Hannah, 'we've only been here half an hour and the kids are loving it. Can't you take Hector to the coconut shy, or to guess the number of sweets in the jar? Throw a wet sponge at the vicar? He's old enough for all that stuff now.'

Matt rolled his eyes.

'What?' said Hannah. 'Don't you think it's lovely? I love all this. Crap village fêtes are part of my DNA.'

'It's all right for five minutes, but it's not exactly the Easter Show, is it? Where's the show bag tent?'

Hannah thought for a moment and then glanced down at her husband's feet. He had his usual Converse on, they'd do.

'OK, here's an idea,' she said. 'Why don't you run home? We'll see you back there.'

Matt's face brightened at the prospect of some exercise and an escape from the suffocatingly twee scene. It wasn't anything like his idea of village people ha ha. It was a shame Pete wasn't there – they could have done an impromptu performance of YMCA. That would jolly things along. Hector knew the arm movements, so he could join in.

He was wondering whether he would rather be the Indian chief or the construction worker, when Hannah nudged him.

'So are you going to run home or not?' she said, sounding irritated.

'Oh, yeah, great, if you're sure you don't mind?' he said.

'Of course not, it's better than you getting all humpy, when we've still got days to go here.'

He leaned down and kissed her cheek.

'I'll be all right, babe, I'm sorry. I've just got to decompress a bit and get used to life in the sticks. You know I'm a city boy and it's always a shock to my system, so much green and space and air and stuff. Not enough people and pollution, makes me edgy.'

'Bugger off, then,' said Hannah. 'Find a car to run behind so you can fill your lungs with noxious fumes on the way.'

Matt handed Nancy back to Hannah, followed by his shirt, which he had shrugged off to reveal a T-shirt stretched tight across his muscular chest. His hands went automatically to the bottom of the T-shirt to pull that off too, but he stopped.

'Better not get topless here, right?' he said.

'Not if you want Charlie ever to let you back into the house,' said Hannah.

'Oh yes, Charlie's rules of decorum. Maybe he wouldn't mind if I got shitfaced first?' said Matt, smiling. 'And then you and Marguerite can show Hector and Nancy how to pretend it isn't happening, eh? Do pass the teapot, Mummy – Daddy appears to be vomiting into the aspidistra.'

'Like I said, Matt,' she replied, also smiling, but only just. 'Bugger off, if you're going.'

She play-kicked his shins and he kissed her cheek again. Although that last comment had been pretty close to going too far, they both knew joking about the weirdness of her parents' situation was much better than ignoring it.

Hannah was grateful to him for showing her there was an alternative to her mother's 'keep calm and carry on' coping technique. She just hoped nothing would ever arise with Matt that she would feel the need to shield their children from, because she knew that approach was what would come all too naturally to her. Button your lip and keep smiling.

But as she watched him jog down the country road in the direction of her parents' house, it didn't seem likely that it ever would. He had pulled his T-shirt off as soon as he was out of the gates, waving it round over his head, in a gesture she knew was for her benefit, before tucking it into the back of his jeans. She wouldn't mind investigating the contents of those jeans later. And the rest of him.

It was hard to say who was enjoying throwing wet sponges at the vicar more, Hector or Charlie.

'Good shot!' said Charlie as Hector hit him on the knee. 'Howzat!'

He hurled his own sponge and it hit the reverend smartly on his right shoulder, then he handed Hector a £5 note for more ten more sponges.

Marguerite sidled over.

'Don't you think Hector's done that enough now?' she said into her husband's ear.

'What? He's having a marvellous time, aren't you, Hec? He's a great shot. Oh, good boy! Bullseye!'

Hector had hit the vicar, whose upper body was pinioned in the wooden stocks which were brought every year for this event, right in the face and was now hurling sponges wildly one after another, with scant regard for where they ended up.

One of them hit the man who was running the stand at very close range and another landed at Charlie's feet. He picked it up and lobbed it at the vicar. Another bullseye.

'Stop it, Charlie,' said Marguerite, tightly, under her breath. 'People are starting to look. Let Hector throw those last ones, but please don't throw any more yourself.'

'Oh, all right,' said Charlie, looking like Escoffier when denied food at the dining table. 'Come on, Hec. Let's go and try our luck on the tombola.'

'Actually,' said Marguerite, her voice getting a little higher as she pictured the myriad bottles of cheap rosé on that stall. 'Nancy's getting a bit fractious and Hannah and I are going to have tea now. Would you like some cake, Hector? You can try lots of different ones and that will help you decide which one you would like to make with me.'

'Cool,' said Hector, throwing the last wet sponge over his shoulder and hitting the vicar right in the crutch.

Charlie was bent double laughing as Marguerite practically dragged him over to the tea tables, smiling graciously at the people gawping at them, as though she also thought it were all a great hoot, when she really wanted to hit her husband over the head with her handbag. And she was fairly certain he hadn't even had a drink. He was just high on excitement and marginally less mature than his grandson.

Hannah and Nancy were well established at a table by a lovely old cherry tree, heavy with bright green new leaves, sharing a large piece of sponge cake and chatting to her parents' nearest neighbour, Anthea. Marguerite hoped her nosy interest in Hannah had distracted her attention from Charlie's latest carry-on.

'Oh, would you look at the little poppet,' Anthea was saying, as Nancy pushed her splayed fingers into the cake and then pulled them out and licked off the cream, an expression of bliss spreading over her face. 'And here's your boy. Hello, Hector.'

'Hello,' said Hector, his face still red from the exertion of soaking the vicar.

'Are you having a nice time?' Anthea asked him.

'Brilliant,' he said breathlessly, 'me and Charlie were just . . .'

'Oh Hector, come quickly, there's only one piece of the chocolate cake left,' said Marguerite, practically dragging him away.

Charlie leaned down to kiss Anthea on the cheek, all too aware that she was one of the few female nuts he had never been able to crack.

'Hello, Anthea,' he said, sitting down at the far end of the table from her. 'Lovely day for the fête, isn't it, and you look radiant, as always. A bloom among the blooms.'

'Oh, what a lot of nonsense you talk, Charlie,' said Anthea, 'but you never give up, I'll give you that. I'm a seventy-five-year-old hag and I look it, but your granddaughter here is such a sweetie . . . So where are you planning to send them to school, Hannah, dear?'

The joy went out of Hannah's day as though someone had switched off the lights. Where the hell was she going to send them to school? She had no idea. Ever since Hector's fourth birthday the previous September it had been a black storm cloud looming on the horizon. One of several things that were keeping her awake at night.

He had to start school this September; it was already June and she didn't have a place for him yet anywhere she could bear him to go. The school nearest them, which he had been offered a place at, was just awful. One of the worst in the borough. He was on the waiting lists at all the good schools, but she knew they had a better chance of winning the lottery than getting him in to any of them.

The problem was they'd managed to move into a flat in an educational black hole. She blamed herself for not researching it properly at the time. They'd been so thrilled to get a relatively spacious two-bedroom which they could afford, close enough to their old place on Columbia Road to feel like the known world, it hadn't occurred to her to look into school catchment areas. That had seemed like the kind of dull conversation other people had, like talking about property prices and interest rates. Now she could think of little else.

She smiled weakly at Anthea, trying not to show her how sick the question had made her feel. She hadn't ever raised the topic with her parents and lived in a constant state of dread of them asking her about it.

'Well, it's not that easy where we live, in East London,' she said.

'*East* London?' said Anthea, as though Hannah had blasphemed. 'Do you mean the *East End*?'

'Hackney,' said Hannah brightly, hoping to throw her off.

'But isn't it ghastly there?' said Anthea. 'All knife crime and drugs and gangs? It's where those terrible riots started. I've read about it in the paper. You can't live there.'

Hannah glanced over to her father for support, but he was gazing off towards the tombola, apparently not listening.

'Well, it is rough in parts, but a lot of young families like us live there now. It's very fashionable . . . We love it.'

It sounded as weak to Hannah's ears as it clearly did to Anthea's.

'But you can't bring up this beautiful little girl in such a dreadful place,' she said.

Hannah was thrilled to see Marguerite arriving back at the table with a tray laden with slices of cake and cups of tea. She'd got back just in time to stop Charlie making his excuses and heading towards the bottle of port which was calling his name on the tombola stand. He was looking at it and unconsciously licking his lips, but a slice of fruit cake distracted him just in time, as Hector held it up right in front of his nose.

'Look, Charlie,' he said, 'I got the lady to cut me a special piece with three of those horrible nuts you like on it. I told her it was for me.'

Charlie grinned.

'Oh, you clever boy,' he said. 'Did you twinkle at her?'

'I'm not sure,' said Hector, 'but I did say please.'

Charlie chucked his cheek and pulled him on to his knee.

Marguerite was busy putting cups and teaspoons on saucers and offering different pieces of cake around, but Anthea wasn't about to be put off her subject.

'Hannah was just telling me that these beautiful children live in Hackney,' she said, pronouncing the word as though just saying it brought the smell of steaming ordure to her nostrils.

'Yes,' said Marguerite, 'the young seem to like it there these days. There are some very interesting shops. Will you have more tea, Anthea? Some cake? Hector and I brought extra plates, so we could all try a little of each. Which would you like to start with?'

'But Marguerite, you simply can't allow them to go to school in such a dreadful place,' Anthea persisted. 'They frisk the children for knives and drugs in those places. There are pushers in the playgrounds . . . and everything is filthy.'

Hannah prayed for a tsunami, or a tornado, anything to stop Anthea's flow and was breathless with relief when one materialised in the form of Fiona, her mother's cleaner.

'Oooh!' she was proclaiming loudly, bustling over in a riot of colour from her scarlet head to the purple toenails in orange sandals, peeping out of the bottom of her full-length strapless sundress in a bold tropical print. 'Let me see that little treasure.'

She swooped down and scooped Nancy up, holding her above her head and waggling her around, which made Nancy shriek with delight.

'Hello, Hannah,' she said, bringing Nancy back to hip level and covering her head in kisses. 'Isn't she gorgeous, your little one? I've been dying to see her again, I was telling Lady Berry just the other day, and is that big boy there Hector? Hasn't he grown? You'll be starting school soon, won't you, sweetheart?'

Hannah screamed silently.

'Yes!' said Anthea, triumphantly. 'That's what I was just saying and he's going to go to some terrible school in Hackney, with knives and drugs and hoodies. It really won't do Marguerite, you must talk sense to Hannah.'

'Well, we're not sure where he's going to go,' said Hannah, sounding pathetic even to her own ears.

'He should come to St Clements in the village,' said Fiona, 'with my granddaughters. It's a lovely school. It's just got another Ofsted Excellent – third time in a row – and they just got their gold in the vegetable growing project. They use the vegies in the school meals and the kids do some of the cooking. It's a wonderful school.'

'Yes,' said Anthea, triumphantly, 'and I know the headmistress. Used to play bridge with her mother. When are you going home, Hannah?'

'Er, next weekend,' said Hannah, feeling like she had accidentally jumped on to a flume ride that she couldn't get off. Oh, why wasn't Matt there? He would have known how to deflect this human nightmare.

'Marvellous,' continued Anthea, her vast bosom seeming to expand even further with satisfaction, 'you can you bring him in for a taster day next week. I'll have them ring Marguerite on Monday.'

Not having been in on the earlier part of the conversation, Marguerite was looking bewildered.

'But Anthea,' she was saying, 'there's no point in Hector having a taster day at a school here. He lives in London. They'd have to live here for him to go to St Clements.'

'Well, that's the other thing I was going to tell you all,' said Anthea. 'That cottage at the end of your drive is vacant. That rather odd couple who've been living there did a midnight flit – leaving the chickens behind – so the people who own it are very keen to get some decent tenants in there. They live abroad and I keep an eye on it for them.

I know they're prepared to drop the rent to get the right people, because they just want to know it will be looked after properly, without them having to worry. It has a lovely garden that would be marvellous for the children. I'll have the agent ring you, Hannah. Right, now I'm going to see if my sweet peas have won, I've just seen the judges go back inside the hall.'

And she got up and left them, without so much as a backwards glance.

# Chapter Fourteen

Ali had a job and a flat. Well, not a whole flat, but a room in a flat. A very small room with a futon on the floor and not a lot else, no window, but it was her room. Her room in London. Five minutes' walk from her job which would pay enough for her to rent it and as it was in a bar that served food, she got at least one free meal a day too. Talk about a result.

The really amazing thing was she'd got them both on her first day and all thanks to Matt's friend Pete, when he'd taken her on a tour of the neighbourhood, in full surroundsound, sensarama and Technicolor after they'd shared the joint Ali had rolled. A nice tight small one.

He smiled when she handed it to him.

'Nice discreet street doobie,' he said. 'Good work.'

As well as knowing someone in every shop, café, restaurant and bar he took her in to look at, he seemed to know a lot of people they passed on the street too. They all seemed pleased to see him, except for a few women, who ignored him or gave him filthy looks. They had to dodge into a bar to avoid one of them.

He'd grabbed Ali's hand suddenly and pulled her into a dark doorway on Kingsland Road.

'Sorry, Als, but that particular lady I really don't want to see. Not feeling strong enough today. Way too high on the Richter scale. Major earthquake merchant.'

He put his head back out of the door to make sure she'd gone and immediately ducked back in again.

'Shit,' he said. 'She's waiting at the bus stop outside. Let's have a drink here to be sure she's gone.'

They sat up at the bar with pints of Guinness. Ali's round.

'Cheers, Sydney chick,' said Pete, clinking his glass against Ali's. 'Thanks for the drink and well done ordering them in pints.'

'I've done my research,' said Ali, clinking back, 'but tell me, Pete. What have you done to all these women that you have to hide from them?'

He smiled, looking more reptilian than usual.

'Shown them a good time,' he said.

'And they hate you for it?'

'They hate me when it stops.'

Ali considered what he'd said for a few sips.

'So are you the sort of bloke who roots a girl a few times and then never phones her again?'

He looked at her and took a swig from his glass before he replied.

'Pretty much,' he said, after he'd swallowed.

'And you think they're angry with you because you're withholding your magic ding-a-ling from their life?'

He nodded. Ali leaned in close to him.

'Maybe they just think you're fucking rude,' she said.

Pete looked at her for a moment, very intently, and then burst out laughing.

'That's hilarious,' he said, smacking his hand down on the bar. 'You're probably right. Ah, that's good. Here's me thinking they're desperate for another dance with the Donger of Doom and they're just disgusted at my appalling manners. I love it. I'll have to get a book of knobbing etiquette. A gentleman must always send a lady a letter of appreciation after they have conjoined in mutual jiggy jiggy . . . That kind of thing?'

'Very funny. Not. But tell me, Pete, why do you do it? I've always wanted to ask an arsehole like you that. I've been done over by non-phoners – all girls have – and it's no fun. I mean it's all right if you both know from the start it's a one-night stand, that can be great for everyone, but are you the sort that romances them a bit? Not red roses and poetry, but in your Mr Cool of Shoreditch way?'

Now Pete looked a bit uncomfortable, pushing his cap up and scratching the front of his head.

'Might be something in that,' he said. 'I suppose I've always thought it was part of showing a girl a good time. Not just wham bam etc, but making her feel good about herself, give her something to remember.'

'And then dump her?'

'You might be right,' said Pete, scratching his hairy stomach through his shirt, where there were a couple of buttons missing.

Ali was starting to wonder if he had fleas. He didn't look very clean, but somehow it was in a cool way. He didn't smell, but with his unshaven jaw and well-worn clothes, he looked like an oversized Dickensian urchin. But it all just kind of worked, the reptile eyes, the big lips, the scruffy brogues with no socks. She could see why they had passed rather a lot of those wronged women. He had an earthy animal appeal.

'Do you want another drink?' he asked her.

Still only halfway down her first pint of Guinness, Ali was starting to feel seriously giddy and found it more and more difficult to stop her eyes closing. Pete caught her just as her head threatened to slump down on the bar.

'Ah,' he said, 'the stupid lag, I'd forgotten. Drinking in a dark dive is the last thing you need. Come on, let's go for a walk, you need to get as much sunshine as possible on that pineal gland, if we can find any. If that fails, we'll get some uppers ha ha ha.'

That was when he got her the job. As they were about to leave the bar a very tall man loomed out of the shadows and greeted Pete with the full honours: double fist-grip handshake and man hug, with back slapping.

'Tom, my man,' said Pete, 'I'm just showing my young friend Ali here the landmarks of Shoreditch and of course, this was our first stop. She's just off the plane from Sydney, going to live here.'

'Hi Ali,' said Tom, shaking her hand warmly, but without the extras. 'What are you planning to do over here?'

'She's looking for a job,' said Pete, quickly. 'She's got loads of bar and waitressing experience, all the coolest places in Sydney, and you know how amazing Aussie hospitality staff are. All the customers love 'em. You got anything?'

Even through the fog of jet lag Ali knew better than to show surprise at Pete's extensive knowledge of her CV. She hadn't told him any of it, but it wasn't too far from the truth. Except the 'coolest' part. The food court in Pitt Street Mall hadn't been that cool. Or the bloody pole dancing, but she didn't want to think about that.

'Yes,' said Tom, nodding and looking Ali over appreciatively. She wondered if she should open her mouth so he could check her teeth. 'I do need someone. Had a rather stroppy girl walk out yesterday. I'm covering tonight, but can you start tomorrow?'

'Sure,' said Ali, trying to sound eager but not desperate. 'What time?'

'Come in at six,' said Tom. 'You can do evenings at first. With your jet lag, you'll still be wide awake when we close at three. I pay the going rate, same as all the bars along here, and you keep your tips. Wear what you're wearing.'

They shook on the deal and Pete and Ali left, after he'd paused at the door for a moment to check the bus stop was clear.


Pete hadn't been joking when he said they were going for a walk. He led her back down to Shoreditch High Street and then turned off by the old church with the funny steeple she'd noticed on her bus ride earlier, along a street she saw was called Calvert Avenue. She got out her notebook and wrote it down, so she could check it out against a map later.

It all looked much fresher and posher than Ali had expected. She thought Shoreditch was supposed to be all grime and urban edginess, but this wide street lined with trees had some quite poncy-looking shops in it and a café with cool people sitting outside it, their bicycles leaning against a lamp post. At the end of that street they came to a very unusual square – actually it was a circle, Ali realised – of red brick buildings around a funny little park with a bandstand in it.

'Arnold Circus?' said Ali, pausing to squint up at the street sign. 'Can a street really be called a circus?'

Pete laughed.

'It can in London, darling.'

The next item to go in her notebook was '*Redchurch Street*', followed by '*Cool shops!!!!*'

She came to a halt, her nose pressed up against the window of one called Maison Trois Garçons, which had some really mad vintage furniture in the window. She could see a tantalising rail of clothes inside and wanted to go in and look at them, but Pete was strict.

'You've got the rest of your life to go shopping, darls,' he said, pulling her away, 'but right now, you've got to stay in the light, or you'll turn to dust. You're a jet lag anti-vampire.'

When they got to Brick Lane – Ali squealing with excitement when she saw that street sign – they bought smoked salmon and cream cheese bagels to eat as they went, suddenly starving after the beer. Somehow Pete could manage the slippery bagel in one hand, texting with the other and not walking into lamp posts or seeming to get them lost.

The texting was beginning to irritate Ali, but she kept quiet, because it was good of him to give her so much time, he'd just got her a *job*, for God's sake, and she was really enjoying the walk. It wasn't exactly fresh air they were breathing in and while it wasn't sunshine as she knew it, it was daylight, and he'd been right, she felt better with every step.

Just being there, being in it, with somebody who seemed to know every square metre personally – although the number of people Pete said hello to decreased rapidly once they left the strict confines of Shoreditch – made her feel so excited, her jet lag was soon forgotten.

Finally they arrived at a park, with grass, trees, the whole bit. It looked pretty big.

'Wow, where's this?' asked Ali.

'Victoria Park,' said Pete, 'Vicky Park, Hackney's lungs.'

'Do you come here much?'

'Hardly ever. Your cousin's always in here, though. He runs round it pushing the baby in her buggy, the wanker. I've told him he should move to LA and do it with a dog wearing sunglasses, but he doesn't see the joke.'

Pete laughed heartily, sitting down and kicking his shoes off. Ali decided she'd keep a safe distance from his sockless feet. They looked very hot and pink and she suspected they would not be exactly fragrant.

She flopped down a few metres away, but she could smell them from there. Rotten cheese.

'Can you put your shoes back on?' she said. 'Or take your feet off? They stink.'

He pulled one foot up towards his nose, surprisingly flexible, and laughed.

'I see what you mean, but hang on a tick.'

She felt like groaning as he stared down at his phone again, sending another text, his thumbs moving at hyper speed and then waiting a moment for a reply. She was about to ask him to put the bloody thing away, when his face broke into a grin and he looked up at her.

'Bingo!' he said, passing her the phone.

She looked down at the text:

> Yes there's still a room here. Pretty basic but there is a bed.
> £90 a week plus bills. I'll be in later if she wants to see it. Fred.

'So now you've got a job and a place to live,' he said, grinning at her.

'Are you serious?' said Ali. 'Is that why you were doing all that texting?'

'Mostly. Also setting up a little company for later.'

'Female company by any chance?'

He nodded and she shook her head, pretending to be shocked.

'But Pete, it's amazing about the place. Is it really sorted?'

He nodded.

'If you like it.'

'I'll like it. Thank you so much. You're like my guardian angel. An angel with stinky feet, but still an angel.'

He shrugged and handed her the phone.

'Send that message on to yourself, then you can ring Fred and set up a time to go and see the place. It's round the back from the bar where you're working and not a million miles from Matt, so I reckon you'll be cool there for a while. Fred's a good bloke. Big gayer, won't jump you.'

She forwarded the message to her new phone number and then, as she was holding his phone, couldn't resist having a look in the 'sent' box. She started laughing.

'What?' he said.

'"Why don't you come over and release that trapped chi you found in my neck last night,"' she read out.

'Hey! You cheeky bitch, give me that!'

She threw the phone to him, still laughing.

'Oh, that's got to be up there with showing her your etchings. You old sleaze. You're just Hugh Hefner in skanky hipster clothes.'

'Well, it can't be that bad, because she's coming round later when she finishes work, massaging rich women in the spa at the Grosvenor House Hotel. I get it for nothing.'

Ali made a fake impressed face. 'Sounds special. But tell me, Pete, will you call this one after your happy ending?'

'If you say so, Sydney Chick. But what do I say? "Thanks for making beautiful music with me"?'

'Well, it depends how you feel about her. You might say, "It was great, but I'm not going be able to see you again, because I'm really busy with work and I have to keep all my trapped chi for that."'

'Watch it,' he said, wagging a finger at her.

'Or, "I've decided to take a vow of chastity." OK maybe not that. How about, "Spending this amazing time with you has made me realise I'm not over my last girlfriend and it wouldn't be fair on you." Or, "I think I might be gay." Or, maybe the truth: "I'm too emotionally retarded to have a sustained relationship and just want to have serial meaningless sexual encounters with as many different women as possible to make me feel more secure in my manhood." But the key thing is to say: it's not you, it's me.'

He looked at her, bemused. He was used to women laying the hard word on him – way too used to it – just not before he'd had sex with them. It was quite an interesting experience this way round.

'Or, then of course,' continued Ali, 'you might say, "I've fallen madly in love with you, please move in and have my babies."'

'That is never going to happen,' said Pete.

'Have you never had a proper relationship?'

'I've had girlfriends, but eventually the baby thing always comes up and I just don't think it's compatible with what I do. Do you want kids?'

'Not right now,' she said, 'but one day, yes, it's what we're here for.' Pete groaned.

'It's not what I'm here for,' he said. 'I'm here to look after me, do my best at that, not taking on someone else's shit – literally – but the other thing you were saying before, about telling women I don't want to take it any further, I'm going to try it. Really. Because in all honesty, it is getting to be a bit of a hassle avoiding people all the time and Matt's not the only one calling me Toxic Pete these days, although it was his wife who originally came up with that one.'

'Why, did you hit on her?'

Pete laughed. 'No, but I bloody would if she wasn't married to my best mate. What a total babe. Mind you, Matt's such a handsome bastard himself, it's a nightmare going anywhere with him. All the women have their tongues hanging out and I have to mention his WIFE and CHILDREN every two minutes to have a chance with anyone.'

'Poor Pete,' said Ali, 'never gets laid . . .'

After a short session of pulling faces and sticking their tongues out at each other, started by Pete, they lay back on the grass and watched the white clouds passing overhead.

'The sky is smaller here,' said Ali eventually.

'Shit yeah,' said Pete. 'God, I miss that Sydney sky. More and more. I love London, it's amazing, but sometimes I feel so caged in here. I know Sydney's really one huge suburban sprawl, but you just have to look up to feel like you've got endless space, or you can go to the beach and the ocean goes on forever. People here think this park is a big deal and pay gazillions for the houses next to it, but it's like a puddle of mud compared to living near the ocean.'

'Do you think you'll ever go back?'

'For sure,' said Pete, turning to look at her, 'and sooner rather than later, but I dread telling Matt. He'll be gutted. We've worked together so long and he always thinks we're on the brink of the big breakthrough, but we're so not. We're just not new and interesting any more and there's always fresh waves of young kids coming up. They're obsessed with the new here, which is weird considering how old and knackered everything is, and we're just part of the Shoreditch scenery now. It's not happening for us and it's not going to. I reckon I've got more of a chance going back to Sydney and being the cool guy there who lived in Shoreditch for ten years.'

'Can't he go with you?'

'How? He's stuck here with the wife and kids – the English wife and the English kids. And she's got a great job, so why would she leave?'

Ali thought about it. She could see both sides of that one. Tricky.

'Don't say anything to him, will ya?' said Pete, looking uneasy, 'but I'm going to go at the end of this so-called summer. Get back for real summer there. I've already given notice on my lease. It's up at the end of August. I've just got to find a way to tell Matt.'

'OK,' said Ali, starting to wish she didn't know all that. 'I promise I'll keep my mouth shut – and Pete . . .'

He turned to look at her, smiling gently.

'Thanks. Thanks for everything you've done for me. It's incredibly nice of you to look after me like this, a total stranger.'

'But you're not a stranger, are you? You're Matt's cousin. That makes you almost family to me. But do you wanna know why I've really done it?'

His eyes were nearly closed, just the lizardy glint showing.

'Because you want to hit on me?'

'Ha ha ha, well I would, if you weren't family, you can be sure of that. You're cute and I like your style. A lot. But the real reason is you remind me of myself. How old are you?'

'Twenty-four.'

He nodded.

'That's just a bit older than I was when I moved to Sydney from deep country New South Wales. I'm forty-one now and it stirs my old bones to know there are still youngsters out there with that same hunger for life I used to have. That complete sense of freedom that comes off you, it's great. It makes me feel more alive just being around it.'

She smiled back at him and reached out her hand. He took it in his own big mitt, which was warm and dry with patches of hard skin on it. He was like a hot-blooded saltwater croc. She squeezed it tightly and then broke away again.

As she did it, she saw his eyes move down her body and stop suddenly. Shit, her skirt had ridden up and she'd forgotten about the scars on her thighs.

'They look nasty,' said Pete, frowning, 'and pretty fresh. How did you get those?'

Ali sat up quickly, pulling her skirt down over her thighs.

'Long story,' she said abruptly. 'I might tell you some time, but not right now.'

'OK,' said Pete, jumping to his feet and putting his hand out to pull her up, 'I won't push you. Now let's get a bus back to civilisation before I do try and get in your pants.'

# Chapter Fifteen

Matt was pacing round the bedroom waving his arms around like a human windmill.

'I'm not moving to the country, Hannah,' he said. 'I don't care if the house is free with a crock of gold in the garden, I don't do country. I don't even like it for a week, how could I possibly live in it?'

'I'm not asking you to move to the country,' said Hannah, trying to keep her voice down. She didn't want the children to hear. Or her mother. And she wanted him to calm down. His movements were getting so wild, Hannah feared for her mother's ornaments, all porcelain treasures she'd restored herself.

'We've got to view the house,' she continued, in as calm a tone as she could muster, 'because Anthea has set it up and it would be very embarrassing for my mother if we wouldn't even walk to the end of the drive to look at it.'

'What is this problem your family has with embarrassment?' asked Matt. 'Everything in this house is about not being embarrassed. Not being embarrassed that your father is a crazy drunk who'd set fire to himself for a brandy and not being embarrassed that your daughter lives in a scary part of London with a Labour-controlled council and hoodies. She's probably had to get over the embarrassment of having a colonial for a son-in-law.'

'Oh, Matt,' said Hannah, getting cross herself now. 'You know that's not true. Mummy might be a bit uptight, but she absolutely adores you. You're so good to her and so understanding and helpful about Daddy.'

'Listen to yourself, Hanns! "Mummy and Daddy". You're nearly forty. You're a grown woman, why do you play this creepy Milly Molly Mandy game here? You all need to grow up. Life's embarrassing, people fart in yoga classes and talk to you with boogers hanging out of their noses, so what? Does it mean the end of civilisation to be embarrassed? Is that the worst thing that can happen to you? My dad went bankrupt, but we weren't embarrassed, we were just fucking poor and furious with him for being such an arsehole.'

This was bad. Once Matt got on to the subject of his father, who had re-mortgaged the house to prop up his failing business without telling his wife and family, and subsequently lost all of them – the business, the house, the wife, the family – he could really go off on one.

He was such a lovely, easygoing guy ninety-nine point nine per cent of the time and hardly ever mentioned the great shock of his childhood, when he'd been thrust from a nice big suburban house and garden into a cramped rented unit. He was reconciled with his dad, but every now and again, if he was really upset, it all came out.

'Can we leave that out of this discussion?' said Hannah, trying to steady herself. She consciously lowered the pitch of her voice an octave, not to be shrill. 'The thing is my mum has to live here . . .'

'In this claustrophobic goldfish bowl of a village.'

'Whatever . . . her life is hard enough with my nutty father and I just don't want her to have the stress of Anthea yacketty yacking at her as well. Can't we just treat it like an anthropological expedition? Take the kids, make it an outing for them.'

'An outing to the end of the drive! Whoopee!' said Matt, throwing himself down on the bed in mock excitement. 'What I did in my holidays . . .'

But as soon as he did that, his body relaxing as it hit the bed, she knew the crisis had passed and she knew exactly how to get him over it completely. Taking advantage of where she was standing by the door, she turned the key in the lock and walked over to to him, unbuttoning her dress as she walked and letting it drop to the floor. Matt smiled and put his hand out to her.

Hannah could hear Hector running up from the far end of the garden.

'Mummy! Mummy! Mummy! Mummy!' he was saying urgently, but he didn't sound upset.

She headed quickly down the path that led under a rose arbour to see what was going on, as he arrived there, cradling something in his hands.

'Look!' he said, opening them, very carefully. A speckled brown egg lay there. 'And it's warm. It just came out of the hen's bottom and I found it. Can I have it?'

Hannah looked over at Anthea and the estate agent, hoping there wasn't going to be an upset. Far from it; Anthea looked delighted.

'Oh, you clever boy,' she said, 'of course you can have it. It's your very own egg and I'm sure Mummy will let you have it for tea, with toast soldiers.'

Hector looked a bit worried.

'I was hoping to keep it as a pet . . .'

Everyone laughed – even Matt, who was standing behind them with his arms tightly folded – and although Hector wasn't quite sure why, he ran with it, always hoping to get another laugh.

'Yes, and I'm going to call it Number One, because it will be my very first pet.'

'Your first pet?' boomed Anthea. 'A big boy like you, with no pets? Well, if you lived here, you'd have all those chickens as pets and I'm sure Mummy would get you a cat and a dog as well, perhaps even a few guinea pigs, that's the very least you should have. And of course, you'd have your Granny's lovely dogs to play with and I've got two seventy-year-old tortoises, so you'd be able to come and see them any time you like in the summer, and my two Shetland ponies, which you've seen before, haven't you? And I've got the rabbits, my dogs, three cats . . .'

Hector's eyes were so wide, Hannah thought they might pop out.

'Would I really have a guinea pig, Mummy?' he asked. 'You know how much I want one.'

Hannah smiled weakly, glancing over at Matt, who now had a face like thunder. Hannah had tried to introduce the idea of having a hamster in the flat, so Hector could have some kind of pet, even a very small one which wouldn't give much back, but Matt had put his foot down, saying he had enough human animals to look after already, without adding the randomly shitting and biting four-legged kind as well.

'Ha ha ha,' said Hannah, hoping to continue the joking nature of the exchange, but Anthea and Hector were looking at her with equal keenness.

'No,' said Matt.

Anthea turned and looked at him as if she were wondering where he'd suddenly sprung from and decided to ignore him.

'Do you like tortoises?' she asked Hector.

'I've never met one,' he said.

Anthea beamed.

'Well, that's something we can put right straight away. They've just come out of hibernation. Is it all right if I take him to meet Porgy and Bess?' she asked Hannah, pointedly not including Matt in the enquiry.

'Yes,' said Hannah, 'that would be a lovely treat for him.'

And it would get you away from Matt, she thought.

'Marvellous,' said Anthea, 'I'll bring him back to your mother's when he's met all the animals and you can tell me what you think about the house. Come on, Hector, and on the way you can tell me if you've ever seen the film *Dr Doolittle*, because that's the nickname some of the people in the village have for me. I have a parrot as well . . .'

Hannah turned back to Matt in time to see him raising his eyes to the heavens, his lips silently moving in what she was fairly sure was a long string of Greek expletives, the only words he knew in his grandfather's native tongue. But before she could say anything the peace was shattered by a loud air raid siren.

'Oh sorry, that's my phone,' said the estate agent. 'Better take the call – got quite a few properties going through today. Carry on looking round on your own, feel free.'

He disappeared down to the end of the garden where the chickens were roaming beneath the fruit trees and Hannah went over to Matt, who was now sitting down on a metal garden chair. Nancy had gone to sleep and he'd put her in her pushchair, under the arch covered in roses and honeysuckle.

'Don't say it,' said Matt, as Hannah went over and put her hand on his shoulder.

'Say what?'

'How adorable Nancy looks under the floral bower. Where the bee sucks there suck I and all that, but it doesn't mean I'm going to move in here. OK? It all sucks to me, a big one, and I think Nancy looks just as adorable on the platform of Hackney Central.'

'Would you lighten up?' said Hannah. 'We're only here for my mum's sake, to mollify bossy Anthea.'

'Dr Doolittle?' said Matt. 'Dr Do-too-fucking-much more like.'

'I just can't believe how you're behaving. We only have to have a look at the house and say we'll think about it and then I'll ring Anthea – or get my mum to, if I can possibly wangle it – to say thanks so much for your generous help, so kind blah blah blah, but it just doesn't fit in with our plans at the moment.'

'Or ever.'

'OK, or ever, but as we're here, we might as well have a look. I love looking at houses. Having a perve.'

'You perve away,' said Matt. 'I'm staying right here.'

'Suit yourself,' said Hannah and turned to walk into the house.

They'd come in through a wooden gate at the far end of the garden which opened from her parents' drive, so this was her first proper view of it. She had a choice of ways to go in, she saw, a set of French windows or one of those barn doors, with the top opening separately from the bottom. She chose the barn door and found herself in the kitchen. It had a bright red Aga, just like her mum's dark blue one.

The floors were stone-flagged and while there was no furniture in there, she could see there would be room for a big table with at least eight chairs. It had a butler's sink and lovely old built-in cupboards and shelves, all painted soft white.

Hannah's hand sprang up to her mouth. Perfect. It was perfect. She opened a door and found herself in a laundry, with one of those drying racks that go up and down on ropes and an airing cupboard big enough to walk into.

Her mind flipped back to the flat in Hackney. The washer and dryer stacked up in the kitchen, delicate items festooned all around the flat to dry. So little food storage space they had to shop for it practically every day.

Another door opened into a back hall, with rows of coat hooks and she tried to stop herself picturing four pairs of wellies lined up there, ranging from very big to really tiny.

Feeling oddly nervous, although she wasn't sure if it was for fear it would be as nice as the kitchen, or disappointing by comparison, she opened the door into what she assumed would be the hall, to find it was big enough for a really enormous Christmas tree. They could only fit a very sad small one in the flat.

There were two sitting rooms leading off from there, both with fireplaces. The one with the French windows on to the terrace where Matt was sitting was bigger and more elegant, the other one smaller and cosier. Starting to feel almost queasy about how gorgeous it was, she headed upstairs to find three bedrooms and a bathroom, which had an old claw-foot bath sitting in the middle of it.

Hannah let out a small whimper. The bathroom was big enough to have an armchair in it and she could see that when you were sitting in the bath you would look out on to a view framed by trees, over fields to the hills in the distance.

She went into what she assumed was the master bedroom and opened one of the windows. It looked over the garden, where everything seemed to be in bloom, the chickens were doing their thing and she could see Nancy snoozing in her bower. As she looked down a butterfly flew past her baby's sleeping face.

It was all perfect. The only blight on the scene was her handsome husband, who was hunched over the garden table, fiddling with something. Looking more intently Hannah could see him rubbing his fingers in small movements. Then he lifted the thing up, rolled it and brought it up to his mouth.

Oh great, he was rolling a joint. She hoped the estate agent wasn't going to come back while he was at it and was relieved that she could see him leaning against the wall at the end of the garden, still intent on his phone call.

Matt lit his illicit ciggie, took a strong pull and then leaned back in his chair, blowing the smoke out. She wondered why he thought this was a good moment to indulge in one of the habits she found least appealing about him, but then thought at least it would relax him. Make him a little less grumpy.

Giving him time to have a few more puffs, she looked round the house again, falling more in love with it all the time. It was ideal for a young family. She could imagine Hector running in and out of that garden in all seasons, not needing to be dragged over to the park by one of them just to get a few lungfuls of fresh air. And going to the village school with its 'Excellent' Ofsted status without any bother about catchment areas and waiting lists.

Just as she stepped back out on to the terrace the estate agent came bustling up to them.

'I'm really sorry,' he said. 'Got a nightmare going on. Chain of six houses completing today and a problem's come up with one in the middle. I've got to go back to the office, but please stay and look at your leisure, don't feel you have to rush. Here are the keys, just lock up when you finish and give them back to Anthea.'

'Thanks,' said Hannah, taking the keys, feeling the weight of them in her hand and squeezing them involuntarily. She wanted those keys.

'And here's my business card,' continued the agent. 'I've written the details of the rent on the back – and I presume Anthea explained that the choice of tenant is subject to her approval? OK, goodbye.'

Hannah nodded, holding the card in her fingers, desperate to see how much the rent was, but at the same time almost not wanting to know. She didn't know which would be worse – if they could afford it, or they couldn't. The moment he left she looked down, then blinked a few times, to be sure she was seeing it right. £450 a month. A month? Their flat was £350 a week. £450 a month for this haven was incredible.

'How much is it?' said Matt, looking at her with slightly glazed eyes.

Hannah snatched the card behind her back so he couldn't see it.

'Come and look round with me,' she said, 'or I won't tell you.'

'All right,' said Matt, getting reluctantly to his feet. 'Reckon we can leave Nancy there? She won't get attacked by the chickens?'

'I don't think so and if she is, we won't be far away.'

Hannah took his hand, leading him through the house in exactly the order she'd explored it, trying very hard not to show her excitement. It was difficult though. Seeing it again with Matt in it made it even easier to imagine them living there. To picture how she would furnish the place with things they already had and others she would have all the fun of finding.

Matt said nothing as they walked around and Hannah had to stop herself asking him what he thought. He was showing only the barest interest and it was hard not to get frustrated. When they got upstairs she decided to leave the bathroom until last and when they walked in it did finally inspire him to say something.

'Very nice,' he said, gently kicking the bath with his foot, 'your dream bathroom, eh, Hanns?'

She allowed herself to nod, still trying to keep hidden how much she loved it. Matt looked out of the window, then put the lid of the loo down and sat on it.

'Your dream bathroom in your dream house?' he asked.

'Well, it is nice,' said Hannah, 'you've got to admit it.'

'So how much is it?'

It took the utmost self-control for Hannah not to squeal the answer. '£450 . . .'

Matt raised an eyebrow, acknowledging it was reasonable for a week's rent for a whole house, only slightly more than they paid for a flat.

' . . . a month!' she added and was gratified with the instant look of surprise on Matt's face, but his expression quickly became blank again.

'And tell me,' he said, 'how long is the commute from here to Great Titchfield Street, do you think?'

Hannah turned round and looked out of the window at the glorious view, hot tears pricking at her eyelids. It was a thirty-five-minute drive to the nearest mainline station and an hour and a half from there. Hopeless.

She wished she'd never seen that bloody house.

# Chapter Sixteen

Pete was so stoked to hear Matt on his intercom he ran downstairs to greet him.

'Hey! Matt, my man! I thought you were down on the farm all week.'

Matt grinned back at him and threw his arms around his best friend. They rocked for a few moments in the advanced man hug, finishing with hearty back slaps and hand grips. Pete wouldn't have been more thrilled to find Kirsten Dunst on his doorstep, naked.

'Came back early,' said Matt, following him upstairs. 'Too much fresh air.'

Pete turned round and looked closely at him.

'You've had a row with Hannah, haven't you?'

Matt shrugged, feeling slightly ashamed of his impetuous decision to come back to London early, leaving Hannah and the kids with her parents. The school thing had been the final straw. What was the point of Hec doing a 'taster day' at some tin-pot bush school he was never going to go to in a village they weren't going to move to? Just confuse the little bugger.

So if Hannah – and her mother – couldn't just front up to that insane old bat who was trying to run their lives and tell her to butt fully out, he thought he might as well leave them to it. And it had started to get to him, how much Hector was going on about the animals. He was obsessed with the bloody things.

'Kinda,' he said.

'Can I have her?' said Pete.

'Get fucked,' said Matt cheerily, throwing himself into one of Pete's old leather club chairs, 'and haven't you had enough on your hands entertaining my kid cousin? She's mad about you – I mean, she doesn't fancy you or anything – but she's raving on about what a great guy you are and what you've done for her. Did you really get her a job and a place to live on her first afternoon?'

Pete shrugged.

'It wasn't exactly difficult. Anyone's going to want to hire a gorgeous young thing like that. Have you seen her? She's got this really cute look going on, kinda messed-up early Debbie Harry, so the job bit was easy. Then I just texted everyone I knew to see if they had a room and Fred came up with the goods. Job done.'

'Fred?' said Matt, sounding alarmed. 'That nutter who does embroideries of serial killers on an Arts Council grant?'

'Fred's all right. I mean, I wouldn't want to live with any of his so-called "artworks" but he's a nice guy and fully gay, so he's not gonna climb into her bed in the middle of the night.'

'I bet you tried.'

'I didn't actually, Matt. I do have my standards – and she's your cousin. That's family. And I'm seeing this masseuse at the moment . . . she's keeping me very busy.'

He smiled lasciviously and Matt had to laugh.

'Poor girl, clearly no-one's warned her, but thanks for helping Ali out like that and thanks for holding back. I was a bit concerned she might have the Toxic Pete treatment and head back to Sydney on the next flight.'

Pete felt a massive pang of guilt as Matt said the words about heading back to Sydney, but still couldn't quite bring himself to tell his friend what he was planning to do. What he was doing. He'd bought the plane ticket the day before. He was really going.

He would have to tell Matt and the sooner the better, but now definitely wasn't the time. He'd just had a big row with his wife, which didn't happen very often and he was looking pretty sick about it, so he didn't need another upset on top of that. No, he'd tell him at a more appropriate moment, when they'd had a few beers and plenty of weed. Chemically cushion the blow.

'So,' he said, 'what do you want to do with your rare night of freedom? Get trashed? Go out and pick up some girls?'

'Ha ha, ha, very funny.'

'Such a waste,' said Pete. 'What you could get up to, you handsome sod, it makes me want to weep. But seriously, what'll we do? Your call. Do you wanna do some work, or shall we go and have us a few cleansing ales?'

'I really want to see Ali,' said Matt. 'I've only spoken to her on the phone once since she flew in and she wasn't at the flat when I got back today. Has she already moved in with Fred? She gave me her mobile number, but it's turned off.'

'Funnily enough, I know where she is right now,' said Pete. 'Follow me.'


Ali was so excited to see Matt when he walked into the bar, she nearly dropped the tray of beers she was carrying. Collecting herself, she puckered her lips into an air kiss and quickly served the drinks, before rushing over and throwing herself at him.

'Mattster! My cool big boy cousin! It's so good to see you – but I thought you weren't coming back 'til Sunday.'

'Hey, Aliboo,' said Matt, lifting her off her feet, just as he had when she was six and he was twenty-three, 'I came back early to see you.'

Her skirt hitched up as Matt held her and Pete's eyes, instinctively drawn to any random display of female flesh, fixed on the horrible red scars on her thighs again. He winced. How the hell had she got those?

Matt put her down again and twirled her round with one finger, like a ballroom dancer.

'Look at you,' he said, 'you're a total Shoreditch babe. How did you get that so right?'

Ali shrugged.

'I just came as I was,' she said.

'Naturally cool, then,' said Matt, 'it's just you and me in the whole family, kid.'

Ali laughed.

'You're not wrong about that, we're the freaks.'

'Always were,' said Matt, grinning at her, 'and proud of it.'

Pete was starting to feel a bit left out of the family love-in.

'What ya drinking, mate?' he asked Matt, sloping off towards the bar.

'Usual,' said Matt, meaning a pint of Guinness.

But Pete had a better idea.

'Give me two Dos Equis and two tequila shots,' he said to the barman, shifting his weight on to his favourite stool and checking out who was in the bar over his shoulder. Nothing to worry about, that was good.

Four rounds of that drink combo later, the two of them were daft drunk and falling about laughing, recalling antics of the early days of their friendship in Sydney, when they'd been in a hopeless band together.

The bar had filled up and Pete's beer-goggled eyes could see quite a few women there he'd like to get to know better – and two he'd already been intimately acquainted with. None of the shouters luckily, but when yet another of his exes walked in, he started to get uneasy. What if they all attacked him at once?

His mood switched instantly to a downer as he was reminded this was one of the many reasons he'd decided it was time to leave London. It was a huge city, but this was the only part of it he wanted to live in and he'd shat in his own nest so excessively he just wasn't comfortable there any more. Time to go home, for a fresh start.

And maybe he would do what Ali had told him to this time around with the women he met. Not get into this situation again. He could see her point, that one phone call letting a woman know where she stood with him, even if it was a brazen lie, could save him a lot of long-term aggro. And bad karma, if you believed in that shit and he certainly didn't. Well, maybe a bit.

He hadn't meant to hurt them. He'd always thought he was making it right being super-nice to them for the duration; he hadn't realised the silent let-down cancelled that out. Yeah, Sydney Chick was on to something. When he got back home, he was going to be a new man. Which reminded him, shit, he still had to tell Matt about all that. Nightmare. He wanted to get it over with now, but not here. Not in a crowded bar.

'Hey, mate,' he said, extracting his pie-eyed friend from the attentions of the striking blonde who was shamelessly hitting on him from the other side. He leaned round Matt to address her.

'Sorry, miss, but his wife just texted me – he's got to go home and change his baby daughter's nappy.'

The woman gave Pete a death stare and stalked off, and he tapped Matt's arm to get his full attention before another one lobbed up. It wouldn't be long.

'Wanna split?' he said. 'Go back to mine, blow some weed? Have a look at some stuff I've been working on?'

Matt nodded woozily and the two of them headed out of the bar, holding each other up, pausing on the way for Matt to hug Ali and tell her he'd see her back at the flat, but probably not until late the next morning.


Pete rolled a fat one. He was feeling a bit edgy after seeing too many of his past conquests in the bar and increasingly twitchy about delivering the big news to Matt.

To try and distract himself he played back a song they'd been working on before Matt went away, which he'd been laying some more tracks over. It still wasn't working.

'I think it needs to be faster,' Matt was saying, snapping his fingers like Sammy Davis Junior. 'Can you speed it up? I think it's more of a dance track. The words are quite fast paced and I think it would sound better up tempo.'

Pete played it back faster and Matt immediately started throwing some pretentious dance moves, which made them both laugh until their stomachs hurt.

'Oh, I hate people who think they can dance,' said Pete, flopping into his favourite chair.

'How dare you?' said Matt, executing a fairly convincing moonwalk. 'I'm an artiste.'

'Stop it!' yelled Pete. 'Or I'll put you on *Britain's Got Talent*.'

They tried the track even faster, then slower again, bringing the drum beat further forward in the mix and burying it in the back, then the whole thing much more slowly with extra strings and then they gave up.

'Just not happening, is it?' said Matt, flopping down on the sofa.

'I think the technical term is "crap",' said Pete.

'Got anything else?' asked Matt.

Pete looked a bit shifty.

'I've been playing with some ideas for lyrics, actually.'

'Bloody hell, mate,' said Matt. 'I leave town for three days and you've already stolen my gig.'

'Well, obviously they're rubbish – like any musical ideas you come up with.'

Matt gave him the finger.

'But I thought you might be able to move them on somewhere. I'll go and get them.'

He loped off to the other end of the space where his bed was. Walking back to Matt he glanced down at the words he'd been playing around with. He knew they didn't work as they were, but there was something he really wanted to express and he was hoping Matt could take what he'd done and bring that out. But it did mean showing them to him and that was a bit cringe-making.

Oh, well, they hadn't been friends for nearly twenty years to let that stop him. He handed the piece of paper to Matt.

He scanned them for a moment and then looked up at Pete with a quizzical expression.

'Bambi?' he said.

'Yeah,' said Pete, nodding.

'Like Bambi the young deer?'

'Yes,' said Pete, getting more defensive.

'Does the mother get shot at the end of the song?'

'Oh, sod off, Matt, you prick,' said Pete, pulling off one of his shoes and throwing it at him.

Matt was racked with laughter.

'Bambi! Oh I love it. Let's bring Thumper into the chorus: "Thumper, Thumper, he wants to hump 'er," he sang. 'Bambi, Bambi, he wants to be a she . . .'

'Shut up!' said Pete, throwing the other shoe at him. 'And get fucked while you're doing it.'

He wanted to play it cool but he was hurt. He couldn't help it. He very rarely got involved with the lyrics, he knew it wasn't his thing, but he'd really had a feeling about this. OK, Bambi might be a bit lame, but it got over what he wanted to say about the special energy of the young. The vulnerability that somehow gave them such power.

Matt had tears of mirth running down his face and was still doubled over. Pete knew it was partly smoking the pot on top of the tequila and the excitement of being off the leash for a night, but it was still pissing him off. He wasn't laughing and it was wrong that Matt wasn't picking that up.

'Well, fine,' he said, after Matt launched into another spontaneous chorus with lines about skunks and funk and birds and words and turds, which all scanned and rhymed perfectly right off the top of his drunken stoned head. Show-off.

'It doesn't matter if you think my idea is shit, actually Matt,' continued Pete, 'because you're going to need to get a new writing partner anyway. I'm moving back to Sydney. In September.'

Matt stopped laughing immediately and stared at him. He looked like a deer in the headlights, which would have been funny in the circs, if it hadn't suddenly all become so terribly unfunny.

'What did you say?' said Matt, briskly wiping away the tears of laughter and sitting up.

'Oh, forget it,' said Pete, 'I'll tell you later, let's have another joint. I shouldn't have shown you those stupid lyrics.'

'No,' said Matt, suddenly looking pale, 'I heard you. You're moving back to Sydney, in September – for good?'

'Yeah,' said Pete, slumping down in his chair and nodding heavily. 'September the first. Sorry, mate.'

# Chapter Seventeen

Hector had a baby rabbit in his pocket and he was beginning to regret it. It was wriggling like anything, which was tickly, and it seemed to be trying to dig a way out scarily close to his willy. It made it very hard to sit still and he got more alarmed as the teacher noticed and came over to him.

'Are you all right, Hector?' she asked.

He gave her his best smile, which was ruined when the rabbit suddenly sank its claws into his leg. He jumped, clamping his hands down on to it.

'Do you need to go to the toilet?' said the teacher, looking concerned.

Hector nodded. He didn't dare say anything because he was convinced the first word out of his mouth would be 'Rabbit!'.

The teacher assigned a boy called Marcus to take him to the loo and he managed to get himself and the bunny safely out of the room with his hand stuffed deep into the pocket, although the rabbit immediately started nibbling his fingers.

'Which way's outside?' he whispered urgently to Marcus, the minute they were in the school corridor.

'Why? Do you want to go home?'

Hector shook his head and eased the baby rabbit out of his pocket to show him. Marcus's eyes opened in delighted surprise.

'Cool!' he said. 'What's it called?'

'Carrot,' said Hector, 'but I think I need to let him go. I thought he would go to sleep in my pocket, but he keeps wriggling like anything and he was trying to bite my winkie . . .'

The two of them started giggling uncontrollably. Which was when Carrot made his escape, jumping out of Hector's hands and bouncing along the corridor at high speed.

'Oh no!' said Hector, and he and Marcus chased after it, but it was much too quick for them.

Every time they nearly caught up with it, the rabbit would manage to leap out of their way. They just couldn't get their hands on it, but it couldn't escape either, because all the doors to outside were locked firmly shut, as Hector found when he tried to open one. He rattled it desperately, but it wouldn't budge and while he was trying to do that, they lost sight of Carrot.

He and Marcus locked eyes in panic as the headmistress came out of her office.

'Boys!' she said. 'What are you doing out of your classroom?'

'I was just taking Hector to the toilet, Mrs Bentley,' said Marcus, looking terrified. The loos were at the other end of the hall.

'So why are you trying to open the door to the playground?'

She came over to them and sat on her heels to talk to Hector, eye to eye.

'Are you all right, Hector? Were you trying to go home?' she asked very kindly.

Hector did the only thing he could: he burst into tears. It worked brilliantly, because Mrs Bentley thought it was because he was missing his mum on the taster day and took him into her office for some biscuits and a story before the bell went for playtime.

Just after Mrs Bentley had opened the door to the playground and all the children had run out, Hector saw Carrot bound out too and disappear into the hedge. He was thrilled he'd escaped undetected but wondered how he would explain to Anthea that he'd lost one of the baby rabbits she'd given to him to look after while he was staying at his granny's house. And he had really loved Carrot.

For a moment he felt like crying again, but just as his lip started to tremble, Marcus came over.

'Did you see Carrot go?' he said. 'He ran straight into that hedge. Shall we go and see if we can find him?'

Hector grinned back, tears instantly forgotten, and raced towards the hedge with his new friend.

Hannah was shelling peas with her mother on the terrace. Nancy was on the lawn playing with a wooden spoon and a cardboard box, wearing a sun hat which had once belonged to her mother. Charlie was having an afternoon nap, after an exhausting morning putting fruit nets over the cherry trees with Hannah and the gardener, and Hector was over at Anthea's house, helping her with the animals, the two of them due to arrive back for tea at any moment.

Marguerite's garden was glorious, the early roses coming into bloom and the sweet peas already in their full glory. Wood pigeons cooed in the trees. Cabbage whites bobbed past and bumblebees went busily from flower to flower.

'Why don't you enter your flowers in the spring show, Mummy?' said Hannah, after taking in the scene for a few moments. 'They're just as good as any of the ones we saw there. Better. Your sweet peas are so gorgeous they almost look fake.'

'Ah yes,' said Marguerite, 'they do seem to like that spot, but I don't grow them for competition, I grow them for their beauty. It would sour the whole thing to put them up for judgement like that. And imagine if my flowers beat Anthea's – life wouldn't be worth living.'

They both laughed at the thought and then Hannah's eyes opened wide as she saw Hector running towards them, Anthea bringing up the rear.

'Oops and here she is,' she said, getting up to go and greet them.

'Look, Mummy!' said Hector, opening the cardboard box he was carrying a tiny crack. Hannah looked in and saw an adorable black baby rabbit, before Hector quickly shut it again.

'Gosh, another one!' she said, momentarily glad Matt wasn't there.

'Yes,' said Hector, 'Anthea gave it to me, to make up for losing Carrot. She wasn't cross at all, Mummy.'

'I wasn't,' said Anthea, ruffling his head as she reached them. 'Well, I suppose it was rather naughty, but it's exactly the kind of thing my nephew Dominic used to do. He once had a pet crow in his bedroom for the whole summer holidays without his mother knowing about it. You remember Dominic, don't you Hannah? He used to come to my Christmas parties with his brothers. Lovely fellow.'

'Er, yes,' said Hannah, remembering a great gang of rather terrifying boys, but none of them in particular.

'He was animal mad, like Hector,' said Anthea. 'Lives in New York now, hopeless for pets there. I'm trying to persuade him to move back here, put some roots down.'

Settling into an old rattan chair, Anthea lost no time asking Hannah if she had confirmed Hector's place at the school and when they were going to move in to Garden Cottage. Marguerite cringed. She'd made a point of not asking her daughter those questions. She knew it was too much to hope for, but still didn't want to hear Hannah say it out loud. Especially not when she'd have to retain her composure in front of Anthea, while also agreeing with her that it was crazy of Hannah and Matt to turn down such a wonderful opportunity.

Marguerite was fairly certain the school taster day was the reason Matt had suddenly departed back to London days earlier than planned, claiming urgent work issues. She'd seen how strained things were between them at dinner the day the headmistress had rung to confirm it and he'd left the following morning. Marguerite very deliberately hadn't asked questions and hadn't referred to the cottage, or the school, since.

But Anthea had no such restraint.

'Isn't it marvellous how much Hector loved the school?' she said, all smiles, stirring copious amounts of sugar into her tea. 'So, when are you moving in? You can have the cottage as soon as you like, it doesn't need a thing doing to it. The previous tenants left the garden in very good order, but if that aspect of it worries you, Hannah dear, I'm sure Marguerite's gardener could lend you a hand, couldn't he? Of course, you might get the bug and want to join the gardening club. We have very good talks, don't we, Marguerite?'

Hannah's throat felt as though it had a tight ligature round it. She sipped her tea, to give herself a bit of time. They were all looking at her keenly, although Marguerite seemed to be trying not to. Even Nancy, now sitting on her grandmother's knee, had turned her little face up to look at Mummy.

She was doing something with her hands, Hannah noticed, first holding a little fist up by her face and then holding them both out to the side, pointy fingers spread, and looking at Hannah with an enquiring expression.

It must have been one of the baby signs she'd learned at those classes with Matt recently, but whatever did this one mean? Oh damn Matt for going back to London early and why wasn't it her who'd taken Nancy to the baby signing classes anyway? She ought to know what it meant. It was all mixed up.

'Well, I don't see how we can move in there,' she managed to choke out eventually, seeing her mother immediately look down at her cup and Hector's face crumple.

'But Mummy,' he said, rushing over and putting his hands on her knees, looking up at her pleadingly, 'if we moved into that house, I would have my own chickens and Anthea said I could have a dog and a cat as well as my rabbit and I would be able to play with Marcus every day and Charlie and make cakes with Granny . . .'

'And go to that lovely school,' prompted Anthea. 'Mrs Bentley thinks you are a delightful little boy. She'd love to have you in Reception in September.'

Hannah wanted to throw her tea at her. She cradled Hector's head, which he was butting against her stomach, like a little goat, and kissed it.

'I know you love all that, darling, and so do I, but Mummy has a job in London and I couldn't go there every day from here. You know how bored you get on the train journey down here – you wouldn't want Mummy to have to do that twice every day, would you? I'd never see you.'

'You never see me now,' said Hector, the truth like a bayonet in Hannah's belly. 'You're always at that stupid job. I hate your job.'

And picking up the box with the baby rabbit in it he ran into the house through the French windows. Anthea smiled fondly after him.

'Animals are such a comfort for children,' she said.

# Chapter Eighteen

Ali, Hector and Nancy were watching the slow loris being tickled on YouTube, all in gales of laughter.

'Look at his tummy!' said Hector, putting sticky fingers all over the screen of Matt's iPad. Ali gently pulled them away. 'Look at his face. He's going Ooh, ooh, ooh! No, don't stop! I like it! Oh, he's soooo sweet, I want to kiss him.'

He did, wetly, and Ali made a mental note to give the screen a good wipe before Matt got in. The mood he'd been in that morning, she didn't think he'd react too well to his precious gadget being slobbered on.

He wasn't grumpy exactly – she'd never seen Matt grumpy – he was just oddly distant and preoccupied and it wasn't like him at all. He was always such an easygoing guy, her favourite big boy cousin, she couldn't imagine what was wrong with him. She wasn't taking it personally, because he'd made her feel really welcome in the flat, he just seemed really distracted and he hadn't got much better, even when Hannah and the kids had come home the day before.

Now it was Monday and with Hannah back at work, Matt had decided to keep Hector out of nursery for the day so he could take Ali and the kids out for a jolly outing to welcome her to London properly. She could see he was trying to snap himself out of his funk and he'd put on a good show of his normal self, but the minute he went into repose, the defeated look would take him over again. Something must have happened, but this mood of Matt's was so strange, she didn't know how to approach it.

'OK,' said Ali, quickly shutting the thing down, before any more damage could be done to it, 'let's see who can do the best impression of the slow loris.'

She lay on the floor, lifting her arms up slowly and then lowering them again with a disappointed look on her face, like the lemur in the video, while making 'Oo oo oo' noises.

Hector joined in with great gusto and Nancy watched them both with a bemused expression on her face, before lying down and putting her own little arms up.

'Watch this!' said Hector. 'Now I'm going to be my rabbit, Tiny. This is how he jumps.'

He set off round the room, bouncing and kicking out his legs and Ali had to lift Nancy out of the way quickly before he landed on her, when Hannah came in, laden with shopping bags and looking hot and bothered.

'Mummy!' cried Hector, running towards her, then remembering he was an animal. 'Look, I'm a rabbit and Ali is a slow loris. What kind of animal are you?'

'A hot and rather cranky one,' said Hannah, 'but I'll be a happier rabbit or whatever as soon as I've washed my hands and had a cup of tea. Hi Ali, are you OK? I hope they haven't worn you out too much.'

'Not at all,' she said. 'We've had a great time. Hector's painted you some lovely pictures. They're in the kitchen. Nancy painted herself, so I had to give her a wash. I had to change all her clothes too, sorry about that.'

'Oh, that's fine,' said Hannah. 'Thanks so much for entertaining them so brilliantly. I'll just put this shopping away. Who'd like a drink and a biscuit?'

'Meeeeeee,' shouted Hector, then reverting to rabbit mode, pretending to nibble a carrot.

'And me,' said Ali, 'but I'll make it, you put your feet up, Hannah.'

Ignoring the last suggestion, which she didn't consider an option until both children were in bed, Hannah dragged the bags of food into the kitchen. She dumped it all on the table and had just pulled out two big bags of twirly pasta to put away, when she caught sight of Hector's picture wall. All the buses were gone.

A year of adorable paintings which had started as red blobs and gradually become more sophisticated bus shapes had been replaced by scrappy daubs. Were they animals? There was something brown with four legs. It might have been a dog. Or possibly a donkey. How had he done so many in one afternoon? Most of them were still wet.

Ali came in while she was still staring at the wall.

'He was on a mission,' said Ali, clocking the expression on Hannah's face. 'He said he had to paint at least one of every animal he loved . . .'

'Have we still got all the buses?' asked Hannah, immediately hoping she didn't sound as upset as she felt. It wasn't Ali's fault, but she'd loved those buses. They were such a connection between her and Hector.

'I put them all on your bed,' said Ali, quickly. 'I didn't want them to get damaged by the new paintings . . . and Hector insisted I take them down.'

He hopped into the kitchen, Nancy following.

'Don't you like your buses any more?' asked Hannah.

'Nah,' said Hector. 'Buses are for babies.'

'Well, these are lovely paintings, darling,' Hannah forced herself to reply. 'I particularly like the donkeys.'

'Eee-ore, eee-ore,' said Hector.

Ali filled the kettle and Hannah carried on putting the food away, giving Hector two teddy-shaped biscuits, as a reward for his splendid paintings, and a couple to herself, as comfort for the abandoned buses.

Nancy was looking at Hannah intently, waving one of her arms around. When she didn't respond, she totted over and hung on to one of her mother's legs, gazing at her and putting her forefinger repeatedly to her mouth.

'Iccie,' she said, 'iccie . . .'

'What is it, darling?' said Hannah, as the little face started to crumple with frustration.

'Ali glanced round. 'I think she wants a biscuit as well,' she said.

'Really?' said Hannah.

'Yeah, it's one of those baby signing things,' Ali said. 'Matt showed me this morning. It's amazing what she can do and I think that one means "hungry".'

'Right,' said Hannah, wondering again why Matt had never showed her what all the signs meant. Oh yes, that was right, because they were never in the flat together at the same time. That would be it.

'Do you want a biscuit?' she asked crouching down next to Nancy. 'Are you hungry like Ali says?'

Nancy grinned and patted Hannah's cheeks with both her hands.

'Hey, Nancypants,' called Hector from the sitting room, 'come here quick, there's some really funny monkeys on the telly.'

Nancy wriggled to get away and set off at a speedy waddle, clutching her biscuits.

Then, suddenly feeling exhausted, Hannah decided not to start immediately on their dinner as she normally would, but to sit at the table with her tea. She looked into the shopping bags and pulled out a packet of chocolate fingers. What the hell.

Ali smiled at her as she drew up her chair.

'Would you like a biscuit?' asked Hannah, opening the packet. 'Or ten, because I should warn you, it's impossible to eat just one of these.'

Ali nodded as she picked one up and took a bite.

'Yum,' she said, through a mouthful of chocolaty biscuit. She picked up the packet and studied it. 'Cadbury's Chocolate Fingers . . . we have these at home, but they taste different here. It's probably the water.'

'So how are you liking London?' asked Hannah. 'Looking after these two this afternoon, you wouldn't have had much chance to do anything. Did Matt take you anywhere this morning?'

'We went to the Geffrye Museum,' said Ali. 'Matt thought it would be a good introduction to historical London. I loved it and the kids seemed to enjoy it too. Hector had this cool trail to follow. We didn't take him to nursery, so I could spend the day with him, I hope that was OK?'

'Fine by me,' said Hannah, 'and a nice change for him. He does love going there to hang out with the other kids, but I do think five days a week is too much at his age. I wish he could spend more time at home really.'

With me, she thought, but kept that bit to herself.

'Well, he certainly seemed to have a good time with us,' said Ali. After the museum Matt showed me where all the Vietnamese restaurants are and we had some pretty great phô in your favourite one.'

'Ah, Song Que. We love it there.'

'I knew you must be regulars because Hector high-fived all the waiters when we walked in and then they brought our food over without us ordering.'

'Sorry about that,' said Hannah, laughing, 'but we always have the same thing. Did Hector come out with his pockets full of boiled sweets?'

Ali nodded.

'So did I.'

'Isn't that right by where you're working?' said Hannah.

'Yeah, Chocolate Bar, it's just a bit further down Kingsland Road, but I didn't realise we were so close to it until we walked past,' she paused for a moment, fiddling with her mug.

'It's funny,' she continued, 'because I've lived in Sydney all my life and I've never had to think where to go, or how to get somewhere, or how it all fits together. It's like I was born with a map of the city loaded into my hard drive. So it's quite weird suddenly not knowing where anything is, how it all connects, or how to get from one bit to another. I make notes everywhere I go, so I can check it out on the map later, but all that's taking up so much of my brain I don't feel like I've got enough head left for thinking. I feel dazed all the time and I don't think it's just jet lag.'

Hannah smiled wryly.

'Welcome to the big bad city,' she said. 'It can wear you down, just living in it.'

'Sydney's a big city too,' said Ali, 'but it doesn't do my head in like this. I suppose I'm just used to it.'

'Partly that,' said Hannah, 'but I was born and bred in London and it still beats me up sometimes. Like today – it was so hot on the bloody bus it was like a Bikram yoga class. I love London, it's part of me, like the sibling I never had, but I always feel like you have to pay a tax with part of your soul for the privilege of living here.'

Ali was listening with interest, but there was a frown line growing deeper between her pretty hazel eyes, and Hannah suddenly realised what a downer she was being. The kid was only twenty-four. She'd just moved there and she still had all the life force needed to cope with the city without trying. She didn't need the cynical view of a nearly forty-year-old who was desperate to spend her time frolicking in a meadow with her children, not sweating on the number 55 bus.

'Don't get me wrong,' she said, quickly, 'it drains you, but it inspires you at the same time. There is a unique energy here and there's so much to see. Have you even been outside the East End yet?'

'I bought my phone in Liverpool Street . . .' said Ali.

'Right,' said Hannah, smiling, 'that's what I mean. I'll take you out and show you another side of London. You can come to one of my work events with me this week, they're usually in pretty glamorous places.'

'Oh, that would be so great,' said Ali, her face returning to its usual brightness. 'I'd love to do that.'

She was like a precious little flower, thought Hannah, with her aura of bleached blonde hair and that perky face with its elfin features and ready smile. A marigold or a cheery little buttercup. No wonder Matt was so fond of her.

Ah, Matt . . . there was another issue. Perhaps Ali knew where he was. She'd been ringing his mobile all afternoon and it had been turned off.

'By the way, Ali,' she said, 'you don't happen to know what Matt's plans are, do you? I'm about to start the dinner and I wondered if he was coming back for it – and would you like some?'

'Oh, no, thanks' said Ali, 'they'll feed me at work later, but good you asked about Matt because I forgot to give you a message from him. He said he had to go and see some people this evening and he'd be back later and not to wait up for him.'

'Is he with Pete?' asked Hannah.

A funny look crossed Ali's face.

'No, it's not Pete,' she said. 'In fact, Matt seems to be really mad with Pete about something. He was quite harsh about him today.'

'Matt's said something harsh about his beloved Pete?' asked Hannah. 'That would be a first.'

Ali nodded. She strongly suspected she knew why Matt was angry with Pete – he must have told him he was moving back to Sydney. But if Matt hadn't told Hannah that yet, she certainly wasn't going to.

'Yes,' she said, wondering how much she should say, before deciding on the truth, without any unnecessary information, 'I suggested we asked Pete to join us for lunch today so I could shout him to say thanks for finding me a job and a place to live, but Matt said I was welcome to hang out with Pete whenever I wanted, as long as I didn't expect him to be there too.'


Hannah puzzled over what Ali had told her about Matt and Pete for the rest of the evening, right through the children's supper, baths and bedtime stories. Those two hadn't had a falling-out the whole time Hannah had known Matt. Pete seemed to have ructions regularly with other people – mainly women – but never with Matt. So this was really peculiar.

She'd thought Matt's odd mood since she'd got home from her parents' the day before had all been to do with the Garden Cottage and school taster day fiasco. Now she was wondering if there wasn't more to it, although she wasn't sure if that was good or bad.

In the little waking time they'd spent together since she'd been back neither of them had mentioned what had happened in the country, which had been a great relief to her. Apart from anything else, it meant she didn't have to tell Matt that she had held on to the keys to the house after that first viewing and had gone back every day until she left for another torturing look. Not even her mother or Hector knew that.

She'd found little opportunities to sneak down to the gate off her parents' drive when they were occupied with other things and every time she'd loved the house more. When the sun was out, it poured in through the windows and on the one rainy afternoon it had felt cosy and snug, even with no furniture in it.

To add to the agony, Anthea had put Hector in charge of checking for eggs, so he'd go off through the gate into the garden on missions of his own each day, coming back triumphant with brown speckled eggs in the chicken-shaped wire basket Marguerite had given him for the purpose.

He'd named all the chickens after characters from his favourite TV shows. Hannah didn't think there would have been a chicken called Basil Brush before, but Hector was blissfully unaware of the irony. He'd cried when he had to say goodbye to them and his rabbit, and only repeated promises from Marguerite that she would ring up with regular reports on their welfare had mollified him.

'And anyway,' Hannah had heard him say to Charlie, as they walked along the station platform in front of her, holding hands, 'it won't be long until we're back to live there forever and then I'll be able to see them every day.'

Charlie hadn't contradicted him and Hannah distinctly saw him squeeze his grandson's hand. It had been very hard to get on the train when it came in.

# Chapter Nineteen

Marguerite was checking for eggs. She hadn't actively agreed to take on Hector's chicken-keeping duties when they'd all gone home, but somehow it had turned out that way. She had to let them out in the morning, feed them, give them water and make sure they were safely back in the run again in the evening. It was quite a performance.

She did get to keep the eggs, but there was a limit to how many she and Charlie could eat and without Hector and Nancy there to lick the bowl she didn't have much heart for baking. Half the Victoria sponge she'd made with him was still sitting in the larder. She'd just have to make lots of meringues and mayonnaise and give them away as presents.

The problem was Anthea was still convinced that Hannah and family were moving into Garden Cottage at any moment. Hannah had left the keys with her to give back to Anthea, but when Marguerite had rung on the Monday morning to ask if it was a convenient time for her to drop them round, Anthea had just railroaded her.

'Oh, just hold on to them for when they move down,' said Anthea. 'with you looking after the chickens and me keeping an eye on the garden, it will all be fine until they're ready. Actually, I think the lawn could do with a mow. Can you have your chap do it next time he does yours?'

'But I don't think they're going to rent it, Anthea,' Marguerite said, starting to feel desperate.

The sooner some other people were installed in that house and the tantalising but impossible notion of Hannah and family being there was entirely banished, the better. The pathetic shred of hope she just couldn't push away while it stood empty was driving her mad. She couldn't settle down to anything until this preposterous situation was brought to an end.

'Hannah has a very good job in London, Anthea,' she said in her firmest tone. 'She's the breadwinner and they simply can't move down here, much as I would love them to, of course.'

Anthea just laughed.

'How could anyone with young children, living in a terrible place like Hackney, give up an opportunity like this? Of course they're moving in there.'

And she'd rung off.


Marguerite had just settled down with the Coalport teapot, which was at the particularly enjoyable stage where she was painting the replacement lid she'd made, to match the pattern on the main pot, when Fiona arrived to do the housework.

She never disturbed Marguerite in her workshop, but it was impossible to miss her arrival even with the door closed and Mahler playing. First there was the speed of the wheels up the gravel drive. Then the slamming of the car door, followed by the kitchen radio suddenly doubling in volume, retuned to a pop station.

It wouldn't be long until the hoover burst into cacophonous action, so Marguerite carefully laid down her brush and took off her glasses, abandoning her work until Fiona had finished hers. She enjoyed her company too.

'Hello Lady B,' said Fiona cheerily, briskly sweeping the kitchen floor as Marguerite walked in. 'Hannah and the kids gone now, have they?'

Marguerite nodded.

'Yes, they left on Sunday. It's rather quiet without them.'

'Oh, it would be,' said Fiona, 'my house would be like a morgue if I didn't have the grandkids running in and out. They drive me mad most of the time, but I'd miss them terribly. Isn't that little Nancy a pet? And

Hector's growing up a lovely boy isn't he? So comical. Lovely to think you'll soon have them here all the time, isn't it? You must be thrilled. Bring some life back into the place.'

Fiona was smiling up at her as she knelt down with the dustpan and brush to collect up the sweepings. Marguerite felt as if she'd been punched.

'Did Anthea tell you they were moving here?' she asked, trying to sound casual.

'No, it was Linda in the shop. She was saying how nice it would be for you to have the family down here. Hector's going to be in the same class as her Tom in September. That'll be another friend for him and Marcus's very excited. They really hit it off those two didn't they? You know I clean for his mum as well . . . She's delighted he'll have Hector to play with.'

Linda in the shop? Marcus's mother? Oh no, it was even worse than she thought. She was going to look such a fool when it didn't happen. It would make people think that Hannah had changed her mind about moving down – and who could blame her, the way Charlie carried on sometimes? Oh, how beastly it all was.


Charlie was lying on his sofa reading *Private Eye*. He looked delighted when Marguerite walked in and not only because she was carrying a plate with a large piece of a Victoria sponge on it.

'Oh, a flower springs forth in the desert of my morning,' he said, dropping the magazine on the floor as he jumped to his feet and came over to kiss Marguerite warmly on the lips, whilst also relieving her of the cake. 'Some tea, my darling? And a slice of this lovely confection?'

Marguerite nodded distractedly and sat down on his sofa, picking the magazine up off the floor. She glanced through it idly, looking at the cartoons, until Charlie came back in with a tray stacked with mugs, teapot, tea strainer, plates and the cake.

'Isn't this lovely?' he said, pouring her a mug of tea, black the way she liked it.

Marguerite took a sip and breathed out. Being with Charlie – a blessedly sober Charlie, as he'd been for a wonderful few weeks now – had calmed her down a little. She didn't feel as if she were facing the mockery of the village quite so alone. Poor sad old dull Marguerite, whose only child didn't want to come and live next door to her and her mad drunken father, even when it was handed to her on a silver platter.

'Is something wrong, my beautiful bloom?' asked Charlie, appraising her intently. 'You don't seem quite your usual serene self. Why don't you tell me about it?'

'It's that bloody house, Charlie,' Marguerite burst out. 'Anthea insists Hannah and the family are going to move in there and they're just not going to. But she won't take no for an answer and I'm having to look after the chickens and now she wants Gary to mow the lawn – as though it were our responsibility. It's outrageous and now Fiona has turned up telling me how excited the whole village is that they're moving down. It's so humiliating.'

Charlie looked crestfallen.

'You think they definitely aren't coming then?' he said.

'Oh, not you as well!' said Marguerite. 'Of course they're not! Hannah can't commute from here to London every day and they could hardly live on what Matt makes, if he makes anything at all; I'm never really sure, are you?'

'Poor Hector,' said Charlie, looking miserable and cutting himself a second slice of cake, 'he'll be so disappointed, poor little chap. As am I.'

'Do you really think I wouldn't love them to move in there too?' said Marguerite, tears stinging her eyes. She was furious with herself; she never cried. 'I can't think of anything nicer than seeing Hannah every day and watching Hector and Nancy grow up – and surrounded by trees and fields and animals, rather than pollution and concrete. I've tried to keep how I feel from Hannah, but I hate them living in a flat with no garden, in that grimy part of London. It was fine when they were just a young couple, but children need space and fresh air.'

'We brought Hannah up in London,' said Charlie.

'But we came down here most weekends and for the holidays – and at least we had a courtyard there – she wasn't shut up in an airless hutch like those children are. They're like battery chickens and they should be free range.'

Then despite all her efforts, the tears came. It was such an unusual event, Charlie was quite alarmed and dropped his cake on the floor as he rushed to comfort her.

'There, there,' he said, awkwardly putting his arm around her and patting her ineffectually, when what he really felt like doing was running in the opposite direction. He was as horrified by tears as she was. 'Come on now, don't cry, that's just silly. Buck up, old girl.'

But Marguerite couldn't stop. She didn't know which aspect of it was upsetting her the most. The idea of those beautiful children stuck in a flat in Hackney, the cruel glimpse of the paradise of having them next door, or another humiliation in the eyes of the village.

Charlie sat next to her feeling absolutely useless. He could think on his feet at warp factor speed in a courtroom, but personal situations rendered him squirmingly mute. The whole point of his education had seemed to be to teach you how to sever contact with your emotions, and expressions of them in other people were still like a foreign language to him. What were you supposed to do?

Finally, with Marguerite now sobbing uncontrollably into a cushion, he had a brilliant idea and after a few more pats and reassurances that he'd be back in a moment, he got up from the sofa and practically ran down the steps out of the granny flat. He half-jogged across the courtyard and into the back door of the house intent on his mission.

And yes! There it was, the bottle of brandy still where he'd stashed it for emergencies after Christmas, secreted at the back of the drinks cupboard in the drawing room, behind some dusty bottles of obscure liqueurs. Safely out of his reach in the flat, but there just in case of a crisis, which was what this was. That's what you gave people for shock, a medicinal tot of brandy.

He thought he'd just have a swift one himself first, to be in better shape for looking after her. Just one. And then perhaps another for good luck . . .

# Chapter Twenty

Hannah and Matt were woken the next morning by Hector bringing Nancy in to them, according to his usual routine. Hannah had gone to sleep long before Matt had got in the night before and her first thought on coming back into consciousness was wondering what his mood would be.

Tucking Nancy in between them, she reached her arm out to Matt's shoulder and pulled him close.

'How are you this morning, big boy?' she asked him, hoping if she got him off to a good start, he'd be more himself for the rest of the day.

He smiled sleepily, his deep-set eyes crinkling up at the corners, and Hannah's heart fluttered a little. He could still do that to her after all this time – and it was all the sweeter as he did seem to be more his usual self. That was a relief. Maybe he'd been out with Pete the night before, making up whatever the problem had been between them.

'I'm good, thank you, beautiful wife,' he replied, 'very happy with my human sandwich this morning, but where's the ham today? I've only got the other piece of bread and the little pickle here.'

It was a family joke – Hector was the ham in the sandwich, Nancy was the pickle. They were the bread. So where had the ham gone?

Hannah sat up as Hector walked back into the room holding something very delicately in cupped hands. He was cooing over it and stroking it with one finger. Hannah and Matt looked at each other in alarm. Had he brought home the nursery hamster without telling them? Found a mouse in the kitchen?

'What you got there, buddy?' asked Matt gently.

'My new pet,' said Hector .

Matt turned to Hannah, his eyes wide, eyebrows raised. He didn't need to say anything, his expression said it all: 'Have you bought him a pet without telling me?'

Hannah shook her head vehemently and shrugged. She couldn't imagine what it was either.

'Let's see, darling,' said Hannah, carefully modulating her voice. She didn't want to be sharp with him until she knew what it was, but she didn't want to piss Matt off either by making him think she was encouraging the pet scenario. In a cramped London flat, she could see his point on that. And she didn't need Matt getting moody again.

Hector walked over to them very slowly, stroking and reassuring whatever was in his hands. He sat down on the bed and looked at them very seriously.

'You mustn't frighten him,' he said, quietly. 'He's very shy.'

'OK,' said Matt, 'why don't you show us?'

Hector opened his hands a crack and Hannah could see something very small, fluffy and pink in there. What the hell was it?

'Oh come on, Hector,' she said. 'Stop farting about now. Let us have a proper look.'

He smiled at her and quickly opened his palm. A pink cotton wool ball was sitting there.

For a moment Hannah was too surprised even to laugh, but then she did.

'Oh Hector,' she said, tickling his ribs. 'You silly sausage, I thought you'd found a mouse in the kitchen or something horrid like that. What's your pet's name?'

'Pinkie,' said Hector as though it was obvious, then adding. 'If I do find a mouse in the kitchen, can I keep him as a pet?'

Hannah turned to Matt, expecting him to laugh, but he was rolling his eyes in exasperation.

'No,' he said, 'you can't have a mouse, or any other pet. The cotton wool ball is fine, your cuddly toys are fine, but I'm getting sick of hearing about pets. We live in a small flat and I'm not having animals in here, OK? Enough. No more nonsense about pets.'

And with that, he got out of bed and headed for the bathroom, locking the door behind him. He hadn't been unkind exactly, but it was so unlike Matt's usual morning behaviour, cheering everyone up with jokes, cuddles and carry-ons, Hannah stared after him crestfallen. Mr Normal Matt hadn't stuck around very long; Mr Moody Matt was back in town. She looked back at Hector to see his face crumpling and fat tears starting to roll down it.

'Daddy says I can never have a pet,' he wailed, 'and I want a pet more than anything. All the other kids at nursery have pets and I haven't even got a fish or a stick insect and the kids at Marcus's school have dogs and cats and guinea pigs and horses and I've got nothing. NOTHING!'

Hannah tried to comfort him, but he just got more and more upset until he was practically hysterical. She was so freaked out – he hadn't had a tantrum like this since he was two – she panicked and made a major tactical error.

'Daddy's right, Hector,' she said. 'It is really hard having pets in a small flat like this one, but it's not like you have no pets, because you've got your rabbit and chickens at Grandma's house.'

Hector's wailing went up several decibels and turned into more of a screech.

'What's the use of having pets a million miles away? No-one at nursery believes I've got chickens and they all said I'm a liar and Anthea said I could have a cat and a dog but you won't let me and you won't let me live in a house with a garden and chickens and grass and rabbits and Granny and Charlie next door and I hate you. I HATE YOU!'

With that he ran out of the room and Hannah heard the children's bedroom door slam followed by thumps, which sounded like things being hurled against it. She slumped back on the pillows wondering what on earth she should do – leave him to calm down for a bit, or go to him right away? She really didn't know.

Meanwhile Nancy was making it clear that she needed some attention too. She was looking up at Hannah and patting her arms against her own shoulders. It was another of those bloody baby signs that Hannah didn't understand. So she had one child who hated her and another one she couldn't communicate with because of her own failure to engage with the signing system the little tot had so cleverly learned. What a useless mother she was.

For want of a better idea, she scooped Nancy up, burying her face in the delicious spot where her shoulder met her neck. Nancy gurgled happily and put her arms round Hannah's neck. Then Hannah got it – that must have been the sign for a cuddle. Nancy had wanted to give her a cuddle. Bless her. She showered kisses on her head.

But now even louder thumps were coming from the room next door. She had to intervene. Getting hastily out of bed, she put Nancy on her hip and knocked gently on Hector's bedroom door.

'Go away!' he shouted. 'I'm not here and I hate you.'

She pushed the door, but it wouldn't open. She rattled the handle and pushed harder, but still couldn't make it budge. How had he done that?

'Open the door, Hector,' she said, as calmly as she could. 'I want to talk to you.'

'No,' he said. 'I'm not talking to you ever. Not until you buy me a chicken.'

'Oh, come on, Hec,' she said. 'Don't be silly. I know you love animals, but we just can't have one here. You've got to be a big boy and understand that. How about if we take you to the zoo at the weekend?'

Hector replied by throwing something heavy at the door. Hannah jumped back in shock. What was he doing in there? He could hurt himself. He could hurt her.

'Stop throwing things,' she hissed through the crack in the door. 'You'll wake Ali up.'

'I don't care,' said Hector, throwing something else.

Matt came out of the bathroom with a towel around his waist and wet hair, and was clearly surprised to see Hannah standing with her ear pressed to the door of the kids' room.

'What's going on?' he asked.

'Hector's having a massive freak-out,' she said. 'He's locked himself in somehow and he's throwing things.'

Matt walked past her into the kitchen.

'Let him,' he said, picking up the kettle and taking it over to the sink. 'You need to go to work, Hannah. Put Nancy in her chair and go and get dressed. I'll make you some brekkie to eat on the bus and I'll sort him out after. Don't worry about him. He can stay in there all morning if he wants to.'

'But I can't even get the door open,' said Hannah. 'How's he done that?'

Matt shrugged.

'Probably wedged it with a Power Ranger. He'll come out when he's hungry or needs a pee and I'll deal with him then. Don't pay any attention to this carry-on, it'll just prolong it. He's got to get the message about this pet nonsense.'

He took Nancy gently from her arms, looking tenderly at them both. That was a relief.

'Don't worry,' he said, putting an arm around Hannah's shoulders and squeezing her in to him. 'I've got this. Just get ready for work, babe.'

'OK,' said Hannah, intensely relieved to have her proper husband back, 'but you won't be too hard on him, will you?'

'Give me a break,' he said. 'You know what a pushover I am with the kids, but he's old enough to know better than this and while I understand he's been brainwashed by your mother's meddling neighbour, I won't be moved on the pet subject. Now, go and get dressed, or you'll be late.'

He kissed her cheek, squeezing her bum at the same time, and gently pushed her in the direction of the bedroom.

# Chapter Twenty-one

Ali was waiting for Hannah outside the ChicClick offices, looking very cute in a silver lamé 1960s cocktail dress, with a pale pink beaded cardigan round her shoulders. She'd backcombed her hair and put it into a messy up-do to show off her dangly diamante earrings.

'Check you out,' said Hannah, giving her a kiss. 'You look gorgeous.'

'You like?' said Ali, delighted. 'I went on a little shopping spree in that big barn of vintage gear down off Brick Lane. You have to sift out all the crap, but there are some real treasures. I took Nancy with me and she loved it. She found these earrings actually, in a basket of old jewellery I gave her to play with while I was browsing. She picked out one of these and squealed until I looked at it.'

Hannah laughed. It was a lovely image and she was very grateful to Ali for giving Matt a break from his baby care duties, but at the same time she felt a tiny pang of something like jealousy. Or not jealousy exactly, it wasn't specific to Ali, more like regret that she hadn't spent the day vintage shopping, with Nancy for company. She really couldn't think of anything nicer.

'Well, I think she's got good taste,' said Hannah, reaching out to touch one of the earrings, 'and I've got a present for you here that will be the perfect finishing touch with all that bling you're wearing.'

She fished in her bag and handed Ali a shiny black cardboard package.

'Sills eetoil?' read Ali, looking up at Hannah with a puzzled expression.

'*Cils Etoilé*,' said Hannah. 'It's French for starry lashes and it's the hottest new beauty product there is, a mascara that twinkles when you move. It's not even on sale yet, but I'm giving you one now so you can bat your eyelashes at people and then when they ask how you get your amazing sparkle you can tell them what it is. You're a product ambassador.'

'Seal eh twarlay,' repeated Ali, hesitantly.

'That's it,' said Hannah. 'Here, I'll hold this mirror while you put some on. Just don't forget to tell people that it's made by Nèriade and the only place they'll be able to buy it until September is on ChicClick, because I got us the sales exclusive. Yay!'

'Great,' said Ali, putting on the mascara, then blinking at herself in the mirror. 'Wow, that is amazing. I look all twinkly.'

'Glad you like it,' said Hannah, 'because you're coming to the launch with me tonight. At Claridges. And I had you come here early so we can walk there and I can show you some of my favourite bits of London.'

She checked Ali's feet and was pleased to see she was wearing Birkenstocks – as was she.

'I've got my heels in my bag,' said Ali, following her glance.

'You're already a Londoner,' said Hannah, smiling and pulling one of her own high heels out of her tote bag to show her. 'Right, come with me.'

'So is this the West End?' Ali asked as they came down on to Oxford Street. It was throbbing with shoppers.

'Spot on,' said Hannah, 'although London goes on for miles in both directions, so it's not really the end of anything. This big crossroads we're coming up to now is Oxford Circus.'

'Right,' said Ali, pulling out a notebook and scribbling in it as they walked, 'another circus, that is so weird. I went to Arnold Circus on my first day. It must be a London thing.'

'I suppose it is,' said Hannah. 'Piccadilly Circus is just at the other end of Regent Street, down there.'

'So that means we're on the famous Oxford Street,' said Ali, stopping suddenly to look up at the street sign and nearly causing a human pile-up behind her. 'Shit, it's crowded – sorry, mate – is it always like this?'

'Pretty much, but it's Thursday, late shopping night, so it's even more extreme today.'

'Same as Sydney,' said Ali, happily, 'but more shops here, by the looks of things.'

'Way more,' said Hannah. 'Some time when you have a day off – but not at the weekend – come down here and walk from the far end there at Marble Arch, back to here and check it all out, it'll blow your mind. But we're not going to do that now, I've got other things to show you.'

Ali felt as though her head was going to start spinning round on her neck as she tried to take everything in. So many amazing-looking shops, so many people, so many taxis and buses, it made Shoreditch seem like a sleepy little backwater. She wasn't sure what it made Sydney like.

'OK,' said Hannah, as they crossed a wide street towards an imposing building like a big old house with gabled roofs and black Tudor-style beams, 'this is Liberty.'

She had been going to add 'my favourite shop on Planet Earth', but she kept quiet. It never worked to oversell things; she wanted Ali discover it for herself. But where to start? After some thought she walked them right through the ground floor, with Ali going quiet with concentration as she checked it all out, to the old wooden staircase at the far end, then up to the women's international designers department.

'Wow,' said Ali coming to a stop in front of one of the wall lights in the shape of a woman's arm coming out of the wall and then again as they came into the shoe department, with room after room of exquisite shoes.

After that Hannah let Ali take the lead until a glance at her watch reminded her they had a mascara launch to go to – and one that was crucially important to her and her job. Hannah hadn't been in on the business negotiations, but Veronica had confirmed the sales exclusive on *Cils Etoilé* – and not just for not one, but three months.

It was an amazing result as it was official confirmation that a major elite brand was taking them as seriously for beauty as leading designers already did for fashion. And Veronica's flowers had been proof that she gave Hannah the credit for it, which was pretty thrilling.

So, starting to feel quite excited about it all – especially as it was the press launch, not the one for retailers, and she would see all her beauty writer pals – she dragged a reluctant Ali out of Liberty, leading her down to the bottom of Regent Street so she could have a quick glimpse of Eros in Piccadilly Circus.

'There you are,' she said, 'another circus for your collection and now I think about it, there's a Percy Circus in Islington as well. It's never occurred to me before.'

'You've grown up with circuses,' said Ali, 'so it's normal to you. I bet you found stuff weird when you moved to Sydney.'

'You're not kidding,' said Hannah, crossing over to take them back up to Burlington Street. 'It was the same in so many ways, but then suddenly something would be dramatically different, which made it almost weirder than going somewhere completely exotic like Vietnam or Bali. Is that how you're finding it here?'

'Totally,' said Ali, 'and I'm loving it.'

'I'm so pleased,' said Hannah, putting her arm round Ali's shoulder and giving her an impromptu hug as they walked along, wondering if this was how it felt to have a younger sister. She liked it a lot.

With Hannah pointing out landmarks Ali should come back to look at properly another time – Abercrombie & Fitch, the turning that would take her over to Dover Street Market – and having to physically pull her away from the windows of the massive Louis Vuitton shop, they walked almost the length of Bond Street.

'That's Oxford Street, up there again,' said Hannah, stopping just as they were about to turn left into Brook Street. 'We've come round in a big loop. If you went up there and turned right, you'd be back where we started.'

Ali's notebook came out again.

'There's just so much to take in,' she said scribbling notes. 'I'll have to look at this route on Google maps tomorrow to get it straight in my head. I just can't get over the scale of it all here.' She flung out her arms to indicate what surrounded them. 'Not just one strip of big beautiful old buildings, but street after street of them.'

'And it keeps on going,' said Hannah, setting off again. 'Wait until you see Claridges.'

# Chapter Twenty-two

Matt and Pete were looking at each other across a table in Chocolate Bar. This alone was a sign things weren't normal between them, because they always sat side by side up at the bar. That's what they'd always done. The bar.

But, having got there first, Matt had decided to go for a table, so he could look Pete right in the eye when he asked him why he was walking out on their songwriting partnership – and their twenty-year friendship.

He was gazing into space, still in a state of shock about the whole thing, when he heard the distinctive gravelly tones of his best friend – or was it his former best friend? – at his shoulder.

'G'day, mate,' said Pete. 'We sitting at a girls' table today?'

Matt just nodded and gestured for Pete to sit down opposite him. A pint of Guinness was already set up there.

Pete wriggled on to the narrow bench seat – some kind of old church pew and horrendously uncomfortable – and raised the glass. Matt didn't respond, just lifted his pint to his lips, took a deep drink and put it down again.

'Oh, come on, mate,' said Pete, 'you've made me sit in a girls' seat and now you're sulking like one. Have you got your period, love?'

'I think you have,' said Matt.

'Look,' said Pete, leaning over the table towards him, 'I know you're pissed off with me and I know I told you I'm clearing out in a really shit way, but I just didn't know how to tell you, so it came out at the worst time and really wrongly. You know I'm not exactly Mr Tactful.'

'But why didn't you discuss it with me first?' said Matt, his face broken up with distress. 'It was such a shock . . . and I feel like such a dickhead. All those times I would have been planning things for us to work on together and you already knew you were going and just let me rattle on like a wanker.'

Pete felt bad in the pit of his stomach. This was all too like the scenes women made with him. All this 'Why didn't you tell me?' stuff. Why didn't he tell them?

'Like I said, I didn't know how to tell you, so I just didn't.'

'Well, tell me now,' said Matt.

Oh god, that hurt-dog look. Pete couldn't stand it. Not from Matt. Not from anyone actually.

'I just feel like I'm at the end of my road here,' he said, pulling his shirt collar away from his neck with his finger. 'I've had a great time in London and you moving over too was the icing on the cake, but it's time to be realistic, we're not going anywhere, Matt. We work real hard, make contacts, get a bit of interest, some minor artist wants to record our stuff, but something always stuffs it up and we never get that big break. I'm forty-one, it's too old to be fooling around. I do my bit of producing, people really seem to like my contribution, but never quite enough to give me the big project. So forever writing jingles? Is that how it's going to be for me? It's like you with your modelling – it's good money and we're lucky to have it, but it's not who we are. I tried really hard to break through here, but it just hasn't worked. So it's time to go home.'

'What makes you think it will be any better there?' said Matt, wincing at the reference to modelling. 'The industry is tiny in Australia compared to here.'

'I know that, but I just need to go home anyway, mate. I must be feeling my age, but this London thing is getting a bit of a strain for me. I'm ready to go back to the sunshine and the surf, where people smile at you. I don't want to grow old in this city. It's amazing for the young, but I want a big bright blue sky to look up at when my body starts to seize up.'

Matt gazed back at him, the crumpled look gone from his face, which was a relief to Pete. He didn't look wounded any more, just sad. Very sad.

'You're homesick,' he said.

'Reckon you're right,' said Pete, 'and my folks are getting real old now and I feel like I need to see more of them. I haven't been back for three years and my dad had that prostate scare, remember? He's OK, but ever since that, I've been thinking maybe it was time to ship out. But it was a hard decision to make, Matt – and a large part of that was leaving you.'

'Well, I appreciate that,' said Matt. 'Thanks, and I do understand about your olds. My dad's got a bit of a heart condition.'

Pete nodded.

'I don't even get on with my dad that well,' he said. 'He's an old bastard, but I still don't want to be over here when he carks it.'

It was Matt's turn to nod. This was rather touchy-feely stuff for them, but it felt good to talk about it. He kept it pushed down most of the time, but he knew it was there really. He loved London with a passion, but all the same, there was that constant little hum of yearning to be among his own people.

'That's why I was so glad to see Ali,' said Matt, 'to have someone here from home who gets all those little references no-one else would get. She's the only other cool person in my family, the rest of them are a bunch of suburban freaks – but they're my suburban freaks.'

'Yeah, mine are bush freaks,' said Pete, laughing. 'My bush freaks.'

'And I worry that my kids aren't going to have any sense of family with my lot,' continued Matt, 'but it's so difficult going back there now we've got the two of them.'

He paused for a moment and took a long drink from his Guinness. He found the next thing hard to say, it choked him up.

'Nancy has never breathed Australian air, Pete,' he told him. 'That does my head in. My little girl . . .'

Pete nodded. He didn't get the whole kid thing, couldn't imagine why Matt had ever tied himself down like that, but even he could see how weird that must be.

'And Hector's got a full Pommy accent,' continued Matt. 'He is a Pom. Who am I kidding? He was born here, he's just a straight-up Pom who happens to have an Aussie dad. It's so weird. I'm desperate for him to spend some time over there, but it's just too hard. If only they could invent that *Star Trek* teletransporter . . .'

'Or drag the UK down to the Southern Hemisphere and anchor it somewhere near Tasmania.'

'Or bring Australia up near the Canary Islands,' said Matt. 'I do like being near Europe and New York too. The tyranny of distance. It's a shitter.'

He rubbed his head until his hair stood up on end, which just made him look more handsome, the bastard. Pete felt something like a stab of pain.

'Shit, I'll miss you, mate,' he said, raising his glass again.

This time Matt lifted his too and gave Pete's a loud clink. They both drained them.

'Shall we have a whisky chaser this time?' said Pete, standing up.

Matt high-fived him and stood up to join him on their usual stools at the bar.

# Chapter Twenty-three

Hannah was in such a good mood she had to remind herself not to sing along out loud with the music she was listening to on her phone as she strode up the street to the office.

It was a gorgeous sunny June morning, she'd just been to a really exclusive breakfast launch for the new Chanel nail colours, and she was wearing a new Dries van Noten skirt and top, gorgeous silk in a mash-up of different prints, with a pair of Chloé platform wedge sandals, all of which had arrived in the office the previous day.

They were the kinds of things she would only have dreamed of finding at sample sales before – the shoes alone were £400 at full retail – but one of the great perks of working for ChicClick was being able to buy any of the designer togs they sold at cost price. And Veronica even gave her some of them for nothing, because looking the part was so important for the job.

'We are what we wear,' was one of Veronica's mantras and she certainly lived up to it herself, never looking anything less than paparazzi perfect. Which was necessary, as snaps of her were increasingly often featured in the 'Best Dressed' pages of magazines and she was a major target of fashion bloggers during the fashion shows. She had framed prints of some of the pictures The Sartorialist had taken of her over the years on the walls of her office.

Pausing to check her reflection in the full-length mirrors which lined the ChicClick reception area, Hannah was confident she would pass muster with her boss today, which was good as she had some great new story ideas ready to present to her, along with a lead for another sales exclusive – and she'd checked she had the details straight this time – on a major new skincare product.

So she was delighted to get to her desk and find a note from Veronica's assistant asking her to 'pop over' as soon as she got into the office. Pausing only to reapply her lipstick and a spritz of her favourite Frederic Malle fragrance, *Musc Ravageur*, she fired up her laptop and headed over to the corner office.

Veronica's face lit up when she saw her.

'Oh,' she said, 'you're wearing the new Dries. It looks fabulous on you. You've got the height for those prints.'

'These help with that,' said Hannah holding out one foot to show off the new shoes.

'Love those,' said Veronica. 'I've ordered them too – and I love that nail polish. Is that new?'

'Yes,' said Hannah, 'it's Chanel's next cult colour. That's where I've been this morning, at the launch. They gave us all manicures – and I was one of only five beauty directors invited, so I think they're starting to see the point of us.'

She took out the sample of the polish that they'd given her and passed it to Veronica, who looked at it with interest and then, without saying another word, dropped it into her handbag, which was sitting on the desk.

Hannah blinked, but said nothing – she'd just have to ask the PR for another one – and waited for Veronica to comment on what she'd just said about making it on to the elite list for the launch. So far Chanel had refused to sell their beauty range to ChicClick and getting them on board was one of their major goals.

If she could get them to do business with ChicClick she thought Veronica would definitely give her one of the bonuses she'd talked about – but she wasn't looking nearly as excited about this latest bit of intelligence as Hannah had expected.

'Great,' she said rather vaguely. 'Now, take a seat, Hannah – actually, could you just push the door to first?'

Hannah closed it and sat down, picking up her laptop and putting it on Veronica's desk, open, ready to start her ideas presentation.

'Shall I start?' she said, looking over at Veronica.

'Well, actually Hannah,' she said, looking more animated again, 'I've got some very exciting news to tell you.'

Her face broke into one of her special smiles and Hannah felt herself smiling back, although she couldn't imagine what this news might be. She didn't have to wait long.

'I've sold ChicClick!' said Veronica. 'Well, not all of it, but 51 per cent.'

'Wow,' said Hannah, wishing her brain could compute all the possible implications of this announcement as fast as she knew Veronica's would have been able to, but she looked so pleased it had to be a good thing.

'Well done,' she added, rather randomly, not sure what else to say.

Veronica was looking at her expectantly.

'Well, aren't you going to ask me how much I got for it?' she said.

'Oh,' said Hannah, realising it hadn't even occurred to her. 'I didn't, er, want to seem rude.'

Veronica laughed.

'You really are an editorial girl at heart, aren't you, Hannah? It's never about the filthy mammon for you. Anyway,' she continued, leaning across the desk and lowering her voice, 'I got forty-five million.'

Hannah's mouth dropped open.

'Forty-five million pounds?' she parroted gormlessly.

'Yep,' said Veronica and she jumped up and did a little victory dance in her sky-high YSL sandals. 'Not bad for a girl who left school at sixteen, is it?'

Hannah got up, walked round the desk and hugged her. It seemed like the only way to react to such amazing news.

'It's incredible going for anyone, Veronica,' she said. 'Well done. You really really deserve it.'

'Thank you,' she replied, returning Hannah's hug and then sitting down again. 'It hasn't been formally announced yet and I'm not going to tell the rest of the team until it's just about to happen, but I wanted to tell you first, as it does affect you, Hannah, more than everyone else.'

For the first time, Hannah began to feel a little uneasy and an important question popped into her head, which she realised she should have asked immediately.

'Who did you sell it to?' she asked.

Veronica's expression immediately sharpened.

'That's the key question, Hannah,' she said, 'maybe you'll be a businesswoman yet – because the thing is, I've sold it to JCAP.'

She smiled, but in an odd, sad what-can-you-do? kind of way, as though Hannah should immediately understand why this affected her in particular. Then she did start to get it. JCAP was a major French luxury brand conglomerate, which owned, along with several of the most famous names in haute couture, one highly prestigious beauty brand – Nèriade.

'Is that why you didn't want me to come to that dinner?' she asked, pennies beginning to drop so fast she thought she might get concussion.

'Yes,' said Veronica, 'they rang me just as I was leaving the office to say that Jean-François was coming too . . .'

She didn't have to explain who that was. Surname not necessary. The billionaire owner and CEO of JCAP was as likely to appear in the party pages of *Tatler* as the business sections of the papers. Hannah knew exactly who Jean-François was.

'I see,' said Hannah, cautiously, still wondering exactly how this affected her, but beginning to be fairly sure it wasn't going to be in a good way – although it certainly explained how Veronica had secured the three-month sales exclusive on the Nèriade mascara.

'Of course I've been talking to them for some time,' continued Veronica, 'but that dinner was when the deal was finally done and the thing is, with them owning Nèriade – and of course the various beauty and fragrance lines of their fashion houses – one of the conditions of the purchase is that we limit our beauty offer to just the ones they own. They want us to carry on exactly as we are with all the fashion labels, to keep our market leader edge, but the beauty offer will be only their brands.'

She looked at Hannah as though this explained everything. It would certainly limit what she could do, she could see that and her brain was already starting to buzz with ideas for how she could make the limitations into an advantage. But before she could put any of it into words, Veronica spoke again.

'So you can appreciate that we won't be needing an editorial beauty director any more. It will be handled by someone in more of a PR role, who we'll appoint jointly, probably from their team.'

Hannah couldn't quite take it in at first – was she being sacked? It sounded like it, so why was Veronica smiling at her?

'Are you telling me I don't have a job here any more?' Hannah managed to choke out.

'I'm afraid so, darling,' said Veronica, 'and I really am sorry, because it has been so great working with you. You are defnitely the best in beauty editorial, I was right about that – and you've really come a long way as a businesswoman since you've been here, but that's the way JCAP wants to structure it and I'm hardly going to argue with forty-five million pounds, am I?'

Hannah felt dizzy with shock, but Veronica was still smiling. Did she have lockjaw?

'Will I get any redundancy?' asked Hannah, sorely aware that the rent was due in a week – and that she'd just spent the best part of £500 on the clothes she was wearing, which didn't come cheap even at wholesale.

'Well obviously, you're not entitled to formal redundancy,' said Veronica, holding up some sheets of paper. 'You'll know that from your contract, because you're still within the twelve-month trial period.'

Hannah felt sick. It would be a year in just under one week's time. She was suddenly so angry she couldn't speak. With £45 million of her own in the bank, Veronica had timed this dismissal so she could kick Hannah out at the least possible cost to the business.

'But in recognition of all the good work you've done while you've been here,' Veronica continued, 'I'm going to give you the discretionary bonus that we talked about when we first discussed the job, which will be the equivalent of three months' salary – and with your talent and experience, Hannah, I'm sure you'll have a new job well before that time is up, so it will be a nice little bit of play money.'

Play money? She had children to feed! She felt like punching Veronica in her Crème de la Mer-plumped face, but she was a lawyer's daughter and wasn't going to do anything or say another word until she'd had a good look at that contract herself. She couldn't remember the details of the twelve-month trial period off the top of her head and she wasn't going to compromise her position by making any comments until she'd checked it thoroughly.

'Any questions?' said Veronica, with a sympathetic look on her face which made Hannah want to slap it even more.

And yes, she had a lot of questions, the most pressing of which were, 'How could I have been sucked in by you?' and 'How do you sleep at night?', but she knew she had to keep her cool.

'Obviously, it's a lot to take in,' she said, in the most measured tones she could muster. Her mother would have been proud of her. And her father for that matter.

'Yes, it must be a shock . . .'

Hannah held up a hand. She didn't want a pity party from a woman with a bank balance rivalled in size only by her sense of entitlement.

'When do you want me to leave?' she said in a monotone, determined not to let her anger out.

'Well, I think it would be best if you went straight away,' said Veronica, as though it were a kindness, 'and of course, the terms of the bonus are that you don't say a word to anyone about the sale of the company until it's been formally announced – I'll let you know when that happens. Also that you don't say anything negative about ChicClick, Nèriade, JCAP, or me, or reveal any information about the business and, of course, you won't work for any fashion and beauty retail portal for eighteen months. I have the agreement here for you to sign and then we can put the money straight into your account.'

She picked up what looked like about twenty pages of A4 and held it out towards Hannah, who was wondering if she was supposed to sign it in her own blood.

'OK?' said Veronica, as though they had been discussing something quite casual.

'I'll have a look at it,' said Hannah, taking it from her without giving it a second glance. Their eyes locked and Hannah could tell Veronica's brain was doing its supercomputer thing, calculating how best to react to her lack of immediate compliance. Should she threaten, cajole, urge . . .? Hannah faced her down.

'Good,' said Veronica, eventually, and Hannah felt a small sense of triumph. She'd made her opt for co-operation. But Veronica hadn't quite finished. 'Oh, and please don't attract questions from the rest of the staff by clearing your desk now. Just walk out as though you were popping off to a meeting. I'll have Lexie pack it all up and send it on to you once the sale has been made public. OK? Anything else?'

'Yes,' said Hannah, standing up and looking down at her from the full height of her Chloé wedges, 'I'd like my Chanel nail varnish back.'

# Chapter Twenty-four

Ali was already surprised to see Hannah and Matt – and Nancy asleep in her pushchair – come into the bar together one quiet Tuesday lunchtime, but their subsequent announcement was a total freak-out. The ginger beer Matt had bought her nearly came down her nose.

'You're doing what?' she asked, spluttering.

'Yeah, I feel like that about it too,' agreed Matt, but smiling, with his arm round Hannah's shoulder, 'but it's true – we're moving to the country. This amazing house has come up right next door to Hannah's folks, for a stupidly small rent and even I have to admit it will be great for the kids. It's got a beautiful big garden, with chickens in it, idyllic really. Hector bloody loves it down there. He'll be stoked when we tell him.'

'And there's a really lovely village school that he can start at in September,' added Hannah quickly, 'and he's already got friends there, so that's perfect too.'

'Be lovely for your mum, Hanns,' said Ali.

Hannah nodded. 'And my dad. He and Hector are such buddies.'

'But what about your job?' said Ali.

Hannah's face fell.

'Well, that's the main reason we're doing it,' she said, crossing her fingers under the table. It was the reason – the only reason – she'd been able to persuade Matt, although he was making the best of it now, but she was really moving into Garden Cottage because she desperately wanted to. 'I don't have that job any more.'

'Are you serious?' said Ali. 'What the hell happened? You're a legend, I've met loads of women in here who work on magazines and websites and when I tell them you're my cousin-in-law, they're all really impressed.'

'Well, that's lovely, Ali, but the owner of ChicClick has decided that she just doesn't need a beauty director after all and it's still within my one-year trial period, so she can do that.'

It nearly killed her to lie about it for Veronica, but she couldn't risk telling even Ali what had really happened. She'd told Matt, of course, but only on the understanding that if a leak about the sale of the website was traced back to her, they might lose out on the measly pay-out she'd been offered – although her gut instinct was telling her not to accept that immediately. She strongly suspected there were a lot of dodgy conditions in that 'agreement' document that Veronica hadn't mentioned to her.

She'd had a quick look at it and her contract, on the way home, but she hadn't been in a fit state to take it in properly. She was going to get Charlie to have a look at it before she signed anything. He'd know what to do – and if he didn't he'd know someone who did.

'But can't you get another job, back on a magazine?' said Ali.

'I probably would eventually,' said Hannah, glancing at Matt, in case he leapt at this suggestion as a lifeline to stay in London, 'but there's nothing available right now and I'm not getting much of a pay-out, so I don't know how we'd live until something turned up. I'll be able to do freelance, but for the time being a very cheap house is exactly what we need, even apart from all the other benefits.'

She was getting a bit sick of hearing herself rehearse all the arguments in favour of the move, so she was glad of the distraction when Pete walked into the bar. He came straight over to them.

'Sorry I'm late guys,' he said, settling into a seat and taking a big swig out of Matt's pint. 'Thanks, mate. I'll get a round in shortly, but first I want to hear what this big announcement is, Mr Mystery.'

Matt told him and his expression instantly changed to incredulity.

'You're going to live in the country?' he pretended to shudder. 'Oh man, are you sure? I grew up in the bush. It's a freaking nightmare.

Nothing to do, dust everywhere, or maybe that would be more mud here, dangerous animals, even more dangerous people . . .'

Hannah gritted her teeth. Thank you, Pete. As usual he could be relied on to say the most annoying thing possible.

'Well, we don't have much choice, mate,' said Matt. 'Apart from the occasional bit of sock modelling by me we've pretty much got no income and the house is – is it OK if I tell them, Hanns?'

She nodded.

'It's actually free. Hannah's dad secretly took over the lease of the place without telling her mum and he's paying the rent. He couldn't bear anyone else to move in there just in case we ever wanted to, so he was paying to keep it empty until we did. He didn't tell anyone, not even Hannah's mum, but it's all worked out perfectly and he's going to keep on paying the rent until we're sorted. And I have to admit it – it's a beaut house. You'll both have to come down. There's loads of room.'

'And there's a lovely school for Hector,' said Hannah, now on auto-pilot, 'and I'll be working at home, so Nancy won't have to go to nursery.'

'Yeah, there's the school thing too,' agreed Matt, 'and, of course, Pete, with you moving back to Sydney in September, there's not much to keep me in London any more.'

Hannah turned to Pete in amazement.

'You're doing what?' she said.

'What he said,' Pete replied, pausing to take another big swig from Matt's pint. 'Moving home.'

Hannah was too surprised to say anything else for a moment.

'When did this all happen?' she said eventually.

'Last week, when I came back from your parents' place in a stupid huff about the house we're now moving into anyway,' said Matt, grinning at her.

She squeezed his thigh under the table. Then somewhere a bit higher. He grabbed hold of her hand and kept it there. Hannah got the giggles and tickled his ribs with her other hand. Pete caught Ali's eye and rolled his eyes indulgently, shaking his head.

'Reckon the prospect of all that pure country air has already got to these two lovebirds,' said Pete. 'Nauseating, isn't it?'

Ali smiled back at him.

'You wouldn't understand,' she said.

Pete stuck his tongue out at her. She thumbed her nose back.

'So tell me properly what happened,' said Hannah, recovering herself.

'Well,' said Matt, 'I deserted my beautiful family and came back to have a big blow-out with my best mate here and instead he sprang that on me. Ruined my night.'

'Yeah, well, I did apologise for that, didn't I? Handled it really craply, as usual,' he said, nudging Ali. 'See, it's not just women I dump badly.'

'So is that why you've been a bit weird and grumpy recently?' Hannah asked Matt.

'Yeah,' he said.

'Why on earth didn't you tell me, you big plonker? I thought you were having the male menopause.'

'I didn't want it to be true,' said Matt, looking sheepish, 'and I thought if I just said nothing, it might go away. But the only thing going away is him.'

He pointed an accusing finger at Pete, who raised his hands in surrender.

'Guilty as charged,' he said.

'You're all going away,' said Ali, plaintively. 'I'm gonna be all on my own in London. Waaaah . . .'

'Well, you'll have me until August thirty-first,' said Pete.

'And we'll always be down the end of a phone,' said Matt.

'And there's something else we want to tell you, Ali,' said Hannah, 'which might cheer you up. The lease on our flat isn't up until December, so we wondered if you'd like to sublet it from us until then? The rent's not too bad by London standards and if you got a couple of flatmates, you'd be fine.'

'Are you for real?' she said. 'Because living with Fred isn't actually that great. He's a lovely guy but he's got these books about serial killers literally all over the flat and that's before you even look at his gruesome artwork. I don't sleep too well there. In a room with no windows . . .'

'Yeah, well I guess that was why it was going so cheap,' said Pete, laughing. 'Right, who wants some tequila?'

# Chapter Twenty-five

Marguerite didn't know whether to hit Charlie or hug him, but she decided on the latter. No wonder Anthea had been so convinced Hannah and family were going to move into Garden Cottage. Charlie had been paying the rent on it ever since they'd gone back to London.

'Why didn't you tell me?' said Marguerite, serving him a bowl of her home-made gazpacho. It was an unusually warm evening for the beginning of June and they were having dinner on the terrace.

'I knew you'd tell me not to do it,' said Charlie, barely suppressing a grin which reminded her so much of Hector for a moment, Marguerite's excitement about them moving in next door swelled up inside her like a balloon being inflated. She felt she might float up from her seat into the blue summer sky.

'But you told Hannah?'

'Not until you told me she'd lost her job,' said Charlie. 'I didn't want her to feel pressured by us, but for my own sanity I couldn't bear to see such a wonderful opportunity just thrown away. Imagine how awful it would have been if she'd finally managed to convince Matt that moving here was the best thing for the kids – and someone else had moved in? It would have killed me.'

Marguerite nodded. She'd been bitterly dreading that too, to the point where she could hardly bear to look at the cottage as she drove up their drive.

'And you know how I've always liked the third way,' continued

Charlie. 'I can't stand things being just yes or no, left or right, in a situation; there's always another way if you can only find it – and after that time when you were so upset about them not moving in, it suddenly struck me that this was the third way in this scenario. So I got the estate agent's contact details from Anthea, did the deal and now it's all turned out splendidly.'

'You're a marvel, Charlie Berry-Downing,' said Marguerite, smiling at him in a way he didn't see very often any more. 'I thought Anthea had lost her marbles, the way she kept saying of course they were going to move in and all the time she knew you'd taken the lease.'

'Well, I did ask her to be discreet about it,' said Charlie, 'but it sounds like that was a lost cause. Why am I not surprised?'

'No wonder she thought we should be responsible for the chickens and the lawn,' said Marguerite and laughed, throwing back her head in a way that reminded Charlie vividly of how she'd looked when he'd met her at the Cambridge May Ball nearly fifty summers before.

He could still clearly remember the moment he'd first seen her, so discreetly beautiful in a teal-blue ball gown which showed off her tiny waist and creamy skin. Hannah had the same skin. And Nancy for that matter.

He sipped his ginger beer. Filthy stuff, but at least it had some bite to it. If he had to drink pop – and he did have to – it was the least ghastly thing. His last binge had been a bad one, even he knew that. Wine he was pretty silly on, beer made him wee himself, but once he hit the spirits he turned quite nasty. That brandy had tasted so good he'd finished the bottle, very quickly forgetting why he'd got the bloody thing out of the cupboard in the first place.

Marguerite had eventually found him in the drawing room, having moved on to a bottle of single malt and although he was glad he couldn't remember the details, he was fairly certain he'd spoken to her in the most unpleasant terms as she threw him out of the house and back to the granny flat to sleep it off. Although she hadn't managed to get the whisky bottle out of his grasp – he'd found it by the bed the next day. Oh pitiful excuse for a man he was.

He took small comfort from knowing he had never been physically violent to her, but when he got into that place where nothing could stand between him and another blissful sip, he knew he could be pretty nasty verbally and he wasn't proud of it.

The shame was always the worst part of the hangover. The physical effects he could handle, but the shame was quite often what led to the next binge. He was perfectly aware of this vicious circle, but had always felt powerless to break it.

As Marguerite handed him the bowl of soup which he knew would be utterly delicious, as everything she made was, he thought yet again what a very fortunate man he was, still to be sitting down to dine with her after all the stupid things he'd done. He didn't deserve it retrospectively, so he must make up for it now.

And with his beloved daughter and those two marvellous little children moving in next door, he vowed to himself this time to stay in control of his urges and out of trouble.

But even as he lifted the first fragrant spoonful of soup to his lips, that uncontrollable demon in his head was telling him how much nicer it would be with a glass of ice-cold dry sherry. Or two.

# Chapter Twenty-six

Hannah pulled Hector's knitted hat low over his ears and wrapped his scarf right round his nose and mouth.

'I can't breathe, Mummy,' he said, yanking it off again.

'You'll get used to it,' said Hannah, pulling it back up. 'I just don't want you to breathe this freezing air straight into your lungs, or you'll get poorly again and have to have more of that yucky medicine.'

Hector's eyes – the only bit of his face she could see – widened in alarm.

'OK,' he said and put his mittened hand into Hannah's gloved one.

They stepped out of the front door into total darkness and Hannah had to go back in to put the outside light on and grab the torch, so they could at least get down to the road without falling over. It was the same every morning but she still wasn't used to it.

'Here, take Sooty's lead a minute,' she said, 'and don't let go of it. He'll run off again.'

'Why is it night in the morning here?' said Hector, as they finally set off.

He was walking so close to her she kept tripping over his feet. With the dog crossing backwards and forwards as well, it was slow progress. She had to keep stopping to untangle them all.

She wished she could have left the bloody dog behind, but the only condition on which Matt had let it stay, after Anthea had given it to Hector without asking them first, was if Hector walked it every day.

Which, of course, meant Hannah, and she had to walk it now so she could work later.

'In London,' Hector was saying, 'there was night and day, but here it's mostly night, isn't it?'

'It's only because it's winter,' said Hannah, 'and there are no street lights here until we get into the village. It's dark in the morning in London now too, but there are so many lights everywhere you don't notice it.'

She panned the torch left and right to show Hector where they were – not far from the sharp bend after which they'd be able to see the lights of the village at last – and then trained it back on the ground right beneath their feet. She had to know where each next step was going to land, or it might be in a pothole of frozen water.

Just as they reached the bend she heard a car coming fast from behind and had to yank Hector and Sooty swiftly off the road and on to the verge, but with care. One morning all three of them had ended up in a wet ditch.

She might have to take up her mother's offer of borrowing the car for the school run until the mornings got lighter after all. She didn't quite know why she'd rejected it in the first place. Some sort of pride about being able to cope without it and wanting to walk Hector to school in the clear country air, because they could. Driving a mile seemed immoral. But what a very long mile it was in the freezing dark of a country February morning.

She already had to borrow the car, or go with her mum, every time she needed to shop for food, a twenty-five-minute drive to the nearest big supermarket. It was that or live on tins of spaghetti hoops and sliced white bread, which was about the best on offer in the village shop. Creamy pasta bake with tinned tuna, tinned sweet corn and frozen peas was a desperation special they'd all become rather too familiar with. And tinned peaches were also featuring all too often.

Somehow her mum never seemed to be reduced to that kind of bedsit eating. She planned her meals ahead for a week and shopped accordingly, but whenever Hannah tried that Matt or Hector would eat some of the key ingredients straight out of the fridge without telling her and all her plans would be wrecked.

Matt kept saying she should order the food online and have it delivered but she hated doing that. She liked to see what she was buying and getting ideas as she shopped, plus she enjoyed the outings with her mum and Nancy. There was something very special about being the three girls out together.

They'd go into the town proper after finishing at the big supermarket, to have coffee – a babyccino for Nancy – in the lovely independent bookshop they were so lucky still to have. It was such a treat to be able to do that with Marguerite, without having to arrange some complicated visit weeks in advance, she relished every moment of it and knew her mum did too.

The other reason Hannah didn't want to give up her weekly trips to the nearest town was she was going a little bonkers staying in the house all the time and she did need to get out occasionally, apart from for the school run. But, she always told herself, that was a tiny irritation compared to the joy of being with Nancy all day, or at least in the same building with her, if she was working and Matt was looking after her downstairs.

Whenever she wanted to see her baby daughter, she could just take a break and go down and see what they were up to, sit on the floor with Nancy and play with her for a few precious minutes and then go back up to her desk again. And they had lunch together every single day. It was exactly what she'd dreamed of all those mornings on the bus going into work.

The joy of that first August morning when they'd woken up in Garden Cottage and Hector had brought Nancy in to them as usual, but then they'd all been able to stay there together as long as they'd wanted to, was still vivid six months later.

Matt had gone downstairs and then brought them all up breakfast in bed, a glorious sticky mess of tea and milk and toast, spread with honey from Anthea's hives. Her housewarming present to them.

A little later he had settled Hector and Nancy in front of a film and come back to bed, a chair wedged under the door handle, to complete the summer idyll, the sun pouring through the window on to their naked bodies.

Now in the grip of winter, the realities of country life weren't quite as magical as they'd been in summer but, she reminded herself, as she navigated around a large frozen puddle, it had been just as grim getting in to the office in the freezing damp each morning. And at least now she didn't have to try to look stylish at the same time as keeping the weather out. Her Uniqlo puffa coat was like her second skin these days and she wasn't carrying a single bag. She didn't even need to take her keys.

After another close encounter with a speeding car – country drivers were terrifying – the lights of the village finally came into view, illuminating the parents and kids arriving at the school. Lots were dropping them off from cars right by the gates, triple parking and zooming off again without indicating. She held tight to Hector's hand and Sooty's lead.

Getting closer to the school, she could see Marcus's mum, Nicola, chatting to some other mothers she recognised but hadn't quite placed yet. When they got to the playground gate, she had to grab Hector by the hood of his coat to make sure she got a kiss before he ran in, shouting to Marcus as he went.

'Hi, Hannah,' said Nicola, as she watched them go. 'Enjoying the weather?'

Hannah laughed.

'Lucky I'm used to it. My husband still finds the English winter an abomination. He seems to think it's all my fault.'

'Oh, yes,' said another woman; Hannah hadn't talked to her before, 'your husband's that gorgeous Australian bloke isn't he?'

'He's definitely Australian,' said Hannah, smiling. 'I'm Hannah,' she added. 'I've got Hector in Reception.'

'Kelli,' said the woman. 'I've got Ethan and Bluebell, years three and five. Pleased to meet you.'

While Hannah hadn't met Kelli before, she'd certainly noticed her. She wore so much elaborate make-up, even in the morning, you couldn't miss her. It always made Hannah wonder if, as a beauty writer, always evangelising about the latest cosmetic miracle, she wasn't some kind of enabler for women like this one.

She had a very pretty face underneath all the slap and although

Hannah loved make-up with a passion, she couldn't understand why anyone would wear so much. She always had high heels on too, even in this terrible weather.

'He comes into the White Hart, that's where I know him from,' she was saying. 'I work in there. He's a Guinness drinker, isn't he? But I only ever see him with your dad. Don't you like going to the pub?'

No, thought Hannah. I hate pubs. Especially country pubs which serve wine you could take your nail varnish off with. And which allow your father to get himself dangerously plastered before they stop serving him. But she'd keep that to herself. The woman's voice had a slight edge to it and she had an idea she was already considered a bit of a snob among the school mums who didn't know her. No point in making it worse.

'It's not that,' said Hannah, 'it's just with the kids, it's easier to let him go out when he feels like it without having to plan it. He needs to have his man time and all that.'

'If I had a man like that, I'd never let him out on his own,' said the woman, laughing.

Hannah made herself laugh along. She was used to women making comments like that to her. Matt was so strikingly, unsubtly handsome, it just went with the territory. She knew they hit on him a lot too, but was confident it was just an irritation to him – they joked about it – and she'd presumed that these country women would be a little less brazen than their pushy London counterparts.

But as she walked up to the post office to pick up her copy of the *Guardian*, Hannah made a resolution to go with Matt next time he went to the White Hart.

# Chapter Twenty-seven

Matt was in his studio, as he liked to think of it, chatting to Pete on Skype. It was five past two in the afternoon in Bumfuck, UK, five after midnight in Sydney town. Prime working time, according to their long-established ritual – but only for one of them. Pete.

He'd had a pleasant Bondi February evening, dinner at his favourite hole-in-the-wall Thai, a few drinks with some people he'd run into there and had come back to his unit, relaxed and refreshed, ready to work.

Matt had spent the day so far entertaining, feeding and changing Nancy, between checking his computer every half hour, hoping to catch Pete on Skype. Finally, Hannah had scooped Nancy up to go to the supermarket with her and her mum, and he'd pinned his best mate down. His image glowed out of the screen of Matt's laptop, bare-chested, tanned and nursing a cold beer.

Every time Pete lifted the frosted bottle to his lips, Matt would automatically raise the mug he was holding and have an unpleasant surprise when his mouth filled with hot tea. The first time it happened he'd spat it out all over his jeans and they were now cold and clammy against his thighs.

He didn't want the sodding tea, but if he didn't have the mug to cradle, his hands would go numb and he wouldn't be able to type. It was too cold to sit still for long in that room and they'd already been at it for nearly an hour. Pete was lazily fanning himself with a magazine as Matt blew on his hands and rubbed them together.

'You cold, mate?' asked Pete. 'Shame I can't send you some of this. It's still twenty-eight degrees here. Can't you turn your heat up?'

'The radiator doesn't work in this room and the chimney's blocked so we can't have a fire in here. I'm going to get a heater, but I've got to go into town to get it, which is like organising a polar expedition, but forget about it, I'll be fine, play that back to me again.'

'I dunno, mate,' said Pete, scratching his stomach. 'I don't think we're in the same place on this track with one of us sweating and the other one getting hypothermia. It's a smooth sort of hot summer vibe, what I was coming in from yesterday when I started it, a long day at the beach, sand between your toes, "Girl From Ipanema" type thing. I'll send you the file later when I've added a few more layers to it and then you can work on it when you've just got out of a hot bath or something and we'll pick up on it again after that . . .'

Matt sighed heavily. He wanted to work now. He'd been looking forward to this ever since he'd got Pete's overnight email saying he'd been working on a really simple riff he felt had great potential and wanted to see what Matt thought.

Matt thought it was really interesting. It was based around one of those catchy little musical phrases that had made Pete quite in demand as a jingle-writer. Not an annoying ear worm, but simple enough to stick the first time you heard it and complex enough to make you want to listen to it over and over to get it straight in your head. It was Pete at his best.

If he could flesh that out with a strong melody for the verse and Matt could come up with a lyrical thread that was equally attention grabbing, it could be something seriously good. It was the most exciting start they'd had for ages.

'But I love this track, Pete,' said Matt. 'I really think you're on to something. I guess it has inspired you going back there.'

Pete laughed.

'Yeah, it came into my head when I was watching girls jogging along the promenade at Bondi on Sunday. It was that corny.'

'We can call it "Music to Watch Girls Go By",' joked Matt. 'Shame someone's already thought of that, but really, it's great, you've given me something very strong to spring off from. Play it again, would ya?'

Pete played the phrase on repeat and Matt typed. And deleted. And typed and deleted. It wasn't happening. He tried to picture Bondi in his head. To feel the heat and salt on his skin and hear the crash of the waves. Smell the sunblock mixed with sweat, a whiff of something frying on the air. The summer ease in his bones. He tried and he couldn't. All he could feel was cold and pinched and all he could picture was how much the light was already fading outside and it was only . . . shit! It was five to three already.

'I've got to go, mate,' he said, his voice sounding as flat as he felt. He couldn't bear to tell Pete why. Bloody school pick-up.

Why did Hannah have to go to the bloody supermarket with her mother this particular afternoon? She'd had some phone interview or something to do in the morning, she'd said, that couldn't be changed. Fair enough, but how come his work always came second to hers?

OK, apart from his modelling, she was still making most of the money they lived on, if you could call it living, but if Matt didn't have enough time for his real work, that would never change. And he could potentially make a lot more money than she ever could. That's what he could never get her to understand.

Living rent-free, thanks to Charlie, was their chance to go for that, but she just wouldn't give in and insisted it was more essential than ever that she kept her profile up in print now she wasn't going to all the bloody launches any more. She used to moan so much about going to them and now it was a problem that she didn't go to them. It was starting to piss Matt off.

Pete didn't look quite as disappointed as Matt felt.

'OK mate,' he said, draining his beer. 'I'll keep working on it and I'll send you what I do later.'

'Can we Skype earlier tomorrow?' asked Matt. 'Or later? This is a bit of an awkward time this end.'

Pete rubbed his neck and looked a bit strained.

'I'm going out tomorrow night. Late one. I'll try and catch you before I go. See ya, mate.'

And he disappeared from the screen.

Matt looked down at his tea, now stone-cold. He drained it and threw the mug at the wall where it broke with a satisfying crash.

# Chapter Twenty-eight

Ali was walking home along Hackney Road after a lunchtime shift at the bar, singing. Mainly because she was just so happy in her new London life, but also to keep warm. She still couldn't believe how cold it was in London in February.

When winter had first kicked in it had seemed really fun to rug up in hats and gloves, and she'd loved Christmas in the crisp cold; there'd even been a dusting of snow.

Going up West – as she now called it, like the local she was – with Hannah to take the kids to see Santa in Selfridges had been just gorgeous, the lights in Regent Street, all the shop windows decorated, such a feeling of excitement in the air, so different from a cruisey summer Christmas in Sydney.

But February was something else. The damp cold seemed to creep into your bones. Ali pulled the collar of her coat up around her chin, glad she'd taken Hannah's advice to invest in a cheap puffa. She'd tried wearing a lovely old tweed thing she'd found in her favourite vintage warehouse, but it was so heavy it was like dragging another person around on her back and not even that good at keeping the cold out. The puffa was hideous, but it kept her toasty warm.

Waiting for the lights to change at a pedestrian crossing, she braved taking off her gloves for a few moments to check Twitter on her phone and was gratified to see she had several new messages – all of them asking what she was doing that night. Huzzah!

One of them was from a cute guy she'd been flirting with in the bar for a couple of weeks and who she was beginning to think just might be the right man to take the big plunge with – the first post-injury love action.

She'd had a couple of pashes over the crazy Christmas party period, which seemed to start in October in London, but hadn't felt ready to take it further with either of them.

Taking her clothes off in front of a man for the first time since the glassing was a big deal, but this guy – some kind of designer, like everyone who came into the bar seemed to be – had a gentle quality to him. He was from oop north, as he said it, and didn't seem as hardbitten as some of the London blokes she'd met.

His tweet was inviting her to meet him at a private view that night and, smiling down at her phone, she immediately replied to say she'd be there, then hastily put her gloves back on.

He was just one of so many cool people she'd met at Chocolate Bar, which made it seem like every minute she wasn't working there was someone great to hang out with, suggesting something really interesting to do.

She'd met her flatties, Minnie and Stewart, there too and it had all worked out really well, with the three of them sharing Matt and Hannah's old place since they'd moved to the country back in August.

Minnie and Stewart had a bedroom each and Ali slept in what used to be the living room. They'd all agreed it was only fair for her to have the biggest room as she'd decided to take on the extra responsibility of being the leaseholder when it came up for renewal in January.

The only sticking point was that for the past three months or so, Minnie's boyfriend had stayed over so often it was almost as if he was living there too. He hadn't actually moved in, so they couldn't ask him to pay a share of the rent or the bills, but he always seemed to be in the bloody bathroom when Ali wanted it.

Stewart felt the same about the situation and they'd agreed each to have a friendly word with Minnie when they had the opportunity, so Ali had been part pleased, part nervous to find her alone in the flat a few days earlier.

'Hi, Mins,' she'd said, joining her in the kitchen, 'want some tea?'

'Got some already,' said Minnie.

So she did. Made with the last of the milk. There was none left for Ali. And that was another thing that was beginning to rile her. They had a joint kitty for loo roll, milk and other basics, but Minnie and her boyfriend never bought them. They'd just use what was there and never think to replace it.

She'd also finished off Ali's butter – and being forced to have a slightly soggy custard cream when she'd been looking forward to hot buttery toast with Marmite probably made her speak to Minnie about the situation a bit more sharply than she otherwise would have. Which in turn made Minnie react very defensively, but Ali thought she'd get over it and see it was only fair.

But when she walked into the flat that afternoon, it soon became clear that Minnie hadn't got over it. The first thing Ali noticed was that her iPod dock, which she'd kept in the kitchen so they could all use it, was missing and so was the electric kettle, which she'd also bought.

Her first thought was that they'd been robbed, but there was no sign of a forced entry and the place hadn't been wrecked the way you'd expect with a break-in. And then, checking to see if anything obvious was missing from the other bedrooms, she walked into Minnie's and found it was completely empty. Everything was gone, even the light bulb.

Ali stood there for a few moments, stunned, then went back to the kitchen and bedroom to see if there was a note she hadn't seen before, but there was nothing. There was nothing in the kitty jar either and they'd all put their £10 in a couple of days before. It was only £30, which wasn't a lot really – well, only £20 really, because £10 of it had been Minnie's in the first place – but it made Ali feel disproportionately upset.

She immediately rang Stewart and he was as shocked as she was.

'That is so crap,' he said. 'They took your iPod dock?'

'Well, somebody has. And the stupid kettle and all Minnie's stuff is gone from her bedroom, so it must be her. I can't believe it. Any idea where they might have gone?'

'Haven't a clue,' he said. 'I'm gobsmacked.'

'Same. We'll just have to find them and demand it all back.'

She heard Stewart blow the air out between his teeth.

'That might not be so easy,' he said.

'Well, they can't just disappear,' said Ali, irritated at his negative attitude.

'They can,' said Stewart.

'How?' said Ali. 'We can ask everybody who knows them and we'll see them around Shoreditch sooner or later, you know how you always bump into people round here, it's a pretty small scene.'

'But London is a very big city,' said Stewart, 'and if she's done a runner, she'll make sure she stays out of our way, Ali.'

'Surely someone will know,' said Ali, as something else dawned on her. 'She owes me two months' rent, Stewart, and this month is due next week.'

'Oh no,' said Stewart, groaning. 'That really is horrendous – and I'm afraid that just makes it even less likely you'll find her.'

'That *I'll* find her?' said Ali, incredulous. 'Aren't you going to help me?'

'Of course I will,' said Stewart, quickly. 'I'll text everyone I can think who might know, but like I say, London's a very big place and if someone wants to disappear, they can. I've known it to happen before. It just swallows them up.'

Ali felt tears prick her eyelids. This all felt very alien. People just didn't disappear like that in Sydney, they always turned up at one of the key bars or cafés eventually and she wasn't going to give in so easily. She hadn't worked all those nights in that horrible strip club to come to London and let those bastards rob her.


A few days later she was sitting in her favourite café, drinking a pretty reasonable flat white and sketching designs for 'Wanted' posters in her notebook.

Despite asking everyone who came into the bar and texting anyone else she could think of since it had happened, Ali still had no leads on where Minnie and her horrible boyfriend might have slunk off to. She had photos of both of them on her phone and was thinking some

*Wanted: Dead or Alive* posters with their faces on them, liberally spread around Shoreditch, could be the answer. Bastards.

She'd just checked her bank balance and was feeling slightly nauseous. Her savings pot was already running low and because she'd signed that bloody lease she was responsible for all the rent they owed, as well as her own share, which would pretty much clear it out.

She was gazing into space, wondering how much a private detective would charge and whether it would save her money in the long run, when Stewart texted her:

> Someone has told me that Minnie was talking about some friends who had a squat near Elephant & Castle tube. They might have gone down there. Worth a try.

Ali clicked her fingers. A lead, at last. Maybe she could be her own Phillip Marlowe. She was having a drink with the nice designer bloke before work, but it was only ten-thirty so, after consulting her trusty Tube map, she put on her puffa and headed over to Old Street to get the Northern Line down to Elephant & Castle.

She came up out of the tube and stood there blinking. She looked around her, wondering which way to go. There were no clues, just scruffy shops, people walking along with their heads down, standing at bus stops, sunk into their coats, hands thrust into pockets. The exhaust from the traffic crawling along in both directions condensed in the freezing air.

She crossed the road and walked along in a random direction, hoping to see a cool-looking café or shop, or someone wearing something vintage who she could ask if they knew about an artists' squat. But there was nothing of interest, just pound shops, bookies and minimarts with miserable-looking fruit and veg outside.

The only café she could find was a greasy-looking place with a couple of old men sitting alone, staring down at empty plates. She ordered a tea and, summoning up her best Aussie smile, asked the man standing by the till if he knew if there were any squats in the suburb.

He looked at her as though he hadn't understood what she meant, then she remembered they didn't use 'suburb' that way in London.

'In the, er, neighbourhood,' she tried again. 'I'm looking for a squat in this area.'

The man's face contorted into a sneer.

'You're one of them filthy squatters, are you? Steal people's houses while they're on holiday? Get out of my shop. We're honest working people here. Go and earn some money, get your own house. Get out!'

He snatched the thick cup and saucer of dark brown tea back out of Ali's hand and threw it into the sink, with a crash. Ali flinched in surprise.

'It's not me,' she said. 'I've got a job, I pay rent. I'm just looking for some people who owe me money.'

'Get out!' the man was saying. 'Bloody foreigners, come over here, steal our houses, go on benefits. Get out of my shop now!'

'Fine,' said Ali, anger rising. 'I'm leaving your filthy dump. You're welcome to it.'

She flounced out, letting the door slam behind her, but her moment of anger immediately subsided, leaving a blank hole in its place. She stumbled back along the street the way she'd come, feeling more lonely than she'd ever felt in her life.

One of the reasons she'd wanted to leave Sydney was she felt there was nowhere in that city she could escape, to be anonymous and free. But she hadn't understood that the freedom could also mean feeling completely unconnected in a negative way, like this.

She tried to argue with herself, reminding the part of her that wanted to curl up in a ball in the next doorway that she had a really cool job, loads of friends – not forgetting the rather gorgeous man she was supposed to be meeting up with later – and a lovely flat. But thinking about the flat just made her feel worse.

Why had she taken over the lease from Hannah and Matt when it came up back in December? What a dumb vanity that had been, just so she could say she had her own flat in London. Now it would cost her the last bit of her savings – so hard-earned – to pay it off.

For the first time since she'd moved to London she suddenly

desperately wanted to be at home, where the air was warm, the cafés were clean and she knew people everywhere she went. She was furious with herself for feeling like that, but couldn't help it. The horrible man in his horrible caff, this depressing street, the realisation that Stewart was right and she was never going to find those thieving bastards, had smashed her confidence like a car bomb.

Taking shelter in a gap between two shops displaying shoddy goods on tables outside which offered a little privacy, she took some deep breaths, determined not to cry in the street. Not in this street among all these defeated-looking people.

She fumbled for her phone and taking off her right glove for as short a time as possible, she dialled Matt's number.

# Chapter Twenty-nine

Matt was still working on lyrics for Pete's cruisey beach-inspired track, with that killer hook on the chorus, and not getting very far. He hadn't been able to find his friend on Skype again for days since their last session, so he'd decided just to keep working at it and get back to him when he had something going.

He'd made a playlist of songs with the right mood and 'The Girl from Ipanema', 'Summer Breeze', 'Waiting on a Friend', 'Golden Lady' and others had been on repeat all morning, but nothing was coming.

He was finding it hard to rise above the fact that he was wearing a green quilted gilet Hannah's father had left at the house acciden-tally, over a thick jumper, a flannel shirt and a T-shirt and still didn't feel warm. It was a little better when he put his knitted beanie on, but he found it hard to think straight wearing a hat indoors. His brain couldn't breathe.

It was a relief when the phone rang.

'Matt?' came a pitiful little voice.

'Hey, Ali all star,' said Matt, delighted to hear from her. 'Are you OK, darls?'

'No,' said Ali, finding she had to fight the tears even harder, now she had a sympathetic voice to talk to, 'I'm not all right and I just needed to talk to a friend.'

'Ah, babe,' said Matt. 'London winter blues got to ya?'

'I suppose that's what it is,' she said, sounding uncertain. 'It's just that my bastard flatmate has done a runner owing loads of rent and she's taken my iPod dock . . .'

'What? Oh, that's no good. And you can't find her, right?'

'Dead right,' said Ali. 'She's just disappeared with her horrible user boyfriend. No one knows where they are. I'm down in Elephant & Castle, looking for a squat where someone thought they might be.'

Matt tutted.

'It's real tough,' he said, 'but London can just swallow people up like that. Very occasionally you'll randomly run into a friend outside your normal zone, but it's so rare you kind of declare a national holiday when it happens. I bumped into Pete like that once in Regent Street and we were both so surprised we headed off to Chinatown and had a massive night. Not like Sydney, eh? Where you run into all your best mates all the time, just on the street.'

'Well, I do see people I know all the time in the bar,' said Ali.

'Yeah,' said Matt, 'that's why everyone in London needs a local. Gives you a tiny sense of community in the great big ocean of people.'

Ali listened intently, feeling a bit better on hearing that this was normal, not some kind of freak ill fortune she'd brought on herself.

'So you reckon I won't find them, then?' she asked.

'You might hear something in the bar, but it's unlikely. If they've nicked stuff, they're going to be the kind of pigs who'll know how to disappear.'

'That's what Stewart – my other flattie, the nice one – reckons,' said Ali. 'So I guess I'll just have to pay the rent she owes and find someone else to move in. How crap is that?'

'It's tough,' said Matt, 'but it does sound like your only option. So, what are you going to do right now to cheer yourself up?'

He hated to hear her sounding so defeated. It was so unlike her.

'Go back to the flat I suppose,' said Ali, her spirits starting to sink again. 'I'm meeting someone later, but not until six . . .'

'I've got a better idea,' said Matt, 'you said you're at Elephant & Castle? OK, get back on the Northern Line, go one stop down to Kennington, then back up on the other branch and get out at Leicester Square, then head east over through Covent Garden, all the way along Longacre into Queen Street and on down there. Then cross Kingsway and head into Lincoln's Inn Fields. Got that?'

'Yeah,' said Ali, standing up a little straighter. 'Lincoln's Inn . . .'

'Fields,' said Matt. 'Lincoln's Inn is somewhere else – Lincoln's Inn Fields is a square with a garden in the middle and in the north-west corner of it you'll find something called the Sir John Soane Museum. Spend a bit of time in there. Then find your way up towards the British Museum and just before you get to it, in Museum Street, you'll find the London Review of Books bookshop. Have a browse in there, then go into the café and have some tea and a nice bit of cake. Then if you've got any more time, go round the corner to the British Museum and just stroll through it. But don't go to the Egyptian bit, it's always full of morons videoing it rather than looking at the exhibits. I like the Abyssinian stuff. Got all that?'

'I think so,' said Ali.

'Don't worry, I'll text the details to you. By the time you get out of the tube at Leicester Square, it will all be there in your phone.'

'Right, thanks, Matt, but why exactly am I going to those places?' asked Ali.

'Because it will remind you why you wanted to move to dank, grey, difficult London,' Matt replied. 'Why it's such an amazing place. Everyone has low days here – even natives – and to get through them, I've worked out things to do to help me keep the faith. This is one of them; I've got others. I'll email them to you, but I think this is the itinerary for today. It's one of my favourite winter walkabouts.'

They said goodbye and Matt sat back down at the laptop hoping he'd helped his young cousin out. Outings like that had got him through a lot of low days the first winter after they'd moved to London, before they'd had the kids, when Hannah had been at work and he hadn't really known what to do with himself.

Talking to Ali had reminded him about those early days, with the rush of being totally elated to be living in that amazing city – so many centuries of history, so many incredible people – then the times when he had felt like it was burying him alive and he longed for the easy pleasures of home. The big sky, friends he'd known since kindie, sun in his eyes, driving down the hill to Bondi.

And that gave him the feeling. Suddenly he could remember what it felt like to drive your car barefoot with no shirt on. Triple J up loud, shades on, the wind from the open window ruffling your hair over your eyes, knowing you were about to lose yourself in the surf.

He started tapping steadily at the keys and the words flowed, in perfect rhythm with Pete's music. Sweet.

Then, as he ripped off the hat which was starting to make his forehead itchy and felt the shock of the cold on his head, he had another flow of ideas. The shivering cold, the bulky clothes weighing you down, the tight hat squeezing your brain and then he went back to the chorus with Pete's great riff.

There and here, here and there
Hot and cold, heart and soul,
Caught between here and there

Far and near, near and far,
Where I want to be, where you are
Caught between near and far . . .

# Chapter Thirty

Charlie was polishing his shoes and giving himself a good talking-to. He could do it. He could. He could go up to London, have the meeting with the fellow who was running Hannah's case for him and come straight back. He could do it without inviting the solicitor to lunch. And without going anywhere near his club. He could. Couldn't he?

He'd been good for so long since Hannah and the family had moved down. Something about having them there went a long way to filling the gap he'd always felt the need to stop up with drink.

Seeing Hector every day, helping him with his reading, was probably the greatest joy he'd ever known. Little Nancy was a dainty darling, just as her mother had been as a toddler, but Hector was something else. Hector was like meeting himself coming back. Such a cheery little fellow, a bright spark and so enjoying school. And such a lucky boy to come home from it each night to his family. Just one year older than him, Charlie had been packed off with a trunk, no teddy allowed, hardly able to read the letters his mother sent him each week.

He put his shoe brushes back in their mahogany box with the tins of polish and soft cloths and stood in front of his open wardrobe to choose his suit. His hand went immediately to his favourite charcoal-grey chalk stripe. He always had a good time in that suit. But a good time doing what? Getting roaring drunk with Anthony at the club, or somewhere sleazier in Shepherds Market.

He stroked the fabric. Such superb quality it had survived quite a few outings when the times had been a little too good. When he'd found himself rolling around on the floor. Or someone had thrown their drink over him. The suit had always bounced back though. A damp sponge, a nice long airing, a good brushing and it was as good as new.

But he could avoid it, all the situations which could lead to the suit needing the special attention. The solicitor chappie's office was in Holborn and the station back home was far nearer to there than the club was. He'd have to go right past the station to get to St James, or close enough to know he was doing it. Surely that would be enough to keep the evil urge in check. Wouldn't it?

He chose a shirt. Strong china-blue with a plain white collar, it looked good with his favourite tie, diagonal stripes in mixed colours on silk twill. Just the cuff links, socks and underwear to lay out and he would be ready for the morning. So the clothes were all ready, but was he?

He heard Marguerite ringing the old ship's bell which was their dinner gong out of the back door and after quickly running his hairbrushes over his hair, washing his hands and adjusting his cravat, he headed down the stairs to join the family for dinner, a flutter of happiness in his heart.

Thursday had become the day they all ate together in Marguerite's kitchen, so cosy in winter with the warmth from the Aga. Hannah and her crew arrived as he did and Hector threw himself into his grandfather's arms.

'Hello Charlie,' he said hugging him tightly round the waist, 'ABCDEFG . . . HIJK . . . LMNOP . . . QRS . . . TUV . . . I don't like the next bit, it doesn't rhyme properly W X, Y and ZED. I think they could have thought of something better, don't you?'

Charlie was laughing and wondering how to answer that when he felt another set of small arms go round his legs. He looked down to see Nancy smiling up at him.

'Oh such riches!' he said. 'A brilliant young boy and now this adorable little girl, who will of course be equally brilliant when she starts school.'

At some cost to his lower back, he scooped them both up and carried them over to the kitchen table, amid much laughter from both of them and pulling of his hair by Nancy.

Marguerite and Hannah smiled, reminding him yet again why he was determined to stick to his plan. Straight to the solicitor. Straight back. Seeing those beautiful faces he loved so much, looking at him with approval and not a trace of the disappointment and hurt they could never quite hide, was the most precious thing he knew. That and the grandchildren. He had way too much to lose now to fall back into his old ways.

Then, over dinner, something came up which filled Charlie with even greater confidence that he could manage to keep himself on the straight and narrow. Hannah was going to London tomorrow too. They could get the train together. So no temptation to stock up on a couple of miniatures in the station café and if he started well, he knew he was much more likely to stay that way.

It all went perfectly. Charlie and Hannah spent the ninety-minute train ride relishing each other's company, chatting, sitting in companionable silence while they read their respective papers and then collaborating on the crossword. The journey had been so enjoyable that when they got out at Charing Cross, Charlie suggested they catch the train back together too.

He hesitated for a tiny moment when Hannah said the earliest one she would be able to make would be the 15.45, but with such a treat to look forward to, and the satisfaction of being met by Marguerite in the same state in which he'd set off in the morning, convinced Charlie it was an excellent plan.

He set off towards Holborn in high spirits.

Having missed the 15.45 and the 16.15, Hannah watched the 16.45 pull out of Charing Cross and wondered what to do. She didn't want to worry Marguerite unnecessarily by ringing to ask if Charlie had forgotten their arrangement and caught an earlier train, so she rang Matt and asked him if he'd heard Marguerite go out in the car that afternoon. He hadn't.

'I'll tell you what,' said Matt, 'I'll go over there pretending I've forgotten what time you're coming back and see if he's already there, or if he's rung her, OK?'

Hannah bought a hot chocolate to try and keep warm in the freezing station. On these day trips up to town she seemed to have even more bags to haul around than ever, so although she wanted to carry on pacing around looking for Charlie, in the end she had to sit down on a cold metal bench.

It felt like ages before Matt called back.

'She's heard nothing and says she doesn't know what time either of you are coming back – but she did say she was expecting Charlie much earlier than this. His appointment was at noon and she said he'd been planning to come back straight after it. By rights he should have been back by now.'

Hannah felt sick.

'It's my fault,' she said. 'He wanted to get the train back with me and I said the earliest I could catch was the three forty-five. He hesitated, Matt, he knew it was leaving too long after the appointment. Hours to be filled in London can lead to only one thing for Dad. I should have said I didn't know what train I could catch. Oh, why did I let him agree to that train?'

'Hey,' said Matt, 'calm down. It's not your fault at all. He wanted to catch the same train as you. It was his idea.'

'We're going to have to tell Mummy,' said Hannah, her heart sinking, 'then she can ring the club, see if he's there. My phone's running out of battery, goddamit. Do you think you can tell her, Matt? I'm really sorry, but I have to preserve what power I've still got on the phone. I'll stay here until she rings me back, OK?'

'It's fine,' said Matt. 'I'll go back over now and tell her. Have her call you.'

Hannah found a seat on the other side of the station where she felt she had a better view of people coming in. A few times she was sure she saw her father, but it always turned out to be just another white-haired man. And none of them as distinguished-looking as Charlie.

She was really cold now and starting to shiver from that and the anxiety. It was fully dark and Charlie on the loose in the city at night had never been a good idea. And as this was his first visit for months, it was really a worry.

When her phone rang, her hands were so numb she dropped it and when she finally pressed it to her ear she could hear the tension in her mother's voice.

'Hannah? Are you there? Is Charlie with you now?'

'No, Mummy, he's not,' she said. 'I'm still at the station, it's nearly two hours after we were supposed to meet and there's no sign of him.'

'He's not at the club,' said Marguerite, 'and he's not with Anthony. Or at least that's what Anthony says. So I think you should come home. I can't think of anywhere else to ring, can you?'

'El Vino's?' said Hannah, her brain dredging up a name that had resounded in her childhood on the evenings when Charlie hadn't come home.

'I tried there,' said Marguerite, 'and the Old Bell. They didn't know who I was talking about at either place.'

Small mercies, thought Hannah.

'Get the next train, darling,' said Marguerite, in a more resolute tone. 'I don't see any point in you waiting there any longer. He'll come home when he comes.'


It was nearly nine by the time Hannah got back. She'd taken a taxi from the station so Marguerite could stay at home by the phone, and directed the driver to her parents' house. As they pulled up, she was surprised to see a police car there.

She opened the front door, her heart starting to race, and Matt came running over to her.

'Oh babe,' he said, wrapping his arms round her. 'Thank god you're back. We didn't want to ring you on the train.'

'What's going on?' asked Hannah, looking up at him in confusion: why did he have that weird expression on his face?

Matt glanced over his shoulder towards the drawing room and Hannah saw her mother sitting bolt upright on the sofa, her face startlingly white. At the same time she heard a police radio crackling. It all seemed to be happening in half time, very slowly, but she still couldn't take it in.

'Where are the kids?' she said stupidly to Matt.

'They're back at the house, Fiona's with them, don't worry, but babe . . . Your dad.'

'What?' said Hannah, getting frustrated.

'The police came to tell us,' Matt said. 'He's gone, Hannah.'

'Gone where? What are you talking about?'

She pushed him away and rushed through to her mother.

'Hannah,' she said, reaching her arms up to her, a crack in her voice that Hannah had never heard before.

The policeman stood up when Hannah walked in. There was a policewoman as well, sitting next to her mother, with her arm round her. Marguerite would so hate that.

'Mummy?' said Hannah, dropping to her knees in front of her. 'What's happening?'

'Your father's dead, Hannah,' she said, her face frozen. Her eyes glassy like a doll's.

Hannah looked round at everyone else in the room, waiting for one of them to say it wasn't true. It couldn't be true.

'Yes,' said the policeman, 'I'm sorry to tell you that your father was hit by a bus this afternoon, crossing The Strand. He died immediately.'

Hannah felt herself falling. She felt stupid as it happened, like she was putting it on for effect, something she'd seen in a film, but she couldn't help it. As she heard those words, she just found herself dropping sideways to the floor.

# Chapter Thirty-one

Charlie's funeral was planned as a small family service, with a few close friends, in the local church where he and Hannah were both christened, and where Hannah and Matt had been married. But the village had other ideas. When Hannah and Marguerite got out of the funeral car, there were hordes of people crowding at the main door to get in.

'Did you know it was going to be like this?' Hannah asked her mother.

She shook her head, looking appalled. Realising Marguerite was going to need all her support, Hannah was awkwardly shifting Nancy on to the other hip, when Ali appeared and wordlessly took her out of her arms. Hannah smiled at her gratefully and took tight hold of her mother's hand.

Matt came up on the other side and put Marguerite's arm firmly through his, and she leaned gratefully into his sheltering bulk. Ali took Hector's hand and the six of them walked through the side door of the church as a tight unit.

There had been extended discussion about whether the children should go to the funeral. Hannah had even gone so far as to arrange for Ali to come down to look after them at home while it was all going on, but Matt was amazed it could even have been questioned. Of course they needed to be at their grandfather's funeral.

In his Catholic/Greek Orthodox family, he'd sat round his grand-parents' open coffins as a child and was surprised Hannah hadn't wanted to go and see her father to say one last goodbye. She'd been horrified at the idea and they'd come close to a row over the whole thing.

In the end it was Hector who made the decision he and Nancy were going to the funeral.

'I heard you talking before,' he'd told them, as they ate dinner, cooked by Anthea, in Marguerite's kitchen, 'and I am coming to Charlie's funeral whatever you say. And Nancy. It's not fair to leave her out. I'm the man of the Berry-Downing family now and I have to be there.'

They all looked at him in amazement. Anthea beamed.

'Well said, Hector,' she said, putting another large helping of rhubarb crumble into his bowl, followed by a generous drenching of custard, 'but where did you get all those grown-up ideas from?'

'From my Charlie,' said Hector, straightening his head, as tears filled his eyes.

Hannah couldn't help hers. They just started rolling down.

'He told me I was his little man and one day I would have to look after Granny and Mummy for him . . .' then he couldn't hold back any longer and started properly crying, 'and I miss him so much. Why did he have to die? He was the best Charlie in the world. I want my Charlie back.'

'Oh, Heccie, mate,' said Matt, jumping up to go to his son, holding him tight on his knee, and rocking him side to side. 'Charlie will always be with you. He loved you so much.'

With Hector's crying getting louder, Hannah now sobbing uncontrollably and Nancy joining in because everyone else was, Marguerite quietly got up from the table and left the room. Ali scooped up Nancy, and Anthea put her arm around Hannah's shoulder and pulled her towards her. Hannah was surprised to find how comforting it was to sob on to that vast expanse of bosom.

'Let it out, darling,' said Anthea, 'much better to let it out. My grandmother was Spanish, she taught me that. We'll have to help your mother to understand it, because if you don't let it out, the misery festers and makes you ill. It's the curse of the English. Wail, make a noise, it's the right thing to do. And not just sadness, you're allowed to be cross that he's gone too. Furious. Charlie died much younger than he should have. Forget all the other stuff that went before. It was an accidental death, much too young. Such a waste with these beautiful grandchildren he so adored.'

So Hannah let herself go, wailing and spluttering, boosted by Hector's racking sobs and comforted by Anthea's no-nonsense reminder of exactly how Charlie had died. Not of alcohol poisoning, or cirrhosis of the liver, or even a heart attack, but in a stupid accident, which she feared had been caused by alcohol-induced impaired judgement, but an accident nevertheless.

And while she felt rather as though her head had been through a spin cycle when she finally stopped, she did also feel a little tiny bit better. Not quite so much like she was holding her breath all the time. Terrified that if she relaxed for a moment everyone in the world would know her father's death was all her fault for agreeing to let him wait around in London with nothing to do, so that he could catch that later train home with her.

Now, as they stood in the front pew of the church and she took in the proximity of her father's coffin, as it was carried down the aisle towards them, she was hoping that outpouring and a few others since had vented enough of her raw grief and guilt to get her through the torturous service without embarrassing herself.

Yet far from feeling intrusive, she found the full church a surprising comfort. She'd always thought her father had been a figure of derision in the village, but glancing quickly over her shoulder, she took in a rather astonishing cross-section of people.

She could see the doctor and her receptionists, the lady who ran the village shop, the milkman, their gardener, the landlord and all the bar staff of The White Hart, including Kelli from the school who wore all the make-up, and the headmistress. Then there were a lot of what her mother called 'county' people and some very distinguished men and women she thought she recognised from his legal milieu. All looking genuinely sad.

Hoping her mother felt the same about the supportive crowd she squeezed her hand and then, getting no return of pressure, turned to look at her. Marguerite was like a statue. Staring straight ahead with no expression.

Hannah's attention was then distracted when she caught the eye of one of the pallbearers, as he turned after placing the coffin on the trestles in front of the altar. Seeing her recognition, he bowed his head and put his hand on his heart, in a gesture of sympathy. She hadn't seen him for years but knew immediately who it was – Anthony. Bloody Anthony!

That sleazy creep who had been such a bad influence on Charlie since they'd met all those years ago. She'd always thought that without Anthony's energetic encouragement, perhaps Charlie wouldn't have got started on his binge-drinking career and become a drinker for whom no amount of alcohol was ever enough.

Her head snapped round to look at her mother again and she nodded to acknowledge Hannah's reaction.

'I gave my permission for him to be a pallbearer,' she said, very quietly. 'The undertaker checked with me and I said yes.'

Hannah didn't think it was the time to ask, the fuck why? But her mother could clearly read the expression on her face.

'Your father would have wanted it,' she said. 'He was his best friend.'

After the service, Anthea was laying on 'refreshments', as she called them, at her house.

'Make sure your mother comes,' she said, to Hannah, as the congregation was filing out, just before the immediate family left for the private internment. 'I've only invited the people you would really want to see for a glass of sherry and a sandwich. I know it sounds bloody, but you must come. It's an important part of the process to be surrounded by people who knew and loved Charlie and to talk about him. You can't let Marguerite duck out of it. And that lovely girl Ali is going to look after the children for you, so you don't need to worry about that.'

Hannah nodded. She knew her mother would detest the idea, but she could immediately see what Anthea meant. The notion of putting her adored father in the cold hard ground was so horrible, she had imagined going straight home to bed and pulling the covers over her head after it, but now she could see that talking about him with people who understood how special he was, despite his deep flaws, would be a much better thing to do.

It would keep his spirit alive somehow, not bury it with the ghastly coffin. And Marguerite didn't seem surprised or bothered when Hannah tentatively reminded her of the plan as they got back into the undertaker's big black car after the burial.

'I'm just so glad I didn't have to arrange it,' she said, patting Hannah's hand absently. 'It's very good of Anthea.'


There was quite a crowd flowing between Anthea's drawing room, large hall and dining room, where a splendid spread was laid out. 'Sherry and a sandwich' turned out to be a full cold collation and people were tucking in with gusto.

Funeral meats, thought Hannah, feeling sick as she looked at the pork pies and slices of rare roast beef, which seemed in the context rather too redolent of the way of all flesh. She chewed on a stick of celery to settle her stomach, taking tentative sips of her glass of sherry.

Anthea came over and gave her a hug.

'Funerals always make people ravenous,' she said, 'reminds them they're alive, awakens all the appetites. Wait 'til the cakes come out, they'll descend upon them like wild beasts.'

Hannah took a bigger mouthful of her drink and found the warmth that flooded her system very comforting. She took a couple more and the feeling of wellbeing increased. Was this how Charlie used to feel, when he had that first blissful taste?

She closed her eyes for a moment, experiencing what felt like a physical blow as she remembered that she'd never be able to ask him now. The permanence of Charlie's death wasn't a concept her brain seemed capable of sustaining and she had to keep repeatedly realising it, with the attendant pain each time.

When she opened her eyes again Anthony was standing in front of her. Eek.

'I'm so sorry about your father, Hannah,' he said, without any preamble.

She just blinked at him. The warm glow in her belly now developing upwards into a slight dizziness. That celery stick was all she'd eaten since the night before.

'I'm more sorry than I can possibly say,' he continued before Hannah could answer. 'Sorry that's he gone – and sorry for all the times I led him astray and contributed to the anguish you and your mother went through with his drinking. He was so lucky to have you both and I'm very ashamed of my part in his bingeing.'

Hannah had no idea how to reply. She didn't have a script for this conversation and it was already one of the longest ones she'd ever had with Anthony. He'd always been a presence in her life, but more as a negative concept than an actual human being. She hadn't physically seen that much of him over the years.

She looked closely at him now, this bogeyman of her childhood. He was wearing a very nice suit, with a crisp white shirt and the appropriate funeral tie, but his white hair was long and wispy, curling down over his collar. It was odd on a man of his generation. And it wasn't as if Anthony was an ageing artist, or a Shakespearian actor, he was a retired barrister like her father.

Snapping back from her stupid superficial beauty editor thoughts – what was she doing, analysing his hairdo? – she realised he was looking genuinely anguished.

'Well,' she choked out, 'thanks, Anthony. You really don't have to . . .'

She was going to say 'apologise', but then she floundered, because he did need to do that, big time – but what was she supposed to say in response, at an event like this? Yeah, you wrecked my childhood, you bastard . . .?

But while she found it very awkward, part of her was rather touched by his unexpected outburst. She was still wondering how to respond when he spoke again.

'I loved him, Hannah,' he said, 'possibly too much.'

Hannah blinked. That really was too much to take on, especially as she could see so many other people she should talk to hovering near, waiting for their moment.

'But I mustn't keep you now,' he said, picking up on it. 'Thank you for listening and for being so gracious. I've wanted to apologise to you for so long.'

He glanced down at his feet and then back up at her and Hannah had a sudden vivid glimpse of him as a boy. There was such a vulnerability in the way he was looking at her from under his brows, his head bowed. Finally, she knew what to say.

'He loved you too, Anthony,' she said. 'Even when we hated you, we always knew that.'

He grasped her hand and squeezed it, looking at her with eyes that looked dangerously close to tears.

'One more thing,' he said, 'before you go and mingle. Will you have lunch with me one day, Hannah? It would mean so much to me.'

Hannah hesitated again. What kind of a lunch did he mean? The kind he used to have with Charlie, that went on into dinner and beyond? She glanced at the glass in his hand. He held it up.

'Water,' he said. 'I've given up drinking. Really. I'm doing AA, the full Monty.'

This time Hannah didn't stop to think, she answered immediately.

'OK,' she said. 'I will have lunch with you, Anthony. Have you got a card? I'll ring you.'

'Actually,' he said, a smile twitching at the corner of his mouth, as he took a leather card holder out of the inside pocket of his jacket and handed her one, 'you can email me. I'm a silver surfer.'

Despite all the sadness and trauma of the ghastly day, Hannah heard a small yelp of laughter escape her. It wasn't particularly funny, but there was just something about the way he'd said it. She was beginning to see why her father had found him such good company. He had a very engaging way about him. After all these years of loathing him, it turned out he was really rather sweet. How weird was that?

'OK,' she said. 'I'll email you then. Charlie would have liked that.'

They looked at each other very sadly for a moment and then, on a sudden impulse, Hannah leaned forward and kissed him on the cheek.

# Chapter Thirty-two

Matt was sitting at the kitchen table staring at his laptop and trying to make sense of all the different emotions that were simultaneously assaulting him. He clicked back to re-read Pete's email and then forward to play the file attached to it again. He was up to five times on both of them.

The track was called 'Bambina' and it included some of the lyrics Pete had shown him that awful night when he'd told Matt he was moving back to Sydney. The words Matt had so soundly taken the piss out of.

Listening to it for the fourth time, Matt decided it was an almost perfect pop song. And it wasn't just him who thought so. It was the number one download in the Aussie charts that week. Pete had finally cracked it – only in the Australian market so far, but it was still more than they'd achieved together – and he'd done it with a track he'd written his own words for.

Matt felt sick. Sick that Pete had done better with his own words than with anything Matt had ever come up with and sick he'd had a number one without him. But at the same time he was incredibly proud of his mate and happy for him. Jeez, it was confusing.

But all that aside, it was a great song. That was all that mattered in the end. The song. He and Pete lived for the song. And the guy who was singing it, a bloke called Abel something or other, he'd never heard of him before, was perfect for it. He sounded young, but there was a gritty quality to his voice that was spot-on for the unrequited love theme of the song. And the arrangement was great. Deceptively simple, crisp, with just enough going on. Classic Pete.

The words were still really dopey – 'Bambi, bambina, sometimes I wish I'd never seen ya, grown-up girl, out in the world, young and free, ooh ooh come to me . . .' seemed to be the gist of it – but it didn't matter. With the catchy tune of the chorus and the croaky wistfulness of the bloke's voice it all worked. Brilliant. Fuck it.

Hannah came down from putting the kids to bed and stood listening to it while the kettle boiled. It was mid-May, getting warmer, but she still had a hot water bottle every night. Deep in grief, she felt chilled to her bones all the time. She could still count the time since Charlie died in weeks. Ten weeks.

'That's a good track,' she said, glad to be distracted. 'What is it?'

'Oh, just something Pete sent me to listen to,' said Matt. 'It's number one over there right now.'

'Mmm,' said Hannah absently, checking the biscuit tin and finding it empty as usual, now Hector had worked out how to stand on a chair to get it down from on top of the fridge. 'Can you play it again? I really like it.'

Matt felt like a knife was being turned in his guts. He really liked it too. And he fucking hated it. Hated that Pete had done it without him. It made him want to rip his skin off in frustration. Not only was he trapped in this dead zone zombie village, his best friend had finally had the success they'd been striving towards together for nearly twenty years and he wasn't part of it.

On top of that he had a wife and son – not forgetting a mother-in-law – wretched with loss. And he was pretty cut up about Charlie himself. He'd loved the old bastard. It was impossible not to, despite his problems with the grog.

Matt just wanted to believe he'd died happy when his head hit that kerb. Part of him couldn't help hoping there was enough brandy coursing around his old veins at the moment of impact for him not to have felt anything. Although it was probably the shock of having a drink after so long off the hooch that had made him misjudge crossing the road like that. Horrible.

Charlie had done such a hero job of staying sober since they'd moved down there. The two of them had got into a really nice routine of going to the pub together once a week since and they'd always had a great laugh with Matt on the Guinness and Charlie on the ginger beer. He'd never had so much as a sniff of the hard stuff those nights at the White Hart.

'I'm properly happy these days, Matthew,' he'd said, as they sat up at the bar together one night. 'So happy having you and Hannah and your wonderful children down with us. I feel like I'm finally having the family life which was taken from me as a child, when they sent me off to that ghastly school – not much older than Hector, imagine – and it's given me the strength to keep my demons down. I'm so grateful to you for giving me that and I do know it's not easy for a city slicker like you living in this cultural wasteland.'

Then he'd smiled his wickedest smile as he flicked his eyebrows over to indicate the barmaid with her heavy make-up and low-cut top.

'Hard enough fighting her off,' Charlie had chuckled. 'I've seen how she looks at you. Like a monkey looks at a banana. Women used to look at me like that. They still do sometimes.'

Matt had roared. Charlie was so right there. The barmaid's less than subtle approaches had made it hard for him to go to the pub without a chaperone and it was great to meet another bloke who understood that it wasn't necessarily a good thing to be constantly hit on. Pete had never got that. But Charlie had a depth of insight that always took Matt by surprise.

'So tell me, Matthew,' he said, after they'd sat in silence for a while, as two particularly obnoxious locals had sounded off about asylum seekers, bloody foreigners and benefit-scrounging immigrants, 'as a bloody foreigner yourself, where do you miss most? London or Sydney?'

Matt didn't even know the answer to that himself, just that either of them would have been highly preferable to where he was. Achingly, pissingly preferable. But it had meant a lot to him just to have that dilemma acknowledged, because ever since the move, Hannah had been a closed book on the subject. Matt just couldn't talk to her about it.

She would close up like an oyster the minute the conversation drifted anywhere near what was great about London and if he dared to raise the topic of missing Sydney and possibly wanting to move back there for even just a little while one day perhaps, to spend some time near his extended family, she always found a way to change the subject – or simply leave the room.

That was a skill she'd learned from her mother. Matt had figured that out years ago. They did it so elegantly, the two of them. Just drifted out like it was the most natural thing to do at that moment. It would be cute if it wasn't so maddening.

But as she sat down at the kitchen table with him now, moving her head in time to the rhythm of Pete's number one song, Matt wished she would leave the bloody room. He was only sitting in there because now the evenings were getting longer it was unbearably gloomy in his so-called studio with its low beams and leaded windows. He felt like a hobbit sitting in there.

'I love this track,' she was saying. 'Can we have it on the iPod?'

'Sure,' said Matt, hoping his lack of enthusiasm wasn't too apparent.

But even in his angst, it was good to hear her being positive about something. It was only two months or so since Charlie had died and she was still like a ghost of her normal self. Hardly eating, so pale and having to make such a big effort to keep things together for the kids.

Hector seemed nearly back to his old self, but they'd found him a couple of times up in Charlie's granny flat, hugging his blue-and-white striped dressing gown and talking to it. Heartbreaking to see, but it seemed to be his way of dealing with it. Matt wasn't sure Hannah was coping at all. She had mentally left the room, just as she physically left it when the conversation made her uncomfortable.

With all that going on, he couldn't possibly tell her that this snappy little tune was Pete's first number one song, written without Matt – because that would mean telling her how wretched it made him feel and that would inevitably lead to how much he hated living in this tiny dot on the map instead of in a big city. And how he longed to go over to Sydney and spend some time with Pete. Maybe get to work on the follow-up single with him.

Matt sat up straight suddenly as the full potential disaster of the situation popped fully formed into his head. Pete would do an album with this guy – he'd be mad not to – and there was no way he could luck out on the lyrics twice. So Matt needed to secure their working partnership, fast, before Pete found someone else, local, to do the words for it.

It just wasn't working over Skype. They needed to share air. Air and a few spliffs. He hadn't even sent him the 'Here and There' lyrics yet. It just didn't feel right if he couldn't work with him on the track in real time.

There was no question about it, he urgently needed to go to Sydney and be with Pete, but there was no way he could lay all that on Hannah now, not when she was already so low. A trip out there would do her the world of good too, but he knew she'd refuse to leave her mum.

Increasing his frustration, she really didn't seem to be about to leave the kitchen any time soon. She'd got some scrap paper out of the recycling box and was making a shopping list.

'I'm going into town with Mum first thing tomorrow,' she said. 'Anything you want me to get?'

A family ticket to Sydney, thought Matt. One way.

'No,' he said, glancing at the clock.

It was nearly eight-thirty, both kids were asleep and a long evening stretched ahead, just him and Hannah and what was becoming a herd of unmentioned elephants in the room. The twin elephants of London and Sydney, now joined by this new one, which had come in on Pete's email. It was getting like Taronga Zoo in there.

Matt tried to work out when Pete had sent him the track. It had come in at some point between the kids' tea and bedtime, while he'd been away from his laptop, and it was about six-thirty in the morning in Sydney now, so he must have sent it in the middle of the Aussie night. Maybe after coming in from a big night celebrating it getting to number one.

Matt drummed his fingers on the kitchen table. He'd really have to get on Skype to congratulate him, give his old mate the praise he deserved, live and fresh. For something this major an email just wasn't enough, but he couldn't do it with Hannah around, or even awake.

She had enough going on without worrying about him having a work crisis, so he'd just have to wait until she was asleep, but knowing he had to do it and couldn't get on with it was making him feel like a caged tiger and he knew she'd pick up on that eventually and then it would all come pouring out roughly. He had to protect her from that.

'Hanns,' he said, suddenly, 'would you mind if I went to the pub?'

'Of course not,' she said, looking pleased. 'It's been worrying me that you don't go there any more. You need to do that. Have your man time away from the family. Like you used to with Charlie . . .'

Matt nodded.

'And I need to get over going for the first time without him,' he said, which was true as well. It wasn't the main reason he wanted to go at that moment, but it was part of it.

Hannah had tears in her eyes now and Matt got up and went round to her side of the table, wrapping his arms around her. As he leaned into her neck and filled his lungs with the glorious scent of her hair, he felt a familiar stirring in his groin. She still had that effect on him, instantly. Maybe that was a better idea than the pub to take his mind off making the call to Pete. He nibbled her ear and slipped a hand down on to her breast.

Very gently, she pushed him away, kissing his cheek, rather as she would kiss Hector's or her mother's.

'Better finish this list before I get too tired,' she said.

Matt pulled back, disappointed but not surprised really. They'd hardly made love since Charlie had died. Was it even twice? For the first time since they met, apart from right after the kids were born, Hannah just didn't feel like it. He wasn't going to push the issue; she was grieving, he'd make any allowance for her, but it was really adding to his general build-up of pressure. He felt like Fukushima, liable to blow up at any moment.

He'd tried dealing with it himself, DIY, but it wasn't the same. He felt like a guilty schoolboy finding stolen opportunities to wank when no-one was around. Once Anthea had nearly caught him in the act, walking into the house unannounced that way she did. That was special – not – although at least it had dampened his libido for a while. Not long enough though. He could feel it building up inside him again, that urgent need for release.

He wondered if he should go up to the bathroom now and snap one off to try and ease some of the tension, but knew it wouldn't be enough. He needed the soft touch of a woman – of Hannah. He felt so empty afterwards, without her familiar body to hold in his arms.

It wasn't her fault. He understood she was in a state similar to deep depression and knew he could only wait until she felt better, but on top of all the other frustrations he was trying to bat off, enforced celibacy was a hard call.


Matt's spirits lifted when he walked into the White Hart. It wasn't a particularly quaint pub by olde Englishe standards and it certainly wasn't cool like Chocolate Bar, or any of his favourite Sydney drinking spots, but with the bar stools, the beer pumps, the sparkling rows of lined-up bottles and glasses, and a scent of stale alcohol in the air, it had enough of the atmosphere of his comfort zones to feel nurturing.

He was also relieved to see that the over-friendly barmaid – Chezza, as he thought of her, because she looked a bit like Cheryl Cole – didn't seem to be in residence behind the bar that evening.

That situation had felt even more awkward after he'd realised he also knew her from the school gate. So she had kids herself – and therefore possibly a husband or partner – and knew he was married with kids, yet still flirted with him brazenly. What was that about?

At least the women who used to hit on him in Chocolate Bar had been young, free and single. He'd considered cycling to the nearest alternative pub to avoid her, but didn't trust himself in the dark country lanes on his bike after a few pints. They were far more dangerous than Commercial Street.

A pint of Guinness with a side of Jack Daniels took the edge off things and a couple of the pub regulars came over to ask how Hannah and Marguerite were doing and to say what a shame it was about Charlie, which was all nice. One of them bought him a pint.

He was at the bottom of that when Chezza made her entrance, looking even more lip-glossed, hair-extensioned and boob-pumped than usual. With glossy brunette hair, dark brown eyes and a curvy figure, she was a good-looking woman. She had a very pretty face underneath all the slap and he couldn't imagine why she did that to herself.

'Want another one of those, darling?' she said, leaning over the bar to give him a better view of her spray-tanned cleavage. It was hard not to look at it – any man would have, it was an automatic reflex – and unfortunately she noticed, smiling to herself with satisfaction. 'And the chaser?' she added picking up his empty shot glass and stroking it suggestively with her ridiculously long-nailed fingers. Forfucksake.

Matt just nodded, determined not to engage in conversation. He'd planned to have three. It was just enough to put him in the zone where the blood sang in his ears a bit, but he wasn't actually shitfaced. He'd be relaxed enough to talk to Pete easily and then fall asleep straight away, not lying awake with a monstrous hard-on caused by the proximity of his wife, or worrying if he would ever make enough money to get out of the hobbit hole and live in a city again.

Chezza wasn't going to let him off that easily though, finding every excuse to come down to the end of the bar where Matt was sitting. He thought about moving to a table, but the whole point of coming out had been to give himself a night off; he wasn't going to have it ruined by her, so he ordered another pint and a double shot and stayed where he was.

'So,' she said, putting the drinks down in front of him and leaning over again, 'tell me, Matt. Is it true what I hear about Australian men?'

'What have you heard,' he answered, 'that we're all gay? Even the happily married ones like me . . . Ask my wife next time you see her at the school gate.'

A swift mention of his wife usually did the trick with women like this. Especially if they'd actually seen Hannah, then they knew they were outclassed, but this one didn't seem in the least bothered.

'No,' she said, raising a heavily pencilled eyebrow, 'I've heard you're all hung like horses.'

Matt stared at her, desperately wanting to laugh but holding it back in case it encouraged her. It was funny though. God, he wished Charlie was there, he would have defused the situation with a witty line and then they would have had a great laugh about it. Or Pete. He would have cracked on to her right off. He could tell him about her when they Skyped later; it would help lighten the conversation if it got tricky.

'I wouldn't know about that,' said Matt, trying to be as bland as possible, 'maybe My Little Pony.'

Hoping that had done the trick, he eased himself off the bar stool. Time for a slash. He felt a bit more tipsy than he expected to as he walked across the pub. It was the most he'd drunk for ages and it seemed he'd rather lost his head for it. He had the odd glass of wine at home with Hannah and gins over at Marguerite's and Anthea's when they went to their houses for dinner, but he wasn't a home drinker. It was all about the bar for him.

And despite the irritating attentions of Chezza he was enjoying himself. It was good to be out of the house, good to be a little bit out of his head. He'd been doing too much thinking, not enough drinking, that's what Pete would say. So when he came back to the bar and she plonked another pint and another shot in front of him, saying they were on the house, he just went along with it. And after than, he ordered another of each. Did that make it six? He'd lost count.

By the time he stumbled over to the men's for the second time, he was properly steaming drunk – over the edge into the place where he didn't realise how drunk he actually was. He reckoned he was pleasantly numbed and happy. How he used to feel when he and Pete really went off on one, which happened rarely enough for it to be a good thing.

And in that state of mind when Chezza came in as he was doing up his fly he wasn't particularly surprised or bothered. It seemed like a normal place for anyone to be at that time. Then, as she took his hand and led him into the cubicle, locking it behind her, that also seemed like a reasonable thing for someone to do.

Even when she unbuttoned the front of his jeans, took out his cock, and wrapped her soft warm mouth round it, that seemed OK too.

In fact, it felt really really good.

# Chapter Thirty-three

Hannah couldn't figure out Matt's mood at all. He wasn't grumpy, like he'd been at first about moving to the country, he was still being super-lovely and incredibly helpful with the kids, as he'd been ever since Charlie died. More so, if anything. He'd even suggested they have Anthea over for supper at their house with Marguerite and had put on a good show of enjoying it – and he'd cooked it.

But alongside all that he was oddly distant. When he wasn't physically required to be there for meals or to look after the kids, he seemed to take every possible opportunity to be out of the house. He would disappear for long rides on his bike, even in the freezing rain, claiming it was to keep his fitness up.

That was understandable, as it was dangerous to run on the country lanes where there were no pavements and all the drivers seemed to think they were Jenson Button, but more surprisingly he'd taken over as Sooty's walker, taking him out twice a day for long hikes, which the dog adored. In fact, the two of them seemed to have become so firmly bonded that Sooty, the unwanted and hugely resented pet, was now very much Matt's dog. That was weird, but the thing that really worried her was when he turned down the opportunity to have sex.

It had happened the night he'd gone to the pub for the first time for ages. Hannah had felt really bad about pushing him away earlier in the kitchen. Matt's appetite for sex was one of the things about him that had made her fall so madly in love when she met him. They'd rutted like wild dogs for their first few months together and then at least once a day pretty much until they'd had Hector. Even after Nancy arrived they still did it far more often than any of her friends with kids seemed to.

She also understood that beyond love and passion, Matt physically had to have sex, or it built up inside him like a dam ready to burst. It made him edgy and uncomfortable in his skin. She used to tease him that he needed to be milked like a cow. Moo, he'd replied and it had become a joke between them. A quiet 'moo' in the ear at dinnertime meant fun on offer in bed later. If not sooner.

So when he came back that night, waking her up as he stumbled into the room, she'd forced herself to make the first move. It was a big effort, as finding extra energy to do anything beyond the necessities had been a real struggle since she'd lost her father, but she knew she had to – for his sake, for their marriage. And she was pretty sure once they got going it would be fine, great even. She probably needed the release as much as he did really.

So she had rolled over to him and started trailing her hand in butterfly touches down his stomach, the sort of move that normally triggered an immediate reaction, but there was nothing. No movement on the home front at all and then Matt had gently taken her hand away from his belly and squeezed it before giving it back to her, like an unwanted gift.

'Sorry, darls,' he mumbled, 'too much to drink. Feel a bit ordinary. Might hurl.'

Then he gave her hip a very asexual pat and rolled away from her. After a long ugly belch and subsequent apology, he'd fallen dead asleep.

Hannah was surprised how disappointed she was and the oddness of the whole situation jolted her into wide-eyed wakefulness. She lay there for what felt like hours staring at the ceiling, which was a particular agony as she'd found sleep her greatest comfort since Charlie had died.

Far from triggering insomnia, her grief had made her sleep much more than usual, as though her body's reaction to all the overwhelming emotion was to close down physically. Waking up – and remember-ing – was the most horrible moment of the day and if it wasn't for the kids coming in, she felt she could have slept all day. Yet despite getting at least eight hours a night, often more, she never felt refreshed by it. She was constantly groggy.

Now feeling preternaturally awake, like she'd just drunk three cans of Red Bull, everything she was trying not to think about came flooding into her brain. Money at the forefront.

How long could they expect Marguerite to carry on paying the rent for Garden Cottage? She had no idea how Charlie's death had affected her finances and couldn't bring herself to raise the subject again. She had tried to talk to her about it once, only to watch her mother float off to her study on some mysterious and suddenly urgent mission.

Hannah had been doing reasonably well freelance, but not being in London made it tricky, as it was hard to stay on top of all the product launches. And if she did go up more than once in a week to try and keep abreast of things, it was hard to find the time to write the articles she'd been commissioned to do. Complicating things further, to go to the more important evening events she had to stay overnight with a friend, which just wasn't fair on Matt, or the kids.

Thinking about all that prompted another of her other major anxieties: how much Matt hated living out of town. She turned to look at him sleeping. He was snoring, which he only did on the rare occasions he'd seriously had a lot to drink. That must be the explanation for the sex brush-off. He really was plastered.

She stroked the side of his face gently with her forefinger, smiling fondly at him. Such a beautiful man in every way. Mind, body and heart. And although growing up with Charlie had made the concept of random male drunkenness challenging for Hannah, she was glad he'd gone out and tied one on that night. He needed to let off steam.

He'd been doing so much looking after her and Marguerite and the kids, keeping it together for all of them, and she knew he detested living in the country, but she just couldn't take that on right now. There was no point talking about it. They had to do it.

They couldn't let the children spend these crucial early years breathing filthy air, living in a cramped flat with no garden and getting their early education at a stressed inner-city school; not when they were lucky enough to have such a glorious alternative. What they might both prefer was irrelevant – and there was no question that the kids absolutely loved it.

They lived in their wellies, spending practically all their time outside, hardly ever watching telly because there was always something more interesting to do in the garden with the chickens and Sooty. She knew Matt could see it was better for them too, which was why he didn't talk about London either, but she lived in a state of permanent repressed anxiety about how much he missed the city. And not just London. There was Sydney too.

Ever since Pete had moved back there, it had been looming between them as another great unspoken subject. She knew Matt wanted Hector and Nancy to spend some of their childhoods there, in his country with his family – and she wanted that too. It had been a given since the kids came along, but how could she possibly leave her newly widowed mother?

That was one unthinkable too many and it seemed to flick some kind of off switch in Hannah's head. Turning away from her husband, she fell immediately into a dead sleep.

# Chapter Thirty-four

Ali couldn't sleep either. The song Pete had emailed her was going round and round in her head. What a great track, so cruisey and summery, after London's never-ending winter.

It was May now and a bit of watery sunshine had been enough to make all the native Londoners throw off their puffa coats and embrace thin summer clothes, but Ali felt like the long cold months had locked a chill into her bones. Between that and a really hectic night at the bar, she felt way too jazzed to sleep, so she got up to send Pete an email:

> How's it going Hugh Hefner Jnr? Got much pork on your fork?
> Thanks for sending me Bambina. It's a great track.
> You're quite talented for a sleazy old reptile.
> Ali xxx

She got an immediate reply, in the form of a Skype call. She clicked to accept it and Pete's smiling face appeared on her screen above a bare chest, and she suddenly remembered to grab a T-shirt herself.

'Damn,' he said. 'You got that on quick.'

'G'day, you old perve!' said Ali, surprised at how pleased she was to see his lizard head. 'Have you got a tan? You don't look as scaly as you did here.'

'I've got an all-over tan,' he said, standing up and undoing the towel that was tied around his waist. He held it up in front of his hips, wiggling them around behind it suggestively. 'Do you want to see?'

'Nooooo!' said Ali, covering her face with her hands. 'Tell me when it's stopped.'

Pete laughed, tightening the towel again and sitting down.

'I'm decent,' he said. 'You can come out now.'

Ali peeped between her fingers and, satisfied Pete wasn't about to flash her, leaned in towards her computer screen.

'Nice place,' she said. 'Can you take me on a tour?'

Pete picked up his laptop and walked around the flat, showing her the rooms – and finally the view from the balcony.

'Can you see it?' he said, turning the laptop back towards his face.

'Not really,' said Ali. 'Just a lot of light and blue.'

'Bondi morning, darling – can you smell the coffee?'

'Oh stop it!' said Ali. 'You're making me really homesick. It's still cold here. Isn't May supposed to be summer in England?'

Pete laughed. 'Well, a few brave little flowers come up, but don't you remember from last year? It doesn't get anything approaching properly pleasant until June. The end of June. In a good year.'

Ali groaned.

'Oh well, at least working in the bar I'm in the dark all the time anyway, so I don't notice it so much – and by the way Pete, everyone in there totally loved your track when I played it to them today. It's brilliant, I can't stop singing it.'

She hummed the chorus.

'I'm glad you like it,' said Pete, looking uncharacteristically modest, 'and I'm happy to tell you a lot of people here like it too. Which is why it's number one . . .'

Ali's mouth dropped open.

'Number one?' she squealed. 'That's amazing. In the pop chart?'

Pete nodded, grinning.

'Wow, you must be thrilled, that's so cool. And you do deserve it, it's such a catchy tune, but not in a stupid annoying way, you just want to keep hearing it so you can be sure you heard it right the first time.'

'Thank you, ma'am,' said Pete, bowing deeply. 'That's exactly what

I was aiming for, but tell me something, Sydney Chick, do you talk to cousin Matt much?'

'I spent Christmas with them and I went to Hannah's dad's funeral – that was really awful, he got hit by a bus, did you hear? Hannah's still in bits . . .'

Pete nodded.

'Yeah, it's really crap. I met him a few times, brilliant old geezer. I guess that's why Matt's not in touch so much. Got his hands full there.'

Ali nodded.

'Yeah, and in all honesty,' she said, 'he sounds a bit flat himself these days. I don't think he loves living in the bush very much.'

Pete shook his head.

'Don't blame him. It's so fucking boring. Oh look, a leaf, how fascinating . . . It's shitty he has to be down there. I mean, I do understand about the kids and school and the free house and yada yada and now I suppose there's Hannah's mum to look after too. Jeez, the poor bastard's really trapped.'

Ali considered what he'd said for a moment.

'I never thought of that,' she said. 'I always just see how happy he and Hannah are together with the gorgeous kids and now with the perfect house and garden and dog and chickens, it seems like what every girl dreams of to me . . . the full fantasy.'

'Is that what you dream of, Sydney Chick?' asked Pete.

'Not exactly,' said Ali, 'not quite that version, but I am a girl and the whole domestic bliss thing still speaks to me. Can't help it.'

Pete nodded slowly, taking it in.

'No wonder I don't understand women,' he said, roughing up his hair with one hand. 'None of you can make your minds up if you want to be Betty Friedan or Betty Crocker. Anyway, have you got any "pork on your fork" yourself, as you so delicately put it? Any romance brewing that will see you chained to a stove with a baby on each hip any time soon?'

'Not really,' said Ali. 'I like the fantasy of the family thing and I'm doing the dating stuff, but not so much the mating at the moment.'

'What? A gorgeous young thing like you? The kiss of the Aussie sun still on you, I thought you'd be beating them off with a stick.'

'Well, I do get hit on in the bar all the time, it goes with the territory, and I have kissed a few frogs – well, Poms – and there was one guy I did really like, northern dude, really cute accent, but in the end no-one's been quite right for the full romance. You could say I've got issues . . .'

Pete leaned closer to his computer, resting his chin on his hand.

'Tell Uncle Pete,' he said firmly.

Ali stood and lifted up her T-shirt to show him her stomach.

'These,' she said. 'I've got them all over my legs and my chest – meaning my tits – as well. I keep getting close to it, but then I just can't bring myself to show them to anyone in a bed scenario.'

'Sheesh,' said Pete quietly. 'I did notice the scars on your legs before, but I didn't realise it went further. How did you get them? You wouldn't tell me when I asked you.'

'Wanker glassed me, in a bar.'

'In Sydney?'

She nodded.

'Which bar?' said Pete, his brows knitted in a deep frown.

She shook her head, her eyes closed.

'I want to know so I can go and beat the crap out of whoever did that to you,' said Pete.

'Oh, forget it,' said Ali, sitting up straight and lifting her chin. 'His punishment is being him every day of his life. I've got all kinds of potions to fade them, so they'll heal better over time and then I'll get back in the lurve saddle. Just taking a break for a while. And being around all those dirty-looking guys in Shoreditch – you know, people like you – I've realised that what I want is a really classic English-type bloke. If I'm in this freezing cold country, I might as well have a wild fling with a Hugh Grant or a Colin Firth to keep me warm. A really pommie Pom. A Pompom.'

'A Pompom?' said Pete, laughing.

'Yeah,' said Ali, 'that's what I want. I want to be wooed by a lovely soppy Pompom.'

'Well, good luck with that,' said Pete. 'There is a reason an ugly slimebag like me was so successful with the girls over there. You might want to think about that . . .'

Ali stuck her tongue out at him.

'So how is your love life now you're home?' she said. 'A bit more competition for you there than London?'

Pete scratched his stomach, the muscles on his biceps flexing as he did it. He was in pretty good shape for his age, Ali thought. Great abs for an old bloke. His body had a lived-in look that was very different from all the twentysomething boyfriends she'd had, with their hairless chests and smooth skin. He looked like the human version of those shoes he wore with the curling-up toes. Beaten up, but seriously cool in his way.

'I'm not really going for it so much at the moment either,' he answered, stretching his arms behind his head, hairy armpits on display. 'Having a bit of a sex sabbatical.'

'Long service leave?' said Ali.

Pete laughed, 'Yeah, something like that, and I'm so into my work at the moment, I don't need the distraction and in all honesty, Sydney Chick, all that stuff you said to me before, I'm taking a bit of time out to think about that. Need to reformulate my operating mode with regard to the lady people. Don't want to mess my own nest again. New start and all that.'

'Well, that's good to hear,' said Ali, folding her arms behind her head and resting her head back against them. 'So we're both having a luuurve lull. Interesting. Keep me posted on that.'

'Same,' said Pete, 'and Ali, seriously, can you check if Matt's OK for me? Let me know?'

She nodded. 'Yeah. I'm thinking to go down and see them. I need a break from work and the city, and after what you've said, I want to make sure he's OK too.'

Pete looked uncomfortable.

'In particular, Als, I haven't heard from him since I sent him that track and I want to make sure he's cool about it.'

'Why wouldn't he be?' asked Ali.

'Because it's the most successful song I've ever put out – and I didn't write it with him.'

Ali made an 'ouch' face. Poor Matt.

'Yeah,' said Pete, 'it is a bit like that. I wanted to work on it with him – the words are shit, I know that – but he just wasn't into it and I really believed in the song, then I found this perfect guy to sing it, so I released it anyway, but I don't want Matt to be pissed off. I don't want to stop working with him. He's still my best mate and my writing partner and I need him to know that.'

But Ali didn't seem to be listening. She was fiddling about on her keyboard not looking at Pete. He wondered what she was doing and then he heard the first chords of his song playing. He smiled shyly at her. She was singing along.

'Bambi, Bambina . . .' she sang. 'Sometimes wish I'd never seen ya . . . I don't think the words are that shit. They're cute and pop-y. I like them.'

'Do you?' said Pete, hoping the resolution on her laptop wasn't too good, because beneath his stubble and his tan, she might see he'd gone a bit pink.

# Chapter Thirty-five

Jogging uphill with Sooty at his side, Matt was trying to physically expiate his sins. Short of wearing barbed wire in his undies, he didn't know what else to do with himself. It was killing him and he couldn't bear to be alone in a room with Hannah in case she somehow knew what he'd done. What he'd allowed to be done to him.

Not that it was any excuse that he'd been led astray, rather than initiated it. He could have pushed that woman away and he hadn't. Well, not immediately. For the briefest moment – two seconds? – he had succumbed to the glorious sensation. And worse. He'd enjoyed it. He could hardly bear to let the thought form in his head, but the whole sleazy scenario, the pub toilet, the utter wrongness of it had been a massive turn-on. He hated himself for it, but that was the truth.

Thank god, though, that even in his drunk and horny state, he'd come to his senses and backed off, doing up his fly clumsily, before stumbling out of the gents and leaving the pub by the back door. There was no way he was walking back through the bar after that. He felt they'd all know. He shuddered at the thought. He wasn't going anywhere near that pub ever again, let alone her – but he couldn't lie to himself, for that very brief instant he'd liked how it felt.

The wave of shame that washed over him at the thought was so intense it made him stumble and he stopped, turning round for a break, looking out over the view, with the village clear in the distance. That wasn't much help. He could see the school, where he'd seen her again for the first time since the 'incident', that morning, when he was dropping Hector off.

He'd seen her look at him, then turn quickly away and he'd done the same, totally freaked at seeing her there of all places, with Hector still holding his hand. He crouched down to look at his son, who was chattering on about the stick insects his teacher had in the class, but really to give himself time to gather his thoughts.

Out of the corner of his eye, he saw Chezza – he didn't even know her real name forfucksake – going into the school's main door with her kids. A boy and a girl, both older than Hec, which was a tiny relief. At least they weren't in the same class.

Once Hector had skipped into the playground, shouting out to his friends, Matt's first instinct was to run for it, but he forced himself to stay where he was. He had to speak to her. That was the price he had to pay, or risk paying a much higher one. He'd seen too many times with Pete what happened when you ignored a woman who felt she had some kind of sexual claim on you, however tenuous.

The crush of parents and children was thinning and Matt played for time, retying his shoe laces and fiddling with Sooty's collar and it worked. As the school bell rang, he saw Chezza walking back across the playground towards the gate.

She even wore towering heels for the school run he noticed, realising his eyes had also travelled up her legs to her round high bottom, clearly outlined in tight skinny jeans. Damn his Neanderthal male brain.

He felt sick with anxiety as she walked towards him, but he simply had to try and reach some kind of understanding about what had happened – to make it clear it had been a mistake, but without offending her. If she wanted to get revenge on him for rejecting her it wouldn't be difficult. She'd only have to tell one person. That was all it would take for it to get immediately round the village and back to Hannah. He shuddered.

'Hello,' she said, playing it cool, but he could see the keen interest in her eyes, 'are you waiting for me?'

Matt got to his feet slowly, still no idea what to say.

'Yeah, er, hi,' he said, like a total drongo.

'Hi,' she said, now looking amused by his discomfort, 'you haven't been in to the pub to see me for a while. I miss you.'

Matt made a noise like a cross between a laugh and a snort. He didn't know what it was.

'No,' he said, pulling himself together, trying to take charge of the situation. 'The thing is, look . . . what's your name again?'

'Kelli,' she said, 'with an i.'

He nodded, saying, 'I'm Matt.'

'I know that,' she said.

'What happened the other night, Kelli,' he forced himself to say it; he had to. 'I shouldn't have done that. I'm sorry.'

'I'm not sorry,' said Kelli, running her tongue over her glossy lips. 'I don't know why you stopped me. I could tell you were enjoying it. I've been wondering when you were going to come back so we could finish it off.'

She took a step closer towards him, pulling back her shoulders slightly so her jacket pulled open and he had a close-up view of the round tops of her breasts peeping out of her T-shirt. Matt started shaking his head. The proffered love muffins were not helping his concentration. He was only human and worse, a man. Shit.

'No, no,' he stuttered, 'it was all a mi . . .' he was going to say mistake, but realised just in time that was absolutely the worst thing he could have come out with. What would Charlie have said?

'. . . a misunderstanding,' he said, inspiration kicking in. 'I've never done anything like that before and I never will again, you just . . .' he paused again to choose his words, 'you just found me at a . . . a weak moment. I mean, you're a very attractive woman, Kelli, and I'm a normal man. You are hard to resist, but you know I have to. So I beg you, please don't tell anyone, it would ruin my life and . . . and my kids. You're a mum, Kelli, you'd understand that, the little ones . . . Please, I mean, thank you, it was really kind of you . . .'

He was gabbling now and he knew he had tears in his eyes. He couldn't help it, so much was at stake. Kelli was rolling hers.

'Kind?' she said. 'Is that what it was to you? Some sort of counselling service? Jesus! If I'd known you were such a wimp, I wouldn't have bothered. I thought Aussie blokes were supposed to be real men. I just wanted a bit of fun. You're hot, Matt, really hot, but I don't want to elope with you. Like you say, I'm a normal woman, I'm single right now and I just wanted to get laid, no strings attached, and I thought you'd be up for that. And, don't worry, I won't tell your wife. I really couldn't be bothered with the hassle. She's welcome to you.'

And she turned on her high heel and strutted off.

Matt dropped his face into his hands for a moment, silently screaming. Nightmare. She thought he was pathetic – but was that good or bad? He had no idea, but at least he'd spoken to her. In some tiny way he felt he'd done one right thing in this horrendous situation. She'd said she wouldn't tell Hannah, that was the main thing. He just hoped she meant it. That made him feel a bit better, but he knew he was still a hostage to her whim. Always would be now. If there was one thing that could have made life in this prison of a village worse, he'd done it. Nice work, Matt.

He looked down at the scruffy little black dog, gazing up at him with pure adoration in his dark brown eyes. Absolutely no judgement there.

'Hey, Sooty, mate,' said Matt, crouching down to scratch him behind the ears, prompting a wild tail-wagging. 'You know what it's like, don't you mate? You're as big a martyr to your gonads as I am, aren't you? Total hormone nightmare. But at least I don't feel compelled to sniff strange ladies' bottoms, that would be embarrassing. I just look at them . . .'

He laughed bitterly. Was he really genetically superior to Sooty? He didn't feel like it. He was just another dumb animal with an even dumber one down his pants.


But while a long high-speed tramp had tired Matt's body – and Sooty was out sparko in his bed in the kitchen – it wasn't enough to calm his conscience. He'd got back to the house feeling as mentally jangled as ever.

Adding to his scattered state as he stood under the shower – pretty powerful by UK standards, one good thing about living in that house – was knowing he still really needed to get in touch with Pete and congratulate him on his success with 'Bambina', but having failed to do it immediately after getting the email he felt increasingly inhibited about it.

Every day he left it – and it was at least five now – made it a bigger problem and harder to know what to say. It had reached the point where he didn't even want to turn on his laptop, in case Pete came up on Skype.

Matt was beginning to wonder if he was turning into an ostrich, there were so many things he wasn't thinking about. He had his head buried in the sand right up to his arsehole. Possibly in his arsehole.

Hannah was up in London for the day, which was a relief – terrible but true – as it gave him some respite from agonising over whether he shouldn't just tell her himself what had happened with Kelli.

He knew it was making him act weirdly around her and he veered wildly between thinking he should tell her because it would be so much better than her possibly finding out from someone else, and then deciding he shouldn't and just hoping for the best.

And why introduce a tiny seed of distrust into their happy relationship, when he really hadn't played any part in initiating it? What had happened in the White Hart was just one stage on from the women who used to hit on him so blatantly in Chocolate Bar.

Hannah knew all about that – the bolder ones did it even when she was there – and while it was irritating, she'd always laughed about it. Said it was a compliment to her choice in husbands.

It had only gone on further with Kelli because he'd been so pissed, not thinking straight. Otherwise, he would have taken control of the situation the moment she'd come into the gents and she'd never have got her hands on him. Or her mouth. And that was still the definitely the worst thing. The guilt about how he'd enjoyed the sensation of Kelli's soft lips and tongue around him.

He looked down at his cock as he soaped it up. Fine mess you've got me into, he told it, before reminding himself – yet again – he hadn't started anything. He was innocent of anything apart from a neurological response to a specific stimulation.

As he towelled himself off, allowing himself a moment's congratulation at what good shape he was in, he made his decision. Now he'd spoken to Kelli and she'd said she wouldn't say anything to Hannah, it was better for him to keep schtum about it too.

What was that thing his Irish nana used to say? Least said, soonest mended. That was his philosophy for this. Now he just needed to work at getting rid of that residual guilt so he could be normal with Hannah again.

# Chapter Thirty-six

Hannah was sitting in a slick modern Chinese restaurant so fashionable and so hard to get a table at, she hadn't even been taken there yet by a beauty brand PR.

But it didn't seem to have been a problem for Anthony, who had been chatting happily to the owner – one of London's leading restaurateurs – when she arrived.

'Shall I order?' he asked, as the waiter handed them menus so big they were more like coffee table books. 'Anything you can't stand?'

'I'm not very keen on tongue,' said Hannah, 'but I don't suppose that features here.'

'Well, they might have deep-fried duck tongues,' said Anthony, smiling. 'I had those once in Taipei, although they're really a Cantonese dish. Rather good if you don't think about what they are. You're eating the quack, really . . .'

'Is Taipei in Taiwan?' asked Hannah, aware she was "making conversation" at a very basic level, but doing it anyway. The whole scenario was so weird, she didn't know what else to do, although she was greatly relieved to be sitting with him in that restaurant and not in one of Charlie's roster of preferred lunch venues, a possibility she'd been dreading.

'Yes,' said Anthony, nodding and playing along with the chit chat. 'I lived there for a couple of years in the early 1980s. Interesting place. Extraordinary museum of Chinese imperial treasures. Endless rooms of exquisite small green bowls.'

Sipping her glass of champagne – Anthony was having sparkling water in a champagne flute – as he gave the waiter their order, Hannah found herself staring at the ring he was wearing on his left pinkie, where Charlie had worn his signet ring. It looked like a real Egyptian scarab, carved from turquoise.

She hadn't noticed it when she'd talked to him after the funeral and now found it hard to take her eyes off the thing. It was really something special and so surprising on a man his age, but it suited him, giving him an arty air which made sense of the overlong white hair licking over his collar.

He might be another retired barrister in his seventies, but with all that and another beautiful suit – Paul Smith, she suspected – and the choice of restaurant, Anthony was a very different package from her father and she was grateful for it.

The food ordered, he continued to keep things light, asking how they had all adjusted to life in the country and what she missed most about London. Hannah was happy to go along with it, but couldn't suppress a rising anxiety that sooner or later he would have to get to the point: why he had wanted to have lunch with her so much. Did he have some dramatic revelation to make?

On top of that, she had things she wanted to ask him. Having taken the plunge to have lunch with him, she was hoping she might be able to get the answers to some questions that had bothered her for years. It was all combining to make her feel slightly nauseous.

The butterflies in her stomach were showing no signs of calming down as the waiter finished laying out what seemed an outrageous number of dishes and she wondered if she'd be able to eat anything.

Anthony took a few moments to explain what all the food was, with Hannah making what she hoped were suitably enthusiastic noises, and then he put his chopsticks down, sat back in his chair and looked at her steadily for a moment. Hannah put her chopsticks down too. He was clearly gearing himself up for the big moment. Meeting her expectant gaze, Anthony smiled at her.

'Thank you for coming today, Hannah,' he said, the smooth flow of his voice, which still had the beautiful lilt from his childhood in South Wales, making her feel a little calmer. It was like a stream over mossy rocks.

'As I said at the drinks after the funeral, I have long wanted to apologise to you for my part in Charlie's excessive drinking and all the difficulties it caused you when you were growing up. It pains me more than I can tell you that it has taken Charlie's death to make it possible for me to do so.'

Hannah opened her mouth to say she had already accepted his apology, but Anthony indicated he had more to say.

'Let me just get this out,' he said. 'This is the hard bit for me. The thing is, I wanted to say sorry anyway, but as I told you before, I'm doing AA. You know, Alcoholics Anonymous . . .'

Hannah nodded. She knew exactly what it was. She'd been reading leaflets about it since she was a child. Leaflets that Charlie had left lying around the house, after finding them waiting for him on the kitchen table the day following a binge.

She could remember coming across one balled up on the floor of the sitting room, when he'd missed trying to throw it on to the fire, and finding it had the words FUCK OFF scrawled all over it in her father's writing. She shook her head quickly to chase the memory away.

'Well,' continued Anthony, 'it's a bit touchy-feely for an old codger like me, but it is really helping me stay off the booze and one of the things you have to do on it is formally apologise to all the people you've hurt because of your drinking. You were top of my list.'

'Well, you can tick me off now,' said Hannah. 'Apology made and accepted – and good for you, Anthony. I so wish Charlie had given AA a go, but he just laughed at the idea. Said it was for weak-minded, self-indulgent egotists who just wanted to talk about themselves.'

'I know,' said Anthony, 'he said that to me when I started.'

Hannah felt her eyebrows shoot up in surprise.

'Did you start before he died?' she blurted out. She'd immediately assumed it was her father's death that had shamed him into it.

'Yes,' he said, 'I stopped drinking nearly two years ago.'

Hannah blinked, trying to figure out dates and timings in her head.

'But what about that time you snuck into his granny flat and the two of you threw all his wine out of the window . . . that was barely a year ago.'

'I wasn't drinking then, Hannah,' he said.

'But why did you start throwing bottles around, in that case?'

Anthony shook his head and smiled ruefully.

'Well, he started it, saying if he was going to give up drinking what was he supposed to do with this all this wine he'd just had delivered? Then he said "How about this?" and threw one out of the window. I tried to stop him, but he wouldn't, so then I joined in because I thought if we smashed it all up there'd be nothing left for him to drink.'

It was Hannah's turn to shake her head.

'But you weren't drunk?' she asked, trying to make sense of it.

'No,' said Anthony firmly.

'But if you weren't drinking, why did you go down to see Charlie like that? Sneaking past my mum . . .'

'I was trying to persuade him to stop drinking,' said Anthony. 'I thought I was the one person he might listen to, but I knew your mum wouldn't believe me, so I had to sneak in like that; I had no choice. I just wanted him to know how much better I felt since I'd stopped – no more waking up to the dread of remembering what you'd done the night before, no more feeling like death until you've had a hair of the dog. I wanted Charlie to know how much more he would enjoy life without drink.'

Hannah sat and thought for a moment, taking it all in.

'Well, he did have a few months of that, at least,' she said. 'From when we moved down the country last August, he managed to stay off it. Seven months. He said having the children there gave him the strength to do it.'

Tears filled her eyes. She couldn't help it.

'You must find that a great comfort,' said Anthony.

'I do,' said Hannah, recovering herself, 'but it also makes it so much harder to cope with the fact that if I hadn't suggested he wait for me to get the later train home when we came up to town together that day, he never would have been tempted to have that first drink and he wouldn't have stumbled drunkenly in front of that bus.'

Anthony looked at her, an appalled expression on his face.

'Is that what you think happened?' he asked quietly. 'Have you been beating yourself up all this time that Charlie's death was your fault?'

She nodded, not able to speak. Anthony leaned across the table towards her and put his hand over hers.

'But didn't Marguerite tell you?' he said. 'The post-mortem showed he had no alcohol in his blood when he died. He wasn't drunk, Hannah, he just missed his step, getting out of the way of a bus, fell and hit his head on the kerb. There were several witnesses. It was a terrible, stupid accident. He wasn't drunk.'

Hannah stared at him.

'Are you serious?' she said.

'Yes,' said Anthony, 'and I must say I'm surprised your mother hasn't told you.'

'She didn't even tell me there was a post-mortem,' said Hannah, shuddering at the thought and furious with her mother for keeping it all locked away, for not sharing such important things with her own daughter. Furious, but not really surprised.

'Well, you know they have to determine the cause of death for the inquest,' said Anthony, 'and I must say I was bloody glad when I found out the result.'

'So am I,' said Hannah, putting her head into her hands for a moment, trying to take it all in, 'you've no idea how much. But how did you find that out, Anthony? Did Marguerite tell you?'

Anthony looked a bit sheepish.

'I was a bit naughty,' he said. 'After all my years in the law, I have quite a few contacts in these areas, so I made some quiet enquiries at the Coroner's Office. I just needed to know, Hannah, do you understand?'

'Absolutely,' said Hannah, 'and I'm so glad you did. Hearing that is the best thing that's happened to me since Charlie died.'

Anthony smiled at her.

'And this lunch is the best thing that's happened to me,' he said.

Then, feeling quite elated, freed of the terrible guilt she'd been hauling around, thinking that she'd helped to cause Charlie's death, Hannah asked Anthony if she could have another glass of champagne to celebrate. Then immediately worried she'd made a dreadful faux pas.

'I hope that isn't inappropriate,' she said, 'me asking for more alcohol when you're not drinking.'

'Not at all, I'm far enough into my recovery now – that's the official term, you know,' he laughed at himself, raising his glass of mineral water and taking a hearty swig, 'that I don't have a problem watching other people partaking. I mean, I wish I could just have two or three glasses of lovely champagne and then leave it there, but I know I can't. I was never your textbook alcoholic – and neither was Charlie – I didn't have to drink to function, I never got drunk on my own, but once I started, I didn't have an off switch. Neither did he.'

And then Hannah knew she had the opening to ask the questions that had been burning inside her and – the irony not escaping her – the Dutch courage from a glass and a half of Taittinger to dare to ask them.

'So, you and Charlie didn't have an off switch,' she started.

'Yes,' he said, 'we behaved like horrendous football hooligans when we were on the razz and I'm not proud of it, but it was partly the pure chemical effect of the booze. It affects people differently. It made Charlie impossible and it made me reckless. I never deliberately led him astray, Hannah, we just set each other off and when we got together, nothing else mattered.'

He paused and looked down for a moment, seeming to gather his thoughts.

'You don't want to hear a lot of old tosh about my lonely childhood,' he continued, 'how I never fitted in at home, at grammar school, or at Cambridge, and what it meant finally to find a friend who really got me. Who admired me just for me, for what I was. Not patronising the bright boy from the valleys, or impressed by my double first and the letters after my name, but the real person inside. Just as I admired him.'

Hannah didn't say anything. She wanted him to keep talking, so she carried on eating, finding her appetite suddenly restored, and he did.

'You see, Hannah, I was still a naïve kid when I started studying for the Bar and Charlie was like my second university. I learned how to learn at Cambridge, but Charlie taught me how to live. It was him who told me to double-barrel my name. I was born plain Williams, so I borrowed the Prosser from my mam's side and bingo – instant posh. He said it was no different from what his family had done, they'd just thought of it a hundred and fifty years sooner.'

They both laughed. Hannah had another sip of champagne and another soft-shelled crab. Delicious. She hadn't felt this hungry for ages. Anthony was still talking, a faraway look in his eyes.

'Deep down I know we both felt very guilty about how our behaviour affected you and your mum – and the really awful thing is, I think that made us behave more badly. In for a penny, in for a pound kind of thing. Push down the guilt with more drink. We grew up in very repressed times, Charlie and me, and in very different but equally stitched-up families and we used the booze to free ourselves. That was one of the things we had most in common, the need to break out.'

'Wow,' said Hannah. 'That's a lot to take in, but amazing to hear you explain it like that. It already makes more sense than it ever has before, the way you two used to carry on. Thank you for being so honest about it all – but what I still don't understand is why Mummy loathes you quite so much. You've known each other so long, she must know you're lovely really.'

Anthony's face froze for a moment and he looked at her very intently, his eyes boring into hers, before his expression softened again.

'Maybe she did once,' he said, 'but over the years my bad behaviour cancelled it out. But let's put all that old stuff behind us now and start a new era. Here's to new friends.'

He raised his glass of water to her and Hannah clinked her glass against his smiling.

'New friends,' she said.

But even as she said it she was wondering how much energy it was going to take to keep all this from her mother, who she knew would not be at all happy that she and Anthony were now friends of any kind.

And then there was knowing the result of the post-mortem to keep quiet about. It was such wonderful news; it had freed her from that terrible guilt, but she couldn't talk to Marguerite about it without telling her how she knew, so she'd just have to keep that all locked inside her too.

Like mother like daughter. And not in a good way.

# Chapter Thirty-seven

Matt thought he'd pop over to Marguerite's to see how she and Nancy were getting on. Hannah had dropped Nancy round there for the morning when she'd gone over to borrow the car, so he could have some time to himself, but after a couple of fruitless hours, he thought he'd rather be with them than staring at words that just wouldn't behave on a computer screen.

Seeing poor Marguerite's shattered face, broken like a piece of the china she so painstakingly mended, might help him put his own self-induced problems in perspective. She was really suffering; his sordid little trouble was trifling by comparison.

He found them in Marguerite's study, which seemed a pretty crazy place to take Nancy. She was at the stage where she would grab anything in her reach and then, for want of something better to do with it, smash it down on to the nearest hard surface. Not very compatible with precious bits of china. .

'Hey, girls,' said Matt, tapping gently on the door, 'just come by to say hi, make sure Nancy's not driving you nuts . . .'

'Oh, hello Matthew, dear,' said Marguerite, looking genuinely pleased to see him. 'How lovely.'

Nancy ran towards him and leaped into his arms.

'Dada!' she squealed. 'Dada! Lovely!'

Matt's heart combusted. Pure molten love.

'Hey Princess,' said Matt, tickling her ribs. 'Having fun with Granny?'

'Working,' said Nancy, in her chiming little voice, 'Nancy and Ganny working.'

'Are you now?' said Matt. 'Are you sure about having Conan the Destroyer in here with you, Marg?'

Marguerite laughed. A rare thing these days, beautiful to see, and the kids were just about the only thing that made her do it, which was almost enough to make him glad they lived down there. It might be hell for him, but it made so many other people happy, it had to be done. End of shitty story.

'She's being a very good girl, helping me sort out some important bits of china and keeping me company.'

Matt looked over to where Nancy had been sitting and saw a tray with a toy tea set on it. Clever Granny. Although he could see she'd already snapped the spout off the tiny teapot. Oops.

'Would you like a coffee?' he said, reluctant to go back to the cottage to face the laptop and all the other reminders of his legion guilts and failures.

'That would be nice,' said Marguerite, 'but actually Matthew, you're just the person I need. Could you give me a bit of help with the computer here? I need to look something up on it and I just can't seem to, well, I can't turn it on.'

She looked so embarrassed, he immediately averted his gaze from her face. He knew how proud and private his mother-in-law was. She'd clearly felt too humiliated to ask him for help before.

'Let's have a look,' he said, putting Nancy down by the tea set, 'might be something wrong with it. Tricky little things, laptops.'

He sat on her desk chair, pulling over a stool and indicating for her to sit down next to him, then fired the thing up.

'It's this little widget here, Marg,' he said, showing her the small button on the side, 'you have to press it real hard to get it going, that may have been the problem. It's a bit fiddly, bad design. Seems to be starting up OK now, let's have a look. What did you need in particular?'

'Hannah bought something for me on her computer and she gave them my email address for the confirmation, so I need to see if it's all gone through.'

Matt opened her email and found the inbox quite full.

'There you go, Marg,' he said. 'All the ones in bold are new and unread. You just need to click on one like this . . . and it'll open and you can read it. Why don't I leave you to have a look at them while I go and make the coffee? If you need me, just shout.'

He turned to smile at her and was surprised at her expression. She was staring at the laptop screen, looking quite astonished.

'All right?' he asked lightly, concerned, but not wanting to pry.

'Yes, yes,' said Marguerite, recovering herself. 'I'm fine, just surprised to have so many emails. I had no idea. I'd better look at them, hadn't I? Might be something important and I think I can see one there from the company I ordered the glazes from, so I'd better make sure they're on their way.'

Matt took his cue and headed for the kitchen, Nancy tripping along behind him chirruping about biscuits.


Marguerite sat staring at the messages in her inbox. She was surprised by how many there were, but the thing that had really made her eyes pop out was the name on this one: Anthony Prosser-Williams.

Anthony! How on earth had he got hold of her email address? And whatever did he want? Hadn't she done enough allowing him to be a pallbearer and to come to the drinks afterwards? The only good thing about Charlie dying was finally getting him out of her life and now here he was again.

Touching the keys of the computer gingerly and looking at the screen out of the corner of her eye, as if trying to lessen the impact of it, she opened the email:

> Dear Marguerite
>     How are you? I hope you don't mind me contacting you
> this way, but it seems less intrusive than the other options.
> So when Hannah told me you were a silver surfer too,
> I thought you would appreciate that.

Hannah? Hannah had given Anthony her email address? How could that have happened? She forced herself to read on:

> You're probably surprised that I mention Hannah, but we had a talk at the drinks after Charlie's funeral. She was kind enough to listen to me while I unburdened myself of some things which have caused me anguish for many years.
>
> I've submitted myself to AA – Alcoholics Anonymous – to conquer my problem with drink and one of things we have to do is to apologise to all the people we have hurt because of our drinking. Obviously, you are one of those people.
>
> So why I am writing to you now, Marguerite, is to ask if you could possibly allow me to apologise to you in person? Could I take you out to lunch?
>
> You and your family are never far from my thoughts. And I miss Charlie like one of my own limbs.
>
> Always yours
> The Awful Anthony x

Marguerite had felt rather as though she were in suspended animation since Charlie's horrible, sudden death. Or behind glass like Snow White, unable to be affected by anything, but Anthony had managed to shock her out of it with his pure cheek.

How dare he prey on Hannah when she was so vulnerable! What state must she have been in, that he could persuade her to give him Marguerite's email address?

She didn't feel cross with Hannah, exactly, just amazed that she would have had anything to do with the man who played such a part in her father's bingeing. Of course, she would have spoken to him at the funeral drinks; it was the right thing to do, as it had been to let him carry the coffin, but anything beyond that, no. Not required. The question was whether she could bear ever to ask Hannah about it. Unlikely.

Without consciously deciding to do so, she found herself reading the email again. One sentence leaped out at her: 'She was kind enough to listen to me while I unburdened myself of some things which have caused me anguish for many years.'

What exactly did he mean by that? For a moment Marguerite felt quite nauseous. Was it only about his part in Charlie's drinking binges? What terrible things from the past had he told Hannah about?

The man was a loose cannon, but she took comfort from knowing that Hannah hadn't shown any signs of being devastated by anything other than her father's death. It didn't seem as though she'd been told any further unnecessary details to add to her anguish. Or Marguerite's.

If only it had been Anthony who had hit his head on the kerb and not Charlie, all that ghastliness would have gone with him.

Narrowing her eyes at the computer screen, Marguerite concentrated for a moment and then, yes, she had it. Delete, that was it. One little tap and Anthony's message was gone. Deleted from her screen and from her mind. He was right, email did have its advantages. A much simpler and cleaner solution to an incriminating communication than slamming down the phone or burning a letter.

Evidence erased, case closed, as Charlie used to say.


Waiting for the kettle to start steaming on the Aga – a stupid bloody system, letting all that heat out just to boil a kettle – Matt was looking idly at the local paper, which was lying on the kitchen bench.

Flicking through the usual headlines about closures at the local hospital, photos of school concerts and the pitiful offerings at the nearest cinema, which was miles away anyway, something caught his eye. It was the listings for church services in the area and there it was, popping out at him: *The Church of Christ the Redeemer. Mass, Sunday 10 a.m. All welcome.*

All welcome, even sinners like him. Most welcome of all actually, if he remembered Father Ignatius correctly. Well, they could put out the flags for him, he'd been tempted by a cardinal sin of the flesh – or was it mortal? Either way it was heavy stuff. Mass was what he needed. Prayer. Holy Communion. Possibly even confession. A cleansing.

With his Greek-Cypriot and Irish heritage, religion had figured large in Matt's upbringing. As the oldest son there had been a bit of a tussle over which church he would be baptised into, but his maternal grandmother had won the day and he was brought up fully Catholic, with mass every Sunday, first Communion hoo hah, the works. And when he'd won a sporting scholarship to a top Jesuit school, his entire family – even the Greek Orthodox side – had wept with pride.

He hadn't been near a Catholic church since he'd left home apart from his nana's funeral, but now, in his time of anguish, he suddenly felt a visceral draw back to it. That was what he needed. He'd go to mass on Sunday and beg for forgiveness.

May the Lord be with you. And also with you.

# Chapter Thirty-eight

Hannah was up in London seeing the solicitor her father had put in charge of her unfair dismissal case against ChicClick. She was sitting in his office in Holborn, which Charlie had visited on the day he died, and it was very painful imagining him sitting in the very same chair she was in now.

She would have found it unbearable without Anthony at her side.

'Your client needs to have this resolved as soon as possible,' he was saying. 'I really can't understand what's holding you up. You just need to unpick that fundamentally illegal employment contract they coerced her into signing at the outset, further aggravated by the unreasonable conditions they subsequently expected her to agree to in order to receive compensation when her employment was terminated without due process.'

He paused for dramatic effect, fitting in a quick wink to Hannah which the solicitor couldn't see.

'A year's salary would settle it,' he continued, 'including, of course, a twelve-month continuation of any benefits and a positive reference. They don't have a shred of a case for anything less. We could seek far greater compensation for stress and damage to her professional reputation, but for the sake of expediency, your client is willing to take the simple option.'

The solicitor grabbed his opportunity to speak.

'There is the complication,' he said, 'that since Mrs Constantinos commenced employment with the company, it has been taken over by JCAP, which is one of the larger international conglomerates in this particular field. So the company she wants to sue no longer exists.'

'Good point!' said Anthony, not missing a beat. 'You can ask for more money. JCAP certainly wouldn't want the negative publicity of someone of Mrs Constantinos's standing in the beauty industry being grossly mistreated now they have taken over the company she worked for – their competitors would love it. And in that context, I would also remind you that she is the mother of two young children, sole bread-winner of a family of four, and the stress of this rambling on, when it should have been settled months ago, is affecting her ability to work to support them. Especially when, as you know, she has recently lost her father, Sir Charlie Berry-Downing QC, who originally engaged you.'

Recently, thought Hannah. Thirteen weeks. The solicitor opened his mouth to speak again, but Anthony just talked over him.

'So what we need is for you to lay out your timeframe for bringing it to a successful conclusion and if it's anything more than one calendar month, I will be serving an incompetence case on you myself. Right, I'm taking your client out for lunch now and I will telephone you at four o'clock for your answer. Save us all a lot of bother, won't you? Get off your bloody arse.'

The solicitor sat there, slightly red in the face and shocked into silence, as Anthony stood up, taking a shiny, latest model smartphone out of his pocket and holding it out to make his point.

'Four o'clock,' he repeated, wiggling the four fingers of his other hand and smiling like a shark.

Hannah had to restrain a giggle. What a performer. He put his hand out to her and she took it, getting to her feet.

'I think that scared the shit out of him nicely, don't you?' said Anthony, as they walked out of the front door of the building. 'I can't imagine why your father engaged such a mimsy moron in the first place. I did try to intervene and suggest someone much more brutal, but he wasn't returning my calls at that point. Nervous that I would lead him astray and spoil the family idyll he was enjoying with all of you. I wouldn't have, as you know, but he never did quite believe I'd really given up the bingeing.'

Hannah reached for his hand and gave it a squeeze.

They had another lovely lunch – their third – and then Anthony said he'd walk her to the station.

They got to Charing Cross just as the 15.45 train pulled out, which was maddening for Hannah, who couldn't bear the thought of hanging around the station for half an hour, with all the horrible memories of the day Charlie hadn't arrived to meet her there, but Anthony immediately distracted her.

'Thirty minutes to the next train,' he said. 'Perfect. We can have coffee, then call that dozy solicitor together.'

As the big clock over the departures board ticked round to four o'clock, Anthony got out his mobile and put it on speaker, beckoning Hannah closer to listen.

'Anthony Prosser-Williams here,' he said. 'What have you got to tell me?'

'They've settled,' Hannah heard the solicitor's voice saying, 'and taking into account the potential damage to my client's elite professional reputation they have agreed that two years' salary would be an appropriate sum. They've also consented to extend the additional benefits for the same term. Your client will have the money in her account on Monday.'

'Thank you,' said Anthony, keeping his voice completely calm, while nodding vigorously and giving a wild thumbs-up to Hannah. 'Good work. I'll leave you alone now. Goodbye.'

He ended the call and Hannah threw her arms around him and they did a little victory dance together on the station concourse.

Hannah called Matt from the train and asked him to invite Marguerite and Anthea round for dinner.

'We've got something wonderful to celebrate,' she told him, 'but I'm not going to tell you until we've got champagne in our hands. Call Mummy and Anthea to come and get that big pot of boeuf bourguignon out of the freezer, but don't worry about anything else. I've got all the treats with me.'

As she pulled up at the house two hours later she was greeted by a banner over the front door, clearly made by Hector with help from Matt, reading: 'We love Mummy!!!' and they all rushed out to meet her. Nancy in her little black velvet Christmas dress and Hector sporting full pirate regalia, complete with eye patch and a plastic cutlass.

'Daddy says we're having a party,' said Hector, launching himself at her while she was getting out of the car with the bags of goodies she'd bought at the M&S at Charing Cross. 'Is it your birthday?'

'Nobody's birthday, just some jolly good luck,' she said bending down to kiss both children.

When they got into the house, Matt had already laid the table and decorated the room with strings of Christmas lights and tinsel. Hannah laughed.

'Do you like it?' he asked. 'You said it was a celebration . . .'

'I love it,' said Hannah, throwing her arms round him, 'and I love you. You're the best husband in the world.'

Matt hugged her back, lifting her off her feet and swinging her from side to side in a way that always delighted the kids.

'Me turn! Me turn!' Nancy was squealing, so Matt took her out into the garden for some full 360° swings, which he then also had to give to Hector.

Marguerite and Anthea had both risen to the occasion, which meant a jade-green silk brocade Chinese jacket and diamond earrings for one, and several extra strings of amber beads for the other. Marguerite's dogs had bows on their collars. As soon as he saw them Hector grabbed some tinsel and tied it on to Sooty's.

Finally they were all seated at the table, glasses of champagne in their hands – lemonade for the children – and it was time for Hannah to make her announcement. She hadn't planned what she was going to say and just launched into it.

'I went up to London today to see the solicitor that Daddy put in charge of the case against my former employer,' she started, glancing at her mother involuntarily as she found she always did when his name came up, 'and I've won it.'

She looked round the table as their faces broke into delighted smiles. This was the moment she'd been looking forward to all the way home on the train and they were reacting just as she had imagined they would – even the kids were cheering – yet she suddenly felt flat about it. She hadn't even told them the really good bit yet, about getting two years of that fat ChicClick salary in one big payment, which was way beyond what she'd dared even hope for, but now the joy had rather gone out of it, because she suddenly felt dishonest.

She wanted to tell them the whole truth, that it was Anthony who'd got her the amazing result, but she just couldn't. Because then she'd have to explain she'd had lunch with him – three times, no less – and she'd discovered there was a lot more to him than the monster she'd grown up believing had led her father so horribly astray. And despite all of that, she'd come to like him. Really like him. But she just wasn't ready to have that conversation with anyone yet. Least of all her mother.

Hannah snapped back to attention when she heard her measured voice breaking through the general jubilation.

'So, come on,' Marguerite was saying, 'tell us the rest. What were the terms of the settlement?'

Hannah smiled at her mother's use of the correct legal terms, so embedded in her from the years with Charlie, and looked over at Matt, who had his eyebrows raised.

'Are we disgustingly rich, Hanns?' he asked, clearly not expecting much.

'We are a bit,' said Hannah, her jubilation about the result returning. 'They're giving me a one-off payment of two years' salary . . .'

Matt's mouth dropped open.

'You're not serious?' he said.

'I am,' said Hannah, nodding fast, 'and it's going to be in the bank on Monday.'

Now they all really let rip with the cheering; even Marguerite was grinning and clapping. Matt was on his feet punching the air, before he came over to hug Hannah, putting his arms round her neck from behind and kissing her on the top of her head.

'You beauty,' he whispered into her ear, 'you little beauty, we've got the deposit for a flat at last.'

Hannah was glad she had her back to him as she felt herself grimace involuntarily. What flat? Where? They hadn't even discussed what they would do with the money, so why on earth was he talking about buying flats? And it wasn't just him; the prospect of that amount of capital had also made Anthea think of property.

'That's marvellous,' she was saying, 'because by the sound of it that would be enough for you to buy this house outright. I happen to know that the owners would like to sell it, so as not to have the bother of it, you know, the maintenance and finding suitable tenants, and I know they're not looking for a huge price. I was thinking of it for my nephew, Dominic, who's moving back from New York at last, but you're already settled here and it's so perfect for the kids. I'll ring the owners in the morning.'

Hannah saw Matt's face darken as he sat back down opposite her.

'We don't want to buy it, Anthea,' he said, 'so don't go to any trouble.'

'Oh, you'd be mad to miss the opportunity,' Anthea continued, 'they have a strong sentimental attachment to the place – it's been in the family quite a long time – and they told me they would take a lower price from a family who would actually live in it, rather than some fly-by-night weekenders.'

'We don't want to buy it,' said Matt, his voice firmer, not rude, but just on the edge of it. 'Renting here is fine, but if we invest in property anywhere, it will be in London – or Sydney.'

Hannah looked over at her mother just in time to see her face crumple at the mention of Sydney. It confirmed what Hannah had long suspected, that the thought of them moving there was Marguerite's greatest fear. The extent of her upset was confirmed when she immediately changed the subject.

'Oh, look at little Nancy,' she said, her face already returned to its normal composure, not a trace of disquiet in her voice. 'She's fast asleep, the little lamb. I'll take her up to bed.'

And that gave her the perfect excuse to leave the room, her sleeping granddaughter in her arms. Hannah was equally relieved to have the previous line of discussion interrupted and glad when Hector gave her an opportunity to leave the table for a bit too. She couldn't cover her confusion quite as quickly as her mother had been able to.

'I'm not going to bed, am I, Mummy?' he said. 'I can stay up for the party can't I?'

Hannah could see how tired he was, blinking beneath his skewiff pirate hat.

'Of course you can, Hec,' she said, 'but why don't you lie down on the sofa and watch a DVD while we do some more boring grown-up talking?'

Hannah fervently hoped Anthea wouldn't bring up the house purchase again while she was out of the room, but when she came back in after settling Hector under a blanket in front of *Shrek 2*, Matt looked distinctly uncomfortable. Not cross, more guilty, like Hector caught in the act of raiding the stash of Kit Kats. Now what?

'Ah, Hannah,' Anthea said. 'I was just asking Matt when the rest of you were going to come to mass with us.'

Hannah couldn't understand what Anthea was talking about. And why was Matt looking so mortified?

'Mass?' she asked.

'Yes, I was delighted to see Matt at Christ the Redeemer last week – I thought I was the only left-footer around here, ha ha ha – so it's lovely for me to find I have another of the blessed as a neighbour. I'm sure he was the most adorable little altar boy.'

Hannah looked at her husband with her eyebrows raised, hoping he would explain later. She didn't want to put him on the spot in front of Anthea, that would be embarrassing for both of them, and she did know Matt was a Catholic, it was just the mass bit that was confusing her. He hadn't been near a Catholic church since she'd known him, except for a family funeral not long after they met.

'Yeah,' said Matt, with a nervous laugh, and a glance at Hannah that seemed to be begging her to go with it, 'I ran into Anthea at mass last

Sunday. I didn't know she was a Catholic either, or I would have cadged a lift. I got a bit hot and sweaty cycling over there.'

Hannah fixed a smile to her face and nodded to show him she was playing along. So that's where he'd gone off to on Sunday morning. She had wondered why he'd been wearing a shirt and jacket for a bike ride.

'Oh, I'd be more than happy to give you a lift this Sunday,' said Anthea.

'That would be great, thanks,' said Matt, a slightly desperate look in his eye.

'So are you planning to go to mass every Sunday now Matt?' Hannah asked, as casually as she could muster.

Matt was practically squirming. What was going on with him?

'Well, yeah, maybe, I just felt like getting back in touch with all that. I suppose it's having the kids . . .'

'Right,' said Hannah, reminding herself what her mother would do in an odd situation like this. 'Now, who'd like some pudding?'

Marguerite came back down to the kitchen just as Hannah was serving up an apricot tart with thick cream, further enhanced by a bottle of dessert wine Anthea had brought them. With everyone tucking in happily, the conversation returned to more general matters and Hannah was finally starting to enjoy her celebration when the phone rang. Matt got up to answer it and then, indicating to Hannah that it was for him, took the phone out of the room.

Hannah was enjoying listening to her mother and Anthea talking about gardening, without any more tensions or weird revelations, when she realised Matt had been gone an oddly long time. She was wondering if she should go and see if everything was all right, when he suddenly appeared in the kitchen doorway. He looked distraught and had tears rolling down his face.

'Hanns . . .' he managed to croak out and she rushed over to him. She took him in her arms and glanced back at the others, nodding to indicate that she could handle it.

She steered her husband into the sitting room and sat down with him on the other the end of the sofa from where Hector was now fast asleep.

'What's wrong, my angel?' she asked, stroking his head.

'It's my mum,' he sobbed out. 'She's had a really bad heart attack. She's in intensive care . . . she's critical.'

'Your mum?' said Hannah stupidly. It was his dad who had the heart condition, not his mum, and she felt as shocked as Matt clearly did. 'Oh my poor darling. You'll have to go home immediately.'

Matt was nodding. 'Yeah,' he croaked out, 'my brother said to get right over there. Fuck, why do I live so far away?'

'I'll get on to Qantas immediately,' said Hannah, 'and I'll book you on the next flight, OK? I think they save last-minute seats for things like this. You'll be on that plane first thing in the morning. I'll drive you to the airport.'

'I just hope I get back in time,' said Matt, tears flooding his face. 'My brother warned me she might not even know me.'

Hannah put her arms round him tight and rocked him until he was calmer. Then she got on the phone and booked that flight.

# Chapter Thirty-nine

Matt planned to get hammered on the plane. It was the only way he could cope with the conflicting emotions which seemed to be holding a prize fight in his heart.

There was the tearing agony of not knowing if he would get home in time to see his mum alive, compounded by guilt that he'd gone to mass to pray for forgiveness for his cardinal sin of lust – but had also added on a plea to be released from the living prison of village life. Now he had been given that parole, but what a price he might have to pay for it . . .

On top of all that was the guilty joy of knowing that in twenty-four hours or so, he would walk out of Sydney airport arrivals and bathe his eyes with the clear bright light of the Australian morning.

In the brief moments of respite from anguish about his mother, he was also thrilled that he would now be able to congratulate Pete on the success of his song personally. It would more than make up for his weird silence to be able to hug his best mate and buy him a few beers in one of the bars they loved. It would also be great to be back in a city – and that one in particular, the beautiful city of his birth.

He would miss Hannah and the kids horribly, but it would be such a relief to be away from that village and the constant terror of the power that predatory woman – he could hardly bear to think her name – Kelli, had to ruin his life.

And now there seemed to be another one cracking on to him. Please not.

When he'd got to the check-in desk at Heathrow he was told he'd been upgraded to business class, which was an amazing bit of luck, and he planned to neck the quality free booze and then spend the flight unconscious – much easier on the nearly flat bed his seat turned into – but the woman now lying on his right had other ideas for him.

She'd first started giving him the come-on in the business class lounge, where they'd been getting drinks at the same time. She'd handed him the Tabasco as he mixed himself a strong bloody Mary.

'Like a bit of spice in it, do you?' she'd said, smirking at him.

What was it about him? Did he have a sign over his head saying 'Available for sex at all times'? He'd never felt less sexy in his life, but his lack of response hadn't deterred her in the slightest.

'Well, well, well,' she'd said, as he'd stood in the aisle looking at his boarding card and the number above the seat, trying to make it not be true that he was seated next to her.

'Look who's going to be lying here next to me. Make yourself comfortable, darling, it's going to be a long ride.'

She'd carried on flirting with him as they took off, whacking into the free champagne with as much enthusiasm as Matt did. Then right through dinner, even though he was watching a film with his headphones on, she kept interrupting, trying to engage him in conversation.

He managed to dismiss her overtures, but after the food was cleared away, the cabin lights dimmed and people started settling down, flattening their seats and going to sleep, it got more difficult. And it was a bit weird, lying there, right next to a total stranger. It was oddly like they were in bed together. Matt closed his eyes and prayed for sleep, but it was no good.

'This is cosy, isn't it?' she said, lowering the folding blind that was the only barrier between their heads and leaning over to him so he got a full blast of her wine-tainted breath. 'So tell me – are you a member of the Mile High Club yet?'

And she put one hand on his crutch and squeezed.

That was it. He couldn't stand sexual harassment on top of everything else. He immediately stood up and headed for the small area in front of the kitchen and the loos. But who to ask for help?

He'd hardly slept the night before after hearing about his mother and that combined with the alcohol he could hardly think straight at all. He stood in the space by the emergency door and put his hands over his face, trying not to cry. He didn't know how long he'd been like that when he felt someone touch his arm. He flinched. Now what? Had she thought he'd headed to the loos to wait for her?

He opened his eyes to see an older woman looking at him with a concerned expression. Grey-haired, with glasses on a chain round her neck. His mum wore one of those. Matt's heart convulsed.

'Are you all right, love?' she asked. 'I'm sitting near you and I could see that woman wouldn't leave you alone.'

'Could you?' he said, breathless with relief that someone had noticed. 'It's very difficult. What can I say to make her back off? And how can I go to sleep lying next to her like that? It's so weird. I'm headed back to Sydney, because my mum's really sick in hospital and I can't cope with this as well. I just don't know what to do.'

Before he could stop it, a tear rolled out of his eye. Could it get any worse?

'Oh, you poor darling,' said the woman, patting his arm gently. 'Let me see if I can sort it out for you. You just stay there. Won't be long.'

Matt put his hands over his face again. It seemed the only way he could get a sense of privacy and he stood there, not caring if he looked like a nutter, until he heard voices next to him.

'This is the gentleman,' he heard the older woman saying.

Matt opened his eyes to see a bloke wearing the steward uniform with extra gold on it and a badge saying 'Purser'.

'Are you having a problem, sir?' he asked.

'Yes,' said Matt, 'the lady I'm sitting next to – well, lying next to – just won't leave me alone.'

'She touched his privates,' said the woman. 'I saw her. I'm sitting just across the aisle. She was that blatant.'

Matt could have hugged her.

'It's really awkward,' said Matt, 'but she just won't get the message I'm not interested and I really need to sleep.'

'He's rushing home because his mum's in the hospital,' said the woman, in her warm, reassuring Aussie accent.

Matt was so grateful he felt tears fill his eyes again and she squeezed his hand. The press of her soft flesh was maternal and comforting, completely asexual, and Matt managed a weak smile. He didn't know what he would have done without her at that moment, rescued by a complete stranger.

The purser took Matt's boarding card and asked him if he would mind waiting while he sorted things out for him.

'Want me to wait with you?' asked the lady.

'Oh, that would be nice,' he said, 'and thanks so much; I just wasn't up to dealing with that.'

She patted his arm.

'I know, darls. It's hard living so far from your loved ones, isn't it?'

Matt nodded, a lump forming in his throat again.

'I've just had to say goodbye to my son and daughter-in-law and my three grandkids,' she continued, 'they live in London. He's got a very good job with an investment bank. They've got a beautiful home and the kids go to private school and all that, but I do wish they didn't live so far away.'

She opened her handbag and pulled out a picture of three young children. Matt looked at it, feeling an agonising stab of longing for his own.

'They're beautiful,' he said.

'Thanks,' said the woman, gazing down at the photo for a moment, before putting it back in her bag. 'Don't know when I'll see them next.'

She looked up at him so sadly Matt couldn't help it, he put his arms round her and gave her a hug. Something about being stuck up there, sealed inside that metal tube full of strangers, seemed to heighten emotions and the lady didn't seem to mind. She patted his back in a way that reminded him so much of his mum again it was almost unbearably poignant. Would he get to hug her one last time?

Then the purser came back, carrying Matt's bag and jacket and indicated for him to follow – through to the first-class cabin. Matt turned round to wave at his saviour as he went, and she smiled at him, waving back and mouthing the words 'Good luck'. He blew her a kiss.


From then on, Matt's trip seemed to have fairy dust sprinkled on it. After so many months of grimness, the upgrade to first class seemed to unleash a chain of good luck, the best of it being that when he finally arrived at the hospital he found his mother out of intensive care, sitting up in bed in a side ward. He knew she must be on the mend because she immediately started telling him off.

'Why did you waste all that money flying over here, Matthew?' she said. 'It must have cost a fortune last-minute like that.'

'Don't worry, Mum,' he said, hugging her carefully around all her drips and so happy he'd come. 'I'll get loads of air miles from it and then I can fly the kids over for nothing next time.'

He sat there with her all day, showing her videos of the kids on his iPad and holding her hand while she slept. After lunch the stream of aunts, uncles and cousins started to arrive, each shouting with delight when they saw Matt. Then all the photos and videos had to be looked at again and the cuteness of Nancy and Hector exclaimed over, which inevitably led to the question: 'So when are all of youse going to move back here?'

Every time someone said it, Matt couldn't help glancing back at his mother, who watched him keenly as he struggled to answer.

'Well, I'd come back tomorrow,' he'd say, 'but Hector has just started school and he's really happy there and Hannah's dad died just a few months ago and we can't leave her mum right now . . .'

He'd then hear himself peter out as whichever rel had asked the dreaded question looked at him with a puzzled expression which clearly broadcast what they were thinking. And then they'd just come out and say it anyway: 'But what about your own mother? How can you live on the other side of the world from her?'

It all made Matt realise just how long he'd been in England. After eight years he must be turning native, because he'd grown completely used to his wife's family – and most Poms, as far as he could tell – and their way of avoiding any discussion of how they really felt about anything.

They seemed to think it was rude and embarrassing to have strong emotions. And as being rude and feeling embarrassed were the two worst things in the world, that just made emotions as a concept wrong. Or at least, if you couldn't help feeling them, it was illegal to show them, let alone talk about them. The whole nation had a broomstick up its arse and now Matt realised he was going the same way. His own rels were embarrassing him with their direct questions and that couldn't be right.

By three-thirty, when there were about ten visitors in the small room, all shouting – his family were incapable of saying anything quietly – the ward sister intervened and said Mrs Constantinos needed some rest and some of them would have to leave. Matt was starting to feel like a spaceman from the jet lag by then, so he gave his mum another careful hug and promised to be back the next day.

He came out of the hospital and got a cab straight to Bondi. The cousin he was going to stay with lived in the opposite direction, in Stanmore, but he had to see the ocean, hear the waves and breathe the ozone, to really believe he was in his city. Until he'd done that he felt like he was in some kind of limbo. Sitting up front in the taxi, a novelty in itself after riding around in the back of London black cabs like a head of state for so many years, he got out his phone to call Pete. Then he realised he didn't know his Aussie number. How messed up was that?

He tapped in the old London number that was still in his favourites list and got the brush-off in that snotty English woman's voice: 'Sorry, it has not been possible to connect you.' Even the bloody phones were uptight over there.

He drummed his fingers on his thighs wondering what to do and then inspiration struck. He emailed him:

Mate
I'm on my way to Bondi in a cab. Fancy a beer?
Call or text me on the usual number.

Then he thought for a moment and sent another one:

I'm serious! I'm really here!

By the time the cab pulled up on the south end of Campbell Parade, he hadn't heard back from Pete yet, but his disappointment disappeared as he climbed out of the taxi and looked around him. Home!

He ran across the road, dodging the traffic, and headed straight down through the park, past the skateboard ramp to the concrete walkway, busy with joggers, power walkers and skaters, even though it was June – winter – and then, after pausing for a moment to pull off his sneakers, he ran down on to the sand.

The feel of it underneath his feet, the slight squeak of it, was like a kind of baptism. He bent down and scooped up a handful of the tiny white grains and let them run between his fingers. Then he rolled up his jeans and jogged down to the shoreline to get his feet wet.

He stood on the wet sand, letting the cold water lick in over his feet and gazing out at the so-familiar ocean view, breathing deeply, abandoned to his senses. He felt happier than he had for months.

After standing there a while, not thinking, just being, he focused his eyes on the surfers. He hoped he could get hold of Pete soon, so he could borrow a board. Watching the few blokes out there, he reckoned he could show them all how to do it, bunch of amateurs.

As he watched another bloke get dumped after a few metres it occurred to him for the first time to wonder if Pete would even reply to his email. Maybe he'd be too pissed off with him for not reacting about the number one single.

They'd never had a silence like this between them before in twenty years of friendship, so he really didn't have any idea what his mate's operating mode would be. He knew what Pete was like with women – presuming if he did nothing it would all go away – so maybe he would apply that same system to Matt's behaviour and just ignore the emails. That would be boring. Worse than that. Heartbreaking.

A wave of jet lag dizziness washed over him and he moved back up the beach and lay down on the sand, flat on his back. He knew it would be disastrous to go to sleep that early, but was finding it very hard to keep his eyes open. He forced the lids wide apart staring up at the big beautiful blue sky.

He blinked to try and get rid of the horrible hot and gritty feeling in his eyeballs, but didn't realise the urge to sleep had got the better of him until he was suddenly jolted back to consciousness by cold water dripping on to his face.

'Well, look what the tide's washed up,' a familiar voice was saying. 'A tasty bit of driftwood for the ladies.'

'Pete!'

Matt sprang to his feet and threw his arms around his friend and his surfboard.

'Mate! I'm so glad I've found you. I haven't got your bloody number or address.'

'That's because you're a shit friend,' said Pete, but with a lopsided smile that was so familiar, Matt almost teared up. It was all cool. Thank god.

'Oh yeah, I'm sorry, mate,' said Matt, hanging his head, 'it's complicated. Can I tell you over a beer? Reckon I owe you a few, or should it be champagne – Mr Hit Maker.'

Pete's grin widened.

'It's a really great track, Pete,' said Matt. 'You deserve to be number one. Even if you did do it without me – and with those shitty lyrics.'

Pete dropped his surfboard on to the sand and raised his fists, but still smiling, and the two of them jumped around, pretending to spar, until Pete stopped and put his hands on Matt's shoulders. Matt did the same to him.

'Oh, it's good to see you, mate,' said Pete, as they smirked at each other in mutual admiration. 'I've really missed ya, you handsome bastard.'

They man-hugged according to their ritual and then as he felt the damp of Pete's wetsuit seep through his shirt, Matt knew what he absolutely had to do. He pulled away and tore off his clothes, until he was standing on the beach in just his grey Calvin Klein trunks.

'Gotta get my head under that water,' he said.

'I've got a better idea,' said Pete, unzipping the front of his wetsuit. He stepped out of it and handed it to Matt.

'Take my board, catch a few waves. I'll see you back in the unit,' he gestured towards Campbell Parade with his head. 'I'm back in the old building, the one where we used to share, just one floor up, number 6. So it's not like you don't know where it is. My dad owns the building, something I may have neglected to tell you before . . .'

But Matt barely took in what he was saying. He was already pulling on the wetsuit, almost shaking with excitement. It was too small for him; his hairy ankles were sticking out of the bottom of the legs, but he didn't care.

'Oh maaaate,' he was saying. 'You have no idea . . .'

'I think I do,' said Pete, laughing and putting on Matt's shirt, 'I lived in London for ten years, remember. I spent my first month back here pretty much living in the surf.'

Pete stopped talking and just looked at Matt for a moment, feeling something like tears pricking his eyes. He'd missed his friend far more than he'd allowed himself to admit. Matt was staring out at the ocean, like a big cat watching its prey, working out the mood of it, remembering how to make it his own. Then something made him glance back at Pete.

'Shit, it's good to be here, Pete,' he said and the two of them whooped and capered around in a crazy dance.

# Chapter Forty

Ali was looking at her laptop screen and feeling slightly sick at what was left in her bank balance after she'd paid her bills for that month.

Her savings had taken a major hit, paying all the extra rent owed by her midnight-flitting ex-flatmate, and although they'd found a temporary one who had so far paid her share on time, Ali's cash stash was pretty much gone – and after rent what she earned in Chocolate Bar was barely enough to live on.

And now her lovely flatmate Stewart had told her he was moving out. He'd had the courtesy to give her a month's notice – and she was fairly sure he wouldn't take any of her possessions with him when he left – but the thought of having to find yet another person to share with was a massive pain.

How could she know they were all right? That thieving freak Minnie had seemed really nice when she met her. It was really sinking in that, since Matt had moved to the country, there wasn't anyone in London she'd known longer than a year. She might as well just stop the first person she saw on the street and ask them if they'd like to move in. It was all too hard.

For a moment she laid her head down on her arms and groaned, hardly able to admit to herself that at that moment she desperately wished she was back in Sydney among people she'd known all her life.

Then thinking about home made her wonder how Matt's mum – Auntie Claire, her mother's older sister – was. She'd heard she was out of intensive care, but decided to give Hannah a ring to see what the latest was and to see how she was coping without Matt. Plus the attraction of hearing a familiar voice.

Hector answered the phone.

'Hey, Heccie boy,' said Ali, smiling as she heard his piping tones, 'how are you, little champ?'

'Is that Ali?' he asked enthusiastically.

'It sure is,' she replied.

'Are you coming down to see us? Daddy's in Australia because my granny there is in hospital.'

'That's why I'm ringing, sweetheart. Do you know how she is?'

'Not really,' said Hector, 'but my mummy's very tired.'

'Oh, that's no good. Is she there?'

'I'll get her,' said Hector, 'but I might be a long time, because she's in the garden. Don't go away.'

'I won't,' said Ali, smiling at the phone. She loved that little boy. He made her want to have five children immediately. But who with? And how, without taking her clothes off in front of them? Like she'd told Pete, she still didn't feel ready for the sex thing.

She'd gone swimming once and had noticed all the eyes flicking over the scars on her thighs, before they looked hurriedly away. A small girl had pointed at her. She was a freak show. The so-called 'healing oil' seemed to be helping a bit, but there was a such large area to rub it on to, she didn't have time to do it three times every day like it said on the box.

Maybe if she could meet her perfect Pompom English posh bloke, he wouldn't mind having sex with clothes on. Weren't those types meant to be a bit pervy like that? She'd have to get some jodhpurs and a riding crop.

But where was she going to meet this Pompom? They were pretty thin on the ground in Shoreditch and the ones who were there were hiding it, dressing like Toxic Pete and talking like the tough guys on 'EastEnders'.

Then as she waited for Hannah to come to the phone, a brilliant idea occurred to her. She'd go down and stay with them for a bit. Not just for the weekend, a week or two, maybe more. She could do with a break from Chocolate Bar, and she could help Hannah and her poor widowed mum out until Matt came back, and spend some extended time with the kids. A perfect trifecta. They were family, after all, it was her duty to help and she wanted to. She loved them.

And where better to meet a classic Pompom than the English countryside? That pub in the village was probably crawling with them, and she could lurk around at farmers' markets and cattle sales. She'd hold up a sign: Broody cow, slightly injured, any bids?

The last time she'd been down there Hannah had taken her to a shop that sold tweed caps and stuff for hens and horses and all that country life gear, to buy some wellies. That would be a prime hunting ground. She could use Hannah as bait.

Thinking about all the possibilities, Ali was suddenly excited, her low mood completely gone at the thought of embarking on a new adventure. It was a great idea for so many reasons – not least of which was that it would give her somewhere to live after she told the estate agent she wasn't going to renew the lease on that bloody flat, which was coming up at the end of the month.

Which she was going to do the moment she got off the phone from Hannah.


Ali was quite shocked by the state of Hannah when she met her at the station a few days later. She'd never seen her look anything less than gorgeous before, but she was a sad sight, her lovely hair lank and unwashed, dark circles under her eyes.

Ali hoped her alarm wasn't showing too clearly and wished the kids were there to act as a distraction – also from the amount of luggage she had with her. But seeing the poor shape her cousin-in-law was in, she decided she'd better fess up about that right away.

'Hi, Hanns,' she said, as brightly as she could, hugging her alarmingly bony body, 'it's great to see you. Sorry, I've brought all my junk with me;

I hope you don't mind. It's just that, well, I've given up the lease on your old place and I've got nowhere to put it until I find somewhere else.'

'That's fine,' said Hannah, sounding as flat as she looked, 'sorry it didn't work out for you there. Matt told me one of your flatmates had done a runner. That's so crap. I remember all that when I first started sharing places; it's horrible. You can leave your stuff with us for as long as you need to. I'm just so happy to see you, Ali.'

And then she did something Ali thought she'd never see. Right there on the station platform, with people all around them, Hannah burst into tears.

'Hey, Hansie,' said Ali, putting an arm round her shoulder, 'let it out, that's good. Do you want to have a cup of tea here and tell me about it?'

'No,' said Hannah, drying her eyes on her sleeve, 'let's go to the car and get home, I'm so sorry, it's just all been too much.'

She started sniffing again, while picking up as many of Ali's bags as she could carry and hurrying off. Ali picked up the rest and hobbled after her.

Once Ali's stuff was stowed in the boot, they climbed into the car and Hannah slumped down with her arms and head on the steering wheel, sobbing again. Ali patted her back and made soothing noises.

'Talk about it, Hanns,' she said. 'Tell me what's going on – I mean, apart from losing your job, your dad dying, Matt's mum being in the hospital and you having to look after the kids on your own and earn a living and leaving London – is there anything else? I mean, all that would be more than enough stress for anyone to deal with, but is there something else as well?'

Hannah shook her head and then, sitting up, she wiped her eyes on her hand.

'No, you're spot on, it's just all that together, it's been too much, and now I think Matt's going to have to stay on in Sydney for a while. I understand why and he needs to be there, because his mum's going to have a triple bypass and there's no point him coming home until that's done, because what would be the point if he came home and then she got critical again and he had to fly straight back? And then on top of that he needs to be with Pete for work. Pete had a number one hit – did you know?'

Ali nodded. 'And Matt didn't write the words for it, is that right?' she said gently.

'That's right,' said Hannah, turning to look at her in surprise. 'How did you know that?'

'Pete told me,' said Ali. 'He felt really bad about it.'

Hannah stared at her for a moment, as if trying to take it all in, then continued.

'Well, Matt didn't tell me any of that until the other day, when he rang to ask what I thought about him staying on there a bit longer. I was just so relieved to find out what had been bugging him, because he's been acting so strangely recently and I couldn't understand why and it turns out it was that. I don't know why he didn't tell me before.'

She sighed loudly and blinked her eyes to try and stop the tears that were threatening to start again, then sat up straight, determined to stay on top of it.

'But the good news,' she continued, 'is that Pete really wants to work with him to do a whole album with this guy, Abel somebody – have you heard of him?'

Ali nodded.

'Yes, Abel Jones. He was just breaking through when I was still in Sydney. I love his voice. He's a great guy for them to work with. Really.'

Hannah brightened visibly at this information.

'Oh good,' she said, 'Matt says it's the best opportunity he's had for years – if ever, really – and they've already recorded the follow-up single using words Matt had written here and Pete thinks it's even better than the last one, the number one, what was it called again?'

'Bambina,' said Ali. 'It is a great track. Really catchy.'

Hannah nodded.

'Yeah, I love it too. Well, apparently the record company are really excited about the follow-up with Matt's words and I'm so happy for him, Ali. And he can live there for practically nothing staying with Pete, because he doesn't have to pay any rent – Pete's dad owns the place.

So it's an amazing opportunity in every way and he really deserves it – but it's just so hard having him away. The kids miss him horribly.'

Mentioning that brought the tears back and she started sobbing again. Ali rubbed her back a bit and then got out of the car, going round to the driver's side and opening the door.

'Move over,' she said gently. 'I'm going to drive. In fact, I don't want you to do anything else today except lie around and eat chocolates – I've brought you some really nice ones – and be with your kids. Leave everything else to me. OK?'

Hannah looked up at her blankly and Ali had to laugh. She had mascara all round her eyes like a panda. It kind of suited her.

'Go on,' said Ali, 'shift over and sort out your eye make-up, beauty writer lady. I think I can remember the way to your place, just shout out if I take a wrong turning.'

# Chapter Forty-one

Anthea was cleaning kidneys for a steak and kidney pie and thinking about Ali. She had a lot of time for that young woman and was so pleased she'd come down to help Hannah out.

She was a rare thing in her generation, a girl who was actually a help, rather than just getting in the way prettily. She'd been marvellous at the drinks after Charlie's funeral. Every time Anthea was about to ask her if she would mind doing something, like open some more white wine, or get some more cheese biscuits out, Ali was already doing it. She'd even known to put the celery sticks in water. Anthea was wondering if she might not be rather good for Dominic.

Although she'd always rather adored staying at his flashy New York apartment with a doorman, she was delighted her nephew was finally moving back to England. Now she just needed to get him to settle down with a good-natured, practical girl and have a family.

If she couldn't have grandchildren – and not having any children herself, she couldn't – she wanted grandnieces and nephews who lived nearby. Preferably walking distance. Dominic's brothers had kids, but they all lived miles away and never came to visit.

Dominic had always been her favourite of her siblings' children and as he was going to inherit her entire estate, she wanted to know it was going to stay in the family. Dominic was her heir and he needed to get his own in place. And not an American one, thank you very much.

If he married one of those flighty girls he'd brought to stay with her over the years, who were so odd about food and wouldn't touch milk or cheese, ridiculous fads, she had a good mind to change her will. They'd only divorce him and take it all.

It was odd how they all seemed to be gluten-intolerant too, those girls, she thought, rolling out the puff pastry she'd made earlier. Strange bloodless creatures. She'd wrung a chicken's neck in front of one of them to see how she reacted. Total hysteria. Pathetic. The girl had left the next day, which was fine by Anthea.

So that was a long-term plan to work on, Dominic and Ali. Anthea mentally rubbed her hands in anticipation, while her real ones pressed the crust down round the edges of the pie plate, but her more immediate concern was Marguerite. She'd never had a problem with her weight, lucky thing, but Anthea thought she was looking dangerously thin these days. She hoped she wasn't ill with something ghastly.

Obviously Charlie's death had been a terrible shock for her, but with Hannah and those darling children around, Anthea would have expected her to be moving on a little by now. Instead she seemed to have got worse recently. She was so pale and her skin was like crumpled tissue paper.

Anthea put the pie in to bake and started to peel a large pile of potatoes, which would be mashed with a lavish amount of butter and cream. It was a strange kind of meal for the time of year, but all those girls next door needed feeding up.


Hector had a funny look on his face. There was a deep frown between his eyebrows, which was odd as Anthea had just put a large plate of food in front of him and he was probably the only child in the world who actively enjoyed eating offal. Steak and kidney pie was his favourite. That was the other reason she'd made it.

'Are you all right, Hector ?' asked Anthea, as no-one else seemed to have noticed.

'I'm just thinking,' he said, putting one finger on his face in a suitably thoughtful pose, but the frown was still there.

Hannah looked over at him, immediately feeling guilty that she hadn't noticed something was amiss with him first. She'd been too distracted by the state of her mother, who was looking so pale and drawn. She knew something was up with her – something beyond Charlie's death – and was wondering how she would ever be able to get it out of her. The sphinx was a chatterbox compared to Marguerite.

But now she was taking notice of her son, his concentrated expression made him look so like her late father puzzling over a crossword clue, Hannah wanted to run screaming from the room. Had she been in her own house, she might have found an excuse to do so, but it wasn't so easy at Anthea's. She glanced at Marguerite, to see if she'd seen it too. She clearly had and was looking down at her plate, pushing the food around, but not lifting any to her mouth.

'Thinking's good,' said Anthea to Hector in her usual jovial tones, 'anything in particular?'

'Yes,' said Hector, 'I was thinking it was true what Charlie said.'

Marguerite dropped her knife and fork.

'Oh yes,' said Anthea, still jolly, 'and what was that?'

'About me being the man of the family,' said Hector, 'and with Daddy in Australia, I'm the only man here now. Well, Sooty's a man, but he's younger than me, so that's it. I'm the man. So if any of you need any help, just come to me.'

Hannah's hand flew up to her mouth. Tears had sprung into her eyes as he spoke, but at the same time it was so adorably funny she started to laugh too. Anthea was already laughing, her head thrown back, one hand slapping down on to the table.

'Oh, that's priceless,' she said. 'Hector, you really are the most marvellous child. I mean, man.'

Ali was also laughing, but Hannah could see the sad look in her eyes too. It was killing, what he'd said, in both ways. Hector was a bit uncertain whether it was getting a good reaction or not and he looked over to Hannah for reassurance. She gave him a thumbs-up.

'Fantastic, Hector,' she said. 'Daddy and Charlie would be so proud of you. How about we get Daddy on Skype later and tell him?'

Hector beamed with delight and Hannah turned to her mother and was relieved to see she was smiling too, faintly, but definitely a smile. It seemed like the first time for ages Hannah had seen her do that. Then Hector couldn't resist the urge to take the successful comment a bit further.

'It's a shame we can't Skype Charlie as well, isn't it?' he said.

Hannah carried on smiling, a little more forced now, but Marguerite rose up from her seat as if someone had pressed an ejector button and left the room without saying a word.

As they heard the distinct sound of Anthea's front door closing, she and Hannah locked eyes. Marguerite had left the building and that was extreme emotional avoidance, even for her.

# Chapter Forty-two

Matt was starting to feel like the man with two brains. After four weeks in Sydney, he missed his wife and family viscerally, desperately – but only when he thought about them. And a lot of the time, when he was hanging out with Pete, working into the small hours, going for a bracing winter surf, having a long afternoon nap, a casual dinner, a few drinks and then back to work, he didn't think about them.

It didn't mean he loved them any less, but he was so fully immersed back in his old life, living in practically the same flat, with the same flattie – he couldn't believe Pete's dad had owned the bloody place all along, the jammie bugger – he felt oddly like the last fourteen years of his life had never happened.

He'd never met Hannah, he hadn't got married or moved to London, he didn't have children, he'd never lived in an English village. He was just a Sydney songwriter surfer dude hanging out with his best mate and doing the odd bit of modelling for spending money. This balcony, this view, this chat, this beer was his universe and it was the only universe.

Then every morning he'd pick up the iPad and Skype them, and seeing his gorgeous kids in their pyjamas, Nancy kissing the screen and Hector holding up Sooty to woof hello – that other world would become real again. His heart throbbed with love and longing for them and then, after Hannah had put them to bed, she'd come back and Skype him again and he'd want to pull her into his arms so badly, he felt like he might jump out of his skin.

Saying goodbye to them was always a torture and he'd feel really unsettled for a little while afterwards, so he'd have to almost physically restrain himself from running out of the flat and flagging a taxi to take him to the airport. But then Pete would emerge from his room, they'd go out for coffee – real coffee, no more of that ceeffo rubbish – sitting outside their favourite café in the winter sun, reading the paper, yacking to people passing by who they knew, checking out the surf, and it would roll off him again. Then he'd stay in Sydney dude brain until the next time they Skyped.

Pete asked him about it one day.

'I'm so glad you're here, mate,' he said, wiping milk foam from his stubbly top lip, 'we're doing the best work we've ever done – but aren't you missing the family? I can remember you rushing home from rocking parties in London just to be there when the kids woke up, but you never mention them here. What gives?'

So Matt told him how it was. Like having two brains in the same head and oddly bearable as long as he stayed in one or the other of them, in the relevant situation. Pete thought for a moment, then nailed it.

'You're like some dude in the army,' he said, 'out on active service. Missing your loved ones like shit, but keeping too busy to think about it. Reckon it's hardwired into the male brain to be able to do that, so we could go off on long mammoth hunts without pining away for the family, what do you reckon?'

'I reckon you're right,' said Matt, 'and I'm going to buy you another coffee, because you've just given me a brilliant idea for some words. "The active service of love . . . love on the front line . . . the front line of love . . ." there's something great in there and I'm the man to find it.'

Pete beamed and raised his palm for a smacking high five.


The next time Matt talked to Hannah he nearly told her about Pete's 'active service' theory, but thought better of it just in time. It clearly didn't work the same way for her. She was being so supportive of him being away, it made him love her more than ever, but he knew she was doing it hard at her end. He'd never seen her looking so tired and drawn, and that was just via Skype.

'When does the new Abel Jones single come out?' she asked him, resolutely positive, although Matt could see how drained she was.

'In a couple of weeks,' he said, excitement fluttering in his stomach, despite his concern about her, 'but it's out on YouTube already and the response has been great. It's looking good, Hanns. Really good. I might actually make some proper money… We're doing the album with him now and I'll have done all the lyrics on it except that one track of Pete's. 'Bambina' has already gone on to iTunes to hit all the big overseas markets and if it does well, they'll want this single internationally too and the album. This could be the big one for us, at last.'

'Yay!' said Hannah, looking genuinely excited. 'I've heard "Bambina" on the radio here and I thought that had to be a good sign. I'm so happy for you, honey. It's brilliant.'

She paused and peered more closely at the screen for a moment.

'You're certainly looking well on it.'

He was sitting up in bed, naked, the iPad balanced on his thighs. He looked as good as when she'd met him, fourteen years before. He flexed his pecs and abs at her like a body builder.

'Pretty good for an old bloke, eh?' he said. 'I'm surfing a lot and running, between working, and I'm really fit. I feel bad telling you that while you're looking after everything there, but as I'm here, I'd be mad not to.'

'Of course you would,' said Hannah, glad she had all her clothes on.

She'd never felt less attractive. She'd lost loads of weight, but not in a good way. Her boobs had just about disappeared and she felt scraggy like an old chicken carcase. Even having a shower was a big effort and she was leaving it longer and longer between hair washes. And it seemed easiest just to put on the same clothes she'd been wearing the day before each morning.

What was the point of making an effort? Who was going to see her? Some of the mothers really went to town with make-up and high heels for the school gate, but she wasn't remotely inspired by that as a venue. Whatever was nearest would do.

Looking at Matt's handsome face smiling out at her, she hoped he couldn't see how awful she looked.

'You're an amazing woman, Hannah Berry-Downing-Constantinos,' he was saying. 'None of this would have been possible without you understanding that I need to do this. Not many women would get it, you know, Hanns. And I would come home on the next plane if you asked me to, you know that, don't you?'

'I do,' she said, nodding, 'and that's probably why I don't ask you to do it – because I know you would if I did. But this is what you've always needed to do, Matt. I've known that since we met. It's the break we've both been waiting for and I'm just so glad it's finally happening for you.'

He leaned forward and kissed the screen.

'Did you get that?' he asked her.

Hannah blew his image a kiss.

'Right back at you,' she said.

'We could have Skype sex,' said Matt, waggling his eyebrows suggestively, 'but I can hear Pete's up . . .'

'Give dear old Toxic my love,' said Hannah, laughing. 'I'm off to bed with my book – and Sooty. He misses you as much as we do, you know. He wouldn't come for a walk with me for the first few days, just sat by the door waiting for you to come in.'

'Fine, loyal hound,' said Matt. 'Give him a good hard tickling. I miss the mutt too. Whodathunkit, eh?'

'You're just a big softie, Matt Constantinos.'

'I'm a big hardie where you're concerned,' said Matt, with his wickedest smile, lowering the iPad to show her where his hand was and what it was doing. He closed his eyes and threw his head back, holding the iPad out and away from him with the other arm, so she could get the whole scenario.

Hannah's belly did a little backflip. A very little one, but it was nice to be reminded of a feeling she'd almost forgotten. Desire.

'Porn star,' she said, laughing and wiggling her eyebrows the way he had before. 'Are you absolutely sure Toxic's up?'

'Yes, unfortunately,' he said, sitting up again. 'I've just heard him belch like the unreconstructed warthog he is. It's put me right off what I was getting up to here. You're disgusting, Pete!' he called out towards the bedroom door, pulling the sheet up over his lap.

Hannah saw the door open behind Matt's shoulder. The sound of a loud belch came through it and then it closed again.

'See what I mean?' said Matt, laughing. 'Warthog!' he called towards the door.

'Well, Skype me earlier tomorrow then, frat boy,' said Hannah, shaking her head, but smiling broadly and looking a bit more like her old self.

'Bye, my angel,' said Matt, leaning towards the screen and planting his beautiful lips on it again.

She blew him another kiss and logged out.

Matt leaned back against his pillows, feeling like a shit. In that moment he was missing Hannah more than he thought possible, but at the same time he couldn't wait to start his chilled-out pretendy bachelor day.

He hadn't even asked her how things were going there, how her mum was, how Hector was doing at school, any of that. He'd really meant to, but he'd just ended up talking about himself and his bloody music. And having a bit of a wank. What an utter git.

Had he reverted to his nineteen-year-old self, unable to think about anything beyond the next surf, the next feed and the next fuck? Or rather, toss-off. He certainly wasn't interested in getting anyone else to help him with that area. It was strictly DIY until he got home – whenever that was going to be.

Perhaps he was just being a selfish bastard staying there and leaving Hannah to get on with it all, while he had a holiday in his old carefree life, indulging his long-term delusion that he would finally make it as a songwriter. He should just forget it and go home.

He pulled the iPad towards him and typed 'Qantas' into the search engine. His mother would be fine now, she'd made a very good recovery from the bypass surgery so far and the specialist had been really encouraging. He knew it was still a big deal, but she had enough other family there to look after her. He should go back and be with his wife when she needed him.

The airline's website had just loaded when Pete walked into the bedroom, fully dressed.

'Come on, you lazy bastard,' he said. 'Get up. Bob from the record label's just called me. They're so stoked about the YouTube response to the new single, they want to have a meeting with us about possibly putting the album out sooner and they need to hear where we're up to with it. So get your arse in gear, matey, I need my topliner there with me when I play them what we've got so far.'

Oblivious to his naked state, Matt leapt out of bed and ran into the shower, all thoughts of home immediately banished.

# Chapter Forty-three

Ali came down the garden at a run, jumping over any chickens which didn't get out of her way fast enough, and burst into the kitchen, where Hannah was putting the finishing touches to a sponge cake. Nancy's face was shiny with cake mix and she had both hands in the mixing bowl.

'Hans! Hans!' Ali was saying. 'OMG I've just met Anthea's nephew – and he's a totally perfect dreamboat posh Pompom, floppy blond hair, everything. Why didn't you tell me? Look at me – I look terrible. Cut-off jeans, a horrible old singlet – the cringe of it! I've got to go and change before I go back there. You could have warned me . . .'

'Is this the famous Dominic?' said Hannah.

'Yeah!' said Ali, making a 'duh' face.

Hannah shrugged, holding up her hands to proclaim her innocence.

'I can't place him. I've met some of her other nephews but I don't remember this one, she's got loads of them. I've heard Anthea going on about Dominic – he's lived in New York for years, working for a bank and he's loaded, I know that much – but I didn't know he was good-looking too. Good for him.'

'Good for me,' said Ali, whose cheeks were a similar colour to the raspberries Hannah was arranging on the bottom layer of the sponge, which was already spread with whipped cream.

Ali reached over to take one. Hannah playfully smacked her hand.

'Leave off, Mrs,' she said. 'Those are for my cake.'

'Naughty,' said Nancy, reaching over and taking one herself.

'Can I borrow a really girly frock?' asked Ali, leaning in close to Hannah's face. 'I need something really old school flowery vintage-y. You've got all that gear, would you mind?'

'Help yourself,' said Hannah, 'but why do you want to wear a girly dress, Ali? You look so great in your own stuff. I love those little Sixties dresses you wear. I wish I wasn't too old to wear that kind of thing.'

Ali sighed theatrically.

'I'm serving the tea with Dominic at the garden party. We'll be wielding the teapots side by side, under the mulberry tree. It's so romantic and I've got to look the part, all floaty and floral.'

Hannah shook her head, smiling indulgently.

'You can borrow a hat as well, if you want to,' she said. 'Perhaps some white lace gloves and a parasol?'

Ali's face lit up.

'Do you mean it?' she said.

'Sure, go and have a look, I've got loads of that gear – well, maybe not the lace gloves and the parasol, but I've got some nice straw hats. They're in the boxes on top of the wardrobe.'

'Ooh,' said Ali, bending down to give Nancy a quick squeeze and a kiss, 'I'm so excited.'

'I'll see you over at Anthea's,' said Hannah, 'as soon as I've finished this cake – and washed Nancy's face.'

Ali looked at her for a moment.

'Aren't you going to change?' she asked.

Hannah looked down. She was wearing white jeans, a stripey Breton top and flat gold sandals. The jeans were distinctly grubby at the edges, but they'd have to do. It would all have to do. No-one was going to be looking at her anyway.

'No, I'll leave all that to you,' she said, 'you're the glamour girl round here. But don't worry, I'll put some lippie on.'

'See you later,' said Ali, running out of the room and up the stairs at breakneck pace.

As she went something else occurred to Hannah.

'Ali,' she called up the stairs after her.

Her bleached blonde head appeared over the bannister rail on the landing, smiling brightly.

'What have you done with Hector? Did you leave him at Anthea's?'

'He's fine,' said Ali, 'dreamy Dominic is teaching him how to bowl.'

'Bowl?' said Hannah, bewildered.

'Yeah, you know – cricket. Dominic says it's never too early to learn your spin and your googlie. He's really good at it, he used to play for his school.'

Hannah shook her head in disbelief and headed back into the kitchen to finish the cake.

She didn't meet Dominic until her second trip over to Anthea's house later that afternoon. The first time she'd taken over the finished cake and Nancy, who was happy to stay on there with Granny, in the exciting bustle of Anthea's kitchen, where multiple batches of scones were coming out of the oven and great piles of cucumber sandwiches were being made for the cream tea, which was Anthea's annual event in aid of her favourite animal charities.

With everything under control at garden party HQ and both children happily engaged over there, Hannah grabbed the rare chance to have some time on her own back at the house. She immediately tried to find Matt on Skype, in case he and Pete were still up having one of their all-night work sessions, but he wasn't online.

Feeling a bit flat, she finished clearing up the kitchen, and then, with just over half an hour until she had to go back, she didn't quite know what to do. It was precious to have any time to herself without a work deadline to meet, but it wasn't long enough to start anything useful, so she checked her emails, tooled around on Twitter for a bit and then had a look at Facebook.

She hadn't been near it for ages and physically jumped when a picture of Matt she'd never seen before, wearing a wetsuit and a huge smile, appeared on her timeline. It was such an odd feeling to see a picture of him that she'd known nothing about. She felt like a voyeur in her own husband's life.

She clicked on it to find a whole album of pics which had been posted by one of their Sydney friends, with lots of shots of Matt and Pete and other surfer dudes fooling around on the beach and then at a dinner at what looked like North Bondi Italian, with a big crowd of people.

He looked really well and happy in all of them, which wasn't a surprise, because she saw him on Skype at least once every day and knew what good shape he was in, but seeing those shots of him having fun at an event she'd had no part in and didn't even know about made her feel incredibly left out.

There was nothing terrible, like Matt with his arm around a woman or anything like that, and she knew most of the people they were with, but it brought home the reality of how weirdly separate their lives were at that moment.

How had they let this happen? She felt like calling him and ordering him to come back immediately, she'd had enough now, but then realised she didn't even know his Sydney mobile number by heart. She'd have to look up her own husband's phone number. This was nuts. A tear rolled down one cheek.

She wiped it away and then the one that had fallen from the other eye, but she didn't start sobbing. It wasn't like that. It wasn't stressed-out desperation crying like the time at the station with Ali, it was pure, calm, sad weeping at the situation that they'd allowed to develop, almost by accident. For the first time since she'd met Matt fourteen years before, she felt there was a distance between them.

There had been times in their busy London lives when she'd felt like they were living on parallel tracks, passing the baton of childcare back and forth, but the closeness stayed intact because whatever had happened the day before, they always woke up together. They'd look into each other's eyes and the connection was always there. Soul to soul. But now she felt that after all these weeks of separation they were drifting inexorably apart through no will of their own, as though caught on different currents.

She opened an email to him, but then closed it again, reminding herself it was never a good idea to send something written in a moment of high emotion. Instead she told herself for the umpteenth time why he was still in Sydney and that he would be coming back as soon as the album was finished, and it was all worth it for him finally to have the success he deserved.

Feeling calmer, but still shaken, she checked her eye make-up – lucky she'd been wearing waterproof mascara this time – tied back her hair and slicked on some pink lipstick, in the spirit of Anthea's garden, now in glorious bloom. The outfit was a bit tired, she acknowledged, catching sight of herself in the long bathroom mirror, but she simply couldn't be bothered to change. The thought of it made her feel like crawling into bed. Instead, she grabbed a bottle of Annick Goutal *Rose Absolue* from her dressing table and spritzed it liberally down the front of her T-shirt. That would have to do.

Making her way rather reluctantly back across Anthea's back lawn, not feeling in the mood for a jolly garden party at all, she spotted a man standing up a ladder by the summerhouse, trying to attach some red, white and blue bunting to the corner of the roof. Hector was holding the bottom of the ladder and gazing up at him in admiration. So this must be Dominic.

Hannah's immediate first impressions were that he was much too old, at least forty-five, and much too straight-looking for Ali. Even from a distance she could see he was wearing ironed chinos.

But taking the opportunity to check him out thoroughly before he saw her, as he struggled with the bunting, she could see what Ali meant about him being handsome in a very particular English way. Tall, with rower's shoulders. Dark blond hair parted on one side and patches of high colour on his well-bred cheekbones. She knew he'd have blue eyes even before she got close enough to see them.

He was just the sort who would be cast as the weak but noble younger son in a film about the Boer War, or the poetic one in the movie version of an E M Forster novel. So predictable, but before she had the chance to make any more enjoyable snap judgements about him, Hector had seen her.

'Mummy!' he called out. 'Come and meet Dominic. We're putting up the bunting. Hey, Dominic,' he called up to him, when she reached the bottom of the ladder. 'This is my mum.'

Hannah glanced up and brown eyes, just like Anthea's, looked back at her. Oops, she'd been wrong about that. He smiled broadly, then dropped the uncooperative flags to the ground and shimmied down the ladder.

'Finally, the lovely Hannah,' he said, taking one of her hands in both of his, which seemed a bit much for a first meeting. She extracted it as quickly as possible without actually wrenching it away, feeling much too grumpy for any such posturing gallantry and, using Hector as a front, she put the hand in question on his bony little shoulder and squeezed it.

He didn't notice, he was so enthralled gazing up at Dominic, while also throwing a tennis ball repeatedly in the air and catching it. Well, sometimes catching it. Oh blimey, though Hannah, not another one. Dominic was getting quite a fan club.

'Yes, I'm Hannah,' she said, hoping it didn't sound as snippy as she felt. She just wasn't in the mood to be patronised. She knew she didn't look lovely. She was dressed in clothes she'd been wearing for three days and hadn't washed her hair for longer. The hastily applied lipstick and scent were hardly enough to make up for it.

'Hector here has been teaching me how to bowl,' Dominic said, ruffling her son's hair. Hannah wanted to smack his hand off Hector's head.

'Yeah,' said Hector, practically spitting with excitement. 'I can do a finger spinner. Look.'

With a snap of his tiny wrist he hurled the bright yellow ball down the garden and Hannah was surprised how far it went. All the way to Anthea's greenhouse where, to her great relief, it bounced off one of the panes of glass and landed in the vegetable patch.

'Oh, good throw, Heccie,' Dominic was saying, 'good man!'

What was with this guy? 'Good man . . .' 'The lovely Hannah . . .' Were they in the 1930s? And how dare he call her son Heccie. That was Matt's name for him.

'Right, Hector,' she said, her voice as clipped as Dominic's was oily, 'that's quite enough of that in Anthea's garden. You can practise at home another day. Now go and ask Anthea if there's anything else you can do to help. I'll be in right away. Run along.'

Hector gave her a disappointed look and raced off towards the house, Hannah turning to Dominic, still feeling as brittle as an icy puddle. She just wasn't in the mood to play smarm-a-long with an English smoothie.

'Well, lovely to meet you, Dominic,' she said. 'I've heard a lot about you. Now I'd better go and see what I can do to help in the kitchen. See you later.'

She turned to follow Hector, but felt Dominic's hand on her upper arm and snapped round to look at him. Excuse me?

'Hang on a mo, Hannah,' he said, smiling at her. He had dimples, she noticed. What kind of a grown man has dimples?

'We've met before,' he said, quietly. 'Don't you remember?'

'Have we?'

'Yes, we used to meet here once a year at Anthea's Boxing Day drinks.'

'We did?' said Hannah, still having absolutely no memory of him.

Dominic was now smirking in a really irritating way, his head was even waggling a bit.

'You might remember me better as Nic,' he said.

Hannah's hand flew up to her mouth. Of course! Anthea's nephew Nick – she'd always thought of him as Nick, as in Nicholas; she'd had no idea it was Nic, short for Dominic.

And she certainly did remember him, she'd been forced to hang around with him and his brothers every year for several hours at those torturous parties, until Charlie would get so drunk they'd have to leave, which was almost a relief for her. An only child at an all-girls school, she'd found the massed maleness of the five brothers very daunting.

'Oh, *Nic*,' she said, 'I'm so sorry . . . of course I remember you, I just didn't make the connection between Dominic and Nic. When did you go back to being Dominic?'

He laughed.

'When I moved to New York. They love the whole English thing over there, so I thought I'd play it up with the full poncy name.'

Hannah found herself smiling. He was the middle brother and he'd always been much nicer to her than the others, but while she now clearly remembered that person, she still couldn't connect him to the man who was standing in front of her.

'I can't believe I didn't recognise you,' she said. 'I'm so sorry. How rude.'

Nick, Nic, Dominic, whoever he was, smiled wryly.

'There's a reason for that,' he said.

Hannah looked at him, waiting for an explanation.

'I was fat,' he said. 'Remember? Really properly fat. I was the ugly fat bastard my brothers liked to torture.'

Hannah opened her mouth and then shut it quickly, realising she had just been about to say, Oh, yes! As in, oh yes, you were really fat, weren't you? Huge!

'Ah,' she managed to change it to, 'well, I thought you looked different, I just didn't remember that detail. When did you transform into the, er, real you?'

'When did I lose four stone, you mean?' he said laughing happily at his own expense. 'In my gap year. I went to Nepal and got the most marvellous case of dysentery. I've never looked back.'

Now Hannah laughed too, all her grumpiness forgotten.

'Well, maybe it was good karma for being nice to me when we were kids. I used to find your brothers terrifying.'

'They were,' he said. 'In fact they still are. Why do you think I lived in New York for so long?'

'That bad, eh?' she said.

Dominic nodded. 'Well, they've mellowed a bit with age, but I try not to see too much of them, old wounds and all that, but I'm glad you say I was nice to you, because you were always very nice to me. Made me feel I might have some qualities beyond the spare tyres my brothers so loved to punch me in.'

'Oh, good,' said Hannah. 'I'm happy to hear it went both ways. Do you remember that time we hid from them in the cupboard under the stairs, playing Monopoly?'

Dominic laughed heartily.

'Yes, I do. That was hilarious. I think you were winning, weren't you, when they found us?'

'Does anyone ever win at Monopoly?' said Hannah.

'Maybe we should have another game in there and decide it once and for all,' said Dominic.

'I think that's something I'll let you do with Hector,' said Hannah, feeling that the extent of her jolly chumminess had now been reached. He didn't seem to notice, although his expression had got more serious, Hannah noticed.

'I'm really sorry about your father,' he said, putting a hand on her shoulder, 'it must have been a terrible shock.'

'Oh, thanks,' said Hannah, 'it has been pretty grisly.'

'He was an amazing chap, your dad,' said Dominic. 'Such a dude. I always thought he was the kind of man I'd like to grow up to be.'

Hannah looked at him, quite amazed. She always presumed everyone thought of her dad as an embarrassment.

'That's so kind,' she said, 'I'm really touched.'

'He was so well dressed and so much cooler than all the other dads. He always wore those really great brown suede boots; I've got some similar myself now. I saw them in a shop and I remembered his. And those knitted silk ties, like Michael Caine used to wear. Loved all that. He gave me a cigar once, when I was about eleven, a big Cuban one in one of those metal tubes. I kept it for years, hidden in my sock drawer.'

Hannah found herself smiling. It was so lovely to hear someone who could remember him like that. And giving a cigar to the fat boy was just the kind of thing she could imagine Charlie doing. She felt a bit teary for a moment, but blinked it away.

'Those were the days, eh?' he said, pushing his hands deep into the pockets of his chinos and rocking back on his heels. 'And it's funny really, all that shared history and here we are again years later back at Anthea's house. You've lived in Sydney and London, I've lived in London, Paris and New York, and now we're both back in this funny little corner of East Sussex. Full circle.'

Hannah nodded. She didn't know about Paris. That was impressive.

'Yes, it is funny when you put it like that and Anthea must love having you here. She talks about you a lot. How long are you staying?'

'A few months,' he said, 'possibly longer.'

Hannah made a surprised face, not sure what to say, as the first thing that occurred to her was: Have you been thrown out of your job too, then? But he answered her question without her having to ask it.

'I'm on "gardening leave",' he said. 'The investment bank I worked for decided I was superfluous to their needs and sent me packing with handsome compensation, but on the condition I don't work for anyone else in the sector for twelve months.'

'Ah,' said Hannah, 'that's quite a familiar story. I'll tell you about it some time. So what are you going to do with your year of freedom? Travel the world? Paint? Go to an ashram?'

Dominic snorted.

'I'm going to make money, of course. It's the only thing I know how to do.'

'Oh, do tell,' said Hannah, rather taken aback at his frankness on one of her family's taboo subjects; maybe the time in New York had brushed off on him after all. 'Me and my husband don't seem to be so good at that.'

'Ah, yes,' said Dominic, slightly too quickly, 'Anthea said you're married to a male model, is that right?'

'No,' she snapped, feeling instantly defensive. She hated Matt being defined as a model as much as he did. And the term 'male model' was so awful, it made him sound like such a himbo. 'Well, he has done some modelling, but he's really a topliner – he writes the lyrics for songs.'

'Gosh,' said Dominic, looking impressed, but with one eyebrow raised rather archly, 'so he's handsome and talented. Would I know any of his work?'

Hannah groaned inwardly. This was a question she had come to dread, as the answer was a definitive NO. Not unless you avidly followed obscure bands no-one had ever heard of, based in the less fashionable parts of east London.

'Probably not,' she said, 'he's collaborated on a lot of different things, just nothing that you'd know, but he's working on a really exciting project at the moment. He's in Sydney, because his mother's been very ill and his long-term writing partner is based back there now. They're doing an album with a young singer who's already had a number one and the new single they've written will be out soon.'

'Yes,' Dominic broke in, 'Hector was saying his father had been away a very long time, possibly forever – his words – how's that been for you?'

Absolutely horrendously crap, thought Hannah, you've got no idea; but she kept quiet, feeling Dominic was getting a little too personal again. She'd just ignore that one.

'Anyway,' she said, hurriedly, 'you haven't told me how you're going to make more money, staying in this back water.'

'Oh, I'm buying a few properties to renovate and then I'll sell them on, or rent them out. Depends what the market's doing.'

He shrugged like it was no more serious than the game of Monopoly they'd played under the stairs thirty years before.

'Great,' said Hannah, wondering what he'd think if he knew she didn't own so much as one flat, let alone "a few properties" and really not wanting to know the answer. It really was time to break this up.

'Well,' she said, knowing she sounded exactly like her mother when she was about to swiftly, but charmingly, exit a situation, 'that all sounds great and if you're going to be here a while, we'll have plenty of time to catch up properly. I better go in now and see what I can do for Anthea.'

And she scarpered.

# Chapter Forty-four

Ali was laughing so much she had to lean against the mulberry tree to catch her breath. Dominic was being so funny and naughty; she hadn't expected that. Not only was he the ideal Pompom poster boy, he cracked her up laughing too.

To be fair she had been close to hysteria to start off with, the whole scenario was so perfectly what she'd imagined and she thought she looked spot on for it in the floral vintage dress she'd borrowed from Hannah, although it was a shame she hadn't actually had the white lace gloves and parasol as well, as they would have been the finishing touches.

Mind you, she'd had to abandon the straw hat pretty early on, because it kept catching in the low-hanging branches of the mulberry tree their serving table was set up under. Plus the wide brim made it hard for her to get close enough to Dominic to hear the hilarious things he was muttering – and getting close to Dominic was the whole point of the exercise for Ali.

In that over-excited state, she did know that even the most mildly amusing remark would probably have set her off, but the things he was saying about the people who came up for their tea were so wicked it was just cracking her up. It was the way he managed to say them under his breath while simultaneously charming the punters with his Pompom smile that was so naughty.

'Do you think I should offer them some tea made with the tears of virgins?' he whispered after one lady was surprised they couldn't offer her any Lady Grey and another expected Lapsang. 'And brewed in the Holy Grail? Using the Turin Shroud as a strainer . . .'

Every single person who came up seemed to have a different demand. I like it good and strong, thank you. Oh, very weak please. Have you got any skim milk? Soya milk? Goats' milk? Do you have any green tea? Herb tea? Darjeeling? Assam? Decaffeinated? It got to the point where Ali wanted to hug every customer who just smiled at her and said, Lovely, thank you, when she handed them a cup of plain English breakfast teabag tea.

Then there were the ones who wanted the milk in first and the ones who wanted it in second. Ali had started off putting milk in all the cups that were out, to save time, but Dominic had tactfully suggested that might not be a good plan, explaining there was a distinct difference between the taste of tea which had the milk in first, or second, and Brits were very thingy about it.

Ali looked at him in disbelief.

'You're joking, right? You Poms are freaks about tea. It's just milk and tea – how can tea and milk be different?'

Dominic shrugged.

'I don't know, it just is.'

'Which do you like?'

'Oh, milk second,' said Dominic, as though it were a stupid question.

'I'm going to try it,' said Ali and she poured some tea into a cup, then added milk. She took a mouthful and swallowed. 'Right, that's definitely tea, with milk.'

Then she poured some milk into a cup, followed by the tea and drank some. Her eyes opened wide and she turned to look at Dominic.

'It does taste different,' she said, amazed.

'I told you.'

'It's sort of creamier if you have the milk in first.'

'Yes,' said Dominic, 'that's exactly why I prefer it the other way, you want the tea to dominate, not the milk.'

Ali hoped she hadn't sighed too obviously. So he had a gourmet palate too.

After that there was a major rush as what seemed like hundreds of people arrived in the garden at once and for a while it was all they could do to keep up with the constant stream of people wanting tea and refills. Then along came the lady who really set Ali off.

'Don't you have any coffee?' she asked crossly, looking at all the pretty tea cups and saucers laid out on the table as though they were something quite nasty.

'No, just tea today,' said Ali as brightly as she could, thinking, just tea, at a cream TEA, are you NORMAL?

'I don't drink tea,' said the woman, as though Ali had insulted her by even suggesting it. 'I'll have some plain hot water.'

'I'm afraid we don't have any of that,' said Ali, feeling the giggles starting to rise in her like a belch you can't keep down, 'they just bring us out the pots of tea and we serve it . . . There's some squash in the jugs there, if you'd like some of that.'

'I don't drink squash,' she replied, now looking really outraged. 'So I've paid five pounds and I won't even be able to have a drink!'

'I'll go and get you a glass of water, if you like,' said Ali, 'and there are lovely scones with clotted cream and home-made jam at the next table.'

'I don't eat cream,' said the woman.

Ali turned away quickly to stop herself screaming with laughter and immediately caught Dominic's eye. He had clearly heard the whole exchange and looked quite delighted by it.

'Oh dear,' he said, in his most grandiloquent Pompom tones, 'so you don't drink tea and you don't eat cream and you've found yourself at a charity cream tea . . . Life's a bitch sometimes, isn't it?'

He was looking at her so innocently – and so bloody handsomely – she clearly couldn't tell if he was being rude or not, even though the particular emphasis he had put on the words 'cream' and 'tea' must have resonated with her. He'd rolled the 'r' in cream quite luxuriantly. Ali couldn't hold it any longer, she ran round to the back of the mulberry tree and bent double laughing. She had tears running down her face.

After a couple of minutes, she peeped round the corner of the tree trunk to check if Mrs Grumpy had gone, to see Dominic grinning at her and gesturing for her to come back.

'It's all right, Ali, you can come out now, she's gone to ask if they've got any scone-free scones. I don't eat scones,' he said, in such a good impression of her snippy voice, it set Ali off again.

Anthea made sure Ali sat next to Dominic at the post-cream tea supper. She'd been delighted to see them giggling together over the teapots earlier and they seemed to be getting on just as well now, which was a very good sign. She poured more wine into both their glasses at every opportunity.

He was about twenty years older than her, which might have been a problem, but Anthea could see by the way Ali looked at him that she was already smitten and she just hoped it was working the other way too. It was hard to tell with Dominic, as he was gregarious by nature and got on with most people, so it didn't necessarily mean he found her attractive in a romantic sense. She'd have to work at throwing them together a bit more. Get it meshed in before he imported one of his frightful American waif women.

That was when she had a brilliant idea. As far as she knew, Ali didn't have a job – so she could be Dominic's assistant on his renovation projects. He'd need someone to help him with all the clerical stuff and to make notes while he went round the sites, that kind of thing.

His Girl Friday, she thought, smiling to herself as she spooned in another mouthful of trifle. Ali was scooping all the sherry-soaked sponge out of her bowl and plonking it on Dominic's, while he picked the raspberries out of his and dumped them in hers. They were like a pair of naughty children together – that had to be a good sign, surely?

She'd have to ask Hannah if she could spare her first, though. That girl was looking so washed out and she hadn't stayed on for the thank you supper, although Anthea had made it an early start especially so the kids could join in. In the end Hannah had taken Nancy home to bed with her, with Ali winning even more points by volunteering to take Hector home later.

And of course Hector wanted to stay at the dinner for the same reason Ali was enjoying it so much – he was besotted with Dominic too. He was missing his father terribly and with Charlie gone, Anthea could see he was desperate for some adult male company, poor little mite.

She was really starting to think it was time Matt came home to look after his wife and family. She would have liked to speak to Marguerite about it, but she was looking even thinner and more washed out than her daughter and had made her excuses and left after the main course.

There was no doubt about it, Anthea decided, after she had bid all her guests farewell – Dominic was carrying the sleeping Hector home for Ali, an excellent outcome – and was padding back to the kitchen to load the dishwasher. Somebody needed to take Marguerite and Hannah in hand before they faded away entirely.

# Chapter Forty-five

Matt was running up the steps by the Tamarama surf lifesaving club-house, listening with great satisfaction to the album tracks they'd finished and marvelling, as he did every day, at the magnificence of the ocean breaking on to the rocks below.

'Here and There' had just finished and he stopped for a moment to watch the waves crashing and listen to 'Least Said'. He really liked that one. The regretful theme of the lyrics really worked in Abel's gravelly voice.

> Least said, soonest mended
> This is not what I intended
> A moment's weakness
> A lifetime's loss
> The smallest pleasure
> At the biggest cost . . .

He didn't like what it reminded him of, but putting his feelings about that stupid incident down in lyrics had helped to work it out of his system. He was sure now he'd done the right thing by not saying anything.

The track ended and the next one starting was 'Active Service', another cracker, but he'd run to that one. It had a faster tempo and he was getting cold standing there.

Now late July, the early evening wind lashing his face was pretty brisk and as he pulled his cotton scarf up higher around his neck, he decided he'd have his run in the middle of the day from then on, when it was warmer. But the thought nearly stopped him in his tracks. What exactly did 'from then on' mean? How much longer was he planning to stay in Sydney?

Counting back, he'd been there six weeks now. With Nancy not much over two, that was a horrendously large proportion of her life to miss out on. What kind of a father was he? It was even quite a big chunk of Hector's life. Coming up towards six, the little fella had been alive for something like 300 weeks and Matt had been away for six of them. What percentage was that? It was certainly way too much.

But Skype really did help. He'd started reading them a bedtime story every night – early morning for him – with them cuddled up on Hannah's knee and him holding the books up to show them the pictures.

For laughs and to try and make it seem more like the real thing, he'd break off from reading and give Hannah stage directions: 'Now kiss Nancy's head, please, Hanns, right on the top there, good, and now the cheek . . .' and 'Please squeeze Heccie's left buttock, he's wriggling too much . . .'

He'd found some great Aussie kids' books, which they loved, and they all particularly liked one called *The Crazy Quokka*. It had a little song in it with the music written out at the back and one morning Pete had played along on his piano – with a few flourishes of his own for fun – as they'd all sung it. That had been really fun.

'Is this the new single, Daddy?' Hector had asked at the end and Pete had fallen off his piano stool laughing.

'Good idea,' he shouted out, 'the lyrics are much better than your father's . . . THE CRAZY QUOKKA WAS A BUSH PUNK ROCKER, HIS FRIEND, GOANNA, WAS HOT ON THE PIANNA!'

With all that carry-on Matt did feel far more connected with his family than he would have if it had just been horrible hot-ear phone calls with an irritating delay, like it used to be, but at the same time, being able to see their beautiful little faces and their soft rounded limbs made missing that physical touch almost unbearable. He'd started going to sleep hugging a pillow. He knew it was pathetic, but it was the only way he could stand it. Pete had caught him at it one time and offered to buy him a teddy. It wasn't such a bad idea.

But while he was physically lonely at night, he wasn't remotely tempted to go out looking for any female company to fill the gap. Not for a millisecond.

And he was hoping that one of the good outcomes of this weird exile would be to enable him to put his guilt about that moment of drunken weakness behind him completely, so he could be normal with Hannah again. Really, the worst part of the whole sordid episode was the way his guilt had made it difficult for him to be natural with her. She'd thought he was angry with her, when really he was furious with himself. What a fuck-up guilt was.

He'd just got up alongside the Icebergs when his phone rang. It was Pete.

'Where are you when I need you, you crazy health freak?' he was shouting.

'Just passed the 'Bergs, I'll be home in less than five,' said Matt. 'Wassup?'

'I'll tell you when you get here, Kunta Kinte, so hurry up!'

'Is it something good?' asked Matt, feeling a bit freaked out by Pete's overexcitement, but he'd already hung up.

Taking out his earbuds and stuffing the phone deep into his pocket, Matt sprinted up the hill as fast as he could and arrived at the unit, puffing, with sweat pouring off him. Pete met him at the door, hopping from foot to foot with excitement.

'So tell me!' said Matt, panting like a dog.

'Oooooh,' said Pete, 'I'm too excited!'

Matt lifted his hands as if he was about to throttle him.

'OK,' said Pete, coming closer to Matt and putting his hands on his shoulders and then reeling away again. 'God, you stink.'

'Pete, just tell me,' said Matt in a low, threatening voice.

'Now where was I?' said Pete, putting a dainty finger on his stubbly chin. 'Oh, yes, do you remember that little song we wrote together? What was it called now? 'Here and There', that's the one.'

'Yes,' said Matt, cautiously. 'I was just listening to it.'

'It's the number one download in Japan!' said Pete, jumping up and down again and then capering around the room like a crazy man. He ran out to the balcony. 'We're NUMBER ONE, people!' he yelled out, 'NUMBER BLOODY ONE!'

Matt was too stunned to speak for a moment.

'But it hasn't come out yet,' he said eventually, finding the news impossible to digest.

Pete bounced back into the room and came over to him.

'The YouTube data was so strong they released it to download there right away as a test market, without telling us, and it's been such a hit – there's even demand for physical copies, can you believe it? – they're going to release it here next week. It's going out to all the DJs today.'

He screwed up his face and danced up and down on the spot like a hobgoblin.

'We're big in Japan,' said Matt, as it finally sank in.

'Yep,' said Pete, 'and here's the best bit – if it works here as well as it has there, they'll release it in the UK, Europe and the States too. We're going global, buddy!'

Matt had tears in his eyes. They'd done it, they'd finally done it. All those years of working together, not giving up despite the constant knockbacks, nearly getting there and then having it fall apart at the last moment. All the weeks away from his family and all the terrible months trapped in that suffocating village were worth it, because 'Here and There', the lyrics he'd written on that miserable cold dark day in his hobbit hole were now part of a number one track.

He was a proper songwriter at last. And he was going to make some proper money. He might not have been a very good hands-on dad the last few weeks, but he was finally going to be a decent provider for his family. That meant more to Matt than he would have admitted to anyone.

'Yay!' he roared, releasing the disappointments and frustrations of the past twenty years in one rebel yell, then he ran out to the balcony. 'We're big in Japan! Suck it up, Bondi!' he shouted. 'Shit, yeah!'

Then he ran back in and wrapped his sweaty arms round Pete and they danced around the room together.

'We made it! We made it! We finally fuckin' made it!' Matt chanted and Pete joined in, and then after they'd yelled it together a few times, he rushed over to the piano and started hammering out some chords in time to the rhythm of the words. Very quickly they formed into a distinctive melody.

'We made it! We made it! We finally fuckin' made it!' they both kept chanting and then Pete stopped and Matt took over, singing it to the tune Pete had bashed out.

'We made it up, we made it win – and now the money's pouring in,' he sang, with Pete adding extra bits to the melody as he went, to scan with the words, 'We made it up, we lived it large, we left the gutter, we joined the stars . . .' sang Matt.

'Loving it,' said Pete, switching on the computer that sat on top of the piano, while playing the riff over and over again, until Matt felt his heart was beating in tune with it.

'Sing it again,' said Pete, still playing with his left hand, while pressing keys on the computer with his right, until a drum beat kicked in, then a bass line. With both hands back on the keyboard, he bashed out the main theme again and when that started playing back through the speakers, he added some more complex variations over the top.

'We made it! We made it! We finally fuckin' made it!' Matt continued, 'We kept it true, just me and you, and finally we've seen it through.'

'OK,' said Pete, 'now the middle eight.'

He played some ascending chords, thought better of it and changed to a rising arpeggio, switching back to fast chord changes at the top. He looked over at Matt, who was nodding, clicking his fingers, feeling it with his whole body.

'Never doubting, true believers, against all odds, the thieves, deceivers,' sang Matt, to the ascending notes.

Pete nodded encouragingly. 'Keep going, keep going,' he said, 'it's happening.'

He played the sequence again and Matt closed his eyes, not thinking, just being, letting it flow into him and right out again through his mouth.

'The ones who said we'd never win, we pushed them out, don't let them in. Just you and me, right to the end. A man's best friend – is his friend.'

Pete's head snapped round to look at Matt and he grinned at him, punching the air.

'Too fucking right,' he said, breaking into a flourish of notes Liberace would have been impressed with, '"Man's Best Friend" – great title. Right, OK, from the top, let's blow it out.'

He fiddled around on the computer and the song started up again from its rough beginnings. He turned up the volume and the two of them sang it through, with Matt adding a few more verses on the same theme and Pete refining the music, ending with a thunderous Harlem roll. Then he clapped his hands together.

'Job done,' he said, beaming with delight, 'let's play it back. Yee haw!'

Matt threw himself down on one of the sofas by the window and Pete cued up the track, then came over, laying himself flat along the other one, staring up at the ceiling, his forefingers in a steeple on his chest. They listened, nodding along, smiles spreading across both their faces. When it finished, they were both shaking their heads in happy amazement.

'I love it,' said Matt.

'So do I,' said Pete, 'I can't wait to record it properly. We'll have to do two versions, of course, like Silo Green, the original and then one where we sing "We finally flipping made it" or something like that, for the radio.'

Matt nodded.

'But mate,' continued Pete, after a moment, 'while I've been lying here I've had a really stupendously great idea.'

Matt raised an eyebrow.

'I want you to sing it for the release,' said Pete.

'Me?' said Matt.

'Yeah,' said Pete, 'this is a song for a man, not a kid. It's a song about not giving up, keeping the faith – our story – and it needs a grown-up to sing it. You're a grown-up and you've got quite a good voice.'

'Really?' said Matt. 'How come you've never mentioned that before – at any time in, now, let me see – the last twenty years?'

'Didn't want you to get up yourself,' said Pete.

'Fair enough,' said Matt, 'but you're not serious about this, are you?'

'Damn well am,' said Pete. He sat up and leaned over the coffee table towards Matt. 'Think about it, with your reasonably acceptable singing voice . . .'

Matt gave him the finger and he flicked a V sign back.

'. . . a great song, my amazing production – and your ridiculous looks, it's a perfect package. We'll leave it now, but tomorrow I want to lay the song down properly and then I'll film you singing it – one take, in arty black and white, tight T-shirt ha ha ha – and we'll run the track over the top and present it to the record company as a video.'

'Aren't I a bit old to be a pop star?' said Matt. 'Introducing, with his back-up band, The Zimmer Frames – Middle-Aged Pop Dad.'

'I've got a two-word answer to that,' said Pete. 'Take That.'

Matt laughed, but he still wasn't sure if Pete was really serious. He lay back for a moment, thinking. It was true he'd always sung his best lyrics out. Once Pete had the basic melody going, he'd let the words flow by singing along to the tune, that's how it had always worked for him – and one of the many reasons he'd found it so impossible to work on his own in the cottage. And if Pete really thought his voice was OK – and he had no reason to sabotage his own success – then why not?

Then Matt had an inspiration of his own.

'Hey, Pete,' he said, sitting up, 'I've had an even better idea. We've written the song together, it's about us – let's sing it together. Or at least, I can sing it while you play the piano and then you can join in on the chorus. It's a song about friendship between men – so it should be sung by two men.'

Pete thought for a moment.

'You don't think my face would break the camera?' he said.

'Don't be stupid,' said Matt, 'you may not be in demand to model gentleman's golfing attire – I'm doing a two-day catalogue shoot for that next week, by the way – but your success with the ladies speaks for itself. Women like dirty old wizened dudes like you. Hannah says you've got a "slept-in" face.'

'Does she?' said Pete, looking delighted. 'Cool. I'm thrilled Hannah likes anything about me.'

'Well, she didn't say she liked it, she just said it looked "slept in".'

'Fuck you very much,' said Pete, throwing a cushion at him, 'but I think you might be on to something; we'll do it both ways and see what works best – and I've just thought of something else. If we sing it ourselves, we'll get more money – the publishing and the performance royalties. Sweet. For our number one in Japan, we're only getting the publishing, which is nice, but with free downloads, it's not the safe income it used to be, so it has to better to have a bigger share of what does come in.'

'Good point,' said Matt, his eyes opening wider as the possibilities of being the performers as well as the songwriters sank in.

'And that's not all,' said Pete, sitting up and leaning over towards Matt. 'If it's a hit and we do an album . . . and if that's a hit . . .' he paused, grinning at Matt, like a madman '. . . we can tour!'

Matt sat up too.

'Ah, mate,' he said, too excited to say anything more intelligent.

'Merchandise,' said Pete, nodding. Matt nodded back.

'The philosopher's stone of the modern music industry,' said Matt, regaining his faculties.

'Yep,' said Pete. 'Your face on mouse mats.'

'Your arse on mouse mats,' said Matt and Pete stood up and wiggled his backside at him.

'Whatever they want, baby,' he said.

Matt sat back on the sofa, his arms behind his head, his thoughts racing. Then he leaned forward again, picking Pete's phone up from the table to check the time. 'Dammit, I really want to ring Hannah to tell her the news about Japan, but it's still too early.'

Pete jumped to his feet.

'Go and have a shower, stinky malinky,' he said. 'You can call her from the bar . . .'

# Chapter Forty-six

It was Ali who finally got Marguerite to admit what was going on. They were in her study so Ali could help her find something on the internet that she'd read about in one of her academic journals. Something to do with using computer modelling to create moulds for the missing pieces to repair ancient ceramics.

'I don't like the idea of it all,' she told Ali, sitting next to her at the desk, 'I can't imagine that the finished repair could have the genuine handmade quality that sits authentically with the original piece, but I must look and understand what they're doing. Someone will only ask me about it and I'll feel like a foolish old woman if I can't give them a considered and informed reply.'

Ali glanced sideways at her as Google loaded. No-one could ever call Marguerite foolish, she had rigorous braininess emanating off her, but as for the old part – she had certainly aged pretty horrendously since Charlie had died. She was so thin and her skin seemed to be sagging on her face. It was awful to see, when she'd been such a handsome woman.

Ali had been so concerned about the state of her she'd spoken to Hannah about it, suggesting she should take her mother to the doctor, but Hannah had just brushed her off, saying her mother would never tolerate any questions about her health, so it was pointless stressing her out any more by asking.

Unbelievable! How could she not talk to her own mum about something so important? What was family for, if not to look after each other?

But then Hannah wasn't looking exactly blooming with life force herself these days. Maybe it was all too close to home.

Jeez, they were a stitched-up lot, these Poms, but she didn't think Dominic – sigh, swoon, pitter patter, lust, faint – was as bad as Hannah and her mum in that way. Anthea was certainly much more open about things, saying what she actually thought, so probably their whole family was different, plus living in New York so long would have made him a bit more comfortable with talking about his feelings. Americans never stopped talking about them.

Not that he'd talked about any particular feelings he had in relation to her, or anything encouraging like that yet, but working with him was totally great. They were spending loads of time together and having such a laugh. The more Ali saw of him, the more she was convinced that Dominic was the man she could trust not to be disgusted by her scars. And since she'd met him she'd been a lot more conscientious about putting the healing oil on three times every day, and they did seem to be fading a bit.

Forcing her attention back to the matter in hand she saw that the site Marguerite wanted to see had loaded, so Ali stood up to let her look at it.

'I won't leave yet,' she said, 'in case you need me to find anything else online for you. I'll make us some tea, OK?'

'Oh, that would be lovely,' said Marguerite, her ridiculously bright tone of voice so at odds with her ravaged face that something suddenly snapped in Ali. It was like watching a puppet show which had the wrong voice for the character and she couldn't stand it any longer.

She paused for a moment by the door and then walked resolutely back to the desk and sat down next to Marguerite, who turned to look at her in surprise, her delicate eyebrows arched. When Ali took one of her hands and held it in hers, they nearly disappeared into her hairline.

'What's going on, Marguerite?' said Ali, firmly. 'You've got to tell somebody. It's eating you alive. What is it?'

Marguerite's mouth opened and closed a couple of times, like a gasping fish. She was clearly trying to frame one of her perfect 1950s hostess replies and then right on cue, her hips began to lift her up from the chair. But Ali was ready for her escapologist routine, she'd seen her do it so many times – and Hannah, for that matter – and was ready for her. She put a hand on her right shoulder and pushed her gently but decisively back down on to the seat.

'No, Marguerite,' she said, shaking her head, 'don't try and run away this time. You've got to tell me what's wrong. Hannah won't ask you, she's too afraid of upsetting you, but I think you'll feel much better if you tell someone. Whatever's going on, Marguerite, you've got to trust us to help you deal with it. Share the load. We want to help you. We love you.'

Marguerite blinked at these appalling words. It was her worst nightmare, this type of personal stuff from a virtual stranger, like something from a ghastly film. She licked her lips. Her mouth had gone so dry she couldn't have said anything even if she'd wanted to and although the urge to flee the room was overwhelming, she knew she didn't have the physical strength. The lightest touch of Ali's hand, still on her shoulder, was enough to keep her pinned there.

'Come on,' said Ali, as though she were talking to a frightened child. 'It won't hurt. Are you ill? Is that it?'

Marguerite shook her head, then from somewhere very deep inside, somewhere she hadn't even known was there, she found a voice.

'It's the house,' she said so quietly, Ali had to lean in close to hear her, 'I'm going to lose the house.'

Ali sat back to take in this revelation and to see if Marguerite would say anything else about it. She didn't, so Ali knew she'd have to carry on dragging it out of her.

'How come?' she asked, very gently. 'Is there a problem with Charlie's will?'

Marguerite nodded and let out a massive sigh. She had never felt so humiliated in her life, but at the same time, she could feel a tiny sense of relief growing inside her, like a dried flower unfurling in a cup of China tea. Already, this terrifying problem which had made it impossible for her to sleep for weeks wasn't sitting quite so heavily on her now she'd told Ali about it. It was rather surprising.

'What's the exact nature of the problem?' probed Ali. 'Is it mortgaged?'

'The house is all bound up in a family trust,' said Marguerite, finding a stronger voice, 'and I did always know that. Charlie's father inherited it from the trust when his father died and then it came to him, but what I didn't understand was that the terms of the trust were really antiquated, with the property automatically passing to the closest living male relative, with no clause for me even to have the right to carry on living in it. Looking back, I realise that while Charlie inherited it on his father's death, he allowed his mother to carry on living here, it wasn't even in question. My problem is that I don't have a son.'

'Holy shit,' said Ali, 'no wonder you've been looking so sick with worry. That's horrendous. What does your lawyer say about it?'

Marguerite looked absolutely anguished at this question, but after taking a deep breath and lifting her chin, managed to answer.

'He says there's nothing we can do. Charlie could probably have changed it while he was alive – and he did speak to our solicitor and the trustees about it, apparently – but he never actually did it. Now he's gone, it's too late.'

Ali exhaled loudly and sat back in her seat. No wonder the poor old girl looked like she was about to cark it; this was a horrendous thing to happen to a woman who'd just been widowed. Especially after what she'd had to deal with while Hannah's dad was still alive, from what she'd heard.

'What about money?' she asked. 'Is that all tied up in the same trust?'

Marguerite nodded, looking absolutely defeated.

'I have a little money of my own, from my parents and my work, but not very much.' she said. 'Enough to live on, but not enough to buy another house. Not even a flat.'

She couldn't believe she was telling this girl she hardly knew the most private details of her finances. Money was a shameful subject, never to be discussed. And problems of any kind were to be dealt with discreetly, or endured without telling anyone. It was such a weakness ever to mention them. Yet, she had to admit that despite all that, she was glad Ali had pushed her to do it. She was mortified, horrified, embarrassed, but also very relieved.

Ali thought for a moment.

'And Hannah doesn't know any of this?' she said eventually.

'Oh, no,' said Marguerite, her hips rising up from the seat again, but she realised and sat herself down again before Ali had to intervene, 'I couldn't possibly worry her with it. She's got enough to deal with herself with Matt being away so long and all that stress she had with her job and now trying to work from home and look after the children on her own – well, you've been the most marvellous help, but . . .'

'Marguerite,' said Ali, interrupting her, 'you have to tell her. Her own mother is about to be thrown out of her childhood home. She needs to know. And there's something else you haven't told me – if you and Hannah can't inherit the house, who does get it?'

Marguerite paused before answering. This was almost the worst part of it.

'Charlie's oldest living male relative – some second cousin I've never even heard of,' she said flatly. 'He lives in Canada.'

'Does he know the full circumstances?' said Ali, incredulous that something like this could happen in the twenty-first century. 'Does he know his second cousin's widow will be made homeless if he takes possession of the house?'

'I don't really know,' said Marguerite, vaguely, not meeting Ali's eye.

Ali wanted to interrogate her further, to find out what she meant by that: how much she actually knew, what she'd done about the situation, but Marguerite already looked exhausted. It must have been a terrible strain for her to tell someone what was going on, but Ali had one more thing she had to do before she could let up.

'I'm so glad you've told me,' she said. 'I knew something bad was going on for you, but Marguerite – you've got to tell Hannah. Today. Now.'

Marguerite didn't need to say anything; what she thought about that idea was obvious – she was appalled at the prospect.

'You have to,' urged Ali. 'She's so worried about you and not knowing what's wrong is adding much more to her stress load than knowing the truth will, however awful it is. Once she knows what's going on, she'll be able to help you do something about it and although this is horrific, it would have been worse if it had been some dreadful illness, which was what I was worried about.'

Marguerite looked down and sighed. She dreaded telling Hannah, giving her yet another reason to feel let down by her father, but she knew Ali was right. In a way it had been selfish of her not to talk about it before.

Apart from anything else, it was Hannah's inheritance too. Presumably she'd been expecting to come into the house and her father's estate one day, so it was better she knew that wasn't going to happen.

Oh, damn Charlie! How he had let them all down! Not just her, but Hannah and the grandchildren too. How could he have done that to his darling Hector? One last shameful thing he'd left his family to deal with, that was his legacy to them.

'You're right,' she said to Ali. 'I will tell her today. I should have told her before, I see that now. It's not just my problem, it affects all of them.'

'That's true,' said Ali, 'but no matter what it was, it still wouldn't have been just your problem. We're all in this together, Marguerite. We're a team, we're family.'

This was the most basic bedrock of life for Ali, she understood that now. She'd always thought her family's connectedness – amplified as it was by the two sisters marrying the two brothers – was too closely bound, but seeing these strange glacial English women, all deep-frozen in their own private miseries, she realised her tight-knit family community was actually like a big protective cotton wool wrapper around them all.

'I'll tell you what we'll do,' said Ali, anxious to maintain the momentum. 'I'll ring Hannah now and tell her that you've got something important to tell her, but I'll stress you're not ill. Then we'll walk over there together with the dogs and you can sit at her kitchen table and tell her what you've told me, while I take Nancy over to visit Anthea's tortoises, OK?'

'OK,' said Marguerite, 'and Ali . . .' she reached out a cool bony hand to squeeze Ali's, looking intently into her eyes, 'thank you so much. You've done me a great favour.'

# Chapter Forty-seven

Hannah was sitting in the pub, sipping a glass of really nasty white wine and eating cheese and onion crisps. They were horrible, but it had been that or prawn cocktail and she hadn't had any lunch. And she needed a distraction.

She didn't feel exactly comfortable in the White Hart – too many bad associations with her father – but at the same time it was good to be somewhere different, away from the cottage and its proximity to her mother's house and all the anxiety that now triggered. So when she'd asked Dominic if they could have a discreet chat and he'd suggested the pub as a venue, she hadn't objected.

She hadn't found a way to bring up what she really wanted to talk to him about yet, so they'd been making chit chat, reminiscing about the old days at Anthea's parties and his awful brothers. She was happy to keep it light for a while.

When he got to the bottom of his pint – she still had a lot of wine to go – he nipped off to the loo. Not wanting another crisp, Hannah picked up her phone and tapped on the icon for Cut the Rope, Hector's favourite game. It immediately started to play some terrible music very loudly and she was fumbling to get rid of it, when someone appeared at her side.

She looked up to see Kelli, the glammed-up mum from the school, perched on the edge of the table next to her. She was laughing.

'Cut the Rope, eh, Hannah? What level are you at?'

'Oh, hi, Kelli,' said Hannah, embarrassed, 'I haven't a clue how to play it. It's Hector's favourite . . . I didn't know you were in here.'

'That's all right,' she said. 'I'm used to being the wallpaper in this place.'

Hannah cringed. She must have walked right past her – that wouldn't help her popularity at the school gate – but Kelli was smiling.

'Just kidding, I was in the kitchen. I spotted you when I came out, but you were deep in conversation and I didn't like to butt in.'

Hannah smiled back at her, relieved, and wondering as she always did why Kelli overdid the make-up so much. She was a very attractive woman, with a pretty face and a good figure, she didn't need all the slap. She'd be a great subject for a 'Less Is More' beauty makeover story if Hannah could place it somewhere. Might boost her school-gate status too if she could make that happen.

'I don't think I've ever seen you in here before,' Kelli was saying. 'Your husband used to come in quite a lot, but I haven't seen him for ages.'

'He's in Australia,' said Hannah. 'His mum was really ill and he had to rush out there to see her.'

'He's been gone a long time, hasn't he?' said Kelli.

Hannah immediately felt uncomfortable, because yes, Matt had been gone an embarrassingly long time now. Getting on for two months. She knew it was cool, but in what had become a bit of a mantra for her she mentally ran through the reasons for his absence: his mum, his work, the album, the single, the number one in Japan . . . But while she knew it was all part of a bigger picture, she was painfully aware how it might look to others.

'Yes,' she said brightly, fully aware she was channelling her mother, 'he's got some amazing work on there, so he has to stay on a bit longer.'

'What does he do exactly?' asked Kelli. 'Isn't he a model, or something?'

For once, Hannah was proud to answer.

'No, he's a songwriter. He's been working on an album with a young singer who's just had a big hit and the new single is coming out in Australia any day now. It's number one in Japan already.'

'Wow,' said Kelli, 'that is exciting. Congrats. I was beginning to think you two might have split up, not seeing him in here . . . It's not easy having them away a long time is it? My kids' dad is in the army.'

'Ooh, that is tough,' said Hannah, feeling an immediate sense of solidarity with her. 'Where is your husband?'

'Afghanistan,' said Kelli, pulling a face, 'but he's not my husband any more actually. I couldn't stand him being away for months at a time and then when he did come home on leave he was all weird, not the man I married. He still sees the kids when he's home and it's fine between us, but we're not together as a couple. I couldn't hack it. If I'm going to be tied down, I want a bloke who's around, you know what I mean?'

Hannah nodded.

'Yes, it does rather seem the point of it,' she said.

'I'd go mad with boredom if my mum didn't mind the kids so I can work in here,' said Kelli. 'It's my only bit of excitement.'

She laughed and Hannah smiled at her.

'Anyway, better get back to my post,' said Kelli. 'See you at school.'

She walked off and Hannah had another horrible crisp, reminding herself how lucky she was Matt was just tooling around in Sydney and not risking his life in a warzone, although she hadn't liked hearing that Kelli had assumed they'd split up.

Presumably that's what everyone at the school thought. Hannah sighed; she knew she needed to make an effort to get to know the other mothers there better, but she just couldn't take that on at the moment, not with everything else she had going on.

To take her mind off all that, she took another sip of wine and must have pulled an involuntary revolted face because Dominic arrived back at the table just at that moment and burst out laughing.

'That bad, is it?' he asked.

'Have a taste,' she said, not wanting to be rude, but not wanting to drink any more of it either.

Dominic took a swig – and spat it straight back into the glass.

'That's filthy,' he said. 'Battery acid. Why ever didn't you say? No, don't answer that, you didn't want to be rude, right?'

Hannah nodded.

'So what can I get you instead? I'm going to have another half of this. Would you like to try that? Or how about a G and T?'

'Oh, gin is a great idea,' said Hannah. 'Much safer bet.'

'Coming up,' said Dominic and headed off to the bar.

Hannah felt like David Attenborough observing Kelli's behaviour as Dominic approached. She jumped off the barstool she'd been sitting on and stuck her chest out like a rooster, looking up at him under her false eyelashes.

Not the most subtle courtship display – but it did explain why she'd given Hannah the third degree about the state of her relationship with Matt. She'd clearly been checking out whether she could make a move on Dominic, or whether he was with her.

Well, good luck to her with that, Dominic was fair game and might enjoy a little dalliance, although from what Anthea had told her, Kelli really wasn't his type. Apparently, he liked them willowy, or as Anthea put it 'terrible drippy waifs'. Hannah smiled remembering Anthea sounding off about the one who had refused her famous Yorkshire pudding on grounds of being gluten-intolerant.

'Barely got out of that alive,' said Dominic coming back with the drinks. 'I've met less predatory sharks.'

'She's split up from her husband,' said Hannah, 'and she's looking for a new man.'

Dominic raised an eyebrow and Hannah continued.

'She's a mother from the school. Her ex is in the army – Afghanistan – and she couldn't hack it.'

'Excellent intelligence gathering,' said Dominic.

Hannah smiled and took a sip of her new drink. Much better.

'So,' said Dominic, putting his own glass down after what was clearly a satisfying mouthful, 'enough of the village gossip, how are things with you? Any news when your globe-trotting husband might be coming back?'

Oh, not that again. Hannah explained about the new development with the number one in Japan and Dominic looked suitably impressed.

'Maybe you'll all have to move back to Sydney, if his career is really taking off there,' he said.

Hannah didn't say anything, but what she was thinking must have been obvious.

'Sorry,' said Dominic, 'easy for me to say that, huh? The unencumbered middle-aged bachelor. Not so easy with a child in school, a little one and a mother recently widowed.'

'Actually, it's my mother I want to talk to you about,' said Hannah, seizing the opportunity to bring it up.

'About the problem with her house?' replied Dominic immediately.

Hannah blinked, amazed he knew – and rather mortified. Did everyone in the village know? What about Kelli over there, back on the stool, picking at her false nails but clearly watching them out of the corner of her eye, did she know?

'Ali told me,' said Dominic. 'Please don't be cross with her. I know how discreet you and your mother are – and as a constipated Englishman myself, I do understand it – but after living away from Britain for so long, I've had the chance to get some perspective on the way we do things here and now I'm not so sure that pulling the shutters down is always the best approach.'

He paused to take another sip of his beer.

'I think it's loosened me up a lot living in the States,' he said. 'They are so much more open there, although of course, they go to the opposite extreme and a total stranger will vomit out their life story to you in excruciating detail the first time you meet them. That's too much, but I'm coming to understand that there is a sweet spot somewhere between those two extremes. And from the time I've been spending with young Ali recently, I'm starting to wonder whether the Australians might not have got it down. You're married to one; what do you think?'

Hannah groaned inwardly again. How had the conversation got back to her and Matt again? Then inspiration struck.

'Yes, I think you might be right there,' she said. 'It's definitely true of Ali . . .'

Perfect. She could turn it into an opportunity to big her up to Dominic. She owed Ali big time for intervening with her mother and now she could report back to her if Dominic said something promising in response.

'She really is a wonder,' continued Hannah, warming to her subject. 'It was her who got my mum to open up about the problem with the house. We all knew something was wrong, but it was Ali who just upped and asked her – I was too freaked out to do it – and I'm so grateful to her for that. She's such a great girl.'

'She sure is,' said Dominic. 'It's a whole lot of fun working with her – and the guys on the building site certainly appreciate her visits in other ways . . .'

Hannah laughed, but she wasn't sure how thrilled Ali would be with that answer. It sounded like Dominic enjoyed her company as a friend and a colleague and nothing more. He'd said 'fun': ouch, all women knew that meant the opposite of romantic feelings.

'Anyway,' he was saying, 'back to you – back to your mother. Have you made any progress?'

'Not really,' said Hannah. 'I've spoken to the solicitors looking after my father's will and they've just repeated what my mum has already told me – it's too late to change it now my father has died. I must say, for a high-ranking barrister he does seem to have had a talent for instructing the most useless solicitors in London. The one he put on my unfair dismissal case was rubbish too.'

'Oh, did you have one of those too?' said Dominic, looking surprised.

'Yes,' said Hannah, annoyed with herself for accidentally introducing an irrelevant subject. She'd gloss over it. 'But it was OK because I got a great pay-off in the end.'

'But I thought you said the lawyers looking after your case were crap?' said Dominic, looking puzzled.

'They were . . .' said Hannah and paused.

And there it was, staring her in the face, the reason she felt uncomfortable talking to Dominic about this. Anthony. If she could only go and ask him for help sorting out the nightmare of her father's will she wouldn't need to ask Dominic for advice.

But there was no way she could get Anthony involved without telling her mother – and that would mean confessing that she'd become friends with him. She just couldn't do it. Hannah hadn't even told Matt about the lunches with Anthony. It was so much easier just to lock it all away inside her.

So Dominic, with his grown-up contacts from international banking, had come to seem like her only possible source of help. Who else could she ask? Matt knew a lot less about law than she did and despite her husband's illustrious career, Marguerite didn't really have any contacts in the legal world herself. Charlie's professional life had been so tightly tied up with his worst behaviour, she'd always kept as great a distance from it as she could.

But while Dominic seemed like the only person she could ask for help, surely his first reaction would be, 'Didn't your father have lawyer friends you could ask for advice?' It was the obvious response and it took her right back to Anthony. Aaagh.

Without thinking, she reached out and took hold of Dominic's wrist, turning it towards her to see the time on his watch. It wasn't until she felt the texture of the hairs on his arm against her fingers that she realised it was a bit intrusive.

'Sorry,' she said, 'I just wanted to see what the time was.'

Dominic was smiling.

'Help yourself,' he said. 'Feel free to borrow my hand any time.'

'The thing is, Dominic,' Hannah launched in, 'I want to ask if you can help us in any way with the house and it might take a while to explain . . .'

She petered out, still not decided whether she was going to tell him about the Anthony complication or not. She needed time to think.

'And you're worrying about collecting the kids?' asked Dominic.

Hannah nodded.

'I'll text Ali,' he said. 'She's doing some work for me over at Anthea's and I'll ask her if she'll pick Hector up from school and – where's Nancy?'

'She's having a play date with the little brother of a boy in Hector's class. The mother's bringing her to the school at home time.'

'Perfect. I'll ask Ali to collect them both and she can look after them until you get back.'

He shrugged and Hannah understood it really was that simple. She'd been about to rush off to fuss about the kids, when all it would take would be one text. Dominic already had his Blackberry out. He sent a message and almost immediately a bleep indicated a reply had come back. Ali probably had her phone strapped to her arm in case he rang or texted at any moment.

'OK,' he said, 'that's sorted and I've had a good idea. Let's go to another pub to talk about this. In another village. I can feel the Bride of Frankenstein's eyes boring into my back and she probably has supersonic bat ears for picking up titbits to share with her regulars. We certainly don't want her to hear whatever it is you want to tell me.'

Hannah laughed.

'You're so right about that,' she said.

# Chapter Forty-eight

Ali was so cross with Hannah she had seriously thought about asking Fred if she could move back in with him and his serial killer needlepoints, but as she walked along the lane towards school with Hector and Nancy on a perfect summer morning, she realised she would miss them too much. She'd grown deeply attached to those kids over the weeks she'd been staying down there.

Hector was counting different wild flowers in the hedgerow for the class nature project and Ali was busy keeping Nancy off the road – even with her reins on, it was hard to keep control of her with one hand while pushing the buggy with the other – and stopping her grabbing at nettles, in imitation of her big brother's botanic activities.

The walk back was much easier, with Nancy consenting to ride in the pushchair. It really was a glorious day and after enduring her first English winter, Ali thought she'd never appreciated the arrival of summer so much. In Sydney, it was always magical when the star jasmine and jacarandas came into bloom, but this felt like a deliverance.

At that time of day the air was still thick with birdsong. Ali closed her eyes for a moment while there were no kamikaze country drivers in earshot, to soak it up, but thoughts about Hannah immediately came rushing into the void and ruined it.

How could she have done it? She'd gone out with Dominic – DOMINIC! – and got absolutely plastered, crashing home in the early hours, giggling with him in the hallway, singing in the kitchen. And all after earlier casually relinquishing responsibility for the children on to her.

Unbelievable. She hadn't even asked Ali if she minded.

Ali did appreciate that she was staying with Hannah rent-free and she'd been really pleased to be able to pitch in to help with the kids while Matt was away, but there had been a high-handedness about the proceedings of the night before that had really hurt her feelings.

The worst of it was that Hannah hadn't even bothered to ring herself to ask – no, *tell* – Ali to babysit. She'd got Dominic to do it. A double blow. Treating her like staff to be ordered around and then rubbing her nose in the fact that she was out having a great time with the man Ali was mad about. Why hadn't it occurred to her to include Ali in the outing?

She knew exactly how Ali felt about Dominic and had been really encouraging about it, always asking if there had been any interesting developments, but when the perfect opportunity had come along to throw them together in a jolly social event, Hannah had casually excluded her. It didn't make any sense. Marguerite could have looked after the kids and they all could have gone out.

Ali had been for a few drinks with Dominic, but it was always with the guys from the building projects as well, so it had felt like work, rather than a proper fun night out. Like the one Hannah – the married woman, married to Ali's own cousin – had just had with him. Unbelievable.

She hadn't even got up for the kids this morning and if Ali hadn't clearly heard Dominic leave the night before – all too clearly, they'd been so noisy, it was a miracle they hadn't woken the kids up – she might have been tempted to peep round Hannah's bedroom door this morning to see if he was in there.

That's how serious it felt, like Hannah had made some kind of a move on him, but surely that couldn't be right?

Ali opened the front door quietly. It would suit her if Hannah was still asleep, as she was dreading seeing her, but Nancy had other ideas, starting to call out 'Mama! Mama!' the minute she got her into the house. Hannah came out of the kitchen to greet her and Ali occupied herself folding up the buggy and storing it in the porch, so she wouldn't have to look at her right away. She was afraid what she might say.

When she couldn't draw it out any longer, she was relieved to see that Hannah had gone back into the kitchen and made for the stairs so she could grab what she needed and head over to Anthea's to start work – although she didn't know quite how she was going to look Dominic in the eye either. But just as she got her foot on the bottom step, Hannah came back into the hall.

'Oh, Ali,' she said, still in her nightie and looking gratifyingly queasy, forefingers pressed into her temples, 'thank you so much for taking Hector to school – and for babysitting last night. I'm so sorry. It wasn't meant to be like that . . .'

'Like what?' said Ali, with what she hoped was a cool neutral expression on her face.

'I didn't intend to go out and get plastered with Dominic last night . . . oh, come and have some tea with me. I feel so sick and so bad about leaving you out . . . It all just happened . . .'

Ali immediately felt a little better. At least Hannah knew not including her was wrong; that went a long way to making amends, but she still wanted to hear more detail.

She followed Hannah into the kitchen and when she saw her struggling even to fill the kettle, she steered her to a chair and made the tea herself, while Hannah sat at the kitchen table groaning, her head in her hands.

The tea made, Ali settled Nancy in her sand pit just outside the kitchen door and sat down opposite Hannah.

'So,' she said, starting to find the situation a little amusing, 'what the hell happened?'

'I asked Dominic to have a drink with me yesterday afternoon,' said Hannah, 'to ask his advice about Mum's problem with the house – thanks for telling him, by the way, it was the right thing to do.'

Ali nodded in acknowledgement.

'It wasn't a social thing at all,' continued Hannah. 'I just wanted to see whether, with all his contacts, he might know any big-shot lawyers he could discreetly ask for advice on our behalf, seeing as the solicitors my father's family have always used seem to be such a useless bunch of twerps and we've already racked up enormous fees with them . . .'

She paused for a moment and closed her eyes, then took a sip of tea.

'Sorry,' she said, fighting a wave of nausea and wondering if this was how her father had felt after his binges, how had he carried on doing it? 'I'd forgotten quite how bad mixing spirits can make you feel. Anyway, so we went to the White Hart, but it's so awful in there and Kelli the barmaid – who's a mother from the school – was listening to everything we said, so Dominic suggested we went somewhere else for some privacy and we went to this great bar he knew in town and it just turned into a big night . . .'

She took another tentative mouthful of tea and when she was sure she could keep it down, continued.

'It was never meant to be like that, but I had to tell him some difficult stuff about my dad so he'd understand the full picture about Mum's situation and I had a few cocktails and I haven't really been drinking much and it just all got really messy.'

'Well, you certainly sounded like you were having a good time, when you were singing in here at one o'clock this morning . . .' said Ali. 'You were like a pair of students. It didn't sound much like a business meeting.'

Hannah dropped her head in her hands again.

'I'm so sorry, Ali,' she said, 'like I say, it just happened. I think I've been so uptight since Dad died and then with Matt being away and my mum being in such a state, I just needed to let off some steam. I really wish I'd called you to come and join us, but by the time it had turned into a party thing, I was already too hammered to think straight.'

'You were living in the moment,' said Ali.

'Yes, I was,' said Hannah, refusing to rise to the challenge, 'and I think I needed to. Look, Ali, I do feel really really bad that you had to babysit while I was gadding about with the man you're crazy for, but it wasn't planned. If only Dominic had asked my mum to babysit rather than you, you could have come out with us . . .'

'Dominic?' said Ali.

'Yes, it was his idea to ask you,' said Hannah, her voice fading out as she saw the look on Ali's face.

'Right,' said Ali, slowly, 'so when Dominic sent me that text, asking me to babysit, it was his idea, not yours?'

Hannah nodded. She'd thought Dominic was so smart at the time, the way he'd sorted out the childcare with one text, but now she could see how it looked to Ali.

'Well,' said Ali, 'at least I know where I stand with him. Turns out he looks on me only and entirely as a member of staff.'

'Oh, I'm sorry, Ali,' said Hannah, feeling awful, but not game to argue with her.

Late in the evening, his tongue loosened by the drink, Dominic had told Hannah he was a bit uncomfortable with the way Ali was around him. He knew she had a crush on him and while he liked her enormously, it wasn't like that. She was too young for him and not his type either. There was no way Hannah was going to tell Ali any of that, but she was relieved she'd now worked it out for herself.

Ali shrugged.

'I think I've been pretty stupid about the whole Dominic thing,' she said, slumping in her chair. 'It just seemed so "meant to be" when he popped up right after I'd decided that was exactly the kind of man I need in my life and I think I've been a bit delusional. He never gave me any reason to think he was interested in anything beyond a jolly working friendship, but he's so lovely to be around I think I let myself imagine something that wasn't there. I reckon his charm is permanently set at full beam. It's his default setting.'

'Rather like my dad,' said Hannah, 'guess they're the same breed, really, except Dominic doesn't have a drink problem. He's got hollow legs. He matched me on the drinks and didn't get anything like as plastered as I was . . . He left the car in town, though.'

'He'll probably want me to go and get it,' said Ali. 'Yessir!'

Hannah laughed. Ali was taking the whole thing brilliantly, but there was one more thing she had to say about it. She reached out and put her hand on Ali's arm.

'Als,' she said, 'you do know there was no funny business with me and Dominic, don't you? We've known each other since we were kids and it was just really easy for me to relax with him. I had a really good time last night – and I think I needed to – but that was it.'

'I know,' said Ali. 'I was just jealous. And anyway, he might be a perfect Pompom, but he wears horrible clothes and he's nothing like as hot as Matt . . . you'd have been seriously trading down.'

'You're so right,' said Hannah, 'and I think I'll go upstairs and Skype my handsome husband right now and tell him he's not the only one having a good time. I've seen pictures of him on Facebook living it up in Bondi, so I think I should remind him that what's sauce for the gander and all that.'

'I think he'd be pleased to know that,' said Ali, smiling, 'but tell me one thing before you go, Hanns – was Dominic able to give you any help about your mum's situation? Did he have any good ideas?'

'Yes,' said Hannah, 'Dominic has given me exactly the solution I needed and that's what I have to get on with, right after I speak to Matt . . .'


Hannah was thrilled when Matt responded immediately to her Skype request.

'Hey, babe,' he said, looking really pleased she'd called unexpectedly and pushing his beautiful face right up against the web cam with his lips puckered. God, he was handsome. Hannah's stomach did a little somersault.

'Look at you, lazybones,' he said, so much tenderness in his eyes, Hannah felt quite giddy, although it could have been the last couple of tequilas from the night before, 'lolling around in bed mid-morning; what time is it there – all of nine forty-five? A big lie-in for you, I'm happy to see it, but what's going on? Are the kids all right?'

Hannah reassured him they were fine and then told him about her big night. She could see he was genuinely pleased for her.

'Good,' he said, 'I'm thrilled to hear you've been out kicking up your heels, makes me feel less guilty about having such a great time here – I'd be lying if I said I wasn't – but who exactly is this Dominic bloke again? Should I be worried?'

'Yeah, suffer . . .' said Hannah. 'He's Anthea's nephew. He lives in New York and he's just over here for a few months. I've known him since I was a kid. I used to see him every year at Anthea's horrendous Christmas party. I was the girl and he was the fat one, so we had to look out for each other.'

'Is he still fat?' asked Matt, grinning.

'No,' said Hannah, 'he's rather handsome now, if you like that sort of thing. Ali thought she did for a while weirdly, but she's over him now. I always thought he was too old for her anyway. And he wears ironed chinos with deck shoes . . .'

'Old, fat, crap clothes . . .' said Matt, 'I like this guy more all the time. Is he bald?'

Hannah laughed, enjoying the very particular physical relaxation a really bad hangover brings on and feeling much closer to Matt than she had for ages. She was in the mood for a really long chat with him and possibly something more – something they couldn't get up to when the kids were around – but he seemed a bit distracted. He kept disappearing from view and then coming back again. Now she could see only the top half of his face and he seemed to be squinting at the small corner of the Skype screen where he could see himself.

'What are you doing, Matt?' asked Hannah. 'Can't you sit still and talk to me?'

'Sorry, babes,' he said, holding his head at a funny angle and fiddling with something at his neck, 'I'm just trying to tie this bloody tie . . .'

'A tie?' said Hannah, incredulous.

Matt's head and upper torso came into view.

'What do you think?' he asked, raising one eyebrow.

He was wearing an amazing black suit Hannah had never seen before, a crisp white shirt and, yes, he was wearing a tie. A slim black satin one.

'Blimey,' said Hannah, 'you look fabulous, but what's it all in aid of? And where did you get that suit? It's divine.'

'It's Dior Homme,' said Matt, shooting the cuffs, 'I treated myself. You likey?'

'I lovey. I've always wanted you to wear suits, you look even more gorgeous than usual in it, but what's brought this on all of a sudden?'

He disappeared for a moment and came back holding up a pair of shiny black lace-ups with pointy toes.

'Look, new shoes too. Helmut Lang. Cool or what?'

'Mega-cool,' said Hannah, starting to feel a bit weird that he had loads of new clothes she'd never seen before. For the past fourteen-plus years she'd been on first-name terms with every item in his wardrobe, down to the last stinky athletic sock. She'd been there when he'd bought most of it. This felt weird.

He sat on the edge of the bed, bending over, clearly putting the shoes on, then he held one foot up to the camera to show her.

'And new socks,' he said, 'silk. Nice.'

'Very nice,' said Hannah, desperate to know, but determined not to ask him again what had brought on this uncharacteristic shopping frenzy. She normally had to use physical threats to get him into a clothes shop.

'One moment,' he said, kissing the screen and then disappearing. He came back a minute later running his hands through his hair, then leaned forwards to check himself out on the computer screen.

'Right,' he said, 'now the finishing touch . . .' and he held up a bottle of Serge Lutens fragrance Hannah had given him the previous Christmas and sprayed some on his neck.

Grinning at the camera he spun on his heel and came to a stop in a corny male model pose. Hannah couldn't help laughing and he sat down on the bed and smiled into the screen at her.

'Pete and I are going to an awards ceremony tonight,' he said, looking so happy Hannah felt a bit teary, in a good way. 'Red carpet, baby, so I had to go out and buy all this gear. It was good fun actually. Pete had to buy smart stuff too, which was really funny. You know most of his clothes look like a tramp's slept in them? Well, he's managed to assemble a formal outfit with that look and spend $3000 in the process.'

Hannah's eyes popped open.

'Wow,' she said, 'that's great, but what's the event?'

'It's the big annual music awards thingo. Pete's up for best single . . . but more exciting than that, we're going to be sitting with the big boss from the record label – the really big boss. He's over from New York for it and he's specially requested to sit with us.'

'Double triple wow,' said Hannah.

'Yeah,' said Matt nodding and looking serious suddenly, 'it could be something really big, Hannah. Massive. I don't even want to tell you about it yet, in case I jinx it, but just keep everything crossed. Very tightly. And if it comes off, we'll be back together again real soon, OK?'

'That would be nice,' said Hannah quietly, feeling almost physically overwhelmed by her longing to feel his arms around her again.

'So, great you called,' he said, 'perfect timing, but I've got to go. They're sending a car for us and it's due about now . . . Oh look! Here comes Burlington Bertie, you can check him out yourself.'

Behind Matt's shoulder she saw Pete come into the room.

'Hey, mate,' Matt said, 'come and show Hannah what you're wearing . . . Cover yourself, Hanns, I don't want Pete to see my wife in her bedtime glory.'

Hannah hastily pulled up the covers as Pete loomed on to the screen. He looked like Johnny Cash in a long jacket with velvet lapels, a black shirt with metal tips on the collar and a lariat tie.

'Hey, Hannah,' he said and she was surprised how pleased she was to see his craggy face, 'how do you like my look?'

'The man in black,' said Hannah, 'works for me . . .'

'Yay, glad you like it,' said Pete. 'Check these out . . .' and he held up one foot to show a Cuban-heeled cowboy boot, with shiny spurs on the back, 'they're real snakeskin . . .'

Hannah was about to admire them when she heard a familiar guitar riff start up. Nirvana.

'Shit,' said Pete, rummaging around in his pocket, 'that's my phone. Reckon that's the driver to say he's downstairs, we better go . . . Wish me luck, Hannah . . .'

'Good luck, Toxic!' she called to him and as he disappeared, Matt's face came back into view.

'Bye, babe,' he said, blowing her a kiss, 'gotta go. Great you rang. I'll email you later what happens. Love you my beautiful angel, bye.'

And the screen went blank.

Hannah lay back on her pillows feeling slightly punch-drunk. She hadn't seen Matt so fired up for years. It was great, wonderful, that he was finally making the breakthrough he'd been striving for so long. She was thrilled for him and reflexively crossed her fingers to bring him luck as she wondered what on earth the really big deal might be. How exciting.

But as she closed her eyes and surrendered to her hangover, as well as the bed feeling too big, she felt like she had a massive hole inside her. The space where Matt should be.

# Chapter Forty-nine

Marguerite was looking across a table at Anthony. She still couldn't really believe she was there, sitting with him in a public place, looking to all the world like two perfectly normal old people having a civilised cup of coffee together.

Although she was glad he'd suggested a good neutral place like the restaurant in Fenwicks and not his flat, or one of the clubs he and Charlie used to go to. Or any of the places she had once gone with him. With Anthony. The secret places they used to go together. The tiny Italian restaurants. The dark bars. The hotel rooms. All the years they'd had that raging affair.

Looking at him now, his eyes meeting hers steadily over his coffee cup, she could remember all too clearly gazing into those eyes in very different circumstances. Anthony in bed. A wild man like a raging beast, so hungry for her. So different from Charlie's rather vague lovemaking, which had always seemed as though he were thinking about something else more interesting.

But the intensity of Anthony's desire, the state of near-madness it seemed to induce in him, had made her feel like Cleopatra. Anthony and Cleopatra: it had been one of their jokes. She'd given him an eighteenth-century ring with an Egyptian scarab carved from turquoise as a farewell gift – how many years before? thirty? – when they'd finally agreed to stop meeting, after so many failed attempts to end the affair. And now, here he was, still wearing it.

Her hand started to shake and she put her cup hastily down on the saucer, spilling some of it. She shouldn't have come. The strain of keeping all that inside her all these years had taken so much out of her. She'd had to lock everything down for fear that opening the tiniest chink would let it all come pouring out. It had been like keeping the lid on Vesuvius.

She could remember family dinners when she'd had to sit digging her nails into her thigh to stop herself screaming it out: Anthony! I love Anthony!

Even years after the affair ended, seeing him, even in the distance leaving Charlie's granny flat, the glint of the turquoise ring on his finger, had always stretched her to her limit. The combination of guilt, shame and frustrated longing had been impossible. She'd had to make him into a monster to be able to bear it.

And now he put out his hand – the left one, with the ring on it – and touched hers, very gently.

'Are you all right?' he asked quietly.

Marguerite nodded, curtly. Still too afraid to open her mouth in case a banshee howl came out, but then she remembered that morning in her office when Ali had made her admit what was worrying her. How surprising it had been to find it actually made her feel better to talk about the problem with the house, rather than keeping it locked inside as a private shame. Could the same principle possibly apply here? Surely not. What would happen if she allowed all her conflicting feelings about Anthony to come out into the open? She might spring across the table and devour him, or strangle him in revenge for the terrifying emotions he'd always unleashed in her.

'I know how hard this is for you, Marguerite,' he said, just stopping himself from calling her Pattie. It had been his pet name for her, short for Cleopatra. Funnier than Cleo. Less obvious. 'It's hard for me too, hard to keep it to business, but don't worry, that's the only reason we're here, Pat . . .' Damn! 'Marguerite . . .'

But it was too late, her head had snapped up at the syllable. He was furious with himself; he could have blown the whole thing with that one stupid mistake, but at the same time, his heart soared. She remembered! She remembered and it still affected her.

She looked down again and he took another sip of coffee to cover a couple of slow deep breaths, calling on all his powers of restraint, the instinct for knowing when to pause that had helped him win so many tricky cases in his time.

'I'm so sorry you have this terrible mess with the house to deal with at such a difficult time,' he resumed, noting that she immediately relaxed a little as he brought the conversation back to a formal discussion of their reason for meeting. He'd play it the way she always did, keep it all skimming along on the surface, that was the ticket.

'Yes, it's been absolutely ghastly,' said Marguerite, her voice a little wobbly, but just strong enough to uphold her dignity.

'I was so glad when Hannah rang me to tell me about it,' said Anthony, 'and so relieved you weren't angry with her for being in touch with me.'

Marguerite almost laughed. Angry wasn't the right word, but she'd never been more horrified than the afternoon when Hannah had suddenly appeared in her study and told her in a great gabbling guilty rush that she'd been meeting Anthony for cosy little secret lunches ever since Charlie had died.

Giving him Marguerite's email address had been bad enough, but this was like a physical blow. Marguerite had been so appalled at what he might have told her, she'd thought she might be physically sick, but then she'd realised that Hannah wasn't upset with her – so couldn't know any of the terrible things she'd always dreaded her daughter finding out. In fact, as she talked, it became clear that the main thing Hannah had found out was just how wonderful Anthony really was.

And it was in this state of confusion – horror that Hannah was in touch with Anthony, yet strangely vindicated that she appreciated his qualities – that Marguerite had conceded that he was the one person who could help them with the house.

'I don't understand why you hated him so much,' Hannah had said. 'He might have egged Daddy on to be silly, but Charlie was an adult of above-average intelligence, it was his own choice to drink like that and it seems odd to me now the way you always seemed to blame it on Anthony . . .'

That was the point at which Marguerite had agreed to meet him as soon as possible. Anything to make Hannah stop pursuing that line of discussion: why she hated Anthony, why she'd always kept him away from Hannah. Although she had found the wit to insist that it would just be her going to meet him, she didn't want Hannah to be there as well.

Hannah had looked a bit surprised by her vehemence on that point, but was clearly so relieved her mother wasn't angry with her that she'd accepted it, along with Marguerite's refusal to speak to him on the telephone herself. To do that in front of Hannah would have required self-control Marguerite knew was beyond even her.

Caught up remembering that strange day, she realised she'd better tune back in to what Anthony was saying. Something about an excellent firm of solicitors he knew who specialised in this kind of case and how he was going to discuss it with them.

'But I have to tell you, Marguerite,' he said, leaning towards her, not sure she'd taken any of it in; she seemed to have gone off into that distant private place of hers, 'I'm not at all sure how much good it will do. Trusts like this are very hard to change after the fact. In the end it may come down to what kind of person this second cousin of Charlie's is. You know I will do everything I can to make this work out for you, but I'm not entirely optimistic. I'm sorry to be blunt, but I think it's best you know that from the start.'

Marguerite nodded.

'Yes,' she said, 'that is pretty much what I've been told so far, but I would be so grateful for anything more you might be able to find out.'

Then she tilted her chin up in a way that was so familiar his heart nearly came leaping out of his chest. That was Marguerite fixing her resolution to stick to the script she had assigned herself and he knew it meant she was about to come out with some tripe about how she had to leave immediately on an urgent errand.

'Well . . .' she said, right on cue, 'thank you so much for seeing me,

Anthony. Do let me know if there's anything else you need to know, but . . .'

'But you've got to rush off,' Anthony, broke in, his head on one side, his left eyebrow raised.

Marguerite looked back at him, speechless for a moment. She remembered that expression so well. That was how he'd looked at her whenever he'd mentioned her leaving Charlie for him and whether Hannah might really be his daughter – and she would categorically refuse even to discuss either subject.

'Yes,' she said, recovering herself, 'I've got a meeting at the Museum.'

'The British Museum?' said Anthony, playing along, anything to keep her there a bit longer. 'So you still work for them?'

Marguerite nodded.

'A little,' she said, 'mainly when they need advice about repairs that were done in pre-historic times, you know, the 1960s . . .'

Her voice petered out as she said it. How could she have made such a stupid mistake? As she sat there, she felt as though she could smell and hear and taste the London they'd been young in together. Young and in love. Or had it just been lust? Whichever, she was back there. She looked down almost expecting to see herself dressed in one of the Ossie Clark dresses he used to love her wearing, always so much more modern than Charlie, and was almost surprised when she saw the wrinkled skin on the back of her hands.

She glanced up again and Anthony was smiling at her so poignantly, she allowed her guard to drop for one tiny moment and smiled back.

'We did have some good times, didn't we, Pattie?' he said.

She nodded, her throat tightly constricted. She couldn't speak, even if she could have thought of what to say.

'Will you see me again?' he continued, praying his instincts were right, that she was ready for this. 'Just like this . . .'

Marguerite felt herself standing up, taking her handbag with her as she rose from the chair on automatic pilot. She desperately wanted to flee, but couldn't quite make herself do it and stood for a moment instead, looking down at Anthony, locked eye to eye. He could see she was fighting the urge to run for it – now, Williams, now!

'I don't know if Hannah told you already, but I've given up drinking, Marguerite,' he said. 'I haven't had a drink for two years.'

He saw the expression that crossed her face before she had time to hide it and knew exactly what she was thinking. Why didn't you do it sooner? We might have had a chance, but you knew I couldn't leave one problem drinker for another. He had to trust his instinct. This was the moment to speak.

'I wish I'd done it thirty years ago,' he continued, 'with all my heart. I wish I'd done it for me and for Charlie, for Hannah – and for you. Most of all for you. I'll never drink again.'

He stopped and looked at her, holding his breath to see how she would react.

Marguerite felt detached from her own body as she heard a voice, which she realised was her own, saying, 'Yes, I will meet you. I would like that very much.'

Then she bent down and kissed him gently on the cheek. Anthony's hand immediately flew up and clasped her behind her shoulder, wanting to keep her there forever, but that was a step too far. She immediately pulled away and walked out of the restaurant without looking back.

# Chapter Fifty

Dominic and Ali were showing Anthea, Marguerite and Hannah round his project. He was converting a large Victorian house which had been full of horrible run-down bedsits into three spacious airy flats and it was nearly finished. Ali was so enthusiastic you would have thought it was her building.

'Look at the sea view, Hanns,' she said, gesturing for her to come over to the window on the top floor, 'it's like Sydney up here.'

'Wow,' said Hannah, gazing out at a great expanse of blue sky and blue sea, 'this is gorgeous. I thought when houses like this were converted, they were always chopped up into as many horrid little rabbit hutches as possible. Couldn't you have got two flats on each floor, Dominic?'

He walked over to them.

'Yes,' he said, 'easily, three if you made poky studio apartments and that is the usual game plan, but I wanted to try something different. I've got two other properties to convert, but I'm doing this one first as an experiment. If it works, I'll do the others the same way. If it doesn't, I'll do rabbit hutches.'

'This is really charming, Dominic,' said Marguerite, joining them at the window.

Hannah had a good look at her in the bright July sunshine which was pouring in. She was looking so much better since she'd had the meeting with Anthony and knew she was getting some proper advice about the house. She'd told Hannah he hadn't been very optimistic about their prospects of changing the trust, but there was no doubt she was looking much rosier now she didn't have to carry the burden of it on her own.

'Do you really like it?' asked Dominic, reminding Hannah vividly for a moment of the eager little boy he'd been. 'I'm so pleased because in all honesty, apart from the investment angle, I've found I rather enjoy the playing dolls houses side of it.'

Anthea walked into the room as he was speaking, puffing from the unaccustomed number of stairs.

'Well, if you like playing house, Dominic,' she said, 'it's time you settled down with a nice young woman and did it for real. You're much too old to be living in a flat and having flibbertigibbet girlfriends. You should be in your own house with a wife and children – and a garden. He's only got a terrace in New York and you can't even go out on it in high winds.'

Dominic caught Hannah's eye and pulled a face that Anthea couldn't see. This was becoming an all too familiar line of conversation from her.

'Don't worry, Aunt Anth,' he said going over and putting his arm around her shoulders. 'I know I've got arrested development, but I will settle down one day soon, I promise. I do know you're right – just stop going on about it, OK?'

He chucked her cheek and they all laughed. Hannah suspected he found Anthea's intrusive nagging much more irritating than he let on and he was very good at making light of it.

In fact, Dominic had a general talent for making life very pleasant, Hannah thought, as they settled into their seats to have lunch in a lovely pub garden on the way home. All of them except Ali, who had stayed behind at the site, something Hannah knew Anthea would be bound to comment on and sure enough, the moment he arrived back at the table with a tray of drinks, she launched in.

'Why didn't Ali join us for lunch, Dominic? I do hope you're not treating her like some kind of serf. You've been keeping her so busy and I was really looking forward to seeing her today. She's such a refreshing young woman, don't you think, Marguerite?'

Marguerite nodded, picking up her drink and lifting it to her mouth in the hope of covering the flush she could feel rising to her cheeks.

She had a lot to be grateful to Ali for. If she hadn't made her admit what was going on with the house, Hannah wouldn't have come clean about seeing Anthony and she wouldn't be having lunch with him the following day. She felt a little sick at the thought of it. Part terror, part pure excitement.

'Yes,' she said, after swallowing a large mouthful of Campari and soda, 'Ali is marvellous. We're all so lucky she came to stay. She's been such a help to you, hasn't she, Hannah, darling?'

Hannah nodded, so happy to see her mother back to something like her normal self. She was verging on the perky.

'Yes,' said Hannah, 'I don't know what I would have done without her, with Matt away so long.'

The moment she spoke, she felt a shift in the mood round the table as the three of them immediately looked at her a little more intently. It was as though Matt had become a taboo subject and they were all slightly embarrassed she'd brought him up. What was that about? It was true she didn't mention him very often, because it made missing him worse – and, now she thought about it, they had all stopped asking when he was coming back. Well, everyone except Anthea.

'Yes, when is he going to come back?' she boomed out. 'You haven't separated or anything dreadful like that, have you, and not told us?'

'No!' said Hannah, slightly too fast and much too loud. Of course they hadn't separated, but seeing the way they were looking at her just a bit too beadily, she wondered if this wasn't something they'd talked about before without her there. She glanced round at them. They all had that keen look – even Marguerite. Unbelievable!

'Well, it is rather unusual for the father of such young children to be away for – what is it now?' Anthea continued, unabashed. 'It must be several months. Aren't you concerned? And isn't it bad for the children?'

'Eight and a half weeks, actually Anthea,' said Hannah tightly, wishing she had Dominic's light touch with her, 'and I speak to him every day on the computer. There's this thing now called Skype, where you can see each other on the screen and it's almost like being with them and he reads the kids their bedtime story every night on it . . .'

She realised how pathetic it sounded as she said it and found herself looking over to Dominic for support, hoping he'd come to her rescue, but he was looking at her as though he were waiting for the 'real' answer too. Bloody hell!

'The reason he's been away so long is that his work is really taking off in Australia at the moment,' said Hannah, determined to make her point, but then glancing anxiously at her mother. She hadn't told her about that before because she hadn't wanted to add to her worries the anxiety that they might all be about to move back to Sydney.

'The modelling, or the songwriting?' said Dominic.

'The songwriting,' snapped Hannah, ready to throw her drink at him. 'They've had a number one single in Japan, as I told you, which is just about to come out in Australia and there's serious interest from America . . .'

Dominic made a sort of 'fancy that' face, while her mother and Anthea looked completely blank.

'It might not sound much to you,' said Hannah, riding a surge of anger that made her feel about fifteen years old, 'but it's a big deal in the music business. He's making some proper money . . .'

He's bought himself a Dior Homme suit, she thought, but didn't bother to say it. They'd have no idea how significant that was. For Matt to spend serious money on clothing meant he must have more coming in than at any time since they'd met.

Hannah hadn't asked him how much – she was her mother's daughter like that – and wasn't that bothered about money for its own sake, but it was really exciting because she knew what it would mean to him.

'Well, as long as you're sure . . .' said Anthea, looking very unconvinced and Hannah couldn't stand it any longer. She left the table saying she needed the loo.

She was standing at the front of the pub, kicking the gravel, cursing and trying not to cry as she realised there would be no phone signal out there in the country, so she couldn't ring Matt for comfort, when Dominic came round the corner.

'Are you all right?' he asked, standing right in front of her and bending his head down to look closely into her face.

'Yes,' said Hannah tightly, having to fight the tears harder. The last thing she needed at that moment was someone being nice to her.

'I'm sorry I wasn't very helpful back there,' said Dominic, 'I suppose I don't really understand your situation and it seemed better to say nothing than say the wrong thing.'

Hannah looked up at him. He still really didn't seem to get it.

'There's nothing wrong to say,' she said, feeling cross again. 'I can see how it might look, but as I keep telling you all, everything's *fine* between me and Matt, he just really needs to be in Sydney right now for work and I'm happy for him, because he so deserves some success, it's just sometimes . . . I miss him so . . .'

And then despite her efforts, one wretched tear managed to sneak out of her left eye. She immediately brushed it away, but she knew he'd seen it. Damn.

'Hey,' he said, putting his arm round her shoulder, 'don't cry . . .'

Hannah immediately stiffened at his touch, feeling simultaneously humiliated and invaded, which wasn't very helpful as she was still fighting the tears. Her first reaction was to shrug his arm off violently with something resembling a kung fu move, but she couldn't let herself be so rude.

Even if it was annoying, she was sure his intentions were kind, but then, as she was still wondering how to react, she realised it actually felt oddly pleasant to stand with him like that. Comfortable and rather reassuring. So she decided to stay there.

'I'm sorry,' she said, 'so embarrassing . . .'

'It's OK,' he said, 'I'm glad I came looking for you. I could see how Anthea's tactless questions were upsetting you – and I do know what that's like.'

'Me and Matt really haven't split up, you know, Dominic,' she said vehemently. 'I know it's a weird situation, but he would be mad to walk away from what's happening with his work now – and I can't just dump my mother when she's got this awful thing going on with the house and drag Hector out of school to be there with him . . . I'd go tomorrow if I could, but I can't, so I've just got to get on with it.'

'You're a good wife, Hannah,' said Dominic, 'most women wouldn't allow their husbands so much freedom.'

'I don't see it like that,' said Hannah. 'I just want him to be able to grab this opportunity – for all of us – and I have my responsibilities here, so we have to be in different places, just for a while. Not forever, but that's how it is right now.'

'He's a lucky man,' said Dominic.

'Is that why you're not married?' said Hannah. 'Do you hate the idea of being trapped by responsibility, like I am?'

After crying in front of him and with his arm still around her shoulder, she felt she had the right to ask such a personal question. She also wanted to deflect the conversation away from herself for a bit.

'Pretty much,' he said. 'Well spotted. So can you explain it to Anthea please? But it's all right really, I love the old girl; I know she means well and since my mum died, she's been like a mother to me. But she missed out on having a family herself and she wants me to make up the slack. I've got nothing against the idea, I do want a family – just when I'm ready, not on starter's orders. Are you ready? Get, set. Breeeeed!'

She laughed, all tension gone, the way he had of doing that.

'It's really not so bad, the breeding thing, you know,' she said. 'Have I got mascara all over my face?'

He shook his head.

'No,' he said, 'you've just got lovely all over it, as usual.'

She glanced back at him, a bit surprised at the comment, to find him looking at her with a rather distant expression she hadn't seen before. What was that all about? Time to break this up. Enough with the cosy sharing.

'I think I'll go and put some more lipstick on,' she said.

'Good idea,' said Dominic, patting her shoulder. 'I'll go back to the girls and see you there. Secret Squirrel . . .'

'Secret Squirrel,' said Hannah, smiling again at his talent for lightening a potentially awkward moment, 'and Dominic – thank you.'

He inclined his head in reply, and she reached up and kissed his cheek. It was only as she turned away to head into the pub that she realised what had been so comforting and familiar about standing close to him like that.

It was the scent of a man.

Underneath whatever aftershave he had on – and it was something nice and citrussy, Eau Sauvage, possibly – was an indefinable spicy warmth. Hormones, pheromones, male musk, whatever it was, Hannah suddenly realised how very much she'd missed it.

When she got back to the table she was glad to see that Anthea was happily distracted negotiating the bones in a Dover sole and that Dominic had moved his place so that Hannah was now sitting between him and Marguerite. He did it all so delicately, thought Hannah, smiling at him to acknowledge that she appreciated his consideration.

'All better?' he asked quietly, as she sat down and picked up her napkin.

She nodded.

'Do you want to hear something that will make you laugh?' he continued in the same low tone.

Hannah nodded again, picking up her fork and holding it over her smoked mackerel salad.

'There's another reason Ali didn't come for lunch with us today. I did invite her, but she didn't want to come . . .'

Hannah opened her eyes wide in anticipation.

'. . . and the reason's name,' continued Dominic, 'is Pavel. He's my carpenter. Lovely chap. Doesn't speak great English, but very charming and very good looking. Got that eastern Europe cheek bone-y thing going on.'

'Oh goodness, that's great news,' said Hannah, 'but I can't believe she hasn't let me in on it. I thought she told me everything about her love life . . . She's been over you for a while by the way, did you know?'

Dominic chuckled.

'Yes,' he said, 'she did kindly tell me that she had been attracted to me for a brief delusional – her word – moment, but had subsequently realised I was much too old and boring for her and I wear horrible clothes.'

It was Hannah's turn to giggle.

'But tell me,' she said, 'does Pavel return her feelings? I couldn't bear her to be disappointed again.'

'Oh, I think so,' said Dominic, 'judging by the noises I heard coming from the bathroom in the top flat a couple of days ago . . .'

Hannah's mouth fell open in thrilled surprise.

'And I strongly suspect that's what they're up to right now,' he continued. 'The other blokes will go off to the pub for lunch and they'll get on with doing what healthy young people do – and with great vigour and enthusiasm, from what I could gather, before I beat a very hasty retreat back down the stairs.'

'Blimey,' said Hannah, 'I'm thrilled for her, but do you think there's a reason she hasn't told me about it? Do you think I can ask her?'

'No idea,' said Dominic. 'I've never understood how you women carry on about stuff like that, all that sharing of gory intimate details you do, but I guess there must be a reason she hasn't said anything to either of us. It is out of character.'

Hannah nodded.

'You're right,' she said, 'so I'll keep my beak shut and she can tell me when she's ready to – and Dominic, don't worry, I won't say anything to Anthea about it either. She'll be furious that the girl she had earmarked for your arranged marriage has got away.'

He burst out laughing and then, as Anthea's head automatically snapped up from her plate on hearing her own name, swiftly changed the subject, asking them all how they were enjoying their food.

# Chapter Fifty-one

Hector was helping Pavel mend the henhouse roof.

'What country are you from, Pavel?' he asked, passing him a nail.

'Most beautiful one,' he replied, 'Poland.'

'Is it the most beautiful one?' said Hector. 'I like England, but my dad says Australia is the best. He's Australian, so I'm half-Australian.'

'And I am hundred per cent Polish,' said Pavel, holding out his hand 'more nails, Hector, please. So to me Poland most beautiful.'

Hector thought it over for a moment.

'So I suppose,' he said, 'I should half-think England is the most beautiful and half-think Australia is.'

'You been to Australia?' asked Pavel.

Hector nodded.

'Twice. I've got loads and loads of cousins in Australia. They're really funny. I love my cousins. I Skype them sometimes, but it's not the same. I wish I could see them again in real life, but it's a very long way to Australia. It takes absolutely ages to get there. Weeks, really.'

'Maybe your mum will take you there soon. Your dad is there now, no?'

'Yeah,' said Hector, kicking the side of the henhouse and suddenly feeling completely bored with the conversation. 'I'm going to see what Ali's doing.'

He dropped the nails into the tool box and ran back into the house. Ali was standing at the kitchen table chopping up vegetables. Nancy had her own little chopping board and a wooden knife and was doing her own version of it, which was mainly resulting in pieces of carrot falling on the floor.

'Hi,' said Ali, smiling at Hector, 'you not helping Pav any more?'

'No . . .' said Hector .

'Do you want to help me?' said Ali.

'No . . .' said Hector, kicking the table leg. He wasn't quite sure why he was kicking things, but it felt like the right thing to do. 'Where's my mum?'

'She's over at your granny's house,' said Ali, 'she'll be back later. Do you want some carrot?'

'No,' said Hector, 'I think I'll go and play in my room.'

He ran out of the kitchen and up the stairs, checking over his shoulder that Ali wasn't following him. When he was sure she wasn't, he ducked into his parents' bedroom and closed the door quietly behind him. His mother's iPad was on the bed – brilliant – she hadn't remembered to hide it from him.

With his heart beating fast, because he knew he wasn't allowed to touch it when she wasn't there, he flipped open the cover. Yes! Up came the bright screen with the picture of him and Nancy in a bubble bath together on it.

With his tongue poking out of the corner of his mouth he scanned the icons until he thought he'd found the right one and tapped it. He jumped when it opened, but was thrilled to see it was Skype. It was easy to find the right place to tap on next because he could read now and it said 'Matt' which meant Daddy. Tap tap and it started making all the right noises. Hector glanced towards the door again and cocked his ear – nobody seemed to be coming, phew.

The noises carried on a bit longer and then – yeah! – there was his dad's face.

'Daddy!' he said. 'It's Hector!'

'Hey, Heccie,' said Matt, grinning at him, 'I thought it was your mum, what a lovely surprise. How are you mate?'

'I'm all right, but Daddy . . .' and before he could get another word out, he started crying, he couldn't help it.

'Oh, Heccie,' said Matt, feeling like a dagger was being stabbed into his heart, 'don't cry, little man, what's the matter? Tell your old dad.'

'I want you to come home,' said Hector, 'you've been gone forever and I want you to come back.'

Through his tears he saw someone walk behind his dad's head and there was loud music playing.

'Everything OK, Matt?' said a man's voice. 'We're ready for you now.'

'Yeah,' said Matt, over his shoulder, 'I just need a moment, won't be long. Wassup, Heccie, what's brought this on?'

'It's just Pavel's in the garden and he's using your hammer and I don't like it . . .'

'Who's Pavel?' asked Matt, bristling.

'He's Ali's carpenter,' said Hector, 'he's good at mending things, but I don't like him using your hammer, Daddy . . . He didn't ask!'

He started sobbing again and Matt felt so bad he wanted to throw his iPad against the wall and smash it. He couldn't bear to see Hector like this. His beautiful son was crying and he was 17 000 useless kilometres away from him. He hated himself.

'Hey, Heccie boy,' he said. 'Where's Mummy? Can you get her?'

'Mummy's at Granny's house and I want *you*, Daddy . . .'

Through his racking sobs he saw Matt glance over his shoulder as the man came back into the room again.

'We're waiting for you, Matt,' he said, 'Pete thinks that top harmony will work better in your voice and we need to record it now.'

'Right, I'm there,' said Matt, 'one tick.'

He leaned closely into the screen, a big frown between his eyebrows.

'Listen, my little man,' he said, his voice gruff with emotion, 'I don't mind Pavel using my hammer – he's allowed, OK? I'm sorry I'm not there with you, darling. I know I've been away a long long time, but I've had work to do here, which will be really good for all of us and I'm coming back real soon.'

'But I want you to come back now.'

He started crying again and through his tears, he saw the door open behind Matt's shoulder again. It was a different man this time. He looked familiar, but it was hard to see clearly.

'Come on, mate,' he was saying, 'they're getting really shitty with me, we've already gone into the next hour and they're not happy, we've got to get this down.'

'I know, Pete,' said Matt, crossly. 'I'm just talking to Hector. I'll be one minute.'

He turned back to the screen, feeling as though he might burst into tears himself.

'Hector, if Mummy isn't there, who's looking after you?'

'Ali,' said Hector miserably.

'Look, you can see the pressure I'm under here, Heccie. I've got to go and work now, there's nothing I can do about it – grown-ups have to work, you're a big boy, you know that. Some drive buses, some are teachers, I do this – so you just go down to Ali and get her to give you a big cuddle and as soon as I've finished here I'll ring you back, OK?'

Hector didn't say anything. It wasn't OK.

'I'll come home as soon as I can, mate, you've just got to be brave a bit longer, like you promised me. Bye Heccie. Love you.'

And then, feeling like the biggest shit on earth, Matt closed the call and ran back into the recording studio.


Sitting at the kitchen table with her mother and Anthony was a lot less weird than Hannah had been expecting. She'd been dreading it, certain her mother would be all uptight and frosty, but she seemed quite relaxed, for her. Even though it seemed the news about the house wasn't good.

'I'm sorry to have to tell you this,' Anthony was saying, 'although I'm glad you're hearing it here and not in some solicitor's office . . .'

'Coffee?' said Marguerite.

Hannah saw a smile flicker across Anthony's face. He clearly found her mother's ability to stick to the social niceties, even in the face of family disaster and financial ruin, as tragicomic as she did.

'Thank you,' said Anthony. 'Black.'

He smiled again as she pushed the coffee cup towards him, followed by the sugar bowl. She knew exactly how he took his coffee. Even if she hadn't remembered from the old days, he'd had it black with two sugars when they'd had lunch the week before. He dropped two lumps in and stirred it slowly, concentrating on that to stop himself leaping up and capering round the room singing like Gene Kelly.

He wasn't entirely looking forward to telling them the final outcome of his investigations into the trust, but at the same time to be sitting at a table with these two beautiful women, whom he had loved from a distance for so many years, was almost overwhelming. Under cover of taking a folder out of his attaché case, he took a moment to compose himself. Deep breaths, Williams, deep breaths. Don't blow it, son.

'Right,' he said, looking up at them both, 'it's not marvellous news, but it's not entirely bad.'

He pulled a piece of paper out of the folder and held it up.

'This is a letter from Charlie's cousin's lawyer in Vancouver. You can read it yourselves, but I'll cut to the chase – he wants the money, but we have managed to get one decent concession out of him.'

He handed the letter to Marguerite, who passed it to Hannah without even looking at it and she passed it back, still unread, to Anthony. He put it down on the table.

'Just tell us the gist of it, please, Anthony,' said Marguerite, 'I'd like to get it over with.'

'All right,' he said, trying not to be distracted by the thrill of hearing her say his name. 'So he insists on inheriting the house and the contents that come with it – not your own stuff, obviously – as is his legal right, and he has instructed the solicitors in London to put it all on the market, with immediate effect . . . I'm so sorry.'

Hannah looked across at her mother. She'd closed her eyes. Hannah reached out and squeezed her hand, but she didn't return the gesture. Hannah glanced at Anthony, who held up a finger to indicate he had more to say.

'But in acknowledgment of the difficult circumstances he has agreed to let you have half the money from the sale, Marguerite,' said Anthony.

'Really?' she said, sitting up.

Anthony nodded, smiling gently.

'Yes, it's quite a good result really and pretty decent of him – proves he shares some DNA with Charlie, I think – and the great thing is it gives you options. If you can raise the funds, you can buy his half from him and stay here. You could even buy any bits of furniture you're particularly attached to. I've done some research and it shouldn't be a problem. There are special mortgages for people in your situation, whereby you borrow now against the future value of the house. It will still make it tricky for you to inherit it outright in the future, Hannah, but you would be able to stay here, Marguerite, that's the main thing.'

Hannah was so excited at the news she jumped up and threw her arms round her mother's neck, leaning round to kiss her on the cheek. She'd be able to stay in the house, with the dogs and all her things and she wouldn't have to leave the beautiful garden she'd spent so many years bringing to perfection. Brilliant! Marguerite patted her arm in her detached way and said nothing. Still excited, Hannah ran round the table and hugged Anthony.

'How can we ever thank you, Anthony?' she said. 'You're a genius and Dominic was so right insisting I had to ask you to help us with this. Thank you so so much. Daddy would be so grateful to you.'

'It was the least I could do for all of you,' said Anthony, kissing her cheek warmly.

Marguerite still hadn't said anything and they both looked across the table at her enquiringly. After a moment she raised her head and looked back at them steadily, with no discernible expression in her eyes.

'But perhaps I don't want to stay here,' she said and with the grace of a dancer, she rose up from her chair and left the room.

Hannah watched her go, incredulous, and then turned to Anthony. He started to laugh, shaking his head.

'Well, I wasn't expecting that,' he said.

'Whatever does she mean?' said Hannah.

'No idea,' said Anthony, 'I'm sure she'll tell us when she's ready to – and not a moment before.'

'You're right there,' said Hannah, 'would you like some more coffee, while we're waiting?'

Anthony smiled to himself as she went to fill the kettle. She was so much her mother's daughter. He wondered if she knew quite how much. And he wondered yet again whether he was more relieved or sad now that he knew that she definitely wasn't his daughter.

It had been agony all those years thinking she was possibly growing up not knowing her real father – and that he might be missing out on his only child – so it was good really to know she'd been with her real dad all along, although on the other hand, it had been a comfort holding on to the hope that he might have a child of his own. But it had turned out that he didn't. Oh well.

Hannah was just pushing down the plunger on the refilled cafétière, when she heard feet thundering down the hall towards them. Then Hector burst into the room, with Ali in hot pursuit and Pavel bringing up the rear, holding Nancy in his arms.

'Mummy!' said Hector running over and sobbing into her lap, 'please don't be cross with me, your iPad was on and I was bored . . .'

'Hey, Heccie,' said Hannah, 'whatever's the matter?'

'Ali caught me on your iPad and she was very cross with me . . .'

'I wasn't cross with him at all,' said Ali. 'I just found him in your room sobbing over it and when I asked him what was going on he just took off over here, so we had to follow… I honestly don't know what's the matter with him.'

'Come on, Hector,' said Hannah, 'calm down and we'll talk about it later. How would you like some of Granny's raspberries to cheer you up?'

'I'll get them,' said Ali, already getting a bowl out of the cupboard.

Hector still had his head buried in Hannah's neck, and she rocked him on her knee, rubbing his back and kissing his head, until she felt his body relax. She pulled up his T-shirt to dry his tears.

'Feeling better?' she asked.

He nodded, sniffing, and she picked up the piece of paper towel Ali had just put on the table with the bowl of raspberries and wiped his nose.

After a couple of spoons of the plump red berries, drenched in cream, he clearly felt better, turning round on her knee to look at everybody. That was when he noticed Anthony.

'Hello,' he said, his tears immediately forgotten at the prospect of making a new friend, 'I'm Hector.'

'Hello Hector, I'm Anthony, lovely to meet you properly at last.'

Anthony smiled as he looked back into the bright little face which had solved the great enigma of his life when he'd first seen it at Charlie's funeral. Just one glance had been enough to tell him that Hector was definitely Charlie's grandson.

And now those lively eyes, so ready and alert for the next bit of fun, were so familiar Anthony's throat felt tight. Charlie in miniature. So while Anthony knew Hannah was definitely not his daughter, he already felt he could love Hector as though she were.

# Chapter Fifty-two

Hannah, Dominic, Ali and Pavel were sitting in the beer garden behind the White Hart drinking watery Pimms and planning a party. Dominic's first property was finished and he wanted to celebrate.

'We've got to have a theme, Dom,' Ali was saying, 'it's not the same unless we get to dress up. How about an Eighties party? I'll come as Madonna in *Desperately Seeking Susan* . . .'

She turned to look at Pavel.

'And you look quite like Aiden Quinn, so that's perfect,' she continued. 'Ooh, I really will need some lace gloves now, Hannah and a leather jacket, have you got one?'

'Who is this Quinn?' asked Pavel.

'A handsome actor,' said Dominic, 'and you do look a bit like him actually, it's the cheekbones, but I don't want a theme, because it wouldn't be fair on the olds. What's Anthea going to dress as, for an Eighties party?'

'Margaret Thatcher?' said Hannah and they all laughed.

'She's certainly bossy enough,' said Dominic, 'and I can be Dennis.'

'And if we got your mum to dye her hair, she'd be a brilliant Nancy Reagan,' said Ali, in all seriousness.

'No, I mean it, Ali,' said Dominic, 'I don't want it to be fancy dress. I want the party to be fun for all ages, but it would be jolly to make it a bit different . . . hmm . . .'

He'd narrowed his eyes and was pushing his tongue into his cheek, 'I think I've had a good idea.'

'Studio 54?' said Ali. 'Chicago? Grease? Woodstock?'

'Well, Woodstock's closest,' said Dominic, 'a barn dance. We're in the country, it's summer – so we'll have a dance, in an actual barn. Anthea knows all the farmers round here, so I'm sure I'll be able to find a really good one to hire and we'll be able to make as much noise as we like, until as late as we like.'

'Ooh!' said Ali. 'That's genius! I'll dress like Marilyn Monroe in *The Misfits* and Pav looks even more like Montgomery Clift than he does Aiden Quinn, so it's perfect.'

'Feel free,' said Dominic, 'and now you mention it, I've got some rather snazzy cowboy boots myself. I bought them in Houston when I went there on a work trip, so I'll be fully boot scootin'. Yee haw!'

'What is barn dance?' asked Pavel and as Ali explained, Hannah wondered what it was like to be in a relationship with someone who had such a limited knowledge of your own mother tongue, let alone any of the cultural niceties.

Clearly, they both spoke the international language of luuuuurve fluently, they could hardly keep their hands off each other, but Hannah couldn't imagine not being able to share nuances of jokes with someone. She and Matt came from opposite ends of the earth, but while they had different accents, childhood references and slang, the language was fundamentally the same.

Although it was exactly the small differences in the shared lingo that could be very entertaining – such as Matt taking every opportunity to use the word 'root' in front of unsuspecting Poms for Hannah's amusement.

Ouch. Remembering the time Matt had made her laugh so much she'd had to fake a coughing fit, when Anthea had been showing them round her vegetable patch not long after they'd moved down, felt like a stab in the guts.

'Yeah,' he'd said enthusiastically, flicking a glance at Hannah, 'I can see the possibilities for some truly spectacular roots here, Anthea.'

Suddenly remembering that sunny August morning threw Hannah into an instant misery of missing him, which was always a shock to her equilibrium, and the way she'd found to cope with his absence.

They still Skyped a lot, but apart from those interludes it was as though she'd wrapped him – and their life together – carefully in cotton wool and put them away, not to be thought about until the next time they spoke, rather like one of the precious artefacts her mother mended, sitting in storage at the British Museum. That was the only way she could deal with it. If she allowed Matt – and the absence of Matt – to sit with her all the time, she could never have got out of bed.

But not much longer now, he'd told her. He and Pete were finishing up whatever it was in the studio that he still didn't want to talk about for fear of jinxing it, the single that had been such a hit in Japan was finally coming out in Australia – and once that was all sorted, he'd be home. They were into the final countdown, he'd promised.

In the meantime, it felt oddly normal to be sitting there in the pub garden with a man she used to play Monopoly with when she was eight, a Polish master carpenter who didn't speak much English, and a twenty-five-year-old Aussie poppet.

Everything was so bizarre in her world – it really bore no relation of any kind to the life she'd been living twelve months before – that it seemed like a perfectly reasonable thing to be doing on a Thursday evening while her kids were with her mother.

Leaning back in her plastic pub garden chair, sipping her really quite revolting drink – how did they manage that with Pimms? – and relishing the warm evening air on the bare skin of her arms, she let Dominic and Ali's chatter wash over her.

Now they were getting excited about how they could decorate the barn and whether they should go all out and have line dancing, or just a regular disco and what kind of food should be served and whether Anthea, Marguerite and their ilk would be comfortable sitting on hay bales, or would they need proper tables and chairs as well?

She glanced at Pavel, who was clearly oblivious to it all and was amusing himself trying to roll the perfect cigarette, starting from scratch every time his Rizla got wrinkled, the circumference wasn't exactly the same all the way along, or the cardboard filter went in wonky. Must be a craftsman thing, Hannah decided. Dominic had told her what a perfectionist Pavel was at work and Ali had told her – in slightly too much detail – how that translated to the bedroom.

Once Ali had finally fessed up to Hannah about her hot romance – she'd been trying out Marguerite-style discretion as an experiment, she said – there was no stopping her. And there was plenty to tell. After not having had sex with anyone for over a year, she was making up for lost time and Hannah heard about all of it.

'Reckon you've got it perfect now?' she asked Pavel, gesturing at the finished ciggie he was holding up to the light and examining from every angle.

He looked surprised and then grinned, realising she'd noticed what he was doing.

'Close,' he said, 'paper little bit messy. Maybe I try one more . . . you want this?'

He held the roll-up out towards her. Hannah shook her head and he tore it up, bending over his packet of tobacco for the next attempt.

'How long have you lived in England?' asked Hannah. She couldn't sit there in silence with him while Ali got more and more animated with Dominic. Now they were on to firework displays.

'One year, little bit more,' said Pavel.

'Do you like it?' said Hannah, getting a bit desperate.

Pavel tipped his head from side to side.

'I like some things,' he said, shrugging, 'others not so much. I like Ali!'

Hannah smiled at him.

'I like Ali too,' she said.

'She is your cousin?' asked Pavel.

'My husband's cousin,' said Hannah, 'but she feels more like my little sister.'

'This is good,' said Pavel, 'in Poland families are more closer. In England, families are too . . .'

He made a scattering motion with his hands.

'Some here, some there,' said Pavel, 'no good. You are good – mother next door. Better in same house, but next door OK.'

'But you don't live near your family, Pavel,' said Hannah.

A shadow crossed his face and she wished she'd kept her stupid mouth shut. Damn her middle-class social compulsions! He'd been perfectly happy working on his masterpiece cigarette, but she'd felt compelled to 'draw him out'.

'No jobs at home,' said Pavel. 'I must make money. Father dead.'

'Oh, I'm so sorry,' said Hannah, cursing herself again, 'my father died earlier this year. It's very hard.'

'My father die before I born,' said Pavel. 'Mother work very hard for me, now I look after her.'

'You're a good son,' said Hannah, wishing there could be a small earthquake. She just needed a medium-sized crevasse to jump into. She'd tried to make light conversation and now they seemed to be playing misery ping-pong.

'I make money, then I go home, buy land, build beautiful houses,' said Pavel, warming to his subject, 'one for me and mother, one to sell. This way, I make good life for family.'

He nodded, looking pleased with himself, and Hannah nodded back encouragingly, wondering how much of this plan Ali knew about.

But before she could think any more about that, she snapped to, realising that the others were standing up, apparently ready to leave.

'What's happening?' she asked.

'Keep up, Hanns!' said Ali, fully overexcited. 'Dom's been on the phone to Anthea and it looks like we might have the perfect barn – we're going to look at it now. Parteeeeeee!'

# Chapter Fifty-three

Marguerite was standing in her hall with the man from Christie's who'd come to value the furniture and paintings which had come with the house, wondering whether it would be very rude just to leave him to it.

He had a copy of the inventory that the trust kept on file, so he knew exactly what was to go to the sale room and she really didn't want to follow him round as he assessed Charlie's family possessions in material and monetary terms. She'd hung up his coat, given him coffee with those nice German dark chocolate biscuits, and put clean hand towels in the downstairs loo, surely that was enough?

'Well,' she said, her mind made up, 'if you're all set, I have some paperwork to see to. I'll be in my office just across the hall – there are no estate items in there, by the way – so let me know when you're finished and I'll arrange a taxi to take you back to the station.'

There! She'd said it and the ceiling hadn't come crashing down on her for her rudeness – in fact, he hadn't seemed bothered at all. He'd just thanked her and returned to his inspection of a gloomy Victorian oil painting of a Scottish landscape which Marguerite had always loathed. She turned towards her study feeling quite skittish.

Closing the door quietly, she looked round the room she had spent so many satisfying solitary hours working in. Would she miss it? Not really. Not as long as she had another room with good light, a sink, enough flat surfaces, and plenty of space for her archives and reference books. And she didn't even need those bulky old books as much as she used to. She'd keep the crucial ones, but there were quite a few she was going to sell when she moved, because with Ali's help, she was feeling much more confident on the computer now and had come to appreciate its advantages.

She sat down in front of the laptop and opened Internet Explorer, which Ali had set to Google, then typed in 'Property for sale Bloomsbury'. Up came a dizzying number of possible websites and she randomly clicked on one. Filling in her maximum budget, keeping some aside for renovations, she was thrilled to see that a two-bedroom flat, with a dining room she could convert into a study, was well within her reach. There was one that looked particularly nice, with a roof terrace, in a building with a lift. How exciting.

All she had to do now was tell Hannah what her plans were.

Marguerite closed her eyes at the thought of it. What would she do if her darling daughter hated the idea and got angry or upset? It was possible. Marguerite felt sad about leaving the place where they'd spent every Christmas of Hannah's childhood – and she absolutely dreaded the prospect of packing up Charlie's granny flat – but after all the difficulties of the past few years, she wanted a fresh start. She needed one.

She'd begun to let go of the place in her head, the moment she'd read that first letter from the solicitor and now felt as though she wouldn't be able to bear to stay there, even if the second cousin changed his mind and gave it to her outright.

But was she being selfish? Ought she to buy the house and somehow put it back in trust for Hector? Is that what Charlie would have wanted? But if so, why didn't he do it? A small voice inside her said that this was one mess of his she wasn't going to clear up – and she decided to listen to it.

She went back to looking at the property websites and was just figuring out how to 'favourite' a particular flat so she would be able to find it again later, when there was a loud commotion in the hall.

'Ganny! Ganny!' she heard a little voice calling out and then the handle of her studio door started rattling. Nancy! She immediately stood up to go to her granddaughter, but then turned back to close down the website first, feeling guilty as she did it.

This situation was making her sneaky – and it wasn't just moving back to London she was covering up. There was the other issue too. That would have to be addressed at some point, oh Lord. Marguerite shook her head to chase the thoughts away, closed the laptop's lid and hurried over to the door.

She opened it to find the hall full of people, or that was how it seemed, although really it was just Nancy, all the dogs, Ali and a young man she didn't know.

'What a lovely surprise,' said Marguerite, as Nancy wrapped her arms around her legs and looked up at her adoringly.

'Hey, Marg,' said Ali, 'this is my, er, friend Pav – Pavel. I don't think you've met him.'

'Lovely to see you, Pavel,' said Marguerite putting out her hand. He was a very good-looking young man. Marvellous bones.

'Hello,' he said, with a good firm handshake.

'Would you like some coffee?' said Marguerite. 'We could have it in the garden, it's such a lovely day.'

She was already drifting towards the kitchen, but Ali put her hand on her arm.

'We've come to take you out,' she said. 'Hanns said the bloke was here to value all your stuff and you don't wanna be here with that going on. She's going to come over in a minute to be on hand in case he needs to ask anything. She said we should just go. We're going to take Sooty with us and your two hounds.'

Marguerite opened her mouth, not sure what to say. Sneaking off to her study to avoid the man from Christie's was one thing, but surely she couldn't just flee from the house altogether? Wouldn't that be going too far?

'Come on,' said Ali, 'we're going to the seaside, I've promised Nancy she can have an ice-cream with a chocolate flake in it and I don't like my chances if I don't deliver.'

Marguerite smiled and ruffled her granddaughter's hair.

'Caterpillar,' she said, looking up at her grandmother with wide but determined eyes.

'The very hungry caterpillar?' said Marguerite, but Nancy shook her head and said it more loudly, an edge coming into her voice.

Ali laughed. 'She means the rollercoaster one – she wants to see if she's tall enough to go on it now. Hector's been on it and Nancy wants a go, so you know what that means . . .'

'It means I'd better get my handbag,' said Marguerite, 'and sharpish.'

As they sped – Ali was driving – through the country lanes in their full summer glory, sun streaming in through the open car windows, Marguerite felt liberated. It had seemed positively rebellious walking out of the house, leaving the man to it with his ghastly clipboard and loupe, but she didn't realise until they set off how happy she was to escape from it. She put her hand over and patted Ali's, on the steering wheel.

'Thank you, Ali, dear,' she said. 'Thank you for rescuing me. You really are a treasure.'

'You're welcome, Marg,' said Ali, 'just thought it would be pretty rubbish to be there while some bloke went grubbing through all your stuff. It's not right what's happening to you, but Hannah said you're not sure if you want to stay at the house anyway now, even if you could buy it back, is that right?'

Marguerite was too surprised to reply. She had said that, in the kitchen that afternoon, after Anthony had told them the final outcome, but because she hadn't elaborated on it further, or ever mentioned it again, Marguerite had thought Hannah might have forgotten it, or dismissed the idea as something silly said in the heat of the moment.

Ali had turned to look at her, that appealing open expression on her face, clearly expecting an answer.

'Yes,' said Marguerite firmly, wishing Ali would keep her eyes on the road. 'That is something I do need to talk to Hannah about in more detail.'

Ali turned to smile at her again, nodding encouragingly.

'Look at road, please, Ali,' said Pavel, from the back.

'Road . . .' echoed Nancy, which seemed to do the trick. Ali looked ahead again, which made Marguerite feel more able to speak freely.

'The thing is,' she said, 'I want a change. I want to live in London again. It was a tremendous shock when I first got the letter saying the house wasn't mine, but I think from that moment, I started to move on. But it's not just about me, Ali. It's Hannah's family home too and perhaps she's been hoping that they would all live in it one day.'

'Oh, I think it's all fine,' said Ali, slowing down to pass some horses and then speeding off again round the blind bends, 'she just wants you to be happy. That's what she told me – but she would like to know what you're planning to do, Marg, so you need to talk to her, that's all.'

'So you think I should just, as you say . . . tell her?' asked Marguerite, turning the idea over in her head as she said it.

Ali laughed.

'Oh, you Poms,' she said, 'you're hilarious. Yes! Open your mouth and tell her what you want to do, is it really that scary? It was OK when you told her what was going on with the house, wasn't it? And here you are doing exactly the same thing again, worrying yourself to death when all you need to do is open your beak.'

'Beak!' said Nancy from the back. 'Tweet, tweet.'

'That's right, Nance,' said Ali, laughing, 'that's what Granny's got to learn to do – sing like a birdie, tweet tweet.'

She beeped the horn in time with Nancy's tweeting and Marguerite couldn't help laughing too.

# Chapter Fifty-four

Ali and Dominic stood at the entrance to the barn, the strains of Patsy Cline filling the air, and raised their beer bottles to each other. With hay bales, tables with red-and-white chequered cloths and a fiddle band setting up their gear on a temporary stage, it looked like the set for a cheesy Elvis musical. Exactly what they'd intended.

'Thanks, Ali pops,' said Dominic, clinking his bottle against hers and then hugging her, 'you're the best. I couldn't have done any of it without you – well, I could have, but it wouldn't have been nearly so much fun.'

'It's been great,' said Ali, hugging him back. 'Well, it was bloody rude that you didn't want to marry me and all that, but thanks for laying Pav on as an alternative, that was generous of you.'

'Consider him your annual bonus,' said Dominic, 'and so lucky for me that he's also a master carpenter.'

'Yeah, wasn't that a coincidence?' said Ali, laughing. 'But I do wish he'd get here, do you think anyone's going to come? It's five past seven and there's usually some freak who gets to a party right on time . . . I want it to get started.'

She drummed her cowboy-booted heels on the ground.

'Hang on a minute,' said Dominic. 'I've got something I want to give you before the hordes turn up.'

He reached in his back pocket and pulled out an envelope, which he handed to her.

Ali opened it, mystified, to see a crisp £50 note, on top of more of the same. She did a quick count and turned to him with her mouth open.

'There's £1000 in here,' she said. 'Is it for the builders? Who do I give it to?'

Dominic laughed, patting her on the shoulder.

'It's for you, dingbat, it's your real annual bonus. As you're working for a banker it seemed only fair to give you one. It's how we do things in my world.'

'Wow!' said Ali and threw her arms around him. 'Thank you so much. I've used up all my savings and it feels so good to know I've got an emergency stash again.'

'Good,' said Dom, 'that sounds like an excellent plan and hold on . . . I think I can hear a car.'

They ran out to see two minibus taxis pull up, containing all the workmen from Dominic's development, plus an assortment of lady companions. Next to arrive were Hannah, Anthea and the kids – plus five dogs. Dominic had insisted the canines were invited, saying you couldn't have a proper family party without dogs and small children on the dance floor.

Hector was dressed as a cowboy, with water pistols in his holsters and he gave Dominic a good squirt in greeting. Nancy was wearing her Snow White dress with a plastic tiara and polka-dot shoes from a Minnie Mouse outfit. She was carrying her best magic wand. Dominic bent down and scooped her up.

'Don't you look beautiful, little princess,' he said. 'Will you do me the honour of a dance later?'

Nancy giggled and hit him on the head with her wand.

'And here are two even more beautiful princesses,' said Dominic, turning to greet Hannah and Anthea. 'Well, maybe, one princess, one queen. Hello, your maj,' he said kissing Anthea on both cheeks, then doing the same to Hannah.

'Where's your mum?' he asked her.

'Oh, she'll be here any minute,' said Hannah vaguely. 'She had, er, something to see to at the house – but she is coming.'

They followed the children and dogs in to the barn to greet Ali and Dominic turned to watch Hannah go past. She was wearing a sleeveless 1950s summer dress, tightly waisted, with a full skirt to mid-calf, and cowboy boots, and looked absolutely gorgeous. In the brief moment of kissing her cheek he'd noticed the freckles on her shoulders. He'd badly wanted to kiss them too.

Her husband must be an absolute idiot to leave her alone for so long. It was over two months now, or something ridiculous. He might be a so-called 'male model' – and Dominic had seen a picture of him in Hannah's kitchen, so knew he was disgustingly good-looking, in a swarthy kind of way – but to have a wife as beautiful and lovely as Hannah and those gorgeous children and then to go flitting off to the other side of the world was just plain stupid. He didn't deserve such a wonderful family.

Dominic watched Hector squirting his water pistols at Ali's boots while she tried to jump out of the way, and Nancy chasing after Hector squealing to have a go. Such great kids. He walked over to them.

'Hey Hec,' he called out, 'give me one of your weapons, then it's me and Nancy against you and Ali . . . WATER FIGHT!'


Marguerite and Anthony were standing in the kitchen waiting for the taxi. He took hold of both her hands in his and brought them up to his lips.

'I can arrive separately, if you prefer,' he said.

Marguerite shook her head.

'No,' she said, 'no more smoke and veils. I've told Hannah that we have become, er, friends and she's happy for us, Anthony, she really is. She adores you and I think she's hugely relieved she doesn't have to feel guilty about that now. She doesn't even mind that it's all happening rather soon after Charlie's death. She said I deserve some fun – I was so touched. But she doesn't know about the past, she thinks it's all a new thing and I really want to keep it that way, don't you?'

Anthony nodded.

'Definitely,' he said, 'I'm all for the new Marguerite who comes right out and says what's going on for her, but only for the here and now – we don't need to go back over the messy past. Another country and all that.'

'I'm so glad we agree about that,' said Marguerite, smiling at him, but then she dropped her eyes and Anthony saw a frown appear between them.

'What is it?' he asked, raising her chin with his forefinger so she would look at him again.

'Oh, Anthony,' she said, tears filling the grey-blue eyes he so loved, 'it's just I still feel so bad about what I did . . . It makes me feel as though I don't deserve this happiness now.'

'What?' he asked gently. 'Tell me, you'll feel better if you do, you know that now.'

'Making myself hate you like that,' she said. 'It was so wrong, but you know it was the only way I could get over not being with you. If I couldn't love you, I had to hate you.'

'It's OK,' said Anthony, 'I know you didn't hate me really . . . I think I even knew it at the time, really.'

'Well, I'm glad to hear that, but I feel so bad that I made Hannah hate you too,' she said. 'I blamed you for all Charlie's excesses, making it all your fault when really I was the terrible one all along, betraying my husband . . . and my child.'

She looked wretched, but Anthony just smiled gently, shaking his head.

'We all did bad things, Marguerite,' he said. 'I betrayed my best friend and he was no saint either, you know that.'

He wondered how much she did know. He certainly wasn't going to tell her the details. He knew them; it was how he'd been able to live with himself all these years. Charlie had been just as bad in his own way – you could almost say worse – but it could all stay buried with him. It was time for them all to move on.

'We did things we regret,' he continued, 'but none of it matters now. And you didn't betray Hannah, you stayed with her father for her, when I begged you to leave him. She need never know about all that and the great thing is, she doesn't hate me now, does she? She didn't hate me from the moment she met me properly, so let it go now, please. We are so lucky to have this second chance and I just want to enjoy it.'

'Are you sure?' said Marguerite.

'One hundred per cent sure. It's all in the past and I'm much more excited about the future these days,' said Anthony.

'So am I,' said Marguerite, realising it was true as she said it.

'So will you celebrate that with me by wearing this?' said Anthony and he reached in his pocket and pulled out a ring.

It was thick gold, with two snake heads meeting on top of the finger. One had a turquoise eye, the other was coral.

'Oh,' said Marguerite quietly, knowing immediately how old and precious it was.

'Is it good enough for my Cleopatra?' he asked, taking her right hand and slipping it on the ring finger, 'we might move it on to the other hand one day, but for now, it can go there.'


Hannah had persuaded Anthea to find a table and claim it as her own. Once she had her settled there, she went to the bar to get them some drinks. She needed a bit of Dutch courage for what she had to tell her, so took up Dominic's suggestion she had a whisky chaser with her beer, cowboy-style, but then he seemed to be sticking around and she needed a moment alone with Anthea.

'Dominic,' she said, 'I'm really sorry, but I've got to go and talk to Anthea – I won't be long, but there's something I must tell her. I'll tell you after, OK?'

'Fine,' said Dominic, looking a bit bewildered, but putting it down to mysterious women's business, he headed off to see what his builder boys were up to.

Hannah sat down with Anthea and took a deep breath.

'Anthea,' she said, her heart hammering, 'I have something to tell you.'

'Is it about your mother?' Anthea answered, smiling broadly.

'Yes,' said Hannah.

'Has she got a fancy man?' said Anthea, picking up her drink and fixing Hannah with a wicked look over the top of the glass.

'Well, yes,' said Hannah, 'but how on earth did you know?'

Anthea shrugged. 'She's got her old glow back. I've known your mother for fifty years, Hannah, since before you were born, or Charlie even inherited the house. I remember what she looked like when she first came down after they got engaged. She was ravishing. She's always been beautiful, but over the years with your father that glow started to fade. In the last few months, it disappeared entirely – but recently it's come back. And I came to the conclusion there was only one possible reason and it had to be male. Who is he?'

'It's Anthony,' said Hannah, astonished, but deeply relieved she hadn't had to spell it out, she'd been so dreading it. 'My father's best friend – remember?'

Anthea roared with laughter.

'Oh, that's priceless,' she said, 'the best friend. Charlie would love it . . .' she looked up to the ceiling and raised her glass. 'Cheers, Chaz, don't worry, she's being looked after.'

'Do you really think he'd be pleased?' asked Hannah.

'Good God, yes,' said Anthea, 'he was always half in love with Anthony himself. Oh, look! Here they are, the happy couple. Ooo oo! Over here!'

She waved her arm in the air as Hannah sat back, feeling rather stunned by it all. She was hugely relieved it had been so easy to tell Anthea, but now she had to deal with seeing Anthony and Marguerite out together in public for the first time.

But the moment she saw her mother on Anthony's arm, all doubts disappeared. She was indeed radiant and the two of them looked so right together. Hannah felt a deep pang to see another man where Charlie used to be, but she was so fond of Anthony already, it wasn't nearly as hard to handle as it could have been. She jumped up and rushed over to them.

'Hello, Anthony,' she said, kissing his cheek and squeezing his hand at the same time, 'lovely to see you.'

Anthony looked so happy and sweetly shy about it all, Hannah had to give him another kiss and whisper in his ear.

'I'm so glad about you and Mummy,' she said, 'now I don't have to be secretive about having lunch with you any more.'

Then she managed to get round to her mother's side to whisper in her ear.

'I've told Anthea, she's cool – and so am I,' and then she dashed off to find Dominic. She wanted to tell him before he saw it. Ali already knew and had agreed to keep quiet, so Hannah could tell him herself. It just seemed the right thing to do, as it was his party and it would probably cause a bit of a stir among the guests and it was still all so new to Hannah, it wasn't something she could just blurt out casually.

She found him outside talking to a group of his builders and sidled up to him.

'Hi,' she said discreetly in his ear, 'can I steal you for a moment?'

Dominic turned to her, smiling.

'Of course,' he said, 'what do you want me to do?'

'I just need to talk to you for a moment,' said Hannah, wishing she didn't sound so melodramatic, 'somewhere a bit more private.'

'I know just the place,' said Dominic and led her off round the side of the barn. It was still light and Hannah could see an old tractor at the far end.

'Is that where we're going?' she said.

Dominic nodded and when they got there, he opened the tractor's door, got in and then reached his hand down to help her clamber up the high step. Hannah sat down in the funny little cabin and giggled.

'Well, this is cosy,' she said.

Dominic smiled and passed his beer bottle to her.

'Fancy a swig?'

'Thank you,' said Hannah, taking a drink and then handing it back.

'What did you want to tell me?' asked Dominic.

'It's silly really,' said Hannah, 'but I just thought I should tell you formally, because it's your party . . . it's just that my mum is, well, she's dating and she's brought her, er . . .' what the heck was he? '. . . boyfriend along tonight. So everyone's going to see them together.'

'Wow,' said Dominic, 'that's good isn't it? She's a beautiful woman,

I'm not surprised some septuagenarian George Clooney has snapped her up. Who is it?'

'Well, that's the other thing. Do you remember that barrister I told you about? The one you convinced me I had to ask to help us with the house, even though it was really tricky for me to approach him because he was my dad's worst drinking buddy and my mother absolutely loathed him . . . Remember all that?'

Dominic nodded, looking a bit puzzled.

'Well, I did ask him – big thanks to you,' continued Hannah, 'and he really helped us and now the amazing thing is, he and my mum have got together, which is insane because she used to hate his guts, but he doesn't drink now, he gave up a couple of years ago and he and Marguerite have found they like each other after all, which is weirdly great, because I adore him too and, as I told you, I felt really guilty about secretly being friends with him when Mummy hated him so much . . .'

She stopped short, realising she was gabbling. Dominic was smiling at her indulgently, rather as he would at Hector telling one of his long, involved and mostly fictitious stories about his school day.

'His name's Anthony,' she added.

'Well, that all sounds terrific,' said Dominic. 'I'm delighted for all of you and very touched you felt you had to let me on it like this.'

Hannah stopped for a moment and just looked at him.

'It's, er, just them being here together tonight for the first time,' she said, 'it's kind of their coming-out ball and I thought, as the host, you ought to know, in case there was any awkwardness. And I suppose I didn't expect Anthea to be so cool about it and thought you ought to know for that reason, but it turns out she had actually guessed Mummy had a "fancy man" as she called it and she thinks it's great.'

She was gabbling again, but it was all so weird, she couldn't help it.

'Yes, she's very intuitive, Aunt Anth,' said Dominic, 'not much gets past her. Well, thanks for telling me, Hannah, it's good to be in on the goss – does Ali know?'

Hannah nodded absently, her thoughts elsewhere. She'd just real-ised why she'd felt compelled to tell Dominic her big news in a formal way and it was freaking her out a bit. She'd come to think of him as the head of the family somehow.

With the three houses so close together, all of them constantly running in and out of each other's kitchens, Ali working for Dominic, Dominic advising her what to do about the house and no other man around, he'd come to seem like the main man. It was odd, yet somehow completely normal.

'Actually Hannah,' said Dominic, turning round in his seat towards her, 'as we're talking about serious stuff, there's something I want to ask you about.'

'Shoot,' said Hannah, quite relieved to be distracted from the other line of thought.

'Well,' he said, 'I was wondering if you would mind if I bought your mother's house? Anthea told me that she has decided to move to London and I would love to buy it, but I want to make sure you would feel all right about that first.'

'Are you going to make it into flats?' asked Hannah, horrified.

'Oh no!' said Dominic, 'I'm going to live in it. I've decided not to go back to New York. Being here with all of you guys, back in funny old England with all its little ways, I've enjoyed myself so much and it's made me realise that Aunt Anth is right, it is time for me to come home. I've got enough money – enough to make more money ha ha – I don't need another job that demands me to have my soul on call twenty-four hours a day. So I can settle down at last and your mother's house would be a very nice one to do it in, plus I'd be next door to Anthea and she's going to need someone around when she gets older. She's been so good to me, I don't want to let the old girl down.'

'That would be great,' said Hannah, pretty sure she meant it. Although while she was genuinely pleased her mother was making the break to start a new life in London – especially as she had promised to come down for regular weekends with them – she hadn't really thought about someone else living in that house.

'No, it really would be good,' she said, warming to the idea, 'much better than having strangers move in. Having you there would be practically like keeping it in the family. I'd love you to buy it, Dominic.'

'That's wonderful,' he said. 'I'm so pleased. I won't say anything to her tonight, but I will press ahead now – result!'

'Well, that was exciting,' said Hannah, 'but shall we go back to the party now? It's getting a bit stuffy in your tractor here and I want to make sure the kids are OK.'

'And I want to take a look at the happy couple,' said Dominic.

# Chapter Fifty-five

Matt was on his way to the airport when Pete rang.

'Maaaaaate,' he said.

'Maaaaaaaaaaaaaaaate,' said Matt back, laughing. It was all part of their repertoire and never failed to make him feel fully earthed and plugged in to his world. 'It's a bit early for you to be up, isn't it?'

'Yeah, well, you woke me up, dragging your stuff around the place like you were shifting dead bodies, so I thought I'd ring to say good-bye – thanks for your farewell note, by the way, I'll keep it always.'

'Yeah, right, in the recycling – but you should hold on to that, it might be worth something one day. Shame I didn't sign it.'

'Well you might be right about that actually,' said Pete. 'Want some good news to think about while you're on the flight?'

'What? Better than "Here and There" being top five in Australia? I'm pretty stoked to be going back with those tidings. Is there something else?'

'Yeah,' said Pete, 'just a little detail for you to tell the wife when you get home. The people at the label love the tracks we put down and they're signing us for an album, with you as the vocalist, me as producer. Australia first up, then . . . the GLOBE!'

Matt was stunned for a moment.

'Are you still there, tosser?' said Pete. 'Don't lose your voice now, when you're just about to become a superstar with it.'

'You're not shitting me, are you?'

Pete laughed.

'No, mate, and it's good money too.'

He said a figure. Matt sat up so fast he dropped his phone on the taxi floor.

'Split 50:50?' he said, once he'd retrieved it.

'No, you moron, EACH – we're making money, my friend. Proper money. Happy landings!'

He rang off and Matt sat staring down at his phone for a bit and then he rolled down the window and started yelling out of it: 'We did it, we did it, we finally fucking did it!'

He was in mid-yell when his phone rang again. Pete.

'Don't tell me it was a joke,' said Matt, feeling a little queasy for a moment.

'No, it's straight up,' said Pete, 'that's not what I'm calling about this time.'

'That's a relief,' said Matt, 'because I've just told every jogger in Centennial Park how happy I am . . . So what gives?'

'I was just wondering,' said Pete, sounding oddly tentative, 'will you be seeing Ali when you get there?'

'Sure,' said Matt, 'she's living at our house.'

'Can you say hi to her from me?'

'No worries,' said Matt, so surprised at Pete's tone. He didn't launch into the teasing attack such a sappy request would normally have unleashed, 'anything else, while I'm at it?'

'Yeah,' said Pete, sounding more himself, 'tell her to Skype the Lizard King. I want to talk to her.'

# Chapter Fifty-six

Anthea was showing them all how to dance Strip the Willow. She'd grabbed one of Dominic's burlier builders to be her partner and once she'd got everyone into two lines – men and boys down one side, women and girls down the other, dogs getting in the way – and after instructing the band what to play, she demonstrated.

Anthony and Marguerite followed her lead and Hannah had to blink back tears, they looked so sweet, holding hands and dancing together. Her mother looked about nineteen when she smiled at him.

'Oh, I remember this now,' said Hannah to Ali, who was standing next to her, 'it's really good fun once you get going and absolutely exhausting.'

'It looks like bush dancing. We had to do that at school and it was rank, but if you say it's good fun, I'll give it a crack.'

'Do you remember it, Dom?' Hannah shouted across to him.

'I think so,' he said, looking dubious, 'wasn't much for the girly skipping myself, but I'll give it a go.'

Then it was their turn to skip up and down the lines of dancers, then up again twirling with each man and woman and Hannah found that she couldn't stop giggling, it was all so silly, then it was down to the bottom to stand clapping until someone came to spin her round again, which seemed to happen with dizzying frequency.

'That was so fun,' said Hector, falling against Hannah in a panting heap at the end of the dance. 'I love willow stripping.'

'It's certainly better than asset stripping,' said Dominic. 'Very jolly – oh, hang on, we're off again.'

Now Anthea, a wicked gleam in her eye, was using Marguerite and Anthony to demonstrate the Gay Gordons. Dominic took Hannah's hands and they assumed the position.

'Forward, two three four, back two three four, skippety skippety skippety skippety, waltzy waltzy waltzy waltzy,' he muttered as they went, with a few 'oh craps' when they trod all over each other's feet.

Hannah was laughing so much she had a stomach ache.

'Agh,' she said, bent double, 'we'll never make it on *Strictly* . . .'

'But it's good fun trying, isn't it?' said Dominic. 'I rather like all this. What's next Aunt Anth, a quadrille?'

'I think we'll try an eightsome reel now, which did develop from the quadrille, Dominic, so don't think you're such a smartie pants, right – you and Hannah, come over here, Marguerite and Anthony, Pavel and Ali, and I'll have my Pole, come on Baltazar, quick sticks, so that's a lovely eight. Everyone get into groups of eight,' she shouted to the rest of the crowd, who didn't dare disobey her.

Hector came over wanting to join their set, so Ali asked Pavel to step aside and took him as her partner. Then Nancy wanted to join in and Dominic lifted her on to his hip.

'Aha,' he said, 'finally, I'm going to get the dance I asked for . . . I'm going to dance with two princesses at once, that's how special I am.'

Fortunately for him, Nancy had had enough after two skips round in a circle and wriggled to get down, running off to join a group of children doing more freeform dancing together.

'Bloody hell,' said Dominic, quite pink in the cheeks, as they tried to make sense of Anthea's instructions to do turns in groups of four pairs, 'this is complicated, I've had a few threesomes in my time, but I'm not so sure about an eightsome . . .'

'A St Andrew's Cross!' Anthea was booming out, 'you have to do a St Andrew's Cross!' before grabbing Anthony and Marguerite to demonstrate with her and her partner. 'It's very easy, in two groups of four, just join your right hands, raised, in the middle and turn, clockwise. That's it!'

They managed to get that together, with Ali, Dominic and Hannah bending down to Hector's level, but by the time they got to the bit where Anthea was shouting at them all to 'do a chain, you hopeless lot, a chain!' they were in a complete mess and Hannah was crying with laughter.

Ali and Hector had lost interest and were doing disco moves to the Scottish music, which just made her laugh more and then she and Dominic joined in, ignoring Anthea's protests.

'Do the pony!' said Ali, demonstrating.

'Do the mashed potato!' said Hannah.

'Do the Monster Mash!' said Hector.

'Disco Inferno!' shouted Dominic when it was his turn.

'Hang on,' said Hannah, 'I know the Zumba moves to that . . .'

She showed them and they all joined in until the band stopped playing and they all came to a sweaty standstill.

'Oh, that was so much fun,' said Hannah, fanning herself.

'I like dancing,' said Hector.

'Good man,' said Dominic, 'very important for impressing the ladies later in life.'

'I'm going to find Pav,' said Ali, 'get him back on the dance floor, if that's OK, Hec?'

'Fine,' he said, looking over to where the children were gathered in a big gang in front of the stage. 'I'm going to find someone my own age to dance with. I can see Marcus . . .' and he ran off.

'And I'm going to brave the loo,' said Hannah.

'Don't worry,' said Dominic, 'Ali made me get the premium portaloos; you could tour Europe in them. I'll go and get us some more drinks.'

When Hannah got out into the beautiful still evening air, she realised how hot she was and stood for a moment, holding her face up to the sky, her eyes closed, relishing the moment. The pure physical fun of the dancing had flooded her blood with endorphins and she felt completely content. The kids were having a great time, Anthea was in her element and far from creating awkwardness, Marguerite and Anthony being together seemed so right. It was all good.

She wished Matt was there, of course; that would have been the perfect last piece of the mosaic, but she was so used to him being away now, it wasn't spoiling her evening not having him there, it just would have been even better if he was.

Although there was a very small voice in the back of her head that wondered whether he would have enjoyed such a hokey party, or whether he might have made scathing comments about it, like he had at the church fête all those months ago. Hayseeds among the hay bales, that kind of thing. She told the voice to shut up and headed for the loos.

When she went back into the barn, the band had been replaced by a DJ and it seemed hot, dark and noisy in there after being outside. She stood at the edge of the dance floor, watching the cavorting people, letting her eyes adjust.

There was Fiona, her mother's cleaner, and what seemed like her entire family. Parents, kids and teachers from the school. Friends of Anthea's and her mother's. The vicar, the doctors, the postmistress and a general mix of people from the village. Kelli from the White Hart was getting on down with one of Dominic's more muscly contractors. Now she could see again in the darkness, she realised she knew practically everyone at the party – and quite a few of them she'd known all her life.

She realised that having gone to school in London and never lived in the village full time until now, only at weekends and in the holidays, she hadn't appreciated before quite how deep her connections with it were. She'd had an inkling of it at Charlie's funeral, but now, for the first time, she realised that in a lot of fundamental ways it was home for her.

Although there was so much she desperately missed about both London and Sydney and she didn't really feel she had much in common with the people who lived in the village, it was still the one place on earth where she felt properly woven into the warp and weft of it all. She understood that now.

Suddenly she felt a terrible pang about Marguerite leaving the house. And if they ever moved out of Garden Cottage, back to London, to Sydney, or wherever, the connection to the village really would be lost and not just to her – also to the kids, who were so happy in such a nurturing nest.

The thought made her feel quite panicky – but at the same time, did that mean she was condemned to spend the rest of her life in a tiny village with one terrible shop and one terrible pub? She didn't know which prospect was worse. Losing the connection with the village, or staying there. Suddenly she didn't feel like dancing anymore.

Dominic came over and handed her a long cool drink.

'I thought you'd like something refreshing,' he said and Hannah took a big gulp expecting water, only to find it was a vodka and tonic, but after the surprise wore off, she found it was just what she felt like and threw it back.

The instantly recognisable first bars of 'Single Ladies' rang out and everyone on the dance floor whooped.

'Do you want to dance?' said Dominic.

'I don't think I do, just at the moment, ' said Hannah, 'the other dancing was so much fun, I don't feel like this kind now.'

She glanced back outside.

'It's such a beautiful night,' she said. 'I think I'm going to go back out there for a bit.'

'Good idea,' said Dominic. 'I'll come with you.'

When they stepped outside Hannah saw that where she had stood enjoying the peace a few minutes earlier was now occupied by a large, rowdy group, made up of several of Dominic's tradesmen and their lady friends. Standing in a circle, clapping and yelling, they seemed to be playing a drinking game.

'I think we might give that a miss,' said Dominic.

Hannah nodded.

'Don't worry, I know where all the good spots are,' he said and led the way down the side of the barn again.

Right at the back was an old trailer, with square bales of hay stacked high on it. Dominic disappeared round the side of it and came back carrying a ladder.

'Up you go,' he said, putting his foot on the bottom rung and gesturing for her to climb up.

Giggling a bit, Hannah did as he said, stepping carefully from rung to rung for what seemed quite a long way and then carefully clambering on to the top of the bales, taking care not to look down. It wasn't very high really, but her head was a bit dizzy from the drinking and dancing.

'Move over,' Dominic called up to her. 'I'm climbing aboard.'

Hannah shifted over to the centre of the flat expanse of hay and looked around her. It was magical. She felt like the only person in the world, looking around into the open air, stars above, the land falling away in front of her, the wooded far horizon just visible in the moonlight.

'Wow,' she said, to herself, just as Dominic's head appeared at the edge of the bales.

'Now for the tricky bit,' he said, 'slightly wish I hadn't had that last vodka, but hup . . .'

He got his knees on to the top and then turned round and crawled over to her, sitting down at her side.

'Aah,' he said, looking out at the view, 'yes, it's just as I hoped it would be. Like a glorious island.'

'It's amazing up here,' said Hannah. 'Did you plan it as a chilling area?'

'Pretty much,' he said, 'meaning yes. I hoped someone would find it and enjoy it and I'm so glad it's me – us.'

Hannah turned and smiled at him.

'Thanks, Dominic,' she said, 'this is just glorious.'

He saluted her and lay back down on the hay.

'Mmmm, now that's even better,' he said.

Hannah took his lead, lying back and gazing up at the stars. Neither of them spoke and it seemed like such a primal thing to do, to lie on a great pile of dried grass gazing up at the night sky.

'This is even better than lying in a meadow looking up at the blue sky on a summer's day,' she said, 'and I love that . . .'

She turned to look at him, to find he was already looking at her. As she smiled at him, his hand folded around hers and it seemed like a natural place to be, lying there with him, on their little hay bale planet, holding hands.

And in that unreal state, it didn't seem any stranger when his head moved towards hers and his lips touched her mouth and rested there.

Very gently at first and then, when she didn't move away, with more pressure, until her mouth spontaneously opened and his tongue snaked in and twined with hers.

As Hannah felt the firm silkiness of Dominic's tongue sliding against hers, pressing slowly deeper into her mouth and then starting to move more quickly, it was as though a car engine had been fired up inside her. A Formula One engine, possibly Apollo 12.

Not thinking, just being, she surrendered to the sensation of their tongues moving against each other. Nothing else existed, except that beautiful feeling and the response it triggered in other parts of her body.

But then, as his hand travelled down to her breast, pulling down her dress and taking her nipple between his fingers, she suddenly came to her senses. That was exactly what Matt would have done; what was she doing letting Dominic have a go?

She immediately pulled away and sat up, yanking up her dress.

'I'm so sorry,' she said. 'I shouldn't have let that happen.'

'I'm glad you did,' said Dominic, reaching out for her hand. Hannah immediately pulled hers away.

'No,' she said, 'I'm sorry, Dominic, but I think I may have given you the wrong impression, coming up here with you, but it's been such a glorious night and it's so beautiful here, I just wasn't thinking clearly.'

'I've never thought more clearly in my life,' said Dominic. 'I've wanted to kiss you since the cupboard under the stairs.'

Hannah said nothing, she was too confused. She knew she had to get away from there as soon as possible, but after sitting up so quickly – and what had just happened – she felt really giddy and knew she couldn't negotiate the ladder feeling like that.

'And now I can tell you something else that I wanted to say earlier, in the tractor cabin,' Dominic was saying, 'but it didn't feel right then. It does now, though. When I buy your mother's house, Hannah, I wonder if you would like to come and live in it with me . . . You and the kids. And Sooty, of course.'

Hannah froze with horror. He still thought she'd meant that kiss. Despite her protests he hadn't got the message that it had been a brief drunken mistake on her part. For the first time since she'd pulled away, she turned to look at him, and saw an expression of total confidence on his face. The master negotiator, he thought it was a done deal.

'Oh,' she said, panic hitting her like a tidal wave, 'no, no. I know I did kiss you back for a moment then, but it was a mistake, the drink . . . I didn't mean to.'

'I know it seems sudden,' said Dominic, reaching for her hand again; she pulled it away, but he didn't stop talking, 'but you can't say it hasn't been building. All the time we've spent together recently, we're already like a couple – this was the inevitable next stage we've been moving towards.'

Hannah's mouth had gone dry. Was that really what he thought? That they'd been courting these weeks, when she'd just thought they were old friends hanging out? Had she led him on without realising it? Oh horribleness. Great terrible horribleness.

'No,' she said, sounding as startled as she felt, 'you've got me all wrong, Dominic. I'm very fond of you, you've been a great friend, but as I keep telling you, I'm happily married to Matt. I'm not going to move in with someone else, not even to my family home. I'm really sorry if you've had that impression and I should never have let you kiss me . . .'

She started to cry. Mistake. It gave him justifiable cause to put his arms round her again. She immediately remembered that afternoon in the pub garden when he'd comforted her, the night they'd got drunk together, all the times they'd gone out on virtual double dates with Ali and Pavel. The dancing . . .

Oh no, he was right. He had every reason to think they'd been dating, when she'd just been using him as a convenient male stand-in. She adored him as a friend, but didn't feel romantically about him at all. Trying not to be any more unpleasant than necessary, she pushed his arms away and sat up straight.

'I'm really sorry, Dominic, but I've made a terrible mistake. As I say, I was carried away by the night and the drinks and the dancing and I should never have let this happen. You have every reason to despise me, but while I'm very fond of you as a friend, I just don't think of you that way.'

Now he looked bewildered.

'But . . . but the way you responded just now . . . You kissed me back . . .'

'I'm sorry, Dominic, it was just an animal reaction. I haven't had sex for months and I'm used to having it . . .'

Her voice petered out; the last thing she wanted to do was to discuss her marital sex life with him. She was used to having it at least every other day. It was the glue that kept her and Matt bound together and she wanted her glue back. Her superglue. Her Matt. What had she been doing with this Prittstick?

'Please can we forget what just happened?' she said. 'Well, keep it as a private – happy – memory between us,' she quickly added, suddenly intensely aware of how important it was not to make an enemy of him. They had to remain friends, or he might want to hurt her by telling Matt. Oh no, it was truly awful. Worse than she'd even realised.

'It shouldn't have happened, but it did,' she continued, 'but that doesn't mean it's ever going to happen again. I'm happily married to the father of my children and I intend to stay that way.'

Dominic sat up too, the look of bewilderment starting to turn into something more upset. Hannah's guts were starting to churn with anxiety.

'But what kind of husband and father takes himself off to the other side of the world for months on end?' he said. 'Don't you think you deserve better than that? A woman like you is a prize for any man – and those wonderful children. Don't you all deserve someone who is there for you, unselfishly, to look after you and provide for you properly like a real man?'

'I've given up trying to make any of you understand that things between Matt and me are fine – if a little unusual,' said Hannah, as coolly as she could manage, desperate to get the tone right, to be firm without getting him offside, 'and as you haven't met him, Dominic, please don't start judging what kind of a man Matt is, OK? And now, if you don't mind, I think I better try and get down from here.'

Dominic sighed heavily and put his head in his hands.

'I'm such an idiot,' he said, 'but I'm not going to let you break your neck. Let me go first.'

He shimmied down the ladder with surprising speed, then stood at the bottom of it while Hannah manoeuvred herself back down slowly. They stood at the bottom looking at each other. Hannah felt sick.

'I'm sorry, Dominic,' she said, 'terribly sorry if I gave you the wrong idea. You've been a really good friend to me and I would like to think we could stay that way.'

He nodded, closing his eyes.

'I'm sorry too, Hannah,' he said, opening them again. 'I think I allowed myself to believe that what I wanted to be the case was true. You didn't lead me on, I deluded myself and I should have known you better than to think you would betray your husband. You're too good for that. And don't worry, I won't say anything to anyone about this, OK? Cross my heart, hope to die etcetera . . .'

'Thanks, Dominic,' she said, smiling in genuine gratitude – and at his unfailing ability to lighten a difficult moment. 'Thanks for that and for everything. You're going to make some lucky woman very happy one day.'

Just not me. She leaned forward and kissed him chastely on the cheek, which felt somehow as though it cancelled out the earlier inappropriate kiss.

'And now,' she said, 'would you mind if we went back to the party separately?'

'Off you go,' he said, slumping down on to his heels and leaning back against the wheel of the trailer. 'I'll stay here a while and work out how I can break it to Anthea that I won't be moving in next door with the perfect ready-made family of her dreams.'

Hannah stood for a moment, taking it in. Even worse than she'd thought. Anthea was in on it. She'd probably been hoping to announce their engagement at this party. At that very moment, she was most likely planning a double wedding, with her and Dominic and Marguerite and Anthony, involving all three houses and gardens. What a total cock-up.

For a moment Hannah felt so sorry for Dominic she wanted to lean down and kiss his cheek again, but thought better of it. So she just raised her hand in farewell and walked off to find her children. Time to go home.

Wherever that was.

# Chapter Fifty-seven

Ali and Hannah were sitting at the kitchen table in their bathrobes, both with their heads in their hands. It was nearly midday. The kids were in the garden playing with Sooty and Hannah wished she could turn down their volume a bit.

The awfulness of what had happened the night before had led to practically no sleep, and that combined with the stupid way she'd mixed her drinks had resulted in a headache like the Seven Dwarves were mining for diamonds around her temples. The long hot shower she'd taken to try and wash her guilt away had done nothing to alleviate the discomfort of that either.

Ali had made a plate of fried cheese sandwiches, which she said always made her feel better the morning after, but even the smell of them made Hannah want to vomit. She was nursing a glass of Hector's chocolate milk hoping the sugar shock might wake her system up a bit.

'I don't know what I would have done if you hadn't come round the corner at that moment last night,' Ali was saying, 'I might be sitting in a police cell rather than here.'

'And I'm just so grateful my mother had decided it was time for the children to go home and had already called a taxi,' said Hannah. 'I couldn't have stayed at that party one more minute. But just tell me again – how did you find out Pavel is married with three children?'

'One of the other Polish guys' wives told me,' said Ali, 'she's English. Met him a couple of years ago, had a torrid sex fest – like me and Pav the Chav – and got married. She went back to Poland with him, but only lasted six months with his mother who did not appreciate having a "foreigner" as a daughter-in-law. But then she found she was pregnant, so he's back here now to be with the kid and he never shuts up about wanting his son to grow up Polish. So he doesn't want to be here and she doesn't want to be there and short of cutting the child in half, one of them has to give in.'

'So, a bit like me and Matt then?' said Hannah.

Ali laughed.

'Yeah, except Poland's only three hours away and fifty pounds on Easyjet.'

'But go on,' said Hannah, rubbing her temples, 'tell me properly how it all came out.'

'Well, we were talking about Polish men and how they compared with Aussie blokes and English blokes and then she said at least I would never be stupid enough to marry Pav or have a kid with him, so I asked what she meant – because of course, I have been planning both of those things in some detail . . .'

Hannah smiled and shook her head. That was a mistake, as the room started to spin. She rolled her eyes instead.

'Right,' said Ali, waving her forefinger in circles at the side of her head, 'what a bloody idiot . . . so, anyway, I asked her what she meant and she gave me a funny look and said "because he's already got a wife and three kids". I was just trying to find him so I could bring the nearest heavy object down on his head, when you came round the side of the barn, looking like you'd just had a similar shock yourself. Except in your case, you were the one who is already inconveniently married, right?'

Hannah nodded and did the same 'crazy person' thing with her fingers.

'I feel so bad that I gave Dominic the wrong idea like that,' she said. 'I really didn't mean to, I thought we were just really good friends . . . You know that, don't you? Please tell me you do? Do you think I led him on?'

'No way,' said Ali, 'but anyone could see he was in love with you. I was sure it wasn't returned from your side, because I know how tight you and Matt are. So I thought he'd quickly realise it was hopeless and get over it – like I did with him – and I didn't need to say anything to anyone about it.'

'That's not like you,' said Hannah and they both laughed. They had to. It was all too ghastly not to laugh.

And Hannah hadn't told Ali the entire story. She'd just said that Dominic had made a move on her and declared himself and she'd rejected him. She'd left out the detail that she had, for one tiny moment, returned Dominic's kiss. And worse, she'd enjoyed it. Really enjoyed it.

OK, she was so seriously sex-starved any kiss would have been welcome, but while she had tried to repress the thought, in the long waking hours of the night she'd been forced to face the truth: Dominic was a sensationally good kisser and for the brief moment she'd allowed it to happen, she'd loved it.

But she wasn't going to tell Ali that. She wasn't going to tell anyone, ever. She just had to hold on to the knowledge that it was a blip, caused by the very odd circumstances and that the subsequent conversation with Dominic had cancelled it out. It had meant nothing to her and she wasn't going to let it turn into a poison of guilt that could affect how she was with Matt when they were reunited.

Ali got up to make them some more tea and Hannah sat staring into space, trying to make sense of it all. Was she being dishonest with herself? With Matt? Undoubtedly, but she was still absolutely convinced that the best thing to do about that tiny lapse was to try and forget about it.

Not all secrets were better shared.

'So how did you leave things with Dominic?' asked Ali, putting the fresh mugs of tea on the table and sitting down again. 'Are you speaking?'

'Oh yes,' said Hannah, pulling her hair back from her forehead to try and alleviate the throbbing, 'I mean, I hope I don't have to see him for a while, or possibly ever, but he was lovely about it – you know the way he is – but I still feel bad. We did hang out a lot and have good times and I was so dense not to realise he thought there was more to it. He really deserves a good woman, I hope he finds one soon. Just not me.'

Then she shuddered involuntarily, remembering the other terrible detail she hadn't told Ali yet, but unlike the true nature of the kiss, she thought sharing this one would make it easier to handle.

'It gets worse,' she said.

Ali's eyebrows shot up and she paused with a greasy cheese sandwich en route to her mouth.

'Spill,' she said.

'Anthea was in on it too,' said Hannah.

'What?' said Ali. 'Details, please.'

'Dominic wants to buy Mummy's house,' said Hannah, revisiting all her mixed feelings about that as she said it, 'and the big plan was for me and the kids to move in with him there. Instant happy families, just add water. So Anthea would have exactly what she wants – Dominic next door, with a suitable wife, two kids and the prospect of more.'

'And they hadn't factored Matt into this scenario?' said Ali, outraged.

'Oh no,' said Hannah, 'they've independently decided it's all over between us, no matter how many times I've told them it isn't.'

'I think I might go and punch Anthea,' said Ali.

'Careful,' said Hannah, 'or you will end up in that cell. She's very good at heart, but she's lonely and getting older and desperately wants to be surrounded by a family – by any means necessary – and who can blame her?'

Ali nodded. 'Too right,' she said. 'I came over here to get away from my crazy suffocating family and now all I want to do is run back to them.'

'So are you really going to go home?' asked Hannah, feeling desolate at the prospect of losing her.

'Sure am, lady,' said Ali. 'It's been great, but I feel like I've done my dash here. I did my cool London thing, that was fun. I tried chasing a proper posh Pompom. Interesting. I rooted an unreconstructed European man – hot – and it got me over my hang-ups about my scars, so I'm grateful to the spunk rat for that. And now, after all that, I've come to the conclusion that maybe Aussie blokes aren't so bad after all. I mean, a lot of them are bastards too, but at least I know where I am with them.'

Hannah raised her mug in a toast.

'To Australian men,' she said.

'Aussie blokes,' said Ali, clinking her mug against Hannah's as they smiled at each other.

At that moment they heard the sound of a car on the gravel outside the house.

'Oh no,' said Hannah, covering her ears with her hands, 'please let it not be Dominic . . .'

'Or Pavel,' said Ali.

'Maybe it's just someone using the driveway to turn,' said Hannah, making no move to stand up, 'or a freak delivery, on a Sunday . . . let's wait and see if they ring the bell.'

No-one did and they relaxed back in their chairs as the children started to squeal and shout in the garden. Hannah sat up again, on instant mother alert, but decided they sounded happy, not injured, so she relaxed again.

The noises got louder and just as she was wondering whether she really should go and check they were OK, a large shape filled the open French windows.

It was Matt, with a very happy child on each hip.

# After

Hannah and Matt were sitting on a blanket in Rushcutter's Bay park on a sunny afternoon, watching the kids play with friends from school.

Matt poured some more wine into Hannah's plastic glass and his own, then nodded in acknowledgement as two women walking past slowed to an involuntary stop when they saw him, nudging each other and gawping.

'Hi girls,' he said, smiling at them.

'Are you Matt Constantinos?' asked one of them, going bright red.

'I think so,' he said, 'ask my wife here . . .'

The women turned to look at Hannah, seeming to notice her for the first time.

'He's him,' she said, smiling and nodding.

'Can I have my picture taken with you?' asked the other woman, immediately turning back to Matt.

He nodded and Hannah did her bit taking the pictures with the women's mobile phones and they went on their way, alight with excitement and chattering like the parrots in the trees over their heads.

'You're so good at all that,' said Hannah, 'the Mr Pop Star stuff . . .'

'Well, I had plenty of time to think about how I would one day deal with glory,' said Matt, laughing, 'although I didn't ever expect to be the singer and all that goes with that. You handle it pretty well yourself. Do you mind being the celebrity's wife?'

'Not if it makes you happy,' she said.

'You make me happy,' he said, pulling her closer so her head was resting on his shoulder, 'but there's something I want to talk to you about before the others get here.'

'Fire away,' said Hannah, turning her face towards the late afternoon sun.

'Are you happy we came back to Sydney?' he asked.

'Of course,' said Hannah, 'very. The kids are both really happy at school, I love Australia and I've found I don't miss the village at all. Now Mum's not there – or Charlie – the ties are broken. I'll always have great affection for it, but without them, it's not home any more. And I'm loving spending time with your family and seeing the kids get to know them properly. It's all good.'

'Is this your home?' asked Matt.

Hannah sat up and looked at him with narrowed eyes, wondering where this was going exactly.

'You're my home,' she said, 'you and the kids. I love our house here – I never dreamed we'd have a house like that anywhere – but it's you three that make it home. That's what I understand now. Once you leave and live somewhere else once, nowhere is really home any more – but if you've got people you love, anywhere can be home, as long as they're there with you. Does that make sense?'

Matt nodded, smiling broadly. She was glad he was pleased with her answer, but still wondered where he was going with these questions.

He took her hand.

'I'd better be quick,' he said, nodding towards the far side of the park, near the yacht club. Hannah followed his gaze and saw Marguerite and Anthony walking towards them, holding hands. Hector had spotted them too and had abandoned his fielding post to run over to them.

'So what is it?' asked Hannah, getting impatient.

'The record label want me and Pete to move to LA,' said Matt, 'and obviously I'm not going unless we all go.'

For a moment Hannah couldn't speak. Another move? They'd only been back in Sydney three years.

'You and Pete?' she asked.

Matt nodded.

'Has he told Ali?'

'If all's gone according to plan, he should be telling her right now . . .' said Matt, pointing to the top of the park, by New South Head Road, where two more familiar figures were walking towards them, the taller one pushing a stroller. Ali and Pete – and baby Jimi.

Hannah saw that Ali's head was turned towards Pete and then she stopped, threw her arms round him and started jumping up and down. Interesting. Looked like she was happy with the idea then.

Hannah glanced back the other way, to where her mother and Anthony were now chatting to the mother of one of Hector's friends. Those two spent hardly any time in their London flat; they were always travelling to exotic places, looking at historic rubble and visiting pals of Anthony's.

They'd just come back from an expedition to the Northern Territory to look at some ancient Aboriginal rock paintings. There'd be no problem about them coming out to LA to visit. Anthony probably had loads of friends there too, he did everywhere else.

And with money no longer an issue, they'd be able to fly Matt's entire family out to see them whenever they felt like it. They'd be able to keep the house in Sydney as a base there too.

She turned back to Matt, who was looking at her anxiously, biting the edge of his lip.

'Great,' she said, leaning forward to kiss him on that beautiful sculpted mouth, 'when do we go?'

# Acknowledgements

This book would not have been possible without the following wonderful people. Love and massive thanks to all of you.

Blair McKichan for his insights into the process of writing pop songs and Tina Matthews for her expertise in the business side of popular music. And for being lovely friends.

James Hodgson, for lending me his beautiful house as a writing retreat, for the second time. Victoria Killay – and Figaro the pug – for keeping me company there.

My sister Mary Watts for her eagle eye on the legal side and my niece, Katy Watts, for her insider knowledge of the cool East End and London bus routes. Jo Fairley for expertise on fragrances.

I am also grateful for the information I gleaned from *China Mending For Beginners*, by Margot Wissler (Bishopsgate Press, 1983).

To my most treasured publisher and friend Julie Gibbs and my editor Jocelyn Hungerford, who is more like a second brain.

My lovely agents at Curtis Brown in Sydney and in London – Fiona Inglis and Jonathan Lloyd.

Pop and Peggy for being my rocks.

And lastly, in strictly alphabetical order, my Ideal Readers: Sally Brampton, Jo Fairley, Victoria Killay and Laline Paul – all wonderful writers themselves. Thank you so much for taking the time to read my first draft and to offer such useful, interesting and disparate advice on it. And for being so loving and supportive, when I felt quite crazed with anxiety. I'm very lucky to have such clever and funny girlfriends.

# SHALL WE DANCE?

Loulou Landers, London's undisputed Queen of Vintage Fashion, meets a man on the eve of her dreaded forty-ninth birthday. He's kind, he's sensitive, he's divinely handsome and he carries a designer suit like George Clooney. Unfortunately, he's barely half her age, and Loulou's just not ready to 'go cougar'.

Then there is Loulou's 21-year-old daughter, Theo, who won't get a job, won't move out, wears chainstore fashion, and hasn't said a civil word to her mother for years. And she is on the verge of her own spectacularly unsuitable affair.

So how will Loulou cope with a daughter who's off the rails, a man who won't take no for an answer, and an ageing process that won't slow down – not to mention a birthday party in a camping ground? Like she always has – with wit, grit and an exemplary sense of style.

Maggie Alderson has created her most magnificent character to date, an unforgettable woman who steps back from the edge of middle-aged oblivion to find wisdom, strength, purpose and romantic love from an unexpected source.

# HOW TO BREAK YOUR OWN HEART

Amelia Bradlow seems to have everything she needs to be happy – a handsome husband, a beautiful home, money, good looks and a glamour job. Everything, that is, except the thing she wants most – a baby.

Ed, her husband, is funny, affectionate and sophisticated but simply not interested in parenthood. He likes his life neat and tidy. And he likes having a wife who attends solely to his needs.

As she approaches 37, Amelia is faced with a life-changing decision, aided and abetted by Kiki, her hopelessly disorganised but ridiculously rich friend. Should Amelia stay in her nearly happy marriage, or expose herself to the vagaries of a single life and the distant possibility of meeting someone who wants to start a family?

Maggie Alderson brings her deep understanding of the human heart to this new novel about the compromises we make in life, and about those rare moments of grace when we decide to risk everything for the chance to be truly, madly and deeply happy.